Outer World

Prairie

Outer World

Prairie

Description

Prairie is one of four outer worlds. An enemy from the distant past has come to these worlds to enslave or kill the people who live there.

On the planet Prairie a young woman has escaped from the enemy but faces certain death on a world she does not know. She is rescued by man she has dreamed about.

Jamee follows Billy on a trek to try and free others who are slaves of the creatures of Prairie. They fall in love and go on an adventure to help save their world and fight for their lives and freedom.

They are pursued by an ancient enemy who wants to enslave or kill all the people of Prairie. They meet others and band together to fight and if necessary die for their world.

The enemy finds that their technology is useless on the outer worlds and they are forced to use weapons from their past. They are on Prairie, the most distant of the outer worlds, to find a mineral that will devastate their old foes and to enslave or exterminate the inferior people that live there.

Other Books by

Dannie C Hill

Tyler Hill's Decision

In Search of a Soul

Outer World

Prairie

by

Dannie Hill

Small Mountain Publishing

http://smallmountainpub.com

http://danniehill.wordpress.com

ISBN-13:
978-0-9826924-4-8
ISBN-10
0-9826924-4-7

Published by Small Mountain
Publishing
Houston, Texas
http://smallmountainpub.com

Cover Art by
Surabhi Singh
http://www.artbysurabhi.com

Interior design by
Small Mountain Publishing

Edited by
Sherry Ruschell

First printing in the United
States of America

About the Author:

Dannie was born in Mooresville, North Carolina. He served in the U.S. Army in a warzone. Dannie has traveled around the world and lived in the Marshall Islands for two years. He now lives in Thailand and Texas. Most of his writing is done in Thailand where the sounds of English are quieted and his daydreams can come to life.

Visit Dannie's blog and enjoy his true stories about **A**

Writer in Thailand   http://danniehill.wordpress.com

Dedication

I want to thank my loving wife – the one woman in this world that was meant to be with me. Without her strength and confidence in what I do I could have never succeeded as an author or a good father. She gives me the time I need to write and is always there when I need her.

I also want to thank my three beautiful children who have grown into fine and wonderful people. They take with them the future and I am proud of them. My three grandchildren and daughter-in-law are family that adds so much joy to my life. And to my mother! I love you all.

I also want to thank Sherry Ruchell, my editor. Without her diligence, great abilities and kind words this and other books I have written would not be the wonderful reads they are!

In memory my father: **Ben Hill**.
He never knew me as a writer but was proud of everything I did.

Acknowledgement
I wish to honor all of the writers in this world. Without authors, imagination would die and so too would our world.

And to the readers! Without you we writers are nothing. I pledge my writing to be the best it can be in story and editing. All that I do is with you, the reader, in mind!

Dannie C Hill

Outer World

Prairie

BOOK I

CHAPTER 1

The ship growled with a deep, resonant throb as it changed attitude and started its descent towards the strange new world. Sergeant Phillips looked at the prisoners crowded into the supply chamber. They were a pathetic looking bunch after three weeks locked in the hole.

He had five men to do the job of twenty but they would be enough if he pushed them. "Corporal Higgins. Get these slaves ready for delivery! I want the cages assembled by the time we touch down. I don't want this ship on the ground any longer than two hours. Those lizards tried to take the last ship and that's not going to happen on my watch!"

Corporal Higgins asked, "Do you think there will be trouble, Sergeant? I heard the last time we were here we gave them plenty to think about when they came at us."

"That's why we're bringing these slaves and weapons. We're trying to make peace with them until we get what we need."

"What exactly does command want from these... these lizards? They sure are an ugly bunch."

"What command is after is none of your business, Corporal. Now get the slaves to assemble the containers." In reality the sergeant had no idea what command was after, except he knew it was some kind of weapon.

After landing, two soldiers stood guard with bows and pikes. Another shoved the slaves into the containers as tight as he could force them, while one man operated the crane and the last two stood on the ground below to disconnect the crane from the containers once they were on the surface.

Private Sheenin looked around and said, "You ever been to this place before, Dole?"

"Yeah, a couple of times but it was always with a full squad. I don't like being out here alone with those two lizards looking at me."

"Nothing but grass as far as I can see. I'd hate to get lost out there."

"Don't worry, buddy. If you get lost you'll only last a day before something eats you. I've seen some of the big cats that roam this prairie and I wouldn't want to come across one all alone. There are also humans out there and they must be fearless because even the lizards stay away from them."

Private Sheenin hefted his bow and said, "I feel ridiculous with this ancient weapon. We're the laughing stock of the Federation. I miss my AS5-3; five hundred rounds firing five at a time. I really miss the sound."

"I know how you feel. We've got all this technology," Private Dole motioned back at the gleaming ship. "You'd think those idiot scientists could figure out why plus-light speed destroys almost anything carbon based, including all our ammunition and electronics. I feel like a fool holding this pike. At least the people we fight aren't any better off. I just hope we don't have to fight the natives of this world. I hear they aren't afraid of anything..."

Sergeant Phillips yelled, "You two men! Pay attention. I want to join up with the company before dark!"

"You and me both," said Private Dole under his breath.

Nine of the ten containers were on the ground and the last one was being lowered by the crane when a guy wire snapped sending it crashing into one of the other containers. Two containers broke open and men and women scattered trying to escape.

The two lizards and the soldiers quickly herded the slaves together because they had no idea where to run. None had ever seen such open ground and all but one simply stopped when they looked around.

The lone girl didn't look around but ran into the grass and didn't stop. Anything would be better than being a slave so she ran until nightfall and crawled into a clump of bushes to hide. Exhausted, Jamee fell into a fitful sleep.

The man came to her again. She had dreamed of the young man with deep blue eyes every night for the past six months. It was so odd because he had no beard like all the men of her world and he was dressed in animal skins. She knew he had come to take her away and protect her, but she always woke with the same frustration. Her life went unchanged until the Voll soldiers came and took her away to the ship.

She woke with a start. Hearing creatures moving around in the dark, she cowered deeper into the thorny bush. If only her dream man was real. She would do whatever she must to go with him and be safe. She wanted his love and wanted him to touch her. A heat warmed her and she drifted off to sleep again. No matter what happened she wouldn't go back to be a slave.

Corporal Higgins reported the slave girl missing to the sergeant and Sergeant Phillips said, "Not to worry. She's tagged. We'll report to the company and they'll send out scouts. She won't live through the night in any event."

It was late afternoon and Billy saw a Koro patrol at the crest of a hill some four miles away. These patrols were becoming more frequent the closer he got to his destination. Billy had started his trek ten days before and had evaded any contact by hiding in the Bookus trees at night.

The Bookus trees were massive, each lower limb reaching out at least one hundred feet from their trunk. For their size the trees were only an average of 60 feet tall. They were the safest place to stay at night out on the prairie.

He had just reached a grove of the giants and was searching for the best branch to climb when he heard a human scream. He looked around until he located the source. He saw a human three hundred yards away, directly in the path the Koros would use on their patrol. He checked the distant patrol and could see that they had increased their speed.

The Koros' vision was feeble but their hearing was excellent. They had thick, leathery skin with pentagonal beaded patterns, much like a lizard. The skin on their faces was plated in the same type of skin as their bodies. They had no hair, walked upright and were very strong. They were also slow in fighting but could move quickly while running.

The Koros had some intelligence, but no one knew a great deal about them.

Billy was tired from the day's journey but he raced to the distant person. As he reached her, he could see it was a girl crumpled face-down in the dirt. She rolled over to face him, covered her face, and continued to scream.

"Be quiet! Please, be quiet."

He grabbed her arms and pulled her to her feet. She opened her eyes and when she realized that Billy was also human she threw her arms around him and started sobbing loudly.

"Be quiet, please. They can hear you," Billy said as calmly as he could.

She quieted down but continued to cry. "I'm sorry. I didn't know."

Without saying anymore Billy took her hand and pulled her along back to the grove.

"Where are we going?" she asked.

"Just come with me. It will be dark in a few minutes."

Inside the grove Billy went to the tree he had picked out earlier and started up. He looked back and saw that she was following. They reached the first level as the first moon rose over the eastern hills.

"Hold on to my belt and follow me," Billy said.

She held his belt firmly and followed without saying a word. They continued climbing from limb to limb. At the fourth giant limb Billy walked carefully to the trunk. The limb was slightly concave on its upper surface. They entered the opening at the trunk that he knew would be there. Billy sat down, drained of all energy.

The girl sat across from him and asked, "Where are we?"

Billy thought that was a strange question because everyone knew about the Bookus trees.

"We are in a water cave, but you should know that."

"I don't know anything about this abominable place. I arrived on Prairie two days ago."

Billy said, "Don't talk now. They may search this area. Lie down and get some sleep."

Billy heard her stirring as she settled down. Within a few minutes he could hear her steady breathing and knew she was asleep. He had a lot to think about on this night, but first he had to check for Koros and then rest.

As the light increased Billy got his first real look at this girl he had rescued. Her syncotton coveralls were torn revealing strong, brown, shapely legs. Her hair was long, black and disheveled. What Billy could see of her face was beautiful; small nose, full lips, high cheekbones and a soft jawline. He had never seen such a beautiful face, even though it was covered with dirt from the prairie. He had lived all of his nineteen years on Prairie and his village had only three hundred and fifty people. Of those, only twenty were women near his age. As Billy watched her, he saw her eyes spring open. They were large, brown, almond-shaped pools and rimmed in white. She jumped up, forgetting where she was, and backed into the side of the cave.

"Take it easy. You're okay now."

She looked at Billy and relaxed. It was then that Billy noticed her body. This was no girl but a young woman. She had a small waist, full breasts, and looked to be about 5 feet 4 inches tall.

"I hope you are enjoying the view," she said. "Maybe we should introduce ourselves before we get too intimate." Her full lips curved up in a smile.

Billy, now as red as the second moon, quickly looked away.

"Thank you for rescuing me. My name is Jamee and I come from planet QB-45, but we call it Ocean. If you hadn't found..." Jamee looked at his eyes and was speechless. His eyes were the color of the ocean on her world—a royal blue. Was this the man she had dreamed of?

Billy, finding his voice said, "I'm...I'm sorry. I didn't mean to stare. My name is Billy Running Wolf and I'm from the Eagle Tribe. My village is far to the south. Why did you come to Prairie?"

She looked away so she could concentrate. "The Volls took me while I was out fishing with my work group. I was put onto one of their spaceships with a group of other people. They brought us here to be given to the Koros as a peace offering. When they were off-loading the cargo from the ship my container fell and broke open and I ran as fast as I could. I hid during the night and traveled all day."

"You're lucky you landed during the day. The Koros would have had you for sure if it had happened at night."

"I never saw a Koro. I don't even know what they look like."

Billy looked outside and said, "We'll wait here today and decide what to do tonight. I'll tell you about my world while we clean up and eat."

"How can I get cleaned up in this? What did you call it?"

"A Bookus tree. We are in a water cave and I'll show you how." He got up and went to the back of the cave. "We only get rain here during the rainy season, which just ended. The Bookus have a large opening at the base of each major limb," Billy explained as he took out a large knife and began to cut through the floor. "That is why we call this a water cave. The limbs funnel water into the opening and the trapped water is filtered into a storage area below the floor."

As Billy talked he cut a circle about four feet in diameter and lifted the three-inch thick floor.

Jamee walked over, peered in and saw clean, clear water.

"How deep is it?"

"Only about four feet to the base, but it continues into the tree for at least ten feet. It doesn't harm the tree to cut the floor as long as you put it back down when you're finished using the water. Use a piece of the floor to scrub yourself."

Without any shame Jamee stripped off her coveralls and walked toward the pool. Billy nearly swallowed his tongue and his eyes locked on Jamee's breasts. They were firm, beautifully rounded and pointed at the tips. Billy dropped his gaze and again turned red.

Jamee laughed with a sweet singing chord. "I hope I didn't embarrass you again, Billy. In my world we swim and bathe with our group."

"In my tribe there aren't many girls and we do not bathe together except with our families," Billy said, still looking at the floor.

He heard a splash and looked up to find Jamee in the pool. "Can I drink this water?"

"Yes. It is clean."

Jamee took several large swallows of water and then said, "Please join me, Billy. I am afraid to be in here alone." All Jamee could think about was this was the man she had dreamed about every night for six months.

Billy was a hunter in his tribe and was afraid of very little. So, maintaining his red complexion, Billy stripped and leaped into the pool. The water was crystal clear and in the morning light streaming into the cave it was impossible to hide his excitement.

Jamee grabbed a hunk of the soft fibers that made up the floor of the cave. It was very light and soft to the touch. It reminded her of the husk material of the coconuts on her planet. Jamee began to rub her face with the fibers. She moved to her shoulders and down her body. A warm feeling ran through her, causing her to look up at Billy. Now it was her turn to glow with the embarrassment she felt.

It was true, what she told Billy about her world, but she didn't tell Billy that in a few weeks she would have been given to one of the men as his mate. She would have had no choice because Jamee had no family and was assigned to a work group. Jamee had been frightened of that day and didn't want someone she had never met to take her virginity. As she thought about this she also realized that she didn't want to die a virgin either.

Jamee moved closer to Billy and really looked at him for the first time. Billy had long, shoulder length black hair. His skin was golden brown with a copperish tint and smooth. He had no beard, which all of the men on Ocean had, a strong jawline and a nose that was bigger than hers but fit his face well. When she looked at his dark, royal blue eyes any doubt that she might have had raced from her. Billy was the man of her dreams. She had to be with him because she knew he would protect her and love her. She was on a world she knew nothing about and she would never go back to be a slave of the Koros. Jamee glanced at Billy as he stared out the cave entrance. This may be her only chance to be safe and she needed someone. She had been alone most of her life and this might be her only chance.

Her dreams had seemed so real and as she thought she made up her mind.

"Billy, how will I ever repay you for saving my life? If you hadn't found me, I would have been captured or worse."

"I'm glad I found you, but anyone on a trek would have done the same. The only thing you owe me is to listen to me when we are moving."

"But it was you and I will find a way to repay you. I promise."

She began to rub Billy's shoulders with the fibers and moved down to his chest. Jamee moved closer to Billy until her body brushed his chest and she spoke into his ear.

"Please don't leave me. I have no one but you. I'll...I'll do anything you ask. Anything."

"I won't leave you. I couldn't. I...I...I've never been with a..." Billy said, turning his head away in embarrassment.

Jamee turned his head with her hands and kissed Billy. It was a soft, gentle kiss and warmed her. Billy pulled her tight against his body.

Jamee looked into Billy's eyes and said, "I don't think I am ready. I would like to wait for the right time."

In the back of her mind she couldn't believe what she had said. Jamee knew that Billy was the one she had dreamed of, but she wanted Billy to feel the same way she felt. Jamee knew she wouldn't wait long.

Billy gently held Jamee away and said, "In my tribe it is forbidden to take a woman if she doesn't want to... I think we had better get dressed." There was tightness in his chest when he looked at Jamee. He wanted her but more than that he felt a pull that was much more than a physical need. He had never had these feelings about any of the girls of his village. He wanted her to stay with him.

Jamee eased herself out of the water and walked out of the cave. Billy jumped out of the water and quickly put his loincloth and leggings on.

He walked out of the cave, not looking at her, and said, "I'll be back. I'll get us something fresh to eat."

"How long will you be gone?"

"Just a short time. I won't leave the tree."

He ran out on the limb, climbed up to the next level and disappeared. Billy ran to the trunk and sat down, letting out a great sigh. His mind was racing. His chest still burned from Jamee's touch. He had never felt so excited and so afraid of a girl before. Here he was on a trek of great importance and now he had a person he felt responsible for. What was he going to do?

Billy needed to collect his thoughts so he gathered two Bookus nuts, sat down outside the cave and began to meditate in the manner he had been taught since he was two years old. He crossed his legs and cleared his mind and from deep inside Billy began to think of how his people came to Korostrata, the original name of Prairie.

It was over ten generations ago when the spacecraft landed and the small group of people were put out. The crew unloaded the many boxes of supplies, a few oxen, and announced to the group they had two hours to move everything away from the blast zone. The people worked feverishly to move all the supplies. At the end of two hours they saw a flash of light from the engines and seconds later they saw the craft lift off and disappear.

Red Cloud, the leader of part of the group, said, "We are where we do not want to be but nonetheless we are here."

"What are we to do now?" cried Two Moons, Red Cloud's wife.

"Why have the whites done this to us?" asked Running Dog.

Red Cloud raised his hands for silence. He then spoke, "We were sent to this land because we are not of the whites and they want to be rid of all who are not like them. We must give thanks to the ones that took us from the killing fields. They risked their own lives to see that our races would not die." Red Cloud continued, "We now have this land to live in peace and it is up to us to survive."

"You do not control my people," said William, a large black man and the elected representative of his group. "But what you say is true. We have a chance to make a new world and we cannot begin it by fighting amongst ourselves." William continued, "How are we to start?"

"Well, I for one ain't gonna live with a bunch of damn Indians!" exclaimed Ray, a small black youth.

"And I will not live with all these Blacks," said Johnny Little.

Johnny had been taken from Atlanta and put with the group just before blastoff. Red Cloud went to William and they both walked a short distance away from the group.

Red Cloud said, "What do you think, William? Can we live as one people?" It was several minutes before William spoke.

He said, "Red Cloud, I honestly don't think it will work, us staying together. Besides, I believe it is important that we maintain our races. I think maybe we should find our own places in this land."

Red Cloud said, "I think what you say is true. But we are two small groups and if we fight each other we will not survive long."

William spoke. "We must make a pact to live in peace and aid one another if the need arises."

And so they returned to their people and split the supplies and the few animals. They moved off together toward the horizon. They had decided...

"Billy...Billy, wake up," whispered Jamee.

"What is it? What are you doing up here?" demanded Billy.

"I heard voices," said Jamee.

"That's impossible, Jamee. There are no people in this part of the prairie."

But now Billy heard the buzz of voices. They were somewhere near the tree.

He thought it must be someone from the Black village but turned to Jamee and said, "Stay here and be quiet. I'll be right back."

"That's what you said last time. From now on I will go where you go."

"No. Stay here!" Billy started out on the limb.

He crouched low and ran out to where the giant leaves enclosed the perimeter of the tree. He moved one of the branches aside and peered down.

He saw two men standing and talking, but what was so incredible was they were white. White... How could that be? There were no white people on Prairie. As a matter of fact, these were the first whites he had ever seen and had only heard of them from tales of the tribe. Billy felt more than heard a movement. He spun with his knife in his hand ready. Jamee crouched there, peering through the leaves.

"What are you doing here?" Billy breathed.

"What am I doing here..? What are those Volls doing here?"

"Volls, what are Volls?"

"They are the soldiers who brought me here. They must be after me."

They both watched the two soldiers. They appeared to be talking but their words did not carry up to Billy and Jamee. The Volls were looking at a metal box and pointing at the Bookus tree that Billy and Jamee were in.

"I have seen that thing before. They are able to track their prisoners with it. I saw a man trying to hide on the ship and they went directly to him," Jamee whispered. "When they found him, he was beaten badly and then they removed a signet from the man's clothes and took him away. The signet must have been some kind of detector. At least that's what our group leader said."

Billy remembered something from the old stories but wasn't sure.

"Do you have one of those signets on your clothes?"

"Yes. I've tried to take it off but I couldn't. It's right here," said Jamee pointing to a small object just below her left breast.

"Let me see."

Jamee came closer and stood up so Billy could examine the signet. Billy took the object in his hand and bent to get a close look at it. The signet was oval, very thin and was hooked to Jamee's coveralls but he couldn't see how. It was only about one inch long and a half inch wide. It had a small design molded into it. Billy had seen the design before in the books that were brought with his tribe from the old planet. The design was a Swastika, an evil symbol of the people from the old world. Billy was so intent on examining the signet that when he felt something brush his cheek he looked up and stumbled back, nearly falling from the limb. Jamee stood smiling at Billy's embarrassment.

"I...I," was all Billy could get out.

"Please, Billy. I think this signet is important and you must get it off. Or will I have to take my clothes off and leave them here?"

Billy collected himself and stood once again. "You're right. I have seen this emblem before and I think it is something evil. I am a hunter of the Eagle Tribe and don't usually act like this. It's just that you are so...so...beautiful," he said at last.

It was Jamee's turn to glow with embarrassment. *Beautiful; he thinks I'm beautiful. He has to be the one!*

Billy moved closer and once again took the signet in his hand. "I have to look at this from the inside of your coveralls, but I don't know how..."

"Here; let me help."

She unbuttoned the front of her coverall and pulled opened the left half, exposing her breast. "Please, Billy, you have no reason to be embarrassed. You have to find a way to get this thing off."

Billy swallowed hard and plunged forward, trying to give the signet his full attention. Once he saw the signet from the back side it looked quite simple. There were four long metal tabs that crossed and locked in the middle. Billy removed his small bleeding knife which he used to cut the neck artery of large game. He placed the sharp point under the tabs where they locked together. With a sharp twist of the blade the tabs broke apart. Billy straightened the tabs and removed the signet without cutting the cloth.

"You did it," whispered Jamee. "Now what should we do with it?" she asked as she buttoned up her coveralls.

Billy had been thinking about the signet, after he finally got his mind off Jamee's body. "I think we have to place it somewhere and then get away from it."

"If only you could throw it miles from here."

Billy turned his attention to the Volls below.

"I must get closer and try to hear what they are saying," said Billy. "Jamee, you must go back to the cave and bring all of my gear up to this level and then wait in the water cave."

"I've already brought all of your possessions up to this level. When I heard the voices, I grabbed everything and followed you."

Billy looked at Jamee in a new light. *She is smart as well as beautiful*, he thought. "Good! Now you must promise to stay here. I swear by the Great Eagle I won't leave you... We will leave tonight."

"I'll wait for you." Jamee turned and walked to the trunk of the tree.

Billy watched as Jamee walked away, her hips tightening her coveralls with each step she took. Billy was happy that Jamee was with him and wanted her to stay.

Billy followed and he fastened the Signet to the wall of the cave. He then began to descend down the tree to a level where he might hear what the Volls were saying. Billy reached the second level, moved out on the limb as quiet as a prairie cat. When he was directly above the two men he lay down and listened.

"Yes, sir! We are more than twenty miles out, in a grove of the biggest trees I've ever seen," said one of the Volls. "Okay. We'll camp here until tomorrow afternoon. Over and out." Turning to the other man he said, "Those bastards are going to leave us out here because they're afraid to travel at night."

The second Voll said, "Calm down, Jesse. We know she's up in this tree. We have to wait here until the other unit shows up and then we'll get her."

"Yeah, Kurt. I'm going to have some fun with this one. Did you see the butt on her when we were back at the landing area?"

"Just so we give her to the Koros in one piece," said Private Kurt Dole.

"Let's set up camp and turn that Homer off. She's probably so frightened she'll never come down."

Jesse, looking around, said, "I wonder why the guys are afraid to come out here at night."

Billy eased back to the transit limb and made his way up the tree. He found Jamee waiting at the entrance to the cave.

"We'll have to leave tonight. There will be more of them here tomorrow."

"Where will we go?"

"We'll go to the south and then turn back northwest. Maybe we can learn why these Volls are here. Let's eat some Bookus nuts and then we'll rest until nightfall."

Billy moved to the back of the cave and brought two large, brown, hairy objects he had gathered earlier and handed them to Jamee.

"What are these things?"

"These are our meal."

He took out his large knife and, using the back of the blade, gave one of the nuts a brisk stroke. Its outer shell cracked completely around. Billy turned his knife and split the nut in two halves. The meat was a light green and had a pleasant aroma. In the center of each half was a full cup of clear liquid.

"Here, Jamee. First drink the juice and then eat the fruit," Billy said.

Without any hesitation Jamee drank the liquid and began to devour the fruit, using her hands to dig out the meat of the fruit. Billy watched in amazement as she attacked the meal.

"You must be very hungry. How long has it been since you last ate?"

Jamee looked up with juice dripping from her chin and said, "I guess it has been at least two and a half days. I haven't eaten since I escaped from the Volls."

"Why didn't you say something to me?"

"Billy, where I'm from, people of my group don't ask for things. We either provide for ourselves or wait until it is offered."

Billy put the other half nut beside Jamee and thought, *What a strange way to live.*

He said, "My people customarily help without asking, but if we need something, we will ask. Jamee, if you need anything and I don't provide it, please ask me."

Jamee had already started on the second half of the fruit when Billy asked," Do you want any more to eat?"

Jamee sat back, wiping her chin, and said, "No, I've eaten enough for now. That was delicious. We have fruit that looks similar to this nut on my world but it doesn't taste anything like this."

"Now I want you to rest because we have a long way to travel tonight and it may be dangerous. I generally don't travel at night because of the Koro patrols and some of the animals that hunt at night."

Jamee asked, "What about the signet? Isn't it dangerous keeping it with us?"

"I don't think so because the Volls turned their box off before I left. We'll take the signet with us until I can think of a way to send it far away." He was already formulating a plan but he still had more thinking to do.

Jamee picked up Billy's knife and moved to the back of the cave where the floor softened under her feet and began to cut a hole in the floor. She completed a small but neat hole just as Billy had done and then pulled the floor up. Billy admired how quickly she picked things up. That wasn't all he admired as Jamee removed her coveralls. She had a taut body with a strong back and shapely legs that made his heart beat faster. Jamee slipped into the water and turned to look at Billy with that impish smile.

This time Billy returned her stare, looking into her beautiful brown eyes and thinking, *She's the most beautiful girl I've ever seen and I want her to stay close to me.*

Billy got up and moved outside to check for any signs of the Volls.

Jamee came to the entrance of the cave and said, "Billy, do you have any clothes I could wear? The coveralls are badly rent."

Billy turned at Jamee's voice. She held the torn garment up to her chin, concealing her chest but not the swell of her hips.

"I don't have any legging but there is a loin cloth and a vest in my pack."

He slipped past Jamee and went to his backpack. He pulled out a vest and a loincloth and gave them to Jamee. "They will be a bit large, but I think they will work."

Jamee dropped the coveralls and began to put the clothes on. Billy couldn't get over the ease with which she exposed her body to him. It was becoming easier for Billy to admire Jamee's body, but he still felt the heat spread to his face. Jamee pulled the loincloth up and tightened the drawstring around her waist, then slipped the vest over her head. The vest was large, but it fit her well.

"It feels wonderful. What kind of skin is it made of?"

"It is from a prairie cat. They are big carnivores and they usually hunt alone. I don't normally hunt them unless they come after me."

"Do you hunt with that small bow?" Jamee asked, pointing at the short bow lying near Billy's pack.

"Yes. This is a Trek Bow and these are the arrows." He pulled an arrow from the quiver and nocked it to the bow string. "We use these short bows when one of our tribe goes on a trek. When we are at home we use a bigger bow to hunt with."

"I've never seen anything like it."

"I'll show you how to use it when we stop tomorrow night. It won't be dark for several hours so we had better get some rest," he said.

Jamee packed her coveralls in Billy's pack and lay down to rest. Billy moved to the entrance of the cave and sat. He looked back and saw the smooth, even breathing and knew Jamee was asleep.

As evening approached, Billy moved to Jamee's side and gently shook her.

Her eyes opened immediately and as she sat up she asked, "Is it time?"

"We will have to leave in a few minutes. When we move out onto the prairie you will have to be very quiet and keep up with me. Just stay close and do whatever I tell you."

Jamee stood up, smoothed her vest. "I'll do the best I can. As long as I'm with you I'll do whatever you ask."

"I want you to carry my pack and bow until we are out of the grove. If we have any trouble with the Volls, I want to be ready."

Jamee lifted the pack and looped the straps through her arms and up to her shoulders.

She picked up the short bow and said, "I'm ready. I owe you my life and I won't let you down."

Billy reached up, took the signet from the wall and put it in his vest pocket. He led the way to the transit branch and started down.

They gained the second level and Billy moved to the trunk.

He leaned close to Jamee and whispered, "We must move to another branch on this level. It's a bit difficult but you can do it."

Billy could smell the fragrance of Jamee's body and before he could move away Jamee kissed him full on the lips. He returned the kiss and then smiled at her. "You are making it hard to concentrate."

Billy grabbed one of the large flakes of bark and found one for his feet. He reached to his left, gripped another flake and continued to move slowly around the trunk. He looked back and saw that Jamee was following close behind. It took ten minutes to reach the next limb but he didn't stop. They continued on to the next limb where they jumped down, walked out to the transit limb and started down.

Billy and Jamee were on the ground moving away when someone leaped on Billy's back. Instinct took over as Billy dropped his left shoulder and lifted his hips. The man came over Billy's head and hit the ground hard. Billy lashed out with a vicious kick and the man stopped moving. Billy knelt down to examine the body. He felt for a pulse and found a strong heartbeat.

"Jesse, are you all right? How long does it take to piss anyway?" Kurt shouted as he moved to where he had last seen Jesse.

He saw Billy and stopped. He pulled out a long knife and said in a commanding voice, "Who are you?"

He saw Jesse crumpled behind the red man and lunged at Billy with a vicious swing as he came in close. Billy ducked under the knife and as it passed over his head he punched full power, striking the man in his solar plexus. Billy heard the whoosh of air escape his adversary's lungs. The man dropped to his knees but held on to the knife.

As the Voll's knees touched the ground, Billy hit him with a left-cross on the chin and the man dropped flat to the ground. Billy took the knife and threw it into the grass and then rolled the man over. He grabbed his belt and lifted upward several times and checked the man's breathing. He did not move but was breathing better. Billy grabbed Jamee's hand and ran towards the edge of the Bookus grove.

CHAPTER 2

Billy and Jamee headed south into the waist-high prairie grass. The prairie was lit in ochre and slowly turning to deeper orange, making the prairie look to be on fire off to the west as the sun settled below the horizon. Both moved at a dead run for half a mile, then slowed to a trot. They came to a dry creek bed and stopped to rest.

Billy leaned close to Jamee and whispered, "Sit down and rest. I'm going to make a trail and double back. I won't be gone long."

Jamee nodded her head and sat without making a sound. Billy moved to the other side of the creek bed and trotted into the grass, making a clear trail.

He ran for about one hundred yards until he came to a large patch of thorny rain berry bushes. The bush's stems grew to about six feet high and had long, sharp thorns covering them. He knew it was dangerous being there at night because of the animals that hunted the large, rabbit-like hoppers. The rain berry fruit were one of the main foods for the hoppers during that time of year. Billy moved into the patch about ten feet, being careful not to wound himself. He backed out slowly and began to backtrack, taking care not to bend the tall grass in the direction he was now traveling.

This effort was time consuming, but Billy knew it must be done to confuse anyone following. Billy was very good at leaving false trails. He and the other young men of his tribe practiced often when they were small boys preparing for their trek and learning to hunt. It took nearly thirty minutes to make it back to the creek bed and when he looked around Jamee was not there.

Billy moved up the creek bed searching for some sign of Jamee. Her movement was hard to follow and he stopped to check the ground. As he knelt down, a small pebble hit the back of his head. Billy spun, only to find Jamee crouching two feet from him. He couldn't see her face but he felt the grin. He turned and started up the creek bed to the east, circling around to the northwest. They traveled for three hours, moving quickly. Billy stopped only once to let Jamee rest. He was impressed with her stamina and she did not complain. She hadn't said a word since they left the tree and did exactly what he indicated. Billy caught the fragrance of pampas flowers and stopped.

He had been searching for this scent ever since they had started up the creek bed. He indicated for Jamee to follow and then moved slowly toward the smell. Pampas was one of the many indigenous plants that grew on the prairie and it was the favorite food of the uteta, a deer-like animal. The uteta stood about four feet tall and standing on its hind legs it could reach over ten feet to get at the flowers and fruit of the pampas. Both moons were up and there was enough visibility to make out the shape of the tall clump of pampas. He signaled Jamee to wait a moment and then follow.

Billy, removing his vest, moved forward slowly until he heard a rustle and chomping noise of something eating. He crawled forward until he could see the uteta. Billy inched noiselessly forward and when he was three feet from the animal he waited. The uteta, engrossed in devouring the flowers, didn't notice the man. When the uteta rose up on its hind legs Billy leaped, throwing his vest over the head of the animal. At the same time Billy wrapped his legs around the uteta's body, taking the animal to the ground. The animal froze in fear and Billy sat up on the uteta's chest.

Jamee came to where the animal lay and Billy quietly said, "Hold the animal's head and don't let go."

Jamee did as she was told and asked, "Are you going to kill it?"

"No. This uteta is going to lead the soldiers away from us."

Billy removed the signet from his vest pocket and pulled out his small bleeding knife. He uncovered one of the ears of the uteta and made four small incisions. He inserted the four tabs of the signet into the cuts and bent them down. Billy took the animal's head and motioned for Jamee to back away.

Billy leaned over to the animal and whispered, "Go, young uteta. Run free and thank you for your help."

Billy stepped back, removing his vest, and watched the uteta spring into the air and bound away.

Billy said, "We still have far to travel tonight and tomorrow. We must hurry from this place in case the Volls have tried to follow."

As Billy put his vest back on Jamee moved close, pressed her body against his and once again kissed him.

"I could get used to your doing that, Jamee."

Jamee smiled, turned and started back toward the creek. Once in the creek bed, Billy took the lead and set a fast pace for over an hour. The creek bed was covered in small rocks, some sparkling in the moonlight. There were pools of water that reminded Jamee of her thirst, but she continued on, staying close to Billy. They slowed to a walk and finally Billy stopped and sat on the ground. He was surprised that Jamee had kept pace with him, even while she carried his pack.

Jamee sat next to Billy and said, "I need something to drink."

Billy took the pack from Jamee, opened the flap and removed a small flask.

He said, "I'm sorry. I've only been thinking about getting us away, not about your needs."

Jamee took the flask, took a few sips of water and started to hand it back.

"Drink it all, Jamee. I will get more at another creek near here. Here, eat this," he said, reaching into the pack and removing a package wrapped in cloth.

Billy removed a small traveling cake and handed it to Jamee. She took a large bite. It was dense but had a sweet flavor.

"This is delicious. What is it?"

"It is a travel cake, made of honey, grain, oats and sometimes pampas fruit." Billy also ate one of the cakes. "I don't eat these unless I can't hunt or find fruit to eat."

"Billy, I have a lot to learn about your world. I hope you will teach me."

"After we travel a few days and I'm sure we are not followed, we will stop and rest for a while. I will tell you about my world and you can tell me about Ocean."

Jamee finished the water and placed the flask into the backpack. She stood and started to pull the pack straps over her shoulders.

Billy said, "No, I will carry the pack now. You have done well, but we must share the burdens of this trip."

He took the pack from Jamee and placed it on his back. He looked down at Jamee and pulled her to him. Her dark eyes stared into his as he bent and kissed her softly. They started out again, moving at a slow trot.

After an hour Billy turned off, heading northwest. It was getting light in the east and as they traveled, more and more of the prairie opened up to Jamee. She had escaped and ran through the prairie for two days but in her panic never focused on the beauty around her.

They were traveling through grass about three feet tall. The grass was dry but soft against her legs. She saw the land was not flat but rolling hills. Some of the hills rose a hundred feet or more. The flora was almost entirely grass of one kind or another

except for clusters of taller bushes scattered about
the hills.

Everywhere she looked was a golden-green
with just a hint of brown as the dry season began.
Jamee followed Billy up a hill and when she crested
it there was nothing but prairie as far as the eye
could see. Far ahead she could see a large grove of
Bookus trees. The prairie relaxed her eyes as she
viewed its strange beauty. They came to a massive
area that looked as though the grass had been cut
close to the ground.

Jamee moved closer to Billy and in a low voice
asked, "Billy, why has the grass been cut here?"

"This was done by a herd of grazing animals
called bovals."

As Billy trotted, he continued to talk. "The
bovals roam the prairie in large herds. They are
peaceful, but it can be dangerous to be around them
if they stampede. I have hunted them many times to
help lay-up meat for the village. Let's stop and rest
for a few minutes."

They stopped at the edge of the grazed area
and sat. Jamee could smell the pervasive odor of
manure and the animals that produced it. The cut
in the prairie was almost a half mile wide and went
out of sight in a winding path.

"These bovals remind me of the giant schools
of fish on my world. They move through the ocean
and eat whatever is in their path, but after they are
gone the other fish return and it's as if the schools
were never there. Billy, this place is beautiful, but it
is so strange to see nothing but prairie everywhere I
look. Is the entire planet like this?"

"I haven't seen all of it, but my tribe lives at
the base of the mountains many days to the south.
A few in my village have been very far to the north
and south. They tell about places of great wonder,

great forest that goes on for days with many different kinds of animals living there.

Far to the north the land becomes cold and covered with ice and snow. There are large beasts roaming the land. To the west there is a great body of water with the taste of salt. From the shore hunters have seen giant schools of fish turning the water into a vast white frothing storm. They said they could see islands far out in the water but had no way to reach them. They feared crossing the water because of all the large fish that swam there.

To the south it grows warm with strange trees and flowers growing all about. There is fruit growing from almost every tree. The long-hunters said it is so beautiful they didn't want to leave, but in the end loneliness brought them back. In all their travels they never saw another human. I have been this far north only once, with my father three years ago."

"Why have you come here now?"

"Every few months we send a hunter from my tribe to make this trek to the north to check on the Koros. The main entrance to their underground mine is many days north of here. We get close and watch their activities. We are afraid that one day they will discover our tribe's location and try to make slaves of us. They've captured many Blacks and some of the People many years ago and took them to the mine. We have tried twice to help them but both times we failed. Some of our men were killed and injured, but we haven't given up."

Jamee said, "It would be good to see the ocean again or travel south to the tropical lands, but I will be happy wherever I am as long as I'm with you." Billy stood, lifting Jamee, taking her into his arms and kissed her gently.

He said, "We must keep moving. We have a long way to travel before it gets dark."

Billy started off at a trot and Jamee ran beside him. Billy couldn't help looking at her as she ran. She was a vision to him and the way her body moved caused tightness in his stomach. They ran for several hours moving generally northwest. They came to another creek bed and Billy turned to the north following the creek. This creek had a number of small pools in it. At a larger pool Billy stopped and removed his pack. He took out his water flask and filled it with water from the pool.

He handed it to Jamee and said, "Don't drink too much. We still have several miles to run." Jamee turned the flask up and took several swallows. She then wet her face and poured water over her legs.

She said, "Thank you. That feels good."

Billy could hear the fatigue in Jamee's voice. "Jamee, you are doing well. I had no idea you had so much stamina."

"I have always loved to run and I can swim a long way, but it will be very good to rest. Before I only ran because I liked to, not because I had to."

"We will come to another grove of Bookus trees in a few hours."

Billy started off at a trot but suddenly turned and kissed Jamee once again.

"I'm glad I found you."

Jamee's heart soared and her steps were lightened. She knew Billy was the one she had dreamed of. They continued down the creek bed, moving through the shadows cast by the hills around them. As they came out onto a flat part of the prairie, Jamee could see a grove of Bookus trees about a mile away. She couldn't get over their size; even from a distance they were massive. Jamee hoped that this was the grove that Billy was searching for. She was looking forward to a cool bath in a water cave. As if reading her mind, Billy turned out of the creek bed and headed for the grove.

Entering the grove of giant trees they slowed to a walk. They moved deep into the grove. All the while Billy searched for a tree with the right signs. He inspected several transit limbs, looking for fresh scrapes made by animals or the carved markings of his people. At last he found the signs that he sought.

Turning to Jamee, Billy said, "Take this pack and go to the second level and rest. I want to look around and find us something to eat."

He removed the pack and handed it to Jamee, unhooking the quiver and bow.

"Will you be gone long? I don't like being by myself, Billy."

"I'll only be gone a short while and I'll be careful."

He watched Jamee climb the limb, admiring the way her body looked wearing his loincloth. He turned to leave, with the image of her burnt in his mind.

He moved out of the grove, heading toward the clump of rain berry bushes he had noticed as they approached the grove. When he reached the bushes Billy prepared his bow. He knelt and picked up a large stone and threw it into the bushes. He heard a loud racket and a hopper burst out, running right past Billy's legs. He turned and released an arrow all in one motion. The arrow found its mark and the hopper dropped. Billy gathered the animal, took out his knife and quickly dressed it out. He skinned the hopper, turning the skin inside out and then covered the animal. After placing it on the ground he began to gather some of the delicious berries. He also picked some herbs he saw growing near the base of a rain berry bush. Heading back to the grove he carefully checked the surrounding area.

Billy entered the grove and went to the trunk of a tree to search around the large roots protruding above the ground. The Bookus tree roots had lifted stones from beneath the surface and this was what he was looking for. It had always amazed Billy how these trees seemed to provide for travelers. That was one reason his tribe held them in such high regard. He found a flat, thin stone that would suit his purpose and returned to the tree where Jamee waited.

Billy climbed to the first level and entered the cave. Moving to the back of the cave, he cut a small hole in the floor and took a long drink. He then washed the hopper and the skin. After he finished cleaning the animal Billy stuffed the body cavity with some of the rain berries and the herbs. He rubbed the outside with herbs and inserted a few stems of sage under the outer layer of meat. He carried everything up to the second level and entered the cave where he had told Jamee to wait for him.

Jamee stood in the back of the cave drying off using her syncotton coveralls. She hadn't noticed Billy enter the cave and he stood at the entrance, taking in the heavenly sight. Her body was perfect; flat stomach and smooth, brown skin glistened in the evening sunlight that streamed through the cave opening. She continued to dry as Billy stood frozen, unable to take his eyes away. Heat had risen to his face. Jamee looked up, seeing Billy standing at the entrance with his arms full, his face glowing and his mouth open.

Slowly covering herself, she laughed and said, "Billy, you're back. What are you carrying?"

"I....I brought us something to eat and a firestone."

Jamee quickly dressed and walked to Billy, taking the hopper from him and giving him a soft kiss.

"How are we going to cook this?" asked Jamee.

Billy knelt, placing the flat stone on the floor and setting the bow and quiver against the wall.

"I will build a fire on this stone. It will protect the tree and the cave will hide the light."

Billy went outside and gathered several large pieces of loose bark. Back inside, he broke them into smaller pieces. Billy reached over, pulled some loose material from the wall and placed it on the stone. He opened his pack, removed a small sparkling stone and a tiny bar of iron. Billy knelt close to the stone and with practiced skill struck the metal bar against the small stone. A spark leaped to the firestone and burned into the material Billy had placed there. He blew on the glowing fibers until a flame appeared. He added small pieces of bark, gradually adding some larger pieces until he had a small fire blazing.

"What can I do to help?" asked Jamee.

"Go and find a few limbs that will hold the hopper while it cooks and I will clean up in the pool."

Jamee went outside, noticing the light dimming as night approached. She was very tired but still excited by the look in Billy's eyes when he had watched her drying herself. She knew he had been watching and felt the heat of his eyes. She had already decided that she would give Billy her gift, not from gratitude but from love.

Yes, she thought, *I love Billy!*

Jamee went down to the ground and out into the grass. She found a nearby bush and cut several limbs that would support the hopper and started back.

She entered the cave and the firelight illuminated the enclosure with a warm glow. Billy was getting out of the pool, water dripping from his body. He was not a large man but his arms and shoulders were well defined and his stomach rippled. While she gazed, Billy looked up and for a moment looked deep into Jamee's eyes. He turned and quickly dressed. Billy picked up the hopper and walked to Jamee, taking the limbs and prepared the animal. He stuck a limb into the floor of the cave and positioned the animal over the fire.

He looked at Jamee and said, "It will take a little time for it to cook and you must be tired. Why don't you lie down and rest. I'll wake you when it's ready."

"No, Billy. There is something I want to give you," Jamee said as she walked toward Billy, removing her vest.

Billy took a step back, saying, "Are you sure, Jamee? You don't have to do this."

"Yes, Billy, I am sure." She molded herself to Billy, kissing him hard.

Billy's shock disappeared instantly and he returned Jamee's kiss and their lips blended into one. Billy's shyness flowed from him as his hand stroked the smooth skin of Jamee's back. He could feel the strong muscles under her skin. Everything about Jamee excited him. As Billy's hand moved over Jamee's body she quivered and a soft moan came from deep inside her. Jamee's hands reached down, grasped the bottom of Billy's vest, broke their kiss and lifted it over his head.

Jamee couldn't believe what she was doing. She had never been so aggressive, but she couldn't stop. She wanted Billy more than she had ever wanted anything.

Billy lifted Jamee, carried her to a clear spot and lowered her to the cave floor. He removed her loincloth, trying not to hurry. Although Billy had never made love before, he knew he couldn't wait much longer. He removed the rest of his clothes and lowered himself to Jamee.

She said, "Billy, you are my first and the women of my group teach a way of easing the pain of the first time. I'll show you if you'll let me."

Billy's ardor slowed at the thought of causing Jamee pain and he said, "Jamee, I wouldn't do anything to hurt you."

"I know you wouldn't. Don't worry; just let me guide you this first time." She rolled Billy over on his back and kissed him.

Her fingers explored his stomach and moved down his body. Jamee kissed his lips, moved down Billy's body kissing his chest and continuing down his stomach. She then moistened him. Jamee quickly positioned herself over Billy and slowly lowered herself onto him. Guiding him with her hand, she felt a sharp, quick pain and stopped for a moment. The passion and need quickly covered the pain as Jamee began to move her body and she felt Billy's body begin to move in response and the pain flew from her leaving only an incredible need.

She crushed her body to Billy's chest. He took her shoulders and rolled her to her back. He rose up on his arms, lowered his head and kissed Jamee. She returned the kiss, filled with a need for him. Jamee could not think. Her mind and body had the same need. She let out a soft moan and felt a tingling begin and it leaped to every part of her body. She shuddered and gasped for air as her release engulfed her. Her cry was met by a deeper resonant cry as Billy shuddered.

He lay beside Jamee, caressing her and said, "You are like no other person I have ever met, Jamee. I am so thankful that I found you."

"You are the one I have dreamed of and I never want to leave you, but my gift was given freely and you don't have to feel obligated for what we have done."

Billy rose up on his elbow and looked into those beautiful brown eyes and said, "Jamee, I've known ever since I found you that I wanted you to be with me. I only hoped you would feel the same."

He leaned over kissing her tenderly. They lay together, enjoying this new experience.

After a few minutes he said, "Let's clean up and eat. Then we must rest. We still have to travel tomorrow."

As he rose, Billy looked over at the hopper cooking and said, "Our meal will be a little burnt on one side."

Jamee laughed and said, "I think that was worth a well done hopper."

Billy turned the meat and added a few pieces of bark to the fire. He then joined Jamee in the pool. They splashed and teased each other, enjoying the other's company. Billy felt a joy he had never known, being with the woman he wanted for a mate. When they returned to his tribe he would ask his father to perform the ceremony that would tie him to Jamee and make her a part of the Eagle Tribe. They sat close, eating their meal, enjoying the closeness.

Jamee said, "This is delicious. You will have to teach me about the plants you've added. On my world I was considered a good cook, but there are many plants here I don't recognize. I will keep you busy, asking questions."

"I'll teach you all I know, but it will take time. The trek we are on will be dangerous, but there will be time to teach and to...learn about each other." Their talk was light and full of soft touches, like that of two lovers who had been with each other for more than a few days.

"We have to rest. In two days we will stop at a place my father showed me and then we rest for a few days."

"I'm looking forward to resting," Jamee said. A glow came to her cheeks. Billy took Jamee's hand and they moved to the entrance of the cave. They lay down together and kissed before settling down to sleep. Their thoughts intermingled as they drifted into a deep, contented sleep.

CHAPTER 3

Jamee woke with a start. Billy was not by her side. She looked around and found half of a Bookus nut lying near her. She relaxed and began to drink the sweet juice and eat the meat. When she looked toward the entrance, Billy stood there smiling.

"I see you."

Jamee returned the greeting. "I see you." She hoped this greeting had the same meaning on this world as hers. *I see you* was a greeting given to fast friends, family and to mates.

"Did you sleep well?"

"Yes, but I missed you when I woke. Where did you go?"

"I wanted to check the area. I didn't see any signs of the Volls. We must leave now if we want to reach the next Bookus grove before dark."

As they moved off into the new day, Jamee felt a slight discomfort from their joining. She smiled to herself, knowing that she was with her mate and that he would protect her and she him. When the time was right she would reveal to Billy the powers that she had, for she would not keep secrets. She would wait a while, knowing it might test the strength of Billy's love.

The prairie seemed to go on forever and as they traveled Billy would pick up plants, explaining what he knew of them. Their pace was slower than the day before, but they covered a great distance. While they walked Jamee noticed the prairie grew less hilly but the vegetation didn't change. At one point they saw a great herd of bovals, stretching away for miles.

The boval were odd looking creatures. Great massive bodies with rather short legs and covered in a tan fur. Large horns reached out four feet or more on each side of the heavy plate on their foreheads. They moved as a herd and left nothing behind them.

The tall hay-colored grass was everywhere as far as the eye could see. The undulating hills and sloping valley walls reminded Jamee of the waves on the ocean. The clumps of bushes and very tall grasses looked like tiny islands. There was a wondrous beauty here, but it was so different from the water world that she came from.

Jamee's mind wandered to the problem of telling Billy about the powers she had. On her world she was feared by the people and officials because of the trouble she could cause. That was the main reason she was put in a work group that took her far out to sea and away from the living centers. The other reason was Jamee's parents had died while fishing in their small work boat during a vicious storm; at least that was what she had been told. She had been only four years old when it had happened. She had rarely used her power except in private or when no one would know that it was anything but natural. She didn't even know if it could be used on this new world.

Jamee had the ability to take over the minds of birds and see through their eyes by just sending out her thoughts. She could will the birds to fly where she wanted them to go, do the things she wanted and probably a few other things she had yet to discover. She had always been afraid to experiment because of the way her group mistrusted her. She would have to try some simple things just to see if her power was brought with her to this strange new world.

As they walked, Jamee let her mind reach out searching for a winged animal. She found a large bird soaring high overhead. Jamee touched its mind and a tremendous jolt sent her mind reeling. She felt the bird drop, dead or unconscious, from the sky. She stumbled and Billy caught her.

"Are you okay, Jamee?"

She sat on the ground letting her mind sort things out.

"Yes. I just felt a little dizzy."

"We'll stop and rest for a moment."

"No, I'm okay. I think I'm just not used to being around so much land."

Jamee rose to her feet and started off at a trot. Billy took the lead but looked back often.

"You're going to fall and break something if you don't watch where you are going. I'm fine."

Jamee wondered if there was something wrong with her powers or did it have to do with the land bird she had contacted. On her world she used seabirds, but on occasion she had used land birds with no harm. She decided to try again but with less power.

She cleared her mind and sent a light thought out with only a small stream of power. She found another large bird and suddenly she was viewing the planet from high above. The bird's eyesight was exceptional and she could see with focused detail. As the bird circled she saw a group of people dressed in gray jumpsuits. *Volls*, she thought. *Where are they?* She increased her concentration a bit and forced the bird to circle wider. She saw three people running about two miles from where the Volls were and they were heading right for them. She forced the bird lower and saw herself and Billy a mile or so away from the Volls. She released the bird and looked up to see the great bird wheeling away.

"Billy, what kind of bird is that?"

Billy looked to where Jamee was pointing and said, "It's a Great Eagle, the bird that protects my people. I've never seen one flying like that."

The Eagle was clawing at the sky, trying to gain altitude. With great sweeps of its wings it slowly became a tiny dot high in the sky.

"What's up ahead of us?"

"There's another creek bed over this hill. We will follow it for a few miles to another Bookus grove. We will stop there for the night."

Jamee tried to think of a way of warning Billy without revealing her secret. She was so afraid that she might drive Billy away with her secret like it did people on her old world. Old world? It sounded strange but she was committed to Prairie now and would not look back. Ocean held nothing for her except one friend and now she only wanted Billy.

"Billy, sometimes I get feelings about things and I'm having that feeling now. There is danger up ahead. I think we should find another way to the grove."

Billy stared at Jamee for a moment, wondering if he should trust her instincts.

He said, "If we go another way, it will take us near a Koro area. That may be more dangerous than anything up ahead. Stay here and I will go and see what's out there."

"Be careful. I know something is there."

Billy moved off at a slow trot. He had traveled about a mile and then he slowed. He too was getting a feeling of danger. He had often gotten this feeling during a hunt and it was usually correct. He slowed to a walk and moved out of the creek bed. He crept through the grass for a few hundred yards and stopped. He heard the flimsy buzz of voices some distance off. He raised his head to the level of the prairie grass and saw a group of eight Volls. He wanted to get closer but he heard movement off to his left. Billy crouched down in the tall grass and waited to see what was coming. It was three Koros striding toward the Volls.

As they approached, the one who seemed to be the leader was growling at the Volls. Billy could not understand the words of the Koro language but the Koro sounded angry. Billy watched the men spread out in a semi-circle. The Koros moved in quickly, still grunting and raising their arms.

Just as the Koros entered the semi-circle, all eight men drew weapons and attacked, cutting down one and badly injuring another. The Koro still standing lashed out with his spear, whirled, cut down one of the men and cut two others badly. The men continued their attack and leaped on the Koros, killing them in seconds. The soldiers grabbed the two wounded men and were trying to lift the dead man when from a distance they heard shouts from more Koros. They dragged the dead man off a short distance, dropping him, trying to hide his body, and ran away from the direction of the shouts carrying the wounded soldiers. Billy was still trying to make sense out of what had happened when two more Koros ran past him in pursuit of the Volls.

Billy waited for ten minutes but heard no sounds. He approached the battle scene carefully. The three Koros were cut to pieces by something extremely sharp. He walked to where the dead man had been dragged and saw he had been speared through his right side by a Koro weapon. He lay face down and as Billy rolled him over onto his back his right arm flopped to the side with a short staff attached to his wrist. Billy had never had a chance to get a close look at a white man before except during the brief fight several days earlier.

He wore a syncotton uniform with detailed insignias on the shoulders. He was like all other men he had seen except his skin color under the torn cloth was very white. Billy reached down and removed the staff and examined it. It looked to be made of some kind of metal but it felt very light and solid. Not wanting to be in the area if the others returned, Billy tucked the staff in his belt and headed back to the creek bed to get Jamee out of the area.

While Billy was gone Jamee examined the creek bed and the area around her. What a strange world this is, with no great bodies of water and only this rolling prairie. It's a beautiful world but so different of her world. She would need time to adjust to it. *If it weren't for Billy finding me, I would be dead by now*, she mused.

Her thoughts went back to their making love in the water cave. She would never have thought that it could feel so good and that she could be so wanton to make the first move. *I gave myself to Billy, not out of gratitude but out of need and love for him.* Jamee had never felt love for a man before and it surprised her how quickly it came. It was true love, of that there was no doubt and making love... She wanted more of that feeling and to please Billy.

On her planet she had dreamed every night for the past six months of a man who would take her away and keep her safe. He had long black hair, a smooth face and eyes the color of the ocean. There was no one on her world like that. All but the very young boys had beards and eyes that were deep brown.

The men in her group all looked at her with disgust and lust. They all knew in a few weeks her eighteenth birthday would come and she would be given to one of them as a wife. Since all the men had at least one wife already, she would become no more than someone to cook, clean and bear more children. The women would have little to do with her because of her power but also because of her beauty. She was not skinny and burnt dark by the sun. Since her fourteenth birthday she had filled out and was taller than the other women. Her skin never darkened past a creamy brown and it had a silky texture. When she bathed she saw the lust in the eyes of the men and the hate of the women. When orders came to give up one woman to the Volls she was immediately selected by the group. The men knew there would be no peace otherwise.

Now Billy had found her and she felt a part of something that could be good. She thought about the coming night when she would be with Billy in another water cave. She blushed and felt warmth in her loins. Jamee never believed she could have these thoughts. She had listened to the other women of her group talking about sex, the things they did to please and the things the men did to satisfy themselves. Jamee could not think of enjoying any of that, but with Billy she knew she could, if only to please him.

As she sat daydreaming a hand grabbed her on the shoulder. Jamee jumped and swung her fist but it was caught in an iron grip.

"It's me," Billy said with a smile on his face.

Jamee's face was flushed as she looked at him.

"You have to be more careful when we're out in the open. I depend on you to watch our back trail."

"I....I'm sorry, Billy. I let my mind wander."

"What were you thinking about?"

She looked deep into his eyes and replied, "Tonight."

Billy's eyebrows came together as he thought about her reply and then flew apart as he blushed in comprehension. Jamee gave a quiet laugh and her white teeth sparkled.

"What did you find?"

"I found Volls and Koros fighting. The Volls killed all the Koros and lost one of their own. Then another small group of Koros gave chase to the Volls. I have never heard of them fighting one another before".

Jamee said, "On the ship I heard some talk about trouble between the Volls and Koros and that was why they were taking us to make a peace offering. What were the Koros going to do with us?"

"I think that they would have put you to work in their mine. That's what we think they do with the people who are captured here. That is one of the reasons I am on this trek, to see if I can find out where they have taken all the people. We have to go now, but follow me very quietly because I don't know if there are more of them in the area."

"I go where you go and I will watch our back trail. I will not think about tonight until tonight," she said with a smile.

Billy led off down the creek bed for about a mile. When he was past the area of the battle he left the creek and ran in a crouch through the tall grass. They kept on for a few miles until they were at the edge of the Bookus grove. Billy told Jamee to wait while he scouted out the area. Billy went to the center of the grove and then headed close to the northern edge. He chose a tree and climbed up four levels to a small cave, dropped his gear and pack and headed back down to the second level. As he cut a hole in the floor for them to bathe, Billy's thoughts ran to Jamee.

He still could not believe he had found a beautiful girl all alone on the prairie and she wanted to be with him. He had never made love to anyone. Of course he had thought of having sex many times. The real thing was so much better than he could have imagined. What had happened took him to places he never dreamed of. He looked down and saw his body responding to his thoughts.

Now you must calm down, little buddy, so I can bring Jamee here without making a fool of myself, he thought.

Billy returned to where Jamee was waiting and as soon as she looked at him, her eyes widened.

With a smile she moved close to him and said with a giggle, "I'm glad you are happy to see me."

Billy blushed, then smiled down at her and kissed her. "I have found a tree for us, my love."

Breathlessly, she could only nod and think, *He called me my love.*

They reached the Bookus tree and started up to the second level.

Outside the water cave Billy said, "We will have to be quiet in here, but I have a cave picked out on the fourth level where we can talk and sleep tonight."

"I hope that's not all we're going to do, my love."

They entered the cave and Billy lifted the floor he had already cut free. They drank their fill and got ready to clean themselves. Jamee stripped and turned to see Billy jump in the water. She walked slowly over, letting Billy see all of her.

She paused and looked down at him and said, "All that you see is only for you, Billy Running Wolf."

She slipped into the water and moved over to Billy and kissed him. She picked up a piece of material Billy had taken from the wall and began to scrub his back and arms. Billy scrubbed his chest and legs and turned to Jamee. He turned her around so he could scrub her back, neck and arms.

He said, "I will have to go and get us something to eat. You go up to the fourth level and find the cave with our gear and wait for me."

"I'll do that but first I'll go down to find a firestone and herbs for the hopper you will bring back."

He kissed her softly and said, "I will never tire of kissing you! I love you, Jamee." He turned and boosted himself up to sit at the edge of the pool and looked into her eyes saying, "I love you, Jamee!"

"Tell me that every day, Billy. I love you too." She moved to him and he was pleased. Afterwards she said with a smile, "Go on now and find us something to eat."

Billy rose, still feeling a little weak and warm, dressed and left the cave. Jamee washed her hair and face, dressed and moved down to the ground to gather the things needed to prepare their meal. She easily found the herbs, roots and a firestone and then headed back up the tree to the fourth level. The water cave was only half as big as the other cave and it was high up in the tree. She found Billy's gear and began organizing the area, making room for the fire and a place to sleep. She took one of the knives and cut a hole in the floor at the back of the cave. As she sat down next to the pack, she saw a metal staff in the gear that she hadn't seen before.

CHAPTER 4

The staff looked vaguely familiar but she couldn't place where she had seen one or its purpose. She picked it up to examine. It was very light but felt strong and was a dull bronze color. At one end there was a small guarded lever. She put her finger under the guard and pushed the lever down. From the other end of the staff a double-edged blade snapped straight out from the end. The blade was about eight inches long and its silvery metal gleamed. She brought the blade close to her face to examine it and lightly touched the edge with her finger. Blood sprang from a deep cut in her right index finger and she dropped the staff. The blade cut into the floor as if it were made of paper. Jamee grabbed her finger, trying to stem the flow of blood. She took some material from the cave wall and pressed it to her finger. The blood stopped flowing at once and the material seemed to ease the pain.

She carefully lifted the staff out of the floor and gently pressed the lever flat again. The blade retracted with a snap and was once again only a staff. At the sound of the blade retracting her memory focused and she remembered that a Voll officer had carried one of these things on a thong around his wrist. She put it away and cut a piece of material from her syncotton coveralls. She wrapped the strip around the matting from the cave wall to secure it to her finger.

Billy moved through the grove and into the high grass. He found a patch of rain berries and quickly had a hopper cleaned and skinned. He headed back to the grove, carefully checking for signs of animals and people. He reached the tree and was soon at the water cave where Jamee should be. As he stepped through he found Jamee ready to spring with a knife in her hand. She relaxed and smiled at Billy. He was impressed at her ability to adapt quickly. He kissed her and sat down to rest a moment.

"We shouldn't light the fire 'til dark. Would you like to see the sunset while we wait?" Billy asked.

"Yes!"

"Come with me then."

Jamee followed Billy out, carefully keeping her right hand from his view.

Billy led the way until they were at the eighth level and stopped at the next transit branch.

"You go first. This is the top of the tree."

As Jamee brushed past him, she let her body rub across his chest and smiled at him. She started up the transit branch and she felt Billy's hand grasp her thigh.

"Let me help you up, my love," Billy said and smiled up to her.

"Thank you," she laughed, wiggling seductively.

As her head came out above the last branch she stopped and gasped. At the top of the tree the limbs tightly intertwined to form a platform, but what was more amazing was the view. She looked out at the prairie to the west and as far as she could see there were rolling hills of golden green grass. Off in the distance she saw another grove of Bookus trees and clumps of small bushes scattered here and there. It was a sight she had never seen before and it was beautiful. The sun was just above the horizon and slowly sinking onto the grassland. She felt a hand squeeze her again. She laughed and continued out onto the natural platform.

"I'm sorry, but the view just froze me for a moment."

"I know what you mean. It does it to me and I've seen it many times. The great thing is it is just a little different each time and when the seasons change so does the prairie. So this is a one-time view and we should enjoy it."

Billy sat down and pulled Jamee down to sit between his legs as she marveled at this new world.

Jamee pressed her back against Billy's chest and rested her hands on his thighs.

Billy said, "When we go to my village after this trek there will be other men there. Many are bigger and some are stronger. They could protect and care for you and...and..."

"What are you trying to say?" Jamee asked.

Billy took a deep breath, wanting to ask but afraid of the answer. He held his thoughts for a moment and finally plunged into his question as best he could.

"I have never been with a woman before you and I don't know if I will be the best person to keep you safe and, more than that, make you happy. You might want..."

Jamee spun to look at Billy's face. There were tears in her eyes.

"Are you saying you don't want me, Billy?"

Billy looked at her tears with a start. "No, Jamee! I want you more than I've ever wanted anyone or anything in my life. I want you all for myself, but I don't want you to think you owe me or have to stay with me. I love you truly. You are too important to me to obligate you or trick you. I guess what I'm really trying to say is you are the most beautiful girl I have ever seen and I don't know why you would want someone like me. I'm not smart around women and I'm not sure how I'm supposed to act. I am a little frightened of your beauty."

Now Jamee could see Billy's eyes glisten. She turned her back to him and pressed in close. She watched the beauty all around her as the sun softened the color of the landscape as it touched the horizon. She tried to put her thoughts in order but what filled her head was the fact that Billy thought she was beautiful and loved her.

On her world she saw the looks the men gave her. They did not look at her as if she were pretty but as a thing of lust. They were not gentle or kind in any way. Now here was the man she had dreamed about and he was afraid of her beauty. What must she do to keep him? Her needs were for happiness, to be cared for and loved by only this man. She also wanted to care for him so she decided that truth was her only hope.

"Billy, no man had ever called me beautiful or even shown me kindness. Now you have done all that. The truth is that for months before I left my world I dreamed of a man with long black hair, a smooth face and eyes the color of the ocean. I dreamed he came and took me away as his own. I didn't know where he would take me, only that I was at peace as I have never been before. Now that has happened and he has a fear that I will want someone other than him."

Still watching the colors of this new world change by the minute with a beauty she never thought possible, Jamee pressed deeper into his arms.

Without turning she told him, "Don't make me into something to be frightened of. Don't worry that you don't think you know how to act around women. I am not other women. I am the woman that loves you only and unless you throw me away I will never leave you. The fact is I am frightened of you, Billy. I'm afraid I'll make a mistake or do something to displease you and I don't want to live like that. The truth is you can never do anything to drive me away if you just love me like I love you."

Jamee sat quietly watching the sun drip below the horizon and the colors fade into pastels and then the silvery grays of evening.

Jamee felt Billy's hand on her waist as he lifted her and turned her to sit on his thighs facing him. In the soft colors of evening his eyes were a deep hue of blue. Billy kissed her softly on the lips and again stared into her beautiful brown eyes.

"This worry ends now. I will also tell you the truth. I have never felt love for a woman until I met you, Jamee. You are the most beautiful girl I have ever seen, but that isn't the only reason I love you. I see someone who I want to be with forever because of who you are inside and out. Yes, I want to hold you, kiss you and make love to you, but I also want to work with you, walk with you, protect you, learn from you and be happy with you. I will never leave you, Jamee, and I will love you forever."

They kissed and held each other until the light of the sunset had turned to night.

Jamee smiled and teasingly asked, "You really want to make love to me?"

Billy laughed, lifting her to her feet and said, "First thing: I really want to eat and then I'll think about your question."

Jamee playfully slapped Billy's behind and started down to the water cave. In the cave Billy started the fire and Jamee prepared the hopper. She set it to roast over the fire and lifted the cover she had previously cut in the floor to fill the water containers. Billy gathered his gear and set it aside. This cave was much smaller than the one on the second level and Billy explained that being higher, the fire light and any noise they made would not be heard or seen. He had gathered some Bookus nuts on the way to the cave and opened one and offered half to Jamee. They sat and enjoyed the fruit and relaxed, waiting for the meat to cook. It was then that Billy noticed the wrapping on Jamee's finger.

"What happened to your finger?"

"I cut it on the staff you brought with you."

Billy took her hand in his and removed the wrapping and the material from the tree she had put into the cut. The cut had neatly healed and only a red line was visible.

Jamee looked at her finger and said, "That's amazing! It was a deep cut only a few hours ago and now it is almost healed."

Billy said, "I have never used the matting from the tree to treat a cut. Where did you get the matting?"

"I took it from the wall here," pointing at the place where she had gathered it. "I didn't know what else to use so I tried it. We use something that looks like this on my world but it only keeps the injury clean until it heals. This material has healing properties I have never seen before."

Billy said, "We'll make sure we take some of it with us when we leave. You said you cut it on the staff. How can that be? There are no sharp edges. I found it under the man who was killed. It was on a thong around his wrist."

"I have seen one once before. One of the Volls on the ship had one and all the other soldiers shied away whenever he passed by. Look, I'll show you what it can do."

Jamee picked up the staff and gripped the end with the small guarded lever. She pressed the lever and with a snick the blade sprang from the tip. She held it up for Billy to see.

As Billy reached for it Jamee said sharply, "Be careful! It is so sharp it will cut deep with only a light touch."

Billy took the staff and examined it with his eyes. The blade was only about eight inches long and not very thick. He picked up one of the sticks brought in to cook the hopper and touched it to the blade. As the piece of wood touched the blade it parted and fell to the floor. Billy tried a few more times, watching closely. He could feel no resistance or truly see the blade touch the stick as it parted.

"This blade is sharper than anything I have ever seen. How did you make it come out?"

Jamee explained about the lever and when Billy tried to push it down he couldn't get his index finger under the guard. He used his little finger and finally was able to push the lever down. With a snap it retracted into the staff. He worked it a few more times but each time it took an effort to operate it.

"My hands are too big for it."

Jamee took the staff from Billy and with little effort her small but strong fingers operated the blade in and out.

"Maybe I should carry this and practice as we go."

"All right, Jamee, but only practice with the blade retracted until you become familiar with it."

"I'll be careful," Jamee said and gave Billy a bright smile. "Thank you for trusting me with this. It will help protect us, I'm sure."

They ate their meal and drank from the pool. After they finished Jamee took a piece of syncotton and removed her clothes and washed herself. She turned to Billy and motioned for him to come to her. Billy moved to her and let her remove his clothing. She gently washed Billy all over. She finished by drying him slowly and then laid the cloth out to dry.

"I guess we should get some sleep," and she started to move away from Billy.

He reached out and grabbed her waist and laughed. "Oh, no! We haven't finished yet."

She giggled as Billy lifted her and moved her away from the pool.

He looked deep into her eyes and said, "Now it is my turn to please you."

Jamee lay back, stretched and said not a word. Although Billy was not experienced, he had thought all day about what he would do. He only hoped it would please Jamee.

Billy kissed her hair, then her forehead and then her eyes softly. He moved to her cheeks, nose and then to her mouth. Jamee opened her mouth wide and tried to probe with her tongue, but Billy moved quickly to her chin and neck.

Jamee's breath quickened, but he took his time as his mouth traveled her body. He kissed her left shoulder, down her arm to her hand and fingers. Softly kissing her wrist, he let his lips slide up to her elbow. He kissed the inside of her bicep and ran his tongue along the ridge of her armpit. Her taste was incredible and he was enjoying his trek across her body.

Billy moved to her right arm and repeated what he had done to her left.

Jamee was trying to relax but the warmth that sprang up from her chest moved to her stomach. She used her will power to remain calm and enjoy every minute. She knew what Billy was doing was his gift to her and she intended to stay in control of herself.

Billy kissed her silky smooth skin and a moan escaped from Jamee's lips and he knew she liked what he was doing.

A fire raced across her chest as Billy's lips gave her pleasure. He lingered at each breast and then moved down her stomach.

Under the creamy softness of her skin he could feel the hard muscles ripple as his lips moved across her flat belly. He paused at her belly button and dipped his tongue in.

He couldn't get over her taste. Her whole body had a flavor so pleasing it would be burnt into his memory. Billy's lips seemed to be everywhere giving her a feeling of need. A new fragrance filled his nostrils. It was the aroma of her flower. His mind was racing to move faster and it took his iron will to go slow. He moved to the hollow at the top of her left leg, kissing her there and letting his lips explore the depression. He traveled down the top of her thigh to her knee and continued slowly to her ankle. Billy started up towards Jamee's calf.

When Billy kissed the back of her knee Jamee bucked and swung her head back and forth. Bolts of lightning passed through her. Never had she thought that being kissed there could feel so good. His lips kissed her inner thigh and paused at the center of her heat.

He started down her right leg and Jamee grabbed at his hair to pull him back. She heard the muffled laugh come from the top of her thigh and released him to let him continue on his journey. Once again the lightning streaked through her body as he came to the back of her knee. Her eyes were closed but she saw streaks of light. Billy moved over her body, lingering at the center of her warmth with soft kisses. Her taste was wondrous.

As he continued his kisses her mind froze, waiting for the release. It came in waves of heat and a humming tingle coursed through her veins. It lasted and lasted, holding her in a grip that was strong and full of pleasure. Finally, trying to catch her breath, Jamee settled back to the floor.

She said, "Billy, I have never felt anything like that and in so many places."

Billy moved up and put his mouth to her ear and said, "My love, I love you so much and it's not over yet."

"What do you mean?" she asked breathlessly.

Then she felt Billy's body move to hers and her mind began to freeze again. Billy's mouth came down on hers and kissed her deeply. Billy could not hold back what had been driving him all day. His need for her seemed to have no bounds.

Jamee's need had returned in an instance, filling her completely. She felt herself building to a release again. It came to her so quickly she was driven by need alone as her body moved against him. Her release took her again and she felt Billy begin his fulfillment that made his whole body throb. They lay together for a long time, holding, caressing and kissing.

How could life be any better than this? Jamee asked herself.

As if reading her thoughts Billy said, "I wish this moment would last forever, because I can't imagine life being any better."

They separated. Jamee laid her head on Billy's chest looking up at him, her breath still ragged.

"Billy, how did you know so much about my body and how to make me feel like that?"

Billy smiled and said, "I just thought about what you did for me and I wanted more than anything to please you. I enjoyed myself and kissed you like I thought you would like and I enjoyed hearing and feeling your pleasure."

"I can't describe what it felt like except to say that I was so filled with fire and need for you. It was like you were driving me crazy with need."

They both lay with their thoughts for several minutes.

When Billy looked down at Jamee, she was fast asleep and breathing easily. He lifted her head and slipped out from under her, gently lowering her head to the floor. He went to the fire and built it up a bit to add more light and then went through his pack and removed a light blanket and placed it close to Jamee. Billy went to the pool at the back of the water cave, picking up the cloth Jamee had left to dry. He washed his body quickly, cleaned the cloth and returned to Jamee. She was lying on her side with her legs curled up and her beautiful long black hair spread out like a fan. Billy pulled her hair up behind her head and gently began to wipe her neck, back and legs. He went to the pool and rinsed the cloth. Returning to Jamee, he turned her onto her back and began to bathe her body.

As he worked he looked at her, still not believing her beauty was his. She was in a deep sleep and as he softly wiped her body he wanted to kiss her softness but didn't. Her body was perfect, with no flaws he could see. Billy wiped her legs and returned to the pool to rinse the cloth. He laid it out to dry and then returned to Jamee. He lay down beside her and in her sleep she rolled over, put her arm over his stomach and moved her head to his chest. Billy breathed a deep sigh of contentment, closed his eyes and was asleep in moments.

The next morning Billy woke to find Jamee gone. He sat up quickly looking around. He found half a Bookus nut close at hand and he smiled. Billy also noticed the staff missing. He went out of the cave and found a fresh cut leaf on the transit branch leading up. He went to the top level and found Jamee sitting nude with her legs pulled to her chest. She turned as he mounted the platform. She grabbed Billy and gave him a deep kiss.

"Good morning, my love. You look well rested and very manly."

Billy had forgotten to dress and he knelt beside her. "Good morning. Did you sleep well?"

"I feel so relaxed. I hope I will be able to walk today. I woke up early and found myself clean and fresh. I've never had anyone care for me like that. You are too good to me."

Billy smiled and relaxed beside Jamee. As he looked around the prairie he saw smoke rising about five or six miles away.

It was a dark smoke that had to come from a large fire.

"Jamee, did you see that smoke when you came up here?"

"No. I looked all around to check for people at first light. It must have just started a few minutes ago. What is it?"

"I don't know, but it can't be good. No one would make a fire that size, especially in the daylight. Come, Jamee. Let's get ready to move out. We'll try to take a look at what has happened. It's to the north and that's the way we are heading."

They went to the cave and ate a quick breakfast while they packed their gear. Billy and Jamee moved to the ground and started north out of the Bookus grove.

"Stay close to me."

They moved off toward the still billowing smoke. Jamee scanned the sky and saw a large bird circling nearby. She reached out gently with her mind and entered the bird. Her vision became sharp and she was looking down over what appeared to be bodies piled up and burning. She quickly checked the area and found no one moving around. She looked further out and to the northeast. Miles away she saw a party of men moving away. Jamee released the bird and her vision returned to herself. She followed Billy as he set a quick pace.

After a few miles Billy stopped to let them rest for a minute. He moved off again, carefully scanning the grass ahead for any danger. When they were a few hundred yards from the still smoking fire he held out his hand, palm out, to signal Jamee to wait. She shook her head no and motioned she would follow. Billy didn't want to argue so he started off again at a slow pace checking all around. When they reached the edge of the grass that had burned away from the fire he stopped. He could clearly see the blaze and the burning bodies of Koros. It took him only a few minutes to view the entire area and then he quickly bypassed the burnt grass and continued on north. Several miles from the fire he found a creek bed and a pool of water. He stopped and motioned to Jamee that they would rest for a few minutes.

He moved close to Jamee and said, "I don't understand what has happened. Those bodies were Koros and I have never heard of Koros burning their own. As far as my tribe knows, they take their dead and we think they are placed in one of the mines they have closed. I just can't think of what might have happened back there."

"Do you think it could have been the Volls that did that? It looked like there might have been a battle, but it was hard to tell with all the burning."

Billy said, "Until yesterday I have never heard of the Volls and Koros fighting. Something must have happened to cause a war. What would cause the Volls to fight the Koros so close to their area? We are going to have to go in closer to where the Koros live and try to find out what is going on. I was sent on this trek to check on them, but I never expected to see anything like this."

They sat close and rested. Jamee was happy to find that she was not tired. She had thought with all the exercise the night before she might be a little weak. The thought made her smile and she turned and kissed Billy.

"What?" Billy asked.

"Oh, nothing."

"Are you ready?"

She nodded and they started up the creek bed heading north again.

The pace was slower and as she followed behind Billy she began to swing the staff in tight circles, getting a feel for it. She did not release the blade, but kept it retracted as she tried new moves. The staff was so light and completely silent that Billy didn't see what she was doing. On her world she had used a longer staff for exercise and spears for fishing so she quickly began to feel confident with the staff.

She had never used a weapon in anger but had fought with other women several times when they tried to abuse her. Jamee had no fear of fighting, as the other women soon found out, and she was left alone. The women of her group found many ways to punish her that didn't include fighting. Every hard job that came along was assigned to her, from hauling in the larger fish to repairing the structures on the floating island. Jamee didn't mind the hard work and it made her body strong. The worst part for Jamee was the loneliness and the looks in the eyes of everyone. They didn't trust her when they learned of her gift.

After miles of walking Billy once again thought it was safe to talk softly. He continued telling her about the plants and the few animals they saw. Jamee listened and took everything in.

As they walked Jamee once again thought about the knowledge she withheld from Billy. She trusted him with her life and was sure they would be together from now on. She felt the guilt of her secret and made up her mind not to hold anything back from him. She decided she would tell Billy that night when they stopped.

As they moved through the creek bed Billy heard a noise in the distance. He held his hand up and moved it to his lips to let Jamee know to stop and be quiet. He motioned for her to wait and when she shook her head he gave her a piercing look and motioned again. This time Jamee nodded her head and moved into the grass beside the creek. Billy moved down the creek bed, searching with his eyes and ears. After about four hundred yards he had an intense feeling of danger. He jumped into the grass just as a spear passed his neck, missing by only a few inches.

Billy had his knife out and was swinging it as the Koro ran at him. He cut the Koro across the chest, brought the knife back around and sliced his throat. The Koro dropped without uttering a sound, but three more moved into the creek bed and advanced toward Billy. Billy dropped his pack and bow to the ground and readied himself for the attack. They came in together with their spears held forward and up toward his chest. Billy dove in low at the center Koro, taking his legs out from under him and whipping his arm out to the right, cutting through the tendons of the leg of the one on the right. Billy continued through, spun and stood facing the lone Koro still standing. He moved quickly in on him, raising his knife arm. As he did this the Koro raised his spear to block the blow and Billy struck out with a vicious front kick that took the Koro just below the ribcage.

Billy continued forward, but the Koro Billy had knocked down in his first attack swung his spear, slicing Billy's left side and into the back of his arm. Billy gasped but his forward motion carried him onto the other Koro. Billy's knife plunged into his chest. Billy rolled trying to get to his feet but his left arm was useless. He knew he was bleeding badly and was in trouble. He rose to his knees to block the spear point that was sure to come. As the Koro moved in on Billy, his right armed dropped from his body and a gaping cut appeared in his side. The Koro dropped and was dead before he hit the ground. Billy's eyes, nearly blind from the pain, looked out at Jamee moving toward the last Koro with the staff in her right hand, blade extended. She quickly killed the Koro, looked around, seeing four dead Koros and nothing else moved in the area. She turned and ran to Billy.

He said in a weak voice, "I told you to stay back there."

He slowly fell back and passed out. She examined his back and arm, grabbed his pack, pulled water, syncotton and matting from the Bookus tree out. Jamee cleaned the wounds, packed the matting into the deep cuts and wrapped his back and left arm with the syncotton. She picked up Billy's bow and pack and slung them over her shoulder, then sat Billy up and put her head under his right arm.

"Billy, try and walk with me. We have to get out of this area as quickly as we can."

Billy could barely walk but with Jamee's help was able to move down the creek bed. They traveled for about an hour and as darkness fell Jamee looked for a place to stop. There were no Bookus trees that she could see so she found a patch of rain berries and carefully helped Billy into the center of the bushes. He lay down and was asleep instantly.

Jamee left the bushes and made her way back to the creek. She brushed their tracks back for over a hundred yards and walked off toward the west until she found a hard, rocky patch of ground. She went off in several directions, backtracking each time. Then she backtracked to the creek bed and moved down the creek, brushing away her tracks as she went. By the time she reached the rain berry bushes it was completely dark and she found Billy just as she had left him.

She removed the bandages and the blood-soaked matting. She could feel that the wounds were already beginning to heal. She used the last of the matting, covered the wounds and wrapped them tight. She gave Billy some water and thirstily drank the remainder of one of the containers. She gathered the bloody material, walked out into the prairie and buried it. Jamee gathered a handful of rain berries and ate them. She pulled the blanket from the pack, wrapped Billy in it and lay down beside him.

As she waited for sleep her thoughts were about killing the Koros. She had never killed anyone, but she did it without thinking. She saw Billy in trouble and it was over before she had time to give any thought to it. She would kill again to protect Billy and herself. She then thought about her power. She would find some way to use it to protect them but she wasn't sure how. Jamee let her mind reach out, scanning the area for a night bird, but fell asleep almost at once.

CHAPTER 5

It was daylight when she woke, still lying beside Billy. His breathing was easy and his body was not hot with fever.

"You should never fall asleep with your mind open, Land thing."

Jamee sat up, looking all around, seeing nothing but the bushes and grass.

"When you leave your mind open many can look into it if they are gifted." Jamee's head snapped around but still didn't see who was talking.

"Who are you and where are you?" Jamee asked. Jamee had the staff in her hand as she stood.

"Would you try and hurt me just for talking?" the voice asked. "I am here."

Jamee saw flashes of color in a bush five feet from her. The display was all the colors of a rainbow and brilliant.

The colors were gone and Jamee peered closely at the bush and saw a small bird staring back at her. She blinked to try and clear her vision, but the bird was still there. Its color was hard to define. The bird was a brownish color that blended in with the bush. As she stared, the bird's color flashed through the rainbow again.

"Yes, I'm the one who is talking. What's the matter? Has a bird never talked to you before?" it asked.

"No," Jamee replied. "What kind of bird are you?"

"I am a Star bird and my name is Flick. You are an odd Land thing, the first I've ever seen who had mind enough to hear me. I have seen many Land things but none with your power."

Jamee said, "I am not from this world but from another. I was brought here and this man rescued me and protects me. My name is Jamee and his name is Billy. I have always had the power to enter the minds of birds to see what they see but never had one talk to me."

"That's because I am one of very few that has power like you do. I think I will stay with you for a while. It might be fun to see what you see and talk to, Jamee. Besides, the man thing, Billy, looks very interesting," replied Flick.

Jamee said, "I would like to talk to you as well, but if you stay with me, you must help us by watching for danger. Some here would try to harm us if they found us. You must be careful of your colors and not alert the others."

"Jamee thing, I am not stupid. I am very old and know this land well."

"I'm sorry and I know you must be very smart, but I don't know anything about you. And my name is Jamee, not Jamee thing."

"Very well. I will do as you ask for as long as I want. Then I will go about my business as I wish."

"Thank you, Flick. You are welcome to stay as long as you wish. If you would watch out for Billy, I would be very thankful. He is important to me. He protects me and we love each other."

"Love? Do you mean to say you mate with each other and he guards your nest?"

"Something like that," Jamee said with a blush.

"I look forward to seeing you mate. It must be different than the way birds mate because he looks too big to climb on your back."

Jamee made no reply.

Billy began to stir. He rolled on his back and opened his eyes.

"How are you feeling, my love?" Jamee asked.

"I feel like I've been dragged across the prairie."

Then remembering what had happened, Billy sat up quickly, wincing and looked around. He didn't recognize the area and started to rise, reaching for his knife.

Jamee reached out and held him down and said, "Take it easy. We're safe and I have dressed your wounds. I couldn't find a Bookus Grove so I brought you here to rest. You've been asleep all night."

"The last thing I remember was the fight with the Koros and you standing there with that staff of yours. How did you carry me and how far away are we from where I fought? " Billy asked.

"We're several miles away. I helped you walk down the creek bed and I found these rain berry bushes. Let me check your wounds."

They both peered at the cuts as Jamee lifted the dressings. Both wounds were almost completely closed but red.

"The matting from the Bookus tree is amazing," Jamee said. "I used the last of it so we will have to get more."

Billy slowly stood and could feel the damage to his side and arm, but he could move without a great deal of pain.

"We need to move away from here. It is too dangerous to stay. They will follow our trail."

"No, Billy. I covered our trail and made several false trails to lead anyone away from us if they try to follow."

Billy looked down at Jamee. Her eyes twinkled and her smile was dazzling.

"How did you know to do that?"

"I have listened and watched everything you have done. I am a fast learner."

Billy pulled her to him and kissed her. "I am proud of you. We make a very good pair."

They gathered up their gear and started back to the north. Billy took it slow for a while, still feeling weak from his injuries. As the day progressed he increased their speed, feeling better and better. By nightfall they found another Bookus Grove and this time they both traveled into it. The pain in his side had increased but he said nothing.

Billy found a good tree and they moved up to the third level. Jamee took Billy's knife and cut a large hole in the floor so they could bathe. She removed the wrapping from Billy's wounds. The arm was completely healed over, but a small amount of blood was coming from the wound in his side. They undressed and jumped into the pool.

Jamee washed Billy and gently cleaned the wound in his side. Billy relaxed and watched Jamee wash herself. Every time he looked at her he was amazed at her beauty.

He reached for her and Jamee came to him but said, "Tonight you rest and let me care for you. I want you strong and healthy."

"I am strong now but you are right. We will rest tonight. I just hope I can sleep with this in the way."

He was looking down and gave Jamee a sad smile.

"You can make it for one day," Jamee said laughing and gave him a quick kiss and sprang out of the pool.

She was dressed and was out of the cave before Billy realized it. He lay back in the pool letting the cool water soak into him and letting his mind float for a moment. Jamee returned quickly with everything needed for a fire and had three Bookus nuts that she laid on the floor. After they ate Jamee cleaned the wound in Billy's side and applied some matting from the wall of the cave. She wrapped it and told Billy to lie down and relax. He lay on his stomach and Jamee gently massaged his neck and upper back. Billy was asleep in moments. Jamee lay beside him, wrapped her body over him to keep him warm. She was so content feeling his body next to hers that she too was asleep quickly.

She woke and saw Billy looking at her.

He was smiling and said, "Good morning, beautiful."

Jamee smiled at him and kissed him deeply, then said, "I could wake up to your eyes every morning, my love."

She rose and began removing the wrap that covered his wound. There was still some blood seeping from the wound and it had turned an angry red and was slightly swollen. Now that she looked closely, she could see the tiredness in his eyes and she could feel the heat from his body.

She said, "I don't understand it. The matting worked so fast on my finger and your arm, but it's not working on your side."

"Don't worry. I will be fine. Let's get ready to go." And with that Billy began to rise, wincing as he moved.

Jamee pulled him back down saying, "Wait for a bit. Let me think about this. There must be a reason the matting is not working. Rest and I'll take a look around before we leave."

Billy didn't argue and lay down on the floor. Jamee left the water cave and headed to the top of the tree. She carefully scanned the area and saw no one. She sat and thought about Billy's injury. She couldn't imagine being without him. They had only been together for a short time, but it felt like her life had begun again when Billy found her.

She thought back step by step from the time she found the staff in Billy's gear. She had cut her finger badly, taken the matting from the wall and wrapped her finger. The only thing different was the other water cave had been on the fourth level. Could that make a difference?

She climbed down to the fourth level and entered the cave at the base of the limb. She pulled some material from the wall. It did feel softer than the matting from the third level and it seemed more alive. She took a handful and moved up to the fifth level. In that water cave the matting was coarse, greenish and hard to pull away so she left it there. When she entered the cave on the third level Billy was asleep but he stirred, holding his left side. Jamee gently removed the wrapping and pulled the matting away. The wound was an ugly red and hot to the touch.

She went to the pool and cleaned the wrapping and returned to Billy's side. Carefully she placed the matting she had gathered from the fourth level against the wound and wrapped it. Then she went back to the pool and soaked a piece of cloth. Jamee wiped Billy's head and body to cool him. She let Billy sleep and went out to gather some food.

As Jamee was gathering herbs, roots and some berries, Flick landed on a branch close to her. She flashed colors at Jamee and peered at her.

"Hello, Flick. What have you been up to?"

Flick said, "When does the mating start? You Land things are not as interesting as I thought."

Jamee blushed and said, "That is none of your business. We are very private and don't talk about such things. Besides, Billy has been wounded and needs to rest. Have you seen anyone about?"

"No. The land around you is clear. I noticed that he was still sleeping. Is that because of the hurt in his side?" Flick asked.

"Yes. Normally we travel all day and rest during the night. How did you know about the hurt in Billy's side?" she asked.

"Well, I can feel these things if I take an interest in something, and besides, I was in the cave with you while you lay together. I was hoping for more of a show than you gave me. He looks interesting. His body is big and his face is pleasing," Flick replied.

"You shouldn't be watching us like that."

Flick said, "You asked me to watch out for you and if I am going to watch then that's what I will do! You know that all work and no play bores me. Don't worry. You won't know I'm there unless you reach out with your mind. I was hoping your mind would be on mating. When will you mate?"

Jamee was unsure how to respond. After all, Flick was just a bird. Besides, whom would she tell? "Flick, you should be helping to protect us, not spying on our private moments."

"Yes, yes, yes..." With that, Flick was gone in a flash. "Flick? Flick?" Jamee spoke but no answer came.

She shrugged her shoulders, moved to the tree and went up to the water cave.

When she entered she checked on Billy. His body was cool and he slept quietly. She started a fire and used a small camp pot from Billy's pack to heat some water. She began adding all the ingredients to make a broth. After it boiled she let the fire die down to let it simmer.

She went to the pool and slid in and rubbed her body clean, feeling the heat of her touch in her breasts and loins. Self-consciously she looked around for Flick but saw nothing of her. She did want to make love with Billy, but his health was more important than her needs. If she had to wait, she would for as long as necessary. After finishing washing and dressing she went out to the platform branches at the top of the tree. Jamee spent several hours watching the surrounding area and relaxing.

Her thoughts wandered. She thought about how lonely her life had been on Ocean, but there were always people around. She had never felt a part of the group and no one had tried to show her any kindness. The only time she had had any kind of companionship was when she was sent back to land to help gather supplies. When she was still a small girl she had wandered the city with no real purpose. She had met an older woman who had shown some interest in her. Her name was Silver and she was a prostitute, although Jamee didn't know what that was at the time. Silver took Jamee to her home, fed her and talked to her. Silver told Jamee about her childhood and it rang similar to Jamee's in the first part of Silver's life.

Silver had no parents and lived in the city using her wits to survive. Some people helped her when she was very young, but after she was around ten she had only herself to rely on. She grew up quickly and as her body developed Silver had to defend herself from the men who roamed the town. One night when she was fourteen three men grabbed her and took her to a ship getting ready to sail. They took her into the forward hold, tied her up and left her there for two days. Then they came to her, warning her not to make a sound or she would be killed and thrown overboard. She was so frightened she couldn't make a sound. The men took turns raping her that night. They gave her food and water before they left her tied and gagged.

The next night they came again, but before they could abuse her another man came to the hold and beat them with a club. He freed her and took her to his cabin. It was a large room at the back of the ship. He was the captain. He told her not to be afraid and he would care for her until they returned to land. He kept his promise but also demanded she be his woman because that was her only protection. He was kind and usually gentle with her and she complied with his wishes. She had no choice and the instinct to survive was strong in her. She learned many things in the ways of having sex from him. He also taught her how to defend herself. She trained daily.

She grew to depend on him and knew the only way she could keep his protection was to see to his needs. The voyage lasted over a year before returning to the city. After the ship docked, that very night he put her ashore and told her never to come back. She was crushed, thinking he cared for her or maybe even loved her. As he shoved her away he told her that she now had a good skill to survive.

Silver wandered the streets of the city and finally went to a house where women entertained men. She was young and beautiful and the owner was anxious for Silver to work in the house. Silver made demands of freedom to choose the men she would be with and a larger than normal percentage of what she would receive. So began her career as a prostitute.

She was very kind and Jamee enjoyed her time with Silver. Jamee would visit Silver each time she went to the city. As she got older, she learned what business Silver was in and began to question her about what she did. Jamee had no bad thoughts about how Silver made her living.

Silver seemed happy enough and only once in a while did Jamee see a look of true sadness in her eyes. Through all their talks Silver made one thing very clear to her: Jamee was never to do what she was doing and always be on guard so that the things that happened to her would not happen to Jamee. She promised Jamee that she would be her friend as long as she did those things. Jamee promised.

While with Silver, Jamee learned all there was to know about sex and men in general. She learned how to do things to excite, please and hold a man if she wanted. Silver also taught her muscle exercises for her flower that would please the man she found. Jamee asked Silver why she taught her these things but then told her not to use her knowledge to make a living. Silver told her she was to save all this knowledge and wait for someone special, someone to give and receive love. Jamee never understood what she meant by love until she had her dreams and Billy found her. Jamee worried that she might be trapping Billy into loving her and the thought hurt her.

When she entered the water cave Billy was sitting up looking refreshed and had no sign of fever in his eyes. Jamee went to him and kneeled down to kiss him lightly. Billy's arms wrapped around her and his kisses were hungry. She molded to his body, letting his warmth seep into her.

She pushed away from Billy, giving him a dazzling smile and said, "I guess you are feeling better. Now let me check your wound and give you something to eat." She removed the wrapping from his side and saw the wound was completely sealed, with only a touch of redness.

"It looks so much better than it did a few hours ago. I think I have discovered what I was doing wrong before."

"What did you discover?" Billy asked as he reached for her.

Jamee giggled, moving out of reach.

"The matting I used the first time came from the fourth level. After I changed your dressing I had to use matting from this water cave and it didn't help. Your wound was getting worse. So while you slept I went out to think about what went wrong. I went to the fourth level and the matting was softer and with a touch of green. I checked the matting on the fifth level and it was green and very coarse. So I used the material from the fourth level to dress your wound again, and look at it. It's almost completely healed."

Billy thought about this for a moment and said, "You may have truly discovered something that no one else knows. This could be very important to my people!"

"I hope so, Billy. Maybe it will help them to accept me into your tribe."

"Don't worry about acceptance; you are already accepted by me."

Jamee brought the pot of food she had prepared to Billy. They sat and ate everything and then had several pieces of fruit. Satisfied, Billy still had a look of hunger in his eyes.

Noticing the day was almost done Billy said, "We will stay here tonight and move out early in the morning." With a smile he asked, "What should we do 'til morning?"

Jamee said, "Let's talk." She could see the disappointment on his face. Jamee started to laugh and couldn't stop. There were tears rolling down her cheeks, and soon Billy was also laughing so hard he had to hold his injured side.

Jamee began to tell Billy about her friend Silver from Ocean. She told him of all the things Silver had done to help her as she grew up. Only keeping a few things from him, like the training and exercises Silver taught her to please the man she wanted to be with. She talked about how much of a friend Silver was while she delayed the real secret she had to tell him.

Billy said, "She sounds like quite a person. I would have liked to have met her."

After Jamee collected herself she gave Billy a look of concern and cast her eyes to the floor.

"What's the matter, Jamee?"

"I have some things to tell you and I am worried that it might make you not want me."

"Whatever it is, it will not change my love for you. Tell me what you have to say and you will see for yourself that nothing could shake my love."

So Jamee began to tell Billy of her power and some of her life on Ocean.

"I have a power that was the main reason for my being so lonely on my world. The others were afraid of me and have distrusted me ever since they found out.

"I can reach out and enter the minds of birds. When that happens I can see through their eyes and control them. I can make them fly where I want them to and do whatever I want them to do. I have found that on this world my powers are much stronger and I have to be careful until I am used to this new strength."

Billy thought about what she said and it did scare him a little.

He kept the fear from his eyes and said, "I have heard of something like this but never believed it to be true. Some people claim to be able to take over the minds of animals, but I have never seen them do it. It makes the people of the tribe afraid to be around those that make this claim, and I think they only say they can so they will have power over others. Can you show me what you mean when you say you can make them do what you want?"

"I'll show you, Billy, but don't be afraid of me, please!"

Jamee let her mind open and reach out. She searched the sky and soon found a very large bird. She gently entered its mind and through its eyes found the Bookus grove. She guided the bird down to the tree.

As Billy waited he looked at Jamee and she just seemed to be sitting there doing nothing. He began to think that maybe this was all a game and she was playing with him.

He heard a great whoosh of air and looked at the entrance of the water cave. There stood a Great Eagle looking at him with a fearsome glare. Billy jumped back but his eyes never left the bird. The bird walked into the cave, dipping its head at the entrance, its eyes never leaving Billy.

"I don't believe it! These birds never come close to humans and never land except to feed," Billy exclaimed.

The Eagle dipped its head to Billy, took one look at Jamee, turned and walked out of the cave.

There was a great movement of air and Billy jumped up and ran outside to see the Eagle climbing through the air to gain altitude. Billy went back into the cave. His eyes were wide and showed a little fear in them. He could see the hurt in Jamee's eyes. He moved and sat next to her.

A moment passed and then Billy said, "I never thought in my whole life I would be that close to a Great Eagle. Thank you, Jamee. I believe you."

Jamee looked at Billy, stunned. She had thought she would drive him away, but he was thanking her, with the fear no longer in his eyes.

She slumped and tears flowed down her cheeks. She made small mewing sounds as she cried. Billy took her in his arms and softly stroked her silky hair.

"Jamee, don't cry. It hurts my heart to see you cry like this. That was wonderful! I do truly love you. Even if you couldn't do that I would still love you," he said with a laugh.

Jamee, still crying, threw her arms around him and buried her face in his neck.

"I was so afraid... I love you, Billy, and needed so badly to tell you the truth, but I was so afraid you would fear me and throw me away."

"You are mine and I will hold you, protect you and love you forever, although it may be you protecting me," he said with another laugh.

Jamee turned her head up and took his mouth with hers and kissed him deeply. She felt Billy's hand take her right breast and squeeze softly. She let out a moan into his mouth and let her hand slip down his body. He started to lay her back to the floor, but she stopped him.

"Billy, I have one more secret but please don't worry. It is nothing like the last one, I promise."

"Tell me when you are ready but have no fear of losing me. I told you, I won't let you go."

"And I will never let you go, my love," Jamee replied. "Now come with me and let me take care of you. I don't want you to hurt your side."

"I'm fine. Can't you see?"

She stood, pulling Billy up and moving him to the pool. After they were in the water she bathed Billy, taking care to wash him everywhere. She then did the same to herself, watching Billy follow her every move. Then she helped Billy out of the water and dried him off. She let Billy dry her in the same fashion.

Jamee could feel the need rising in her body. They made love gently with soft touches and kisses. Jamee did all the things that would please Billy. As they relaxed she looked into his eyes and smiled weakly at him. She lay her head on his chest and let her breathing slow. Jamee felt so satisfied knowing she had pleased him. Wet tears again flowed from her eyes. As she looked out at the cave with unfocused eyes a flash of color caught her attention.

She looked again and saw a rainbow of vivid colors flashing on the wall of the cave. She looked intently where the colors had been and finally was able to see Flick blending in with the surroundings. Jamee's face blushed red as she watched Flick streak from the cave.

Billy lifted her head in his hands and said, "What's wrong? Why are you crying again?"

"They are tears of joy. Did I truly please you?"

"Never worry about whether or not you have pleased me. I am pleased with everything you do. I only hope I can make you feel the same way."

They held each other, enjoying the closeness of each other while savoring the ebb of their joining. Jamee thought about Flick and what she would say to the inquisitive bird. They slowly separated and went to the pool to wash each other.

Billy said with a smile, "Now I must go find some meat for us to eat. We have to keep up our strength."

"I still have herbs and everything else we need. I will get the fire started."

After Billy reached the ground he headed off to the grass. His mind was still on their lovemaking and his body still felt the heat of Jamee's touch. She was so young and could do all of those incredible things. He wondered how she had learned all that. He cleared his mind and concentrated on finding them something to eat.

Back in the water cave Jamee busied herself preparing for the food Billy would bring. She thought again of Silver and silently thanked her for all her training in the ways of pleasing her man. She would never use this to control Billy, she told herself. She wondered how Silver was doing.

When she last saw her, Silver was growing tired of her life in the house where she worked. She told Jamee she was thinking about finding one man to live with and learn to cook, clean and take care of a home. When Jamee first met Silver she had thought she was much older than herself, but as she grew she realized that Silver was only ten years older. Jamee grew and she soon was taller than Silver by several inches. As her body developed she also saw that Silver was more slender and fragile looking than she was. She knew that those looks were deceiving.

Silver was strong and lethal when she had to be. She had been training for years with some of their world's best fighters and she had given this training to Jamee as part of her lessons. Silver had become a master of several fighting techniques and was as deadly as she was kind. She was strong-willed and would do as she pleased. She had always shown Jamee kindness, giving her protection while she was there. Her advice and training was unusual, but to have a friend Jamee would learn whatever she taught. Silver's advice was always toward being with one man and how to keep him. Silver told Jamee that being with many men was bad for the soul and would never bring happiness. She also told Jamee that their time together brought her more peace than she had ever had. She thought of Jamee as her little sister. Jamee did miss her and hoped she was happy.

Jamee heard a noise and spun around to find Billy staring at her, holding a hopper in one hand.

"Someday you will have to tell me what you think about. You looked like you were lost in a dream."

Jamee smiled brightly, stood and took the hopper from Billy. As Jamee prepared the meal Billy relaxed nearby. He was nodding off when he felt Jamee's lips touch his.

Looking down into those deep royal blue eyes Jamee said, "It's time to eat, my love."

They laughed and talked as they enjoyed the food. Both thought of how lucky they each were. It was just past sundown but they lay together touching and caressing and were soon fast asleep.

Before the sun was up they set off to the northwest and were moving across the prairie as the sun rose in the east. The prairie slowly opened before their eyes. The grass turned from gray to golden green and the rolling hills caught the beams of light at their crest leaving the hillsides in muted shadows. It reminded Jamee of the rolling waves of her ocean world. She missed the sound of the waves marching to shore, but to see their color she only had to look in Billy's eyes. They traveled at a steady pace, letting the miles of grass flow behind. They stopped for a quick meal of meat and fruit from the previous evening meal and then continued with their mile-eating pace to the northwest. Billy told Jamee they were heading for a large plateau that dropped into a valley. The valley was called Green Hiding.

CHAPTER 6

It was still several hours before sunset when Flick flew past Jamee's face, catching her attention.

"What do you want?" Jamee asked, still perturbed at Flick.

"There are four Land things up ahead, only a short distance away. They appear to be hurt and very dirty," Flick said.

"What kind of people are they? Are they white skinned or scaly?"

"Well, they are not the things that live to the north. They are people like you and the nice Billy, who is your mate. They are covered in mud so now their color is gray. They are injured and don't appear to have weapons."

"Billy! There are people just ahead of us," Jamee exclaimed.

"What? How do you know that?" Billy asked.

"I was told by a bird."

"I thought you could only see through birds' eyes."

"There is one bird here that can talk to me and -- oh, I'll explain later. Right now you have to decide what we should do. I don't think they are armed. They are injured and covered in mud."

"I would like to go ahead by myself but I know that you will follow me anyway. Let me lead but keep your staff ready."

They slowly moved forward through the waist-high grass, looking for any signs of others. Billy stopped and listened. He could hear what sounded like a cough and small cries of pain. He moved ahead with his knife in his hand, ready to kill if necessary. As he parted the grass he could see what looked like a clump of dark gray mud with arms and legs. He looked closer, still crouching about twenty feet from the clump. As he took in the details he could make out three or four individuals lying in the grass. Someone was crying softly, obviously in pain. Billy stood up making a quick check of the area, searching for any others that might be about.

He said in a calm voice, "What are you doing here?"

From out of the clump a very large man moved quickly into a crouch prepared to fight. His brown eyes looked about with fear and came to rest on Billy. He didn't say anything, just stared out of his mud-covered face.

He saw Billy was not a Voll or a Koro and finally said, "We are running from the Volls. Who are you and what do you want?"

Billy moved forward with caution, knife still at the ready, saying, "We are not Volls and maybe we can help, but first tell me if you have any weapons."

The large gray man held out his hands wide so Billy could see he had no weapons on him. He swung his left arm toward the others huddled in the grass and said, "We are not armed and if you are offering help, we will take any you can give us."

He lowered himself to a sitting position, holding his right arm. Billy could see a trail of blood running down his arm. As he took in the others he could see what looked to be two children and a woman, all covered in a thick gray mud.

Jamee brushed past Billy, going immediately to the children. She started examining them and found cuts and scratches. Some cuts appeared to be deep. She then looked at the woman and found the same condition on her. She moved cautiously to the man and found a deep cut in his right shoulder and upper arm.

"Billy, we have to take them to water and get them cleaned up so I can treat their wounds. Is there a Bookus grove nearby?"

"No, but we can take them down into Green Hiding. There will be water and food there." Looking at the man he asked, "Can you walk?"

The big man said, "I've come this far. I can go on, but the two small ones can't. The other woman is in a little better shape. She has been helping carry these two," nodding toward the two children.

Billy looked at Jamee and said, "The path down to Green Hiding is about thirty minutes from here but we need to hurry. The trail down is dangerous to travel in the dark."

The big man stood slowly and lifted the larger of the two children.

The woman rose and started to lift the small child, but Jamee came to her, touching her arm and said, "I will carry her. You follow me and bring your packs."

The woman picked up the two packs that were lying next to her feet and was ready to follow.

Billy leaned in close to Jamee and said, "Jamee, lead off in that direction and be ready in case these people aren't all they seem. I will bring up the rear, covering our tracks and keeping an eye on the man."

They started off, Jamee in the lead, followed by the woman, man and finally Billy. She walked at a quick pace, looking back to be sure the others could keep up. The child in her arms was so light, she was no burden. The others kept pace but she could see they were tired and nearing the last of their endurance. Billy covered their trail and kept a careful watch on the big man.

Billy thought as he walked, *What am I going to do with all these people? I'm supposed to be traveling alone to see what is happening in the north, but we can't abandon them out here. This will make for interesting talk if we ever get back to my village.*

As they neared the drop-off to Green Hiding, Billy moved up next to Jamee.

"Be careful. The edge appears suddenly."

They had taken only a few more steps and Jamee stopped abruptly. She stood at the edge of a sheer cliff that dropped off at least two hundred feet. At the bottom of the cliff the floor of a beautiful valley stretched out as far as she could see. Her breath caught as she took in the sight. The floor of the valley was covered with forest, glades and a winding river, all in different shades of green. The cliff was about two miles long, in a crescent shape.

"It's so beautiful."

"Yes. I've only been here once before, but it is a place everyone on a trek makes a point to stop at. We will find plenty of game and vegetation to eat and we can rest here for a few days without worrying about anyone seeing us. It's so big, once we're down there we'll be safe. The Koros have never been seen down in the valley."

He told everyone to rest for a few minutes so he could scout the trail down.

They lowered themselves gratefully to the ground. Billy gave Jamee a knowing look of caution and headed down the trail. He was back in a few minutes and sat down beside Jamee.

He said, "The trail down is steep, but the footing is good. Go slowly and there won't be any problems. We have enough time to make it to the bottom before nightfall."

Standing, he took the child from Jamee and told her to take the packs from the woman. He took the lead and started down the trail. The others followed and all but Jamee took no notice of the surrounding area. They looked ready to drop.

It took an hour to reach the floor of the valley and the sun was just setting, leaving the valley in dusky golden light. They traveled about a mile to a cave in the cliff face. The back of the cave was hollowed-out where they could build a fire without letting light reach the front. Billy quickly built a small fire from wood that others had stored there. Once the fire was going he picked the child up and motioned for the others to follow. He led the way to the edge of the river. The only light came from the first moon as it rose above the rim of the valley. He handed the child to Jamee and told all of them to clean up and let Jamee wash their wounds.

He went back to the cave and retrieved his bow and then went downstream to a calm pool and looked around. He could see no game about but noticed large dorsal fins of fish in the pool. He laid his bow down and crept to the edge of the water, reached in and quickly had two large fish flopping on the bank. He dressed them, picked up his bow and headed back to the cave. As he was preparing to cook the fish he heard noises of the group returning.

When he turned to look all he could see was the giant of a man in torn syncotton clothes. He was white. Billy had his bow with an arrow nocked and the bowstring stretched in an instant. The big man stopped, wide-eyed, and held his hands out from his sides.

Billy said, "You're white!"

The man lowered his hands slowly, in obvious pain and replied, "Yes, but I am no threat to you. I escaped just like the others. If the Volls find me, I am dead. I have no love for them and I give you my word I mean you no harm."

Billy relaxed his bow, but kept it ready.

"What are you doing on Prairie if you are not a Voll? No white men have ever lived here."

The big man replied, "I guess that is true and, yes, I was a Voll but not from my choosing. I was ordered into this service. I spent several years on my world fighting in conflicts between factions of the Federation. It was mostly limited conflicts, but they were bloody. I became very good at what I did, even though I was one of the older draftees. I'm forty-two. I was sent from my world to the outer world Voll Group. I had no idea that they would bring me to the outer worlds and I had no idea there were people living here. I never saw a brown man until I came here. When I was told we were to enslave the people of these worlds, I refused to help. I was put in prison for disobeying orders and had been there for one year. I was being transported, just like these others, to work in the mines."

Billy looked at Jamee and saw she had closed in near the man and had her staff ready.

He smiled at her and then looked at the man, asking, "How do I know you are telling the truth?"

"Ask the others," the man replied.

Billy looked to the woman, who stood behind the big man. She was not from Prairie. Her skin was dark brown and her hair was a tangle of tight curls. She had large, dark, almond-shaped eyes. Her syncotton coveralls were also torn, revealing a strong body.

She began to talk in a quiet, husky voice. "If he hadn't helped us, we would all probably be dead now. He wore the same clothes as us, not the uniform of a Voll, and was forced into the same containment hole as me. He is not one of them, although he sure looks like them. We were all afraid of him and no one would get close to him on the voyage here, except that little girl," pointing at the small child. "Hell, I didn't even know he could talk 'til he dragged us through the grass after he killed the four Volls who were attacking the three of us. I trust him with my life!"

Billy looked at the older child, but she lay unconscious on the ground.

He then looked at the small child and asked, pointing to the man, "Do you know anything about this man?"

The child looked up at Billy with beautiful black shining eyes and said, "Red is my friend."

The little girl also had brown skin but she was much lighter than the woman. Billy looking at Jamee, saw her nod and lowered his bow.

He went up to the big man with his right hand extended and grasped his right forearm saying, "Then you will be my friend as well, Red. I need to check all your clothing."

As he looked up at the big man he could guess why his name was Red. He had short-cropped hair that was a dark reddish brown color. He had massive shoulders, chest and arms. His hands were big and scarred. Billy would not like to be on the wrong side of his anger. Starting with Red, he checked for the homing insignia. He then moved to the others, checking their clothing carefully.

Red said, "I removed the homing tags the first night out." Billy felt more at ease with Red as he finished his check.

Jamee moved the group nearer the fire and began to clean and dress the wounds. The girl, who still remained unconscious, was laid down on a blanket Billy had removed from his pack. Her face was battered, eyes swollen shut and bruised. Her clothes were torn and there was swelling and bruising all over her body. As Jamee examined her, she pulled her coveralls open and revealed a firm, mature pair of breasts. Opening her clothing more showed her that this was no child but a small, willowy woman. The hair over her flower was silky, black and cropped short. Jamee turned her over, saw deep purple bruises and lash marks all down her back and legs.

She looked up at Red and asked, "What happened to her? She looks like someone tried to beat her to death."

"That's exactly what happened. I think some of the Volls were trying to rape her. All I know is they dragged her into camp, beating and kicking her. Then these two went crazy and ran to her and attacked the men, trying to make them stop. The men turned on the child and woman and began beating them. I had already worked my bonds loose so I could escape when the time was right. I'm not sure what happened next. I kind of went berserk. When my eyes cleared the Volls were all dead and I had this cut on my shoulder and arm. We grabbed up a few packs, the small woman and ran out of there."

He took a deep breath and continued, "We ran south for two days, only stopping to rest a bit, with me carrying this little woman the whole way. Today we were still running and ran into a swamp or bog. It was all I could do to pull everyone out. We kept running for a couple of hours and we stopped to rest. I guess we all fell asleep. Then you found us. I don't think we could have gone much further."

Jamee said, "You must be starving. Billy, cook the food and let me dress these wounds. That's enough talking for now."

Billy put the fish over the fire, ran to the river pool and pulled out two more and then hurried back to the cave.

Jamee dressed a deep gash on the unconscious woman's thigh using the matting from the water cave, then checked the other woman and dressed a deep cut in her back. She checked the child and found only bruises, scrapes and one deep cut, which she dressed. She asked Red to pull his coverall down so she could look at his wounds. He had a very deep wound in his shoulder and arm. She didn't know how he had traveled so far in that condition. She only had a small amount of matting left but used it all dressing Red's wounds. She was very gentle and he smiled his appreciation.

When the meal was ready everyone except the unconscious woman ate hungrily. Soon all but Billy and Jamee were asleep. They moved out into the night and Billy brought Jamee into his arms and kissed her. She returned the kiss with her own eagerness.

"How is this going to work with all these people around?"

"Don't worry; I won't let you suffer," she laughed quietly. "I need you as much if not more. We will find a way to be alone."

They sat holding each other close, talking softly of their love for one another. They rose together and Billy told Jamee to go in and sleep and he would keep watch for a while.

He sat in the dark, feeling his excitement soften and said, "You'll just have to relax for a while, little buddy."

He laughed and settled in to keep watch. Jamee, standing by the entrance, heard his comment, smiled and went in to sleep.

Morning came and Jamee woke to find Billy curled up into her back, molding himself to her. She smiled and enjoyed the warmth he provided. She wasn't too happy that suddenly they were not alone to enjoy each other whenever they liked, but she knew they were doing the right thing. She was proud of Billy and so happy he included her in the decisions that had to be made. She rose and went down to the river to bathe. The water was cool and sent shivers through her. She heard a noise and turned, expecting to find Billy.

The dark-skinned woman stood on the bank looking at her.

"You are very beautiful and lucky to have a man like that one back there," the woman said.

"Thank you," Jamee said. She was embarrassed, standing in the water nude. She said, "My name is Jamee and the man I am with is Billy."

"My name is May," the woman replied. "Can I join you?"

Jamee nodded her head, watched May strip off her torn coverall and move into the water. She had a beautiful, strong body, even with the cuts, scrapes and bruises. May was taller than Jamee by around 3 inches. Her body was dark all over and her muscles were taut as she moved through the water. May had beautiful large almond-shaped eyes and high cheekbones that told Jamee that she was from people similar to her own, but her tightly curled short hair was different from any she had seen before. As the cold water swirled around her legs Jamee could see the strength in her body. Her breasts were large and firm. May's legs and butt were large but strongly muscled.

"Is Billy all yours, Jamee?" May asked.

"We are together and I am all his. Why do you ask?"

"Now, don't get me wrong! I had to ask. You have done so much for us already and I didn't want to make any mistakes," May replied. "You know he is a fine looking fellow and well... if he wasn't attached, I might like to have a go at him. But don't you worry, Jamee. My hands are off!"

Jamee didn't reply, but thought about what May had said.

"I'm going down-river a little way to see if I can catch some fish," Jamee said.

She rose from the water, dressed and moved down the bank of the river. She found a quiet spot. She sat and thought, *Do I really have a claim on Billy?*

They had eagerly agreed they would be together, but now that there were other women around, would Billy still feel the same? It worried her. She rose and went back to the cave to examine the injuries of the new arrivals.

She found that Billy had made a broth of fish and herbs and was feeding it slowly to the unconscious woman while May lifted her to a sitting position. She checked the woman and found her wounds were nearly healed, but the bruising was still dark purple. She moved to Red and felt the heat from his body as she turned him over. The wounds were an angry red and still seeping blood. She had used all the matting on the woman and May except for the small amount she had left.

She went to the packs that May had brought with them and checked the contents. All she found were two small hunting knives in sheaths and some syncotton clothing. She washed his wounds, reused the small piece of matting and rewrapped them. She saw Billy was finished with the woman and motioned for him to follow her.

They went out of the cave into a secluded area and sat.

She said, "Billy, we have to have more of the matting from a Bookus tree. Red has a fever. His wounds are infected and I don't have any more matting. How far is the nearest grove?"

"The grove we were at is the closest and it is a day's travel. I will leave at once."

Jamee grabbed his arm and looked into his eyes saying, "You can't go. You have to watch over these people. No one else can do it. I can't protect them and Red will be no help if something should happen."

Billy shook his head no. "I won't let you go alone. You could get lost and there is a lot of danger out on the prairie that you don't know about. It's too much for you, Jamee. You don't know the way!"

"I have a good idea where to go. I have my staff and I won't be alone. I will have a guide."

"What do you mean, you'll have a guide?"

"I have a friend I haven't told you about." She turned her head and said, "Flick, show yourself."

As Billy looked around, not knowing what to expect, a bird appeared right before his eyes. The bird was small and a beautiful royal blue in color. It landed on Jamee's shoulder and was staring right at Billy.

"What is that? I have never seen that color on a bird before," Billy exclaimed.

"Her name is Flick and she is a Star bird and we can talk to one another. She came to me several days ago and just started talking. It shocked me because I've never been able to communicate with birds before."

Flick said, "Billy looks different with his clothes on. I think I like him better without them. I do like him."

Jamee smiled and blushed a bit.

Looking at Jamee, Billy said, "What?"

"Flick was talking to me, and she says she likes you."

"I didn't hear anything," Billy said, looking from Flick to Jamee.

"It's hard to explain but we use our minds to talk, but you can speak directly to Flick. I'll have to answer for her."

Billy was having trouble taking it all in but replied, "That wasn't so hard to explain."

He turned his head to look at the bird and was startled to see it was now a brilliant yellow color.

"She is beautiful!"

Flick instantly turned a pinkish blush color and Jamee let out a laugh.

"I think she is blushing. Maybe you should introduce yourself to her."

Billy turned to face the little bird and said, "Hello, Flick. I'm Billy."

Flick instantly turned back to a royal blue and bobbed her head.

Flick said, "Tell Billy that this is his color and yours is yellow. We can work out a color system so I can warn him of danger or if you are in need of help. Also tell him he looks very nice and I would like to watch you mate again."

Jamee gave Flick a hard stare and said, "Flick says hello. The color you see now is your color and I am yellow. She also says we will work out a system of communication with her by the colors she shows you."

"How many colors does she have, Jamee? I've never seen anything change like that."

Flick flashed all the colors of the rainbow and many others as well. Then she turned royal blue on the top half of her body and yellow on the bottom and let the color line move up and down in a slow rhythm, all the time looking at Jamee.

"What does that mean?"

Jamee blushed, giving Flick a hard stare and said, "I have no idea." Quickly continuing, "We will work out a system to let you know how I am doing while I am gone. Flick will go with me, but she can fly very quickly and return to you if I need you. Can you see that it must be me to go and get what we need? We have to have more of the matting."

"I can see the need, but how will you protect yourself?"

Jamee lifted the staff she always carried and whirled it in a blur, stopping an inch from Billy's neck.

"I've been practicing while we walked," Jamee said.

Billy's eyes were wide in amazement and said, "I can see that! Very well, but you must be careful. If something happened to you, I would be lost, my love."

Jamee kissed him deeply and moved her body against his. "I won't do anything that will keep me away from you."

Jamee explained to Billy what the different colors Flick made meant, so he would know if he was needed.

They returned to the cave and while Jamee checked the injured again Billy prepared a pack for Jamee to take. They then left and began the climb to the top of the cliff trail. Jamee led the way and Billy couldn't take his eyes off her as her hips moved with the rhythm of her walk. He was excited when they reached the top. Jamee turned, looking at him, and with a tinkling laugh moved close to Billy, placing her hand on him.

"I can see you'll miss me as much as I'll miss you. Don't let him go snooping around while I'm gone," she said through her laughter.

"What do you mean by that?"

"Nothing, my love. I will travel as fast as I can and try to be back by sundown tomorrow. Billy, I love you with all my heart!"

"You are my heart," Billy said, kissing her softly on the lips.

Jamee turned and loped off with Flick flashing colors above her head for an instant, then disappearing. Billy watched until Jamee was out of sight, then slowly turned and headed back down the trail. He hoped that this was not a mistake, knowing he would never forgive himself if something happened to Jamee.

As he arrived back in the cave, May asked, "Where is Jamee?"

Billy sat down and told them of the decision for Jamee to go after more medicine.

May asked, "Is this medicine so important that she would go off like that alone?"

Billy replied, "Look at the girl's and your wounds. They are almost completely healed because of the matting Jamee used to treat them."

May removed the wrapping on the child's wound and was amazed to see the wound completely healed. She did the same to the unconscious woman and found the same condition.

"That is unbelievable! That stuff she put on us did all that?"

"Yes. We only discovered the healing qualities of the Bookus tree a few days ago. Jamee used the last of it on Red but only had a small amount. Red's wounds aren't healing well and they are getting infected. We decided that Jamee was to go because she knows what to look for and where it is located in the tree."

May said, "That must be some kind of good tree! I've never heard of a Bookus. What does it look like?"

Billy explained all about the Bookus tree and how important it was to his tribe.

Red had been listening the whole time and weakly said, "Billy, we owe you and Jamee our lives. I only hope I will be able to repay you."

The child walked over to Billy and gazing at him with her dark shining eyes put her arms around his neck and said, "Thank you, Billy. You and Jamee are my friends."

May wrapped her arms around Billy and kissed him on the mouth.

"You...You are all welcome," said Billy.

He blushed and May laughed and said, "Don't worry. I won't bite. I was just trying to say thank you."

It was late morning when Billy sat down next to Red and asked, "How are you feeling?" Red was lying on his side and looked up at Billy with fevered eyes.

"I've been better, but I'll be all right in a couple of days. Billy, I need to tell you something. I don't know where Jamee got that staff she carries with her but I know what it is."

"What can you tell me about it?"

Red raised his head and saw that May and the child were not in the cave.

He laid his head back to the blanket and said, "That is a *Steer*. It is only carried by high-ranking Volls. It is a status symbol of rank and it is very dangerous."

"We know about the blade," Billy replied.

"Good. When traveling between worlds the ships go very fast. It's called *light speed-plus*. For some unknown reason no weapons that we use on my world work when the ships slow down. Many pieces of electronic gear are worthless as well. Even explosives are unusable.

"The military developed the Steer. It has to do with cellular layering. The staff and blade are very special and I was told the blade will not break and never needs sharpening. It takes a lot of time and expense to make. Very few are made because of this and only high-ranking Volls have them for special missions. What I'm trying to say is if the Volls see Jamee carrying it they will make a great effort to get it back!"

"I don't understand much of what you just said, but I understand the danger of Jamee carrying it. How would they know that it is a Steer?" Billy asked.

"By its color and the way it shines. If you could change its color or maybe wrap it in some way, then it would be hard to recognize until the blade is exposed."

"I will think on this, Red. Thank you for helping."

"Like I told you, Billy, they will kill me if I'm caught and I have no love for what they are trying to do to the people of the outer worlds. I want to gain your trust and truly be your friend. I hope I will be able to start a new life here. If everyone on this world is like you and Jamee, I think I have found a home."

"It might be hard for you until people get to know you. Whites are feared because of the old stories of what they did to my people. Only a few have ever seen a white man, but the distrust will be there. I will speak for you when we get to my village. Now rest. I have much to think about."

Billy went to check on the others. The small woman was still unconscious but had no fever. The swelling in her face had lessened only a little, but her wounds were almost completely healed.

He walked out of the cave and went in the direction of the river. As he approached he heard laughter and stood at the edge of the trees and looked out at May and the child playing in the water. They were nude and Billy caught himself looking at May's body. She was very pretty and her body was strong and easy to look at. Her movements were fluid as she threw water at the child. Her rear was full and firm and her legs were nicely muscled. When his eyes came up to May's face she was staring directly at Billy.

She said, "Come in and join us."

Billy, now blushing, stepped back and turned to go. "No...No, I will check the area."

He heard her laugh as he hurried off downstream.

He found a quiet place to sit and rest not too far away. He didn't want to go too far in case he was needed. He thought about all that Red had told him but found his thoughts straying back to the curves of May's body. He shook his head to clear his thoughts and concentrated on the problem of the staff. He was worried about Jamee and he already missed her greatly. He had finally come up with a way to disguise the staff when he heard a soft rustling behind him.

Turning quickly with his knife in his hand, he saw May standing not five feet from him with a smile on her face.

"I give up, Billy. You got me."

Billy put the knife away and asked, "What are you doing here?"

"I just wanted to talk to you alone."

She moved to sit next to him and moved even closer and said, "Billy, I want to tell you something. You are a handsome man and those eyes make my knees quiver, but what I want to say is that I know you and Jamee are together and I'm not looking to make trouble for you or her. You both have done more than most people would to help me.

"Where I come from I was just a body to work and guide people through the forest of my world. I wasn't treated as a person because my skin is so dark. Most of the women looked at me like they would a beast from the forest. The men looked at me as something to satisfy their sexual needs. I learned to fight and hide when I was very young and would let no man touch me. My parents were good to me, but I was taken away when I was five to be trained as a forest guide. You are the first man that I've met that I would be interested in being with, but I'll tell you right now that I'll not come after you because of what you and Jamee have done to help me."

She turned and looked into Billy's eyes and said, "I want to be your friend and help you if I can! I'll still look and you can even look if you want, but I think I need friends more than anything else right now. I may not know how to act around you but I'm gonna try. I've never really had a friend, except for little Nuuna."

Billy said with a smile, "I will be your friend, May, and thank you for understanding about Jamee and me. I love her so much that she is in my thoughts almost all the time. You're a very pretty woman and someone will be lucky to win your affections. Who is Nuuna?"

"That's the little girl with us. I don't know much about her, but we've been together ever since we were put in the holding area waiting to be transported... Billy, I've got to know something. Are there any more men here with eyes like yours?"

Billy, still smiling, said, "As far as I know, I'm the only one with blue eyes. Some from other villages keep their distance from me because of them. They think I've been touched by spirits.

You're the second person who has looked at me with pleasure, I guess."

"I bet I can guess who the first was, but I also think there are plenty of young women back where you live who are missing you!"

They rose and walked back talking and smiling. When Billy got to the cave he picked up his bow and told them he would be back soon.

Billy went through the forest looking for game. After about a mile Billy saw a small uteta, a deer-like animal, walking on a game trail. Billy nocked an arrow and as the uteta came in range, he shot it through the heart. It ran a few feet and dropped.

As he moved to pick up the uteta he caught a movement to his left. He had another arrow nocked in a blur, aimed and shot a prairie cat that was moving to take his game. Normally Billy would not have killed the cat, but he had a special purpose in mind for its skin. He quickly dressed and skinned the uteta and then skinned the prairie cat. He thanked both animals for the help they provided. Carrying the load back to the entrance of the cave he laid the animal on the ground. He went into the cave and asked May to come outside. When she arrived she saw the carcass and skins and smiled.

"I guess we'll have meat tonight!"

"May, do you know how to prepare this?"

"You bet I do! I'll have it cut up in no time. Just let me get a knife."

Billy took a rope from his pack and with May's help strung the carcass up on a limb of a nearby tree.

"I have something I need to do, May."

"You go on; I can take care of this!"

Billy picked up the skins and headed to the river. He staked out both pelts, scraped the fat and pieces of meat from them using a spoon-shaped tool made for that purpose. He continued to scrape the cat's skin until it was quite thin. He then hung it in a tree to dry. He went to the cave, gathered up ashes from the fire and carried them to the uteta's skin. He rubbed in the ash until the skin felt dry. He would finish his work the next day when both were dry.

Billy went back to the cave to find that May had already cut the meat up and was preparing a large roast for the fire. She had also sliced very thin strips of meat and hung them near the fire on racks to dry. She had taken some herbs and salt from Billy's pack and rubbed them into the roast and strips of meat.

"You really do know what you are doing, don't you?"

"Yes, I do," May said with a proud grin. "I hung the rest of the meat in the back of the cave to keep it cool and I'll cook it in the morning."

Billy went outside, worrying about Jamee. He hadn't seen Flick so he had to believe that she was all right. She wasn't due to return until tomorrow evening. Even with people around his feeling of loneliness was strong. He felt as if there was an emptiness in his chest and he didn't like the feeling. He had only been with Jamee a short time but it felt like years instead of only a week or so. Love for her came quickly, but he knew in his heart it was for a lifetime. Billy sighed and turned back to the cave to check on the others.

Red's fever was worse and the small woman was still sleeping. He worried about her the most. If she didn't wake soon, he had no idea what to do. Nuuna came to sit in his lap and he took her in his arms and rocked her. She hardly spoke but seemed to sense what the others were feeling. She was a great comfort to him in that moment. May was making a broth from the meat and herbs to give to the unconscious woman. He hoped it would help revive her.

Red ate only a little of the meal and was soon sleeping restlessly. Billy, Nuuna and May enjoyed the delicious meal. May beamed as she watched the other two eat. She was beginning to feel like part of a family-- a feeling she hadn't had for many years. After they finished, May with Billy's help fed some broth to the woman. She drank it down without ever opening her eyes.

"Billy, I'm worried about her! Isn't there something we can do to wake her up?"

"I don't have any idea what to do, May. I'm also worried. Hopefully she will wake up on her own. What is her name?"

"I don't know. I saw her talking to Nuuna a few times but she mostly kept to herself. They put her on the ship just before we left."

Billy got up and told Nuuna and May he would check the area and sit outside for a while. When he returned later that night everyone was asleep and the fire was burning low. He lay down but sleep didn't come to him for several hours. In Billy's dreams he saw Flick with the royal blue and yellow colors moving up and down her body and knew she had watched Jamee and him making love. He smiled in his dreams.

The next morning Billy was up with the sun and was still smiling. *What an odd little bird*, he thought. He started the fire again and left to check the area. When he returned May was wiping the other woman down trying to soothe her with the cool water from one of the containers. She had her clothing opened and was moving a cloth across her chest. Billy could see the well-formed breasts that fit perfectly with her small body.

May looked up, smiled and said, "She is so beautiful. Wait 'til her face and body are healed. She'll take your breath away."

Billy turned away and smiled. "I'm sure she will."

He was thinking that he had seen more breasts in the last week than he had his whole life before. *I wish Jamee would hurry back*, he thought. He ate some meat left from the meal the night before and went to check on Red.

Red was awake but still looked feverish and weak.

"How do you feel?"

Red gave a weak smile and said, "I think I'll live. Sorry I haven't been much help."

"You just take it easy. There will be plenty for you to do when you're feeling better."

Billy worked around the cave helping May and Nuuna gather firewood. He went to the river with them to wash up. The girls removed their clothes and jumped in the water.

May turned to Billy. "Come on in and get cleaned up. Remember we are friends and I will be a good girl. I promise."

Seeing the sincere look on May's face and the happy face of Nuuna, he removed his clothing and moved quickly into the cool water.

Nuuna swam to him, kissing him on the cheek and said, "Let's play, Billy."

Soon they were all laughing, splashing water and swimming about. May did not try to get close to Billy or tease him. It was an enjoyable time for them all. As May and Nuuna walked out of the water and began to dry off, Billy couldn't help but notice the flaring hips and firm rear of May.

As she dried off she said, "Come on out and dry off, Billy."

"I'll be out in a minute. You two go ahead to the cave. I'll catch up."

May laughed and with a friendly wave moved off to the cave.

Billy thought, *You better stop doing that, little buddy. I really miss Jamee!*

In the afternoon he scraped the uteta skin again, took the prairie cat skin to the river and submerged it in the water. A few hours later he hung it again to dry. The pelt was beautiful. It was a yellowish-tan, tinted dark gray within light gray square patterns all over. It would be perfect for what he wanted to do.

He was returning to the cave when Flick darted by his face and landed on a limb near him. Flick looked directly at Billy and her colors were moving between royal blue and yellow.

"Is Jamee coming?"

Flick continued her display a moment longer and flew away heading up the cliff.

CHAPTER 7

Billy ran to the cave, grabbed a water container and headed for the trail. He ran the whole way up and was winded as he reached the top. Looking around, he couldn't see anyone. Disappointed, he sat down and waited. It was a short wait and then he saw her trotting toward him. He was up and running and took Jamee in his arms, lifting her up and holding her close. He said, "I see you."

"I see you."

When he put her down and looked into her smiling face he could see Jamee was near exhaustion. He sat her down and gave her the container of water. She drank greedily.

Catching her breath, she asked, "Did you miss me, my love?"

"Jamee, I don't ever want to be away from you again. I have been worried since you left."

They kissed and held each other for a moment, and then Jamee said, "I've been running all day with only the thought of getting back to you."

Jamee looked dead tired but stood and said, "Let's go down. I have everything we need to help the others."

Billy lifted the packs and helped Jamee to the valley below.

As they entered the cave Jamee could smell the meal cooking and realized how hungry she was. The others turned and May and Nuuna ran to Jamee and hugged her.

May said, "It's so good to see you back safe. We've missed you!"

A little surprised at the warm greeting, Jamee hugged them back.

May said, "Here; you sit down and eat something. You look worn out."

"Let me take care of Red first and then I will eat whatever that is that smells so wonderful."

She moved to Red as Billy handed her the packs.

Red looked up and said, "Hello Jamee. It's good to see you again."

She could see his fevered look and said, "This should fix you right up."

She let May help her with the dressings and then moved to the woman.

"Has she woken up yet?"

May said, "No, but we have been giving her broth and she takes that just fine."

Jamee looked her over and saw that the swelling to her head had not gone down at all. Her eyes were still swollen shut. She examined her other wounds and found them completely healed. The bruises over her body were beginning to heal, but she worried about the head wounds.

"That beating she took might have cracked her skull."

"They were beating her with large sticks and hit her on the head a couple of times."

"We'll just have to let her rest until she comes around. Her wounds are healing everywhere except her head," said Jamee.

May gently lifted Jamee by the shoulders and moved her to a log she had placed near the fire. She then went to the fire, cut some meat off the roast and put some broth in a bowl and brought it back to Jamee.

"Jamee, now you have to eat and then get some rest. I'll deal with everything else." Jamee looked up to May's smiling face and nodded her thanks.

May had changed since she had left. She could feel the warm friendship and was glad for it.

She took a bite of the venison and looked up in surprise. "This is delicious! I'm glad you are here."

"I'm glad I'm here too, but I'm happier that you're back. Billy has missed you something awful.

We've missed you, too! I really want to be your friend. You and Billy have done so much for us."

Jamee looked over at Billy, wondering how much help May had been to him. Billy couldn't take his eyes off Jamee as she ate; touching and rubbing her back to make sure she was really there.

After Jamee finished eating, Billy took her by the hand and said, "Let's get you cleaned up and then you must rest."

Jamee rose and walked out of the cave into the night. The night was bright from the light of both moons overhead. She held Billy's hand as they walked to the river's edge. She turned Billy to face her, kissed him deeply and squeezed him tight. Billy helped her remove her vest and loincloth and quickly removed his own. They stepped into the water, letting the cool water swirl about them. Billy had brought a cloth with him and began to rub Jamee's body. As he cleaned the trail dust and dirt from her he caressed her and could feel her breathing increase. Jamee lowered her hand, rubbing him.

"Oh, Billy, that feels so good! It seems like such a long time since I've felt your touch."

"I love you with all my heart." Reluctantly he added, "You need to rest, my love. Let's go back so you can sleep."

"Not yet."

She put her arms around his neck and lifted her body up and slid down on him.

"I've missed you so much," she said in a husky voice.

He lifted her with his hands and softly kissed her. "That feels so good!"

As they kissed and moved together, heat ran through their bodies. It was all Billy could do to remain standing, but it was an effort he barely noticed. Their movements were frantic through the end.

Jamee stepped back into the water. She took the cool water in her cupped hands, cleaned him and then herself. "I see he has been a good boy while I was gone," she said with a giggle.

"He is only for you."

They walked back to the cave and Billy helped Jamee lie down on a blanket away from the others. She was asleep before her head touched the ground. May looked over at Billy and smiled. She thought, *That must have been a good bath.*

The next morning while Jamee still slept Billy got a bone needle and cord from his pack. He took Jamee's staff and left the cave without a word. Once he retrieved the prairie cat pelt, he laid it out and cut the pelt using the staff as a pattern. He went to the river, held the pelt under the water until it was completely soaked.

Billy sewed the pelt together skin side out. The seam was thin and tight. Turning his work fur side out, he slid the staff into it. With his knife he carefully cut out a place for the guard to slide through. The hole was purposely smaller than the guard, so the pelt protruded upward slightly. When he finished he took it back to the cave and hung it from a rock on the face of the cave opening to dry.

Billy went inside and found Jamee eating. He picked up a pack, motioned for her to follow him out and they walked off into the trees holding hands.

"Where are we going?" asked Jamee.

"I want to be alone with you and I have something to show you."

They walked for an hour along the bank of the river, heading upstream towards the center of the long curve of the cliff wall. As they walked Jamee began to hear the sound of rushing water. The closer they got, the louder the noise became. The river was churning but she couldn't see ahead. They moved around a boulder blocking their view with Jamee in the lead and as she rounded the boulder she saw the source of the noise.

Water was boiling out of the river near the base of the cliff. A column of water rose up at least fifty feet into the air, cascading down in a circle around the column. The water was crystal clear. She stopped and Billy's hands went around her waist. She backed into Billy and pressed her back to his body.

"Billy, it's beautiful!"

"I thought you would like to be the first of our little company to see it. When I came to the valley before, I came here to see where the river came from. This time it is much more beautiful." He pressed his hand onto her belly and caressed. He kissed the back of her neck.

"Where does the water come from?"

"I don't know for sure, but I think there must be an underground river that runs beneath the prairie. Come," he said.

He led her to the cliff face and around the back of the column. The spray swirled around them and cooled their skin. They came to a steep stairway that had been carved out of the rock-face. It led up to what looked like an opening high above them. Billy let Jamee go first so he could admire her as she worked her way up. Her vest fell away from her body and welcomed warmth filled him. He reached up with his hand and placed it on her rear.

"Are you helping me, Billy?" She laughed.

"Yes, my love."

As they reached the opening in the cliff, Jamee saw a brightly lit cave going into the rocks.

They moved in and sat facing the column of water. Jamee looked out and could see a bowl of water formed in the top of the column where the water fell back to the river making a circular waterfall. It was almost ten feet across.

"Billy, I have been around water all my life, but I have never seen anything so beautiful."

"I have never seen anything as beautiful as you."

Jamee turned with bright, shining brown eyes and gave him a dazzling smile.

She grabbed his vest bottom and jerked it up and off. She then stood him up and pulled his loincloth off. Jamee held him in her hand and kissed as Billy looked down across his belly and saw her beautiful eyes staring up at him. It was almost more than he could stand, but he pulled her to her feet and kissed her hungrily. Billy worked frantically at her vest and loincloth. He removed his boots and hers and lay her down on a blanket from his pack. His lips, mouth and hands worked and massaged every part of her.

Jamee shivered at his touch and pulled his head back and said in a husky voice, "Wait."

She moved him onto his back and swept her leg over his head, began to kiss him with an urgency her body demanded. Billy found the source of her heat and kissed softly and then with a quickened pace. She let a soft moan escape her lips. She felt the tingling bolts course through her as Billy shuddered and the humming ran through him as well. As the glow began to dim, she spun on Billy's belly and kissed him tenderly on the lips. She raised her head and let herself drown in those royal blue eyes.

"I love you," they said at the same time and then laughed together.

They sat close together, watching the water fall back into the river, and Jamee said, "You make me complete. I want this to last forever."

"It will, my love. You are the most beautiful woman I have ever seen and I am yours."

Jamee spoke, not looking at Billy. "I wasn't sure if you would still want me after the others came. May is beautiful. Her body is so strong and full and there will be others when we reach your village. I...I was afraid you might want more than me."

Billy turned her to face him and said, "Jamee, I want you to stop thinking that, please. It's important that we trust each other. We depend on each other! I know we haven't been together long, but I also know I have been waiting for you all my life. Never worry about my love for you. I promise you I will love you with all my heart and only you. I will be yours. Although," he said with a smile, "it's hard not to look at the others."

Jamee punched Billy in the shoulder and laughed. "I won't stop you from looking, but I plan on keeping you too busy to do much of that."

"I'll do my part, too, to keep your eyes on me."

They both began to laugh and touch. Soon they were kissing, caressing and heating each other's bodies. They made love again, but this time it was slow and soft, until the end.

When they finally started back down the natural stairs at the cave entrance Jamee turned to Billy and said, "This time you may have to really help me get down. I can run all day long, but making love with you makes my body weak, but happy."

They made their way back to the others smiling, talking and touching the entire way back.

Near the entrance Billy said, "Go on in. I have something I want to check on."

He went to the rock where he had left the staff and pelt drying. The pelt was completely dry and stretched tight over the staff. The opening he had cut for the guard fit perfectly. He trimmed the ends and took it into the cave. As he walked up to Jamee he held it out to her.

"I made this for you."

Jamee took the staff, felt the soft fur and admired the beautiful pattern. She gripped it and found the fur tight and not slippery at all.

"Oh, it's beautiful, but why did you do this? You must have been thinking about this since I left."

"Red recognized the staff right away. It is something the Volls would know by its color and they would try hard to get it back."

May came up to them and said, "The woman woke up for a little while an hour ago. She muttered that the light hurt her eyes and then drifted back to sleep. I put a cloth over her eyes to shield the light. She seems to be resting a little better."

Jamee went over to check her.

"Has she eaten any more, May?"

"Yes. I fed her again and she ate a full bowl of broth. I tried to give her some meat but she wouldn't eat it."

Jamee pulled open her coveralls and looked at her bruises. She rolled her on her side to check her back. The woman let out a sigh at Jamee's touch.

"Her body appears to be healing, but the swelling in her face is the same."

She gently rolled her to her back and covered her again.

"Billy, I would like to try putting some of the matting in a broth and feeding it to her. Do you think it might help?"

"I don't know, but it shouldn't hurt. People use the matting to clean their teeth and sometimes chew it to take a bad taste from their mouth. We need to do something because we will have to move before too much longer."

Jamee and May began to brew water, adding herbs and some matting. Billy left to check the area again.

As Jamee went to check on Red, May said with a smile, "Jamee, you look rested. Did you and Billy have a good time?"

Jamee gave her a sharp look but didn't reply.

"Oh, Jamee, I was only teasing. I know what you mean to Billy! We had a long talk while you were gone. I want you to know you are a lucky girl to have someone like him and I think he is lucky to have you too! I think Billy and I are becoming friends and I really want for you and me to be friends as well. You don't have to worry about me. Even if I wanted something from him, he wouldn't give it. I don't want anything from him or you but friendship. Do you think we could be good friends?"

Jamee looked up at May and saw tears in her eyes. She smiled, stood and gave May a hug. "Yes, May, I would like that very much. You are a beautiful woman, inside and out."

May let out a sob and hugged Jamee back.

"Thank you, Jamee. I won't let you down."

They moved to check on Red and saw him smiling up at both of them.

"Hey, I need friends too." He held out his arms for a hug. With laughter they both gave him a big hug.

Jamee said, "I think you are feeling better."

"Hugs from pretty women will do it every time for me."

He sat up and moved his arms around smiling. "I feel like a new man. That stuff really works." Jamee checked his wounds and found them healed. Only a little redness was showing.

"That matting is like magic. I've got to see the tree you got it from," Red said.

"They grow out on the prairie in large groves. They are giants and a source of water as well. We only discovered their healing qualities a short time ago by accident."

"Well, count me as a true believer," Red said rising to his feet.

He felt a little dizzy from lying so long but could feel his strength returning.

Nuuna ran to him, jumping into his arms. "Oh, Red, you look good again. Do you think a hug from a little girl will help?"

"You just can't get too many hugs, darling, and little girl hugs are the best!" Red said as they all laughed happily.

Red carried Nuuna outside to sit in the sunlight, laughing and tickling her.

"That's the most I've heard her say at one time since I've known her," May said. "Maybe that white man ain't too bad."

Jamee checked the broth they had set aside to steep and cool.

"Give me a hand, May. Let's give this a try."

May lifted the small woman up in a sitting position with the cloth still covering her eyes and Jamee put the bowl to her lips. She drank it thirstily until it was gone. May laid her back down and the woman was back asleep instantly.

"I hope this works," Jamee said.

As the sun set in the west, they gathered around the small fire and had a fine time eating and talking. Jamee walked down to the river with Billy and they bathed and snuggled in the water. They saw May, Nuuna and Red pass by to find another spot to clean up.

"It will be interesting to see how May and Red get along," Billy said. "She told me a little about the way she has been treated by white people."

Jamee replied, "Oh, I think they will get along fine. May needs friends and doesn't seem to have a mean spirit."

"I like her too, except she's too tall,"

Jamee laughed and splashed water in his face.

That night as Jamee lay in Billy's arms sleeping she awoke at a noise. Lifting her head, she looked around. It was too dark to see anything, but she heard the noise again coming from near where the fire had gone out. She rose and moved to the sound and found it was coming from the small woman.

"Where am I? Is anyone there?"

Jamee knelt beside her, touching her arm saying, "You are with friends and safe. You were hurt badly and we were all worried about you."

The woman replied, "Only one person I've ever known worried about me, but thank you for your help. Can you stay with me? I don't like being in the dark not knowing where I am."

"Yes, I'll stay with you for a while," Jamee said and lay down beside her.

Jamee felt the small hand wrap around her arm and softly cling. She relaxed and was soon asleep again. Jamee woke in the early dawn, the soft dim light of day drifting in from the mouth of the cave. She was surprised to find herself lying next to the small woman with her arm across her chest. She lifted up and checked the woman, felt her face and found the swelling had gone down quite a bit. The woman stirred slightly but remained asleep. Jamee rose and went to lie next to Billy, feeling his warmth and snuggling close.

Billy said softly, "I thought you had gone out last night. I got up and found you lying with the woman. You looked so comfortable I didn't disturb you. I guess I have to share the medicine woman."

She looked up and saw the teasing smile on his face.

She laid her head back on his chest and said, "You will never have to share me, my love, and I won't share you either."

She pinched his side lovingly. They heard May get up and move about, starting the fire and preparing a morning meal.

Red soon rose and helped May, giving her a big hug and said, "What about you and me go for a swim?"

"Not now, white man, maybe later," she said with a laugh.

Billy and Jamee rose and went out to take a morning walk and be alone for a while before the day's activities started.

Billy said, "I am going to have to go soon and scout around the Koro's mine to the north."

"Don't you mean we? I will go where you go now that the others are getting healthy," Jamee replied.

Billy looked down at the determined face and nodded his head saying, "You're right. It might be dangerous, but you have proven your value to me. I go where you go."

Her eyes sparkled as she kissed Billy and gave his little buddy a rub.

Billy laughed. "I don't know how I lived without your touches." Then he squeezed her gently. They both laughed and continued their walk.

When they returned they saw Red and May playing with Nuuna. She was giggling and enjoying all the attention. Jamee glanced over at the small woman and was surprised to see her sitting up, eating a meal May had prepared.

CHAPTER 8

Her back was to Jamee as she walked over and placed her hands on the petite woman's shoulders.

"Feeling better?"

A small hand reached up to grasp hers and she turned to face Jamee.

The shock on Jamee's face was obvious as she dropped to her knees, took the woman in her arms and whispered, "Silver!" Jamee was in tears and she couldn't find the words to say.

"Yes, Jamee love, it's Silver."

They were hugging and kissing as Billy walked over and stared at them.

"I guess you are feeling better."

Jamee grabbed his hand and pulled him sharply down to their sides.

Finding her voice through her tears she looked at Billy and said, "This is the woman I told you about, my only friend on Ocean. Billy, this is Silver."

Billy looked at the woman and now that her face was not swollen he could see a beautiful pair of bright gray eyes, almost the color of silver looking at him.

"Hello. I'm Billy."

Silver said, "You must be Jamee's dream man. The eyes give you away. It's so good to meet you. While I was sleeping my dreams were terrible, but every now and then I thought I heard Jamee and she was telling me she had found you. It gave the only comfort I had in my dreams."

Silver's face was still blotched from the bruising, but Billy could see she was a rare beauty.

Jamee's stories of her came back to him and he said, "Thank you so much for being Jamee's friend when she needed someone. I will be in your debt forever."

Tears sprang to Silver's eyes and she cried along with Jamee. She smiled at Billy but no words would come. That was the first time in a very long time Silver was speechless. May and Nuuna watched in astonishment.

Before Jamee had walked over to Silver, Red had left for the river to wash up. As he entered the cave, Silver looked up to meet his eyes. He stopped dead in his tracks, speechless. Silver, already at a loss for words, could only stare back into Red's eyes. When Jamee looked at Silver and followed her stare she thought that Silver was afraid at the sight of a white man standing there.

"Silver, it's okay. This is Red and he is the one who rescued you and carried you for three days. Red, come over and say hello to Silver."

Red continued to stand and stare.

"Red, are you okay?" Nuuna asked.

Red jerked and said, "I...I... What? Yes... I'm okay."

He walked toward Billy, Jamee and Silver, his eyes never leaving Silver's.

"Uh oh!" May laughed.

Jamee looked at May in confusion and then back to Red saying, "Red! This is Silver. Won't you say hello or something?"

Red nodded his head and said, "Hello."

They waited for him to say more, but it was like he was struck dumb.

"Red, what's the matter with you?" Billy asked.

Red's face was covered in sweat and he looked like he might pass out at any moment.

"Sit down, Red. Is your fever back?" Billy asked.

Red blinked one time and said, "Got to go." And with that he turned and nearly ran out of the cave.

Billy jumped up and said, "I better go check on him! He didn't look good."

May was laughing so hard she tilted over and slapped the floor with her hand. Jamee looked at her like she had lost her mind but turned to Silver, who was still staring straight ahead like in a trance.

"Silver, what is the matter? Are you okay?"

Silver finally turned her head toward Jamee and asked, "Who...Who was that?"

"Who was who?" Jamee asked back, but she got no reply from Silver.

May, still rolling and laughing, began to whoop trying to catch her breath.

Jamee spun on her and barked, "What is going on? May...! May! Talk to me."

May finally controlled herself long enough to say, "You people are dumber than a box of rocks," and started laughing again.

"May, you're making me mad. Please tell me what you are talking about."

May finally sat up and saw the fear, anger and concern in Jamee's eyes. Wide-eyed she said, "Jamee, don't you know dumb, lightning-struck love when you see it?" Jamee sat there in a state of confusion until it finally struck her.

She whirled back to look at Silver and asked, "Is that what this is? You're in love with Red?"

Silver asked again, "Who was that?"

Jamee looked hard at Silver and then began to laugh. It was so funny that she had to lie back. Soon May crawled over to Jamee and joined her, laughing and rolling on the floor.

After they both calmed down, Jamee sat up and hugged Silver, kissing her cheeks and said, "That was Red. He's the one who saved you and brought you here."

Silver turned her head to Jamee and said, "That's very interesting. He looks like a nice man."

Once again Jamee and May were caught up in laughter.

Silver asked, "What's the matter with you two? All I said was he looks like a nice man."

At the same time Jamee was prying the truth out of May, Billy caught up to Red. "Red, what is wrong with you? You looked like you were about to faint."

Red shook himself and asked Billy, "Who was that?"

Billy gave Red a look like he was crazy and answered, "That's the woman you carried around for three days. Don't you remember?"

"That's very interesting. She looks like a nice woman."

Billy, dumbfounded, said to Red, "Come back with me. We need to talk."

As Red turned back to the cave entrance he suddenly stopped and told Billy, "No! I have to check on something."

He spun around, ran to the trees and disappeared. Billy couldn't believe his eyes. *What is going on around here?*

As he entered the cave he saw May and Jamee laughing and hugging each other. Silver sat looking as if nothing had happened. He stormed into the cave and demanded someone tell him what was going on. Jamee and May looked up at him and began to roll on the floor laughing even harder. Billy went to Silver, sat down and asked her what was happening.

She said, "I have no idea."

He turned to the pile of laughter and threw up his hands.

He rose and started to leave when Jamee called to him, "No, Billy, don't leave. Come here and sit with me."

He moved to Jamee and sat down with an angry look.

Jamee said, "They're in love!"

"Who's in love?"

"Silver and Red. They just don't know it yet."

It hit Billy like a bright light from the sky and he started to laugh saying, "I see it now"

May asked where Red was and Billy said through his laughter, "I asked him what was wrong and all he could say was, 'Who was that?' and then he took off running through the trees. I better go find him. He might get into trouble."

"Leave him be. Who or what in their right mind would take on something as big and crazy as Red is right now?"

"I guess you're right, May. He'll be all right. I just hope he comes back."

Jamee said, "Oh! He'll be back," and looked over at Silver.

They were all worn out from the excitement and soon May and Nuuna went off to sleep. Jamee asked Billy if it would be all right if Silver lay down with them just for the night. He agreed and Jamee brought Silver over to their blanket. They lay down with Billy against Jamee's back and Silver against her front. They were all soon asleep.

The next morning they all woke and noticed Red was not there and it didn't look like he had slept in the cave.

Silver, now fully recovered from last night said, "I think I should go and find Red. I have something to tell him."

Jamee said, "I'll go with you. You don't know your way around and I don't want to lose you again."

They walked out of the cave and headed for the river. As they approached, along the trail they spotted Red sitting on a rock along the bank of the river.

Silver turned to Jamee and said, "Let me do this alone. I can find my way back."

Jamee kissed Silver and said, "I love you." She headed back to the cave.

Silver waited until Jamee was out of sight and then went forward. She stepped out of the trees and Red jumped to his feet.

"Don't leave, Red. I would like to talk to you."

Red dropped his eyes to the pebbled shore and said, "I'm really sorry about last night. I must have looked like an idiot."

"No, you didn't, and even if you did, I looked the same way."

She walked up to Red and smiled up at him. Red towered over Silver but he stood quietly and not looking at her. She took his hand and asked if they could sit down. Red took her to a large rock and made room for her to sit with him.

Red started, "Silver, when we were being transported here I never really got a look at you or talked to you. When I looked into your eyes last night...."

Silver put her fingers to his lips and said, "Let me talk first, please."

She said, "Red, when I saw you last night, it was really for the first time. I didn't notice anyone coming here except Nuuna. I was in a very bad state of mind. When you walked in and looked at me, I felt something I have never felt towards a man. I felt a need to go to you and hold on to you from now on. I knew you were the one I have been waiting to come into my life. Does that make sense to you?"

"Yes. Now that I've sat out here all night afraid to go back, it makes perfect sense, because I feel the same way about you. I've had a few girlfriends but nothing ever came of it. Your perfect beauty stopped me cold, but the warmth in your eyes made me realize you are the one I've been waiting for. I am not a very good man. I'm forty-two years old and you are still a very young, beautiful woman. I have no right to expect you to feel the same way as I do."

Silver looked into Red's eyes, then rose up and kissed him softly on his lips.

She said, "I am 26 years old and have lived a lifetime already. I have a past that will probably turn you away, but I won't start anything with you until I tell you the whole truth about me. After I have, you can walk away from me and hopefully we can become friends."

"I can't think of anything that would change my mind about you."

"There might be something that would do that. Let me speak, please. Don't interrupt and don't let my tears influence you."

Red nodded but said nothing.

Silver began with her childhood, how she had been on her own since a very young age. She had lived by her wits and the little kindliness she had known. She took a deep breath and told him about being abducted and how she had made her living up to this point. She told him everything about being a prostitute in a house on Ocean and about the money she had made.

She told him how she had learned to manipulate men into getting what she wanted and how she felt like she was paying them back for what had happened to her as a young girl. She told him everything, not holding back. She told him of being kept by an important man on her world and how his wife had found out and made him send her away as a slave to this world.

She also told him about Jamee, meeting her one day when Jamee was just a child and how Jamee had become her only friend. How she made sure Jamee would not end up in the life she was living. Silver did not cry until she looked up at Red and told him that was everything. She could see the concern in his eyes and it hurt her to think she had lost her one chance at finding true happiness.

Red said, "Now you must listen to my story."

He told her of his privileged life as a kid and how he had grown up not wanting for anything. His mother used to tell him old stories about people of color and how the white race had treated them. As he grew he became mean and because of his size he felt he could treat people any way he wanted because of his family's status.

Both his parents were killed in a plane crash when he was twelve and his life was turned on its head. Suddenly the other family members would have nothing to do with him. They cheated him out of the money that was due him and kicked him out on the streets.

He learned fast how to take care of himself. He was already as big as most men and learned how to fight and steal to survive. At eighteen he became a bodyguard for the call-girls of one of the pimps he knew. He became a friend with one girl, who had a story similar to Silver's. One day she was killed by a man who refused to pay her. Red had been off getting drunk while she was beaten to death. This drove Red crazy with guilt. He gave up drinking and tried to use his education to get out of the life he was living.

He met a man who took him in, gave him a job and became Red's mentor. The man was an activist, trying to get the government to return many of the people who had been cast off the Earth. He had many enemies but survived for a number of years.

Between the words of his mother and mentor, Red lost his respect for the white race. When he was thirty he was drafted into the military and trained as a fighter. It was something he liked because he was able to help crush the more extreme white faction. He was promoted a number of times and had many men following his orders.

He began to question the reason for fighting certain faction. Some were like his mentor; wanting the laws changed to include the rights of the non-white. He was sent to the outer world VOLL defense system.

On his first assignment he refused to capture non-white groups for extermination. He was put in prison where he began to learn about all the different people that he himself labeled non-whites. He also began to love these people and their different cultures. That's when it was decided to let him receive the same punishment, by sending him to the mines on Prairie.

When he finished he said, "If you still want a life with a man like me, I am yours. Silver, you have done nothing but survive your life. I believe you when you say that life is in the past and I believe that you feel for me what I feel for you. If you let me, I will do everything I can to make the rest of your life better in so many ways. If you'll have me, we can start a new life today."

He looked down and saw her tears and tears came to his eyes as well.

"Red, I will give you all the love I have in me. I've been saving it up for a long time and there is a lot to give. Today my heart is singing for the first time. It sings of a love I have never known before."

"I will give you all of my love and all of my heart. You have just described what I am feeling. I couldn't put it into words, but now I know what the words are. My heart sings!"

They came together and kissed deeply. They hugged and held each other for a long time.

"Do you think we should go back and tell our friends so they'll stop worrying about us?" Silver asked with a laugh.

"I'll be the proudest man on this world to walk into that cave with you on my arm." They started back to the cave.

They came upon Jamee and Billy working on an uteta skin.

Billy looked at Jamee and said, "I think they have discovered what we knew last night."

Red laughed. "Yes, I think we have. I hope you have enjoyed seeing me make a fool of myself. I want you to be the first to hear it from my lips. I love this woman!"

Billy grasped Red's forearm and said, "It's good to see your eyes clear. You had me worried last night. I thought you had run off and I would never see you again." He gave Red a big hug.

Jamee was crying, hugging and kissing Silver and said, "I'm so happy for you, Silver. You are like my big sister and now I will have a big brother, too!"

Silver moved to Billy and kissed him hard on the mouth. "I wanted to do that last night for the words you spoke to me. Then Red walked in and I became an idiot."

Billy turned red and moved over to Jamee's side. "Your sister is a good kisser."

Jamee laughed and said, "Well, don't get used to her kisses. I have too many to give to you."

Red said, "How do Silver and I get married on this world?" He looked down at Silver and said, "I guess I better ask you first."

He kneeled down on one knee, smiled and asked Silver, "Will you marry me, Silver? All the words I said earlier and my pledge to you; I love you and will tell you every day."

Silver stared wide-eyed for an instant, her eyes filled with tears as she answered, "Yes, I will marry you and love you forever."

They all laughed and hugged again.

"I am so happy for you, Silver. You deserve to be loved by a great man like Red," Jamee exclaimed.

Billy said, "The marriage will have to wait until we get to my village, but until then you two can't be messing around. A kiss now and then and holding hands are all that's allowed."

Jamee punched him hard and laughed. "That's not what you told me. Don't listen to him,

Red. You and Silver are as one now so start getting to know each other."

Red turned a bright red and said to Jamee, "Yes, ma'am."

Red and Silver continued on to the cave to see May and Nuuna.

When they entered May exclaimed, "Well, we gotta start looking for a man for me!" She laughed, rushing over to hug Silver and Red. "I don't generally like white men, but you are an exception. I'm so happy for you both." She reached up, pulled Red over, gave him a deep kiss, and then said, "Yep, I gotta to get me a man!"

Silver laughed while Red blushed. Nuuna ran to Red and jumped up into his waiting arms. She kissed him on the cheek, leaned out and kissed Silver.

"We will be a big family!"

"Yes, we will, Nuuna. I'm glad you're happy." Red said.

Nuuna, who always had a smile on her face, jumped down and went back to tending the fire.

Billy had taken the uteta skin to the river to soak, then brought it back and staked it out hair side up. The wood ash had done its work, loosening the hair. Billy scraped and the hair came off the skin easily. When he finished, he hung the skin to dry.

Jamee said, "I want to eat fish again. Do you have any hooks?"

Billy reached into an inside pocket of his pack and produced a strong hook.

"I made this myself. I enjoy fishing in the river near my village," he said as he handed the hook to Jamee.

Billy went to the edge of the trees and found a sapling and cut it. He trimmed the branches and skinned the bark and then went to his pack and found a thin twine ball and handed it all to Jamee.

"While you're off fishing I will get some more meat."

"Take May with you, Billy. She needs a break from all the work she has been doing."

"Okay. She told me she was a forest guide on her world. I'll put her to the test."

Billy went to the cave and asked May if she would like to help him gather some meat. She jumped at the chance to get out and see some of the country. Billy grabbed a small pack, putting water and some dried meat in it. He gathered his bow and they started out. May had her knife with her. They made their way to the trail going up to the prairie. He let May take the lead but soon wished he had gone first.

As he followed May up the trail he watched her firm rear and legs work in the rhythm of the climb. She was a pretty woman and had a body that attracted attention. She had put on a new pair of coveralls from the gear they had brought with them, but it did little to hide the swell of her hips and her breasts straining against the syncotton. He was glad when they reached the top. As they stood at the rim of the cliff May just smiled at Billy, knowing where his eyes had been.

"Billy, will you let me use your bow? I'm pretty good with one."

Since Billy had brought May to see how she handled herself, he agreed. He handed his bow and quiver to her and she tested the strength of the bow. She pulled an arrow from the quiver and examined it.

"This is a very nice bow and the arrows are beautiful and straight."

Billy smiled with pride as he told May he had made them himself.

"Where do we go from here?"

"We'll go check the clumps of bushes out there," he said, pointing out into the prairie.

"You lead off. I think your eyes need a rest."

Billy smiled and led off.

May laughed and said, "You're a good man, Billy! I hope there is at least one more like you around here."

As Billy and May moved through the grass he named and explained the different plants he saw. May was taking it all in.

"I've never been in such open country. It's beautiful, but I can see I have a lot to learn."

As Billy neared a clump of rain berry bushes he turned and said to May, "We should find a few hoppers here. You move in and see what you can find. Be careful of the thorns."

May moved ahead and just as she came to the edge of the bushes a hopper streaked out to her left. In a blur, May nocked an arrow and let it fly. The hopper went down in a tumble. Billy was impressed and looked at May. She pointed at him, then to the hopper and continued on into the bushes. Billy went to retrieve the hopper and his arrow.

While he dressed the hopper he heard the bowstring twang twice in rapid succession. He moved to the edge of the bushes and waited. May emerged with two hoppers, cleaned and dressed.

"Let's try for something bigger," May said.

Billy looked around and saw a pampas clump about a mile away and moved off toward it. May took the lead and they soon arrived at the tall bushes. They moved quietly into the clump and saw a small herd of utetas. She nocked an arrow and moved slowly into the bushes. He admired the way she moved without making a sound. Billy watched her kneel, aim and fire all in one smooth motion. An uteta ran toward him, falling at his feet, dead. May returned with a wide grin, pulled out her knife and began to dress out the uteta.

She looked over at Billy and said, "That ought to be enough for a few days, don't you think?"

Billy replied, "I think it will. I am very impressed. I don't think I can teach you much about hunting."

"I can hunt, but I need your knowledge of this country! This is my home now. Now, if I can only find a man like you!" She said laughing.

Billy picked up the uteta, placed it across his shoulder and started off. May carried the three hoppers tied together with a strip of leather. Billy continued talking to May about the things they saw. He also told her about other animals on Prairie. When they reached the valley floor they were tired and sweaty. May led the way to a secluded spot by the river. She hung the hoppers on a nearby tree and helped Billy hang the uteta.

"Now," she said, "Let's get cleaned up before we go back."

She began to undress and then walked out into the cool water, turned and looked at Billy. Billy didn't quite know what to do and just stood there looking at the ground.

"Billy, I told you before you could trust me and we agreed we would be friends. We need to clean this blood and dirt off before we go back, don't we?"

Billy looked up at her and said, "Yes... Yes, I guess we do."

He slowly removed his shirt, loincloth and walked into the water.

"Wow! Now, that's a real nice ... uh... set of muscles you have."

Billy quickly dropped in the water to his chest.

"May, you're not making this easy."

"We're friends. Don't worry. Now, come over here and let me wash your hair."

Billy slowly moved to May and she shoved his head below the water, brought him up and she began to scrub his hair, shoulders, arms, chest and back.

She turned, dipped her head under water and said, "Now me."

Billy scrubbed May's head and noticed how coarse her hair was. It was different than any he had ever seen, but it had a nice feel. He rubbed her neck, shoulders and back. She turned to him and he looked down at her breasts and gulped.

"You can handle the rest."

He cleaned his body as May finished. She walked from the water and began to dry herself.

"Come on out, Billy, and I'll dry you off."

"Uh... not right now."

May laughed and pulled her coveralls on.

"You really enjoy teasing me, don't you?"

"I do enjoy laughing! Come on out, Billy. I'm sorry."

Billy reluctantly walked from the water.

"Don't take this the wrong way, but you are a real man!"

Billy grabbed the cloth, dried quickly and dressed, not saying a word. As they picked up their gear and game, they looked at each other and laughed.

When they entered the cave they were still smiling. Jamee looked them both over and noticed the wet hair and clean skin.

"Did you have fun hunting?" she asked with a serious look on her face.

She couldn't hold the stern look and smiled at Billy.

Billy blushed and said, "We had to clean up a little before we came back." Quickly changing the subject he said, "Look what May brought us. She made every kill!"

Jamee walked over to Billy and kissed him sweetly and asked, "Is she really that good?"

Billy, not catching the double meaning, said, "Yes. She is as good as me with a bow." Then, after realizing what else the question had meant said, "What? No...! I mean, we just got cleaned up."

May and Jamee laughed and Jamee said, "I know what you mean. Don't worry. I trust you and May."

May hugged her and took the hoppers to cook. Billy took the uteta outside and hung it up on a limb.

He turned to Jamee and kissed her and said, "I missed you, my love. What did you do today?"

"I didn't go fishing but...come and I'll show you." Jamee replied.

She took his hand and led him into the trees. They walked about two hundred yards away to an area of thick bush. Jamee pulled him through to the center and stood while Billy's eyes widened in amazement. The entire center of the brushy area was cut down to the ground. Every piece of wood was cut into small pieces.

"What happened?"

Jamee lifted her staff and said, "This happened. I decided not to go fishing but I wanted to try out some of the moves I have been practicing. This is an amazing weapon!"

Billy looked around at the destruction, then stepped back to the edge and said, "Show me but without the blade."

Jamee moved to the center of the cleared area and began to thrust, whirl and stab with the staff. Her movements were slow but each move looked practiced and deadly. Then as she moved back to the center she started over again, but this time the staff was a blur. She finished with the staff stopping a fraction of an inch from Billy's neck. The look in her eyes was lethal but quickly turned to a beautiful smile.

"How was that?"

"That was beautiful. You've learned quickly!"

"This fur you've covered the staff with is wonderful. It helps my grip, and when I tried to wash it, the water ran off without wetting the fur."

"That's why I used the pelt of a prairie cat. It is a prized fur among my tribe for that reason. Let's walk, Jamee."

They continued on through the trees and Billy said, "We will have to leave tomorrow. We shouldn't be gone more than four or five days. After we come back we can rest for a few days and then head for my village."

He looked deep into her beautiful brown eyes and said, "Red did something yesterday that I forgot to do. I have known you and I would always be together but that's no excuse."

He stopped and went to one knee and looked into Jamee's eyes and said, "Jamee, I love you with all of my heart and I will love you more every day we are together. Will you marry me?"

Jamee was taken back and tears flowed as she replied, "You don't have to ask, but yes! I'll be your wife and make you happy. I love you more than my life, too. We will make a life together that will be filled with love and joy."

Billy came to his feet and kissed Jamee.

She pulled away slightly and said, "I need you now!"

Billy raced with Jamee to a glade filled with flowers. Each tore at their clothes as they ran, nude by the time they reached the glade. Falling to the ground they made frantic love. They lay together, kissed and lightly touched afterwards.

Billy stood, pulled her up with him and walked naked to the river to bathe. After they cleaned one another, Jamee took his hand and pulled him back to the glade.

"More" was all she said and lay down on the grass.

Billy kneeled down and kissed her soft, supple body. As he did, Jamee rose up on one elbow, bent over Billy, kissed his hair and neck and rubbed his back.

He rose up, kissed the back of her neck and then lightly bit her ear letting his hot breath flow around her. That sent an excited chill through her. His mouth slid to her shoulders, kissed and bit softly. All the time his hands caressed her. He turned her onto her stomach as his fingertips made circles down her back. He kissed her silky soft skin and enjoyed her taste.

Jamee let out a soft moan. "Billy, I need you so much. That feels incredible!"

Billy slowly finished his travels with his lips, took her hips, lifted her to her knees and moved his body behind Jamee. He began moving in a deliberate, slow motion. As Jamee tried to quicken her movements Billy held her hips tight and forced her movements to slow. He continued his slow action but then he could no longer hold back. He looked down at her beauty; the swell of her hips, the track of her creamy brown back and her long neck. Her long hair was flung to the left side of her neck and it swayed as she reacted to him.

Jamee could stand no more as she matched his movements with an urgency she did not want to control. She felt his thighs pressing against hers and the jolts flashed through her with vibrations starting deep within her flower and spreading throughout her body. She began to collapse, but Billy felt his own need begin to peak and held her hips up until he too felt the humming course through him.

After he was complete, he lowered Jamee to the grass. Billy rolled Jamee onto her back and smiled down at her. Her face was pale. Her breath was shallow and she looked like she would faint.

Billy jumped to his knees and lifted her head and cried out. "Jamee! Are you all right?"

She smiled up at him and said, "Leave me alone for a minute. I'm okay, my love. You took my breath away. Let me rest for a minute."

She closed her eyes and Billy lowered her head to the grass and watched her carefully.

Her breathing became steady and deep and then she opened her eyes again and smiled up at him.

"I'll never do that again. I don't want to hurt you."

Jamee sat up and kissed Billy softly. "No, Billy, you didn't hurt me. You made me feel more than I've ever felt before and don't say you won't do that again. You make me feel so good. Really, my love, I want that feeling again and again but not right now." She kissed him. "Help me up."

Billy gently helped her to stand, still concerned. She took his hand and led him back to the river.

They bathed and Jamee said with a big grin, "I hope we can find our clothes." They searched the woods near the glade, found their clothes and quickly dressed.

"We better get back. They will think something happened to us."

As they walked through the woods Jamee saw the rainbow colors of Flick as she flew through the trees. She blushed but said nothing to Billy.

They entered the cave. May looked closely at Jamee and said, "You're glowing, Jamee. That must have been some walk!"

Jamee ignored May and went to sit down.

Nuuna walked over to her and put her arms around Jamee's neck. "You do look happy, Jamee."

Jamee gave her a hug and kiss and sat Nuna down in her lap.

Billy walked to the middle of the group and said, "Jamee and I must make a trip to check on the Koros. It will take us five or six days. While we are gone keep a careful watch and protect each other."

May asked, "Why can't we come?"

"We have to move fast and quietly. Two people can go in without being seen. A larger group would be dangerous."

Red moved over to Billy as Silver sat next to Jamee. He said, "Billy, I understand a small group will be better, but why are you going near that place at all?"

Billy motioned for Red to follow him outside.

They sat near the entrance in the last of the sunlight.

"This is the reason I am here. My tribe sends out a hunter from time to time to check on the

Koros. We want to know if they are planning a move that would bring them closer to us. Also, we would like to find a way to free the people they have working the mine and find a way to get the Volls to leave."

Red replied, "They will never move from where they are. The way I understand it is the mineral they mine can only be found in that one location. That is the only reason the Volls have anything to do with the Koros. It took them a long time to make contact with the Koros after it was discovered what they could do with the mineral."

"We have some of the thing you are talking about. We call it Green Rock. It is only of little use to us. Why is it so important?"

"The Volls call it *Verdance* and it absorbs sunlight and stores the energy like a battery; only it seems to multiply the power of the sun many times. It is very powerful!"

"I don't know what a 'battery' is or why it's so important. Tell me more about what it can do."

"The Volls can make the green rock provide power for lights and run their machines. They were trying to develop a way to make it a weapon when I left and getting very close to succeeding. I told you before that they couldn't bring their weapons with them because when they arrived they were useless. Using knives, spears and a long knife is not something the Volls are used to. You have no real defense against the weapons the Volls have on Earth. With them they can destroy many people from far away. Be glad that they haven't found a way to bring them here."

Billy asked, "Why do they need these things here?"

"The Volls were sent to the outer worlds to capture or kill all non-white people. They want to return many to Earth as slaves. Your people are lucky in a way. Prairie is far from the other worlds and it is believed there are no more planets where people can live so the Volls have no real interest in this place, except for Verdance."

"How is it you know so much? I know you were a Voll once, but you seem to know a great deal about them."

"I was a very high ranking non-com. That means I wasn't an officer who could have a Steer but I had a lot of control and power over the men. When I refused to obey orders it caused many problems in the ranks of the Volls. The officers were quick to put me in prison and then later transport me here. There are others who feel like I do, but they have no power. Billy, if the Volls ever catch me, I am a dead man, so this is my world now. Meeting Silver is like a dream come true for me. I never thought I had a chance at a good life, but thanks to you, Jamee and Silver, I have that chance. You can trust me."

"I have already given you my trust and you are my friend." Billy smiled and said, "I am happy you have found Silver. I'm just finding out what someone I love as a mate can do for my life. I hope you and Silver will feel the completeness that I feel. I know a little about the hard life Silver has had and it pleases me to know she can have the happiness she has missed all her life. She was Jamee's only friend and helped form her as she grew. Jamee is young but she's more mature than most women twice her age. A lot of that has to do with how Silver loved her. I will always love Silver as a sister and now you are my brother! It will be up to you to protect this group of ours while we are gone."

"It is hard for me to understand the trust you give so quickly, but if the others of this world are like you, I know I have found a true home and I won't let you down." They stood and Red picked Billy up in his arms, smiled and said, "You can count on me, my brother." They walked back in the cave to eat. It was already dark.

CHAPTER 9

The next morning Billy and Jamee shouldered their packs and headed across the prairie. They ran all day and slept in a clump of rain berry bushes that night. They moved out at first light heading due north. In the distance they could see the beginnings of a vast mountain range.

Billy said, "We will make it to the mountains by nightfall and camp in the foothills. We are approaching the Koros' range so keep a sharp lookout for anything that can cause us trouble."

"What are those mountains called?"

"The mountains are known by us as the Slave Mountains."

Flick flashed past Billy's face and Jamee said, "Don't worry; we have help."

Billy asked, "Does Flick watch us all the time?"

"Yes. Unfortunately she sees almost everything we do." Jamee said with a soft laugh.

"I think maybe she sees too much from the colors she makes around me."

"Flick really admires you. She says you have a big..." Jamee said giggling like a little girl. "I think so, too."

Billy said nothing but smiled to himself.

As they approached the foothills Jamee said, "Flick says we need to go into the valley farther east of here. She says there is a Koro patrol in the valley we're heading for."

Billy changed their direction to the east and continued to run. Once they were in sight of the next valley he slowed to a walk and looked carefully around. They moved into the valley and walked to the northern end. He found a place for them to camp in a cluster of boulders that formed a narrow opening and had a small hole in the back where a boulder leaned against another. The hole led out and would make a good escape route if needed.

As they settled in for the night Billy asked Jamee, "Can you ask Flick to come here and sit on my shoulder?"

"I'll ask, but she has a mind of her own."

Flick flew directly to Billy's right shoulder, landed and looked in Billy's eyes. She was royal blue and seemed unafraid of Billy.

Billy quickly leaned his head over and kissed Flick on the head. "Thank you for your help, Flick."

Flick fluttered her wings and turned a striking shade of pink.

Jamee laughed softly and said, "She's blushing."

Flick looked at Jamee, launched into the air and disappeared.

Jamee settled in next to Billy, kissed him and said, "You're a good man." They ate the last of the meat that May had packed for them and Jamee lay down with her head in Billy's lap. She was soon asleep. Billy kept watch while Jamee slept, contented to have her cuddled next to him.

While Billy looked out into the night he thought about all that had happened on this trek. He wondered what it would be like in his village when he returned with five people in his care. His tribe had lost much of their old culture and taken up many new ways. When they were brought to Prairie there were people from many different tribes. No one tribe could dominate the others so they decided to try and combine their customs. Over the generations much was lost but new standards were set. They became a peaceful people but always maintained their fighting skills as part of their heritage. The Eagle tribe had been isolated for many generations. Their only contact with the other tribes was a gathering that took place every three years.

The tribes gathered to exchange information and trade. They would celebrate and have games of skill between the young men. The women would show their handiwork and some would also show their fighting skills. There would be challenges between the hunters, but the fights were not to the death. It was a happy time and always remained peaceful. Young men of each tribe would often display their skills just to impress the young women of other tribes and find wives to take back to their villages.

The next gathering was due in a few months. He worried about bringing Red into the village and keeping him safe until he was accepted. It would be easier with the women but it would take much explaining. The village elders would make the final decision, but he would not give up Jamee. If they would not let them stay, then he would leave with them, but he felt in his heart they would be able to stay.

He woke Jamee a few hours before dawn and asked her to keep watch while he slept. He laid his head in her lap and was asleep in seconds.

When dawn was just turning the gray light to soft pastels Billy woke and they made ready to head out. The surrounding foothills quickly rose into bare rock strewn mountains with deep massive cuts running up their sides. Billy led them up into one of the cuts. They climbed until midday and Billy found the place he was looking for.

He motioned for Jamee to sit and rest and leaned close to her ear, saying in a whisper, "This opening leads to a cliff and we can look down at the cave where the Koros have their mine. We must be quiet but it should be safe."

Jamee nodded. After a few minutes' rest they entered the cut. The sides were shear and closed at the top by fallen rocks. It took almost four hours of slow walking to reach the other end of the cut. As Billy stepped out he saw three Koros sitting not five feet from him.

The Koros jumped to their feet as Billy pulled his knife and threw himself at them. He sliced the throat of one as another grabbed him from behind. The third one had his short spear raised and lunged at him. He never made it. Jamee ran past Billy, taking the head off the one with the spear and turned on the other holding Billy. The Koro loosened his grip for an instance and Billy whirled, stabbed him in the stomach and lifted the blade to his chest. He was dead before he hit the ground. He saw Jamee checking the area nearby, but all was quiet.

"Are you okay?"

Billy nodded and motioned for Jamee to follow.

He moved quickly down the slope to the edge of a cliff. They moved to the left following the ledge but stayed back from it so they would not be seen from below. After they traveled for almost two hours Billy saw a rock outcrop across from a deep cut in the cliff surface. The cut went straight down and was about eight feet across.

He asked Jamee if she could make the jump. She looked at the opening and said yes. Billy removed his pack and threw it across and then threw Jamee's pack across as well. He stepped back about ten feet, ran and leaped across. He moved to the edge and motioned for Jamee to come. She moved back, ran, leaped and just reached the edge. Billy was there to pull her to safety. They worked their way to a column of rocks rising above the cliff. He climbed to the top of the column and found a flat surface. Jamee was right behind him and knelt beside Billy.

He whispered, "I should have checked before stepping out of the cut. We will be all right here as long as we're quiet. We will have to stay here tonight and find another way back out tomorrow." They moved to the edge, lay down and peered below at the entrance to the mine.

Jamee could see an open area about eighty feet below the top of the cliff. It was a flat and about seventy-five yards wide with a road cut into the face of the cliff that followed the mountainside as it curved away to her right.

On the other side of the roadway the edge dropped away in what looked like a straight drop at least a thousand feet down. She could see a river winding far below. The chasm was ¼ mile wide and a boiling mist came from it near the entrance of the mine. She guessed that there must be a waterfall somewhere below the mine.

It must have taken great effort to build the road. The roadway was cut into the side of the mountain and continued around until the view was blocked by other mountains in the range. She turned over and could see that the mountain rose several thousand feet to its peak where it joined other peaks. The mountain range was barren rock except for an occasional stunted tree or bush holding on to life with determined strength. The top of the peaks looked to be covered in ice and snow. Everywhere she looked was barren, desolate mountains. She wondered how anything could live there.

They could see at least twenty Koros outside the entrance of the mine, but even more surprising, there were about fifty Volls setting up camp away from the entrance of the mine at the edge of the far drop-off. They saw a group of people hauling boxes out of the mine and stacking them near the Volls' camp. It was obvious that the group of people were captives. They looked as if they were hardly fed, dirty and watched closely. As they stacked the boxes near the edge of the drop-off, two Volls carrying long steel-tipped spears moved in front of the boxes to guard them.

Jamee whispered, "What do you think is in the boxes? They must be important."

"I don't know, but you are right; they do look important."

As they continued to watch, a large Koro walked to a Voll wearing a different uniform from the rest and began making hand gestures and speaking. He pointed at the boxes several times and held his hands out as if expecting something. The Voll turned and shouted to a soldier standing by a tent. The soldier entered the tent, came out and carried a long metal box to the Voll in charge. He set the box down, unlatched it, opened the lid and stepped back. The Koro knelt down, examining the contents. He lifted out several long knives and what looked like spear tips. He put all the weapons back except one of the long knives and stood.

He pointed at a slave and called to a Koro standing guard over them. The guard went to a slave who appeared to be a man in very bad shape. He grabbed him by the arm and dragged him over to the large Koro. The man's head drooped and he was barely able to stand.

The guard grabbed his right arm close to the shoulder and raised it up. The large Koro swung the knife over his head and brought it down across the captive's hand and then his forearm. The slave's hand and forearm dropped to the ground. Billy and Jamee could hear the scream from where they were. As the blood gushed from his arm, the large Koro pointed to the drop-off. The guard reached down, picked up the severed arm, dragged the man to the edge and threw him over. He then tossed the arm and hand after him, turned and walked back to the group he had been guarding. Jamee was so horrified at what she saw she turned her head and wept.

Billy continued to watch as the large Koro picked up the box and started for the cave entrance.

He whispered, "I don't know what is in those boxes but they must be valuable! The knives and spearheads are worth a great deal. It must be the Verdance Red told me about. He told me that the only reason the Volls come here is to get those green rocks. I'm still not sure what they do with them, but Red said they were trying to make something that could kill many people."

"We have to do something to help those people!" Jamee said.

Billy looked at her and kissed her forehead. "Jamee, there is nothing we can do to help them right now, but maybe we can make life harder for the Volls and Koros. I've been looking at the cliff face and I think I see a way down. If I can sneak down there tonight and push those boxes over the drop-off, it will cause a lot of problems for them."

"Don't you mean we?"

"Jamee, it is too dangerous for you."

"What if something happens and you can't come back here; what will I do then?"

Billy thought about what Jamee said. "You're right. We will go down tonight and you will stay right by my side... Right?"

"Yes, my love."

Billy looked around and asked, "Where is Flick?"

Flick landed on Billy's shoulder, looked at him and then turned her head towards Jamee.

After a few moments Jamee said to Billy, "Flick says she is very sorry for not warning us about the Koro patrol. She was on the other side of the cut checking on some others she saw."

"Tell her that it is okay. She can't be everywhere."

Jamee replied after a moment, "She says it won't happen again. She also says you can talk directly to her. She's a very smart bird, you know."

Billy smiled and kissed Flick on the head. "Smart and beautiful!"

Flick was jet black when she arrived and Billy could see just a touch of pink now.

"Flick, we need to find another way out of here. Tonight Jamee and I will go down there and we will need a quick way out when we're finished."

Flick leaped from Billy's shoulder and was gone.

Jamee said, "She will meet us at the top of the trail we will use."

"Why is she black?"

"It makes her hard to see, even though she can be almost invisible. She wants you to look at her when you talk. She really likes you, Billy," Jamee whispered.

They continued their watch of the activity below as the light of day died. Billy took a long cord from his pack and tied it to the packs, bow and quiver. He tied a small rock to the end of the cord and threw the rock into a small bush on the side of a short outcrop nearby. The cord stayed in place. Billy sat next to Jamee to rest and wait for early morning. Jamee wondered what he was doing but remained silent.

Around two in the morning Billy touched Jamee and motioned it was time. There was a weak light coming from the second moon as it passed overhead.

They climbed down the outcrop and Billy led the way to the place where they would descend. It was a narrow crack in the cliff face. There were many handholds to help them down and they made their way silently. It took thirty minutes to reach the roadway.

Billy looked around the campsite, which was about sixty feet away. He motioned for Jamee to follow and crept to the back of a tent near the boxes. He could see a guard sitting close to the boxes but he appeared to be asleep. He motioned for Jamee to wait, lifted the tent bottom, looked quickly around and disappeared into the tent. He was back in a few moments with the end of a coil of rope in his hand and two long knives in sheaths. He slid the two knives into his belt. They moved to the boxes a few feet away and he tied a tight loop around one of the boxes. Just as he finished tying the box the guard stirred and stood up.

He was only a few feet from Billy. The guard looked around, but before he could react, Billy's fist lashed out and caught him on the chin. The guard dropped and didn't move. Billy looked at Jamee and pointed to the place where they had descended and pushed her in that direction. She nodded and headed off. He waited for a moment to give Jamee time to reach their escape route and then lifted two of the boxes and heaved them over the side. He quickly grabbed two more and did the same. Finally he picked the last box with the rope tied to it, tossed it over the side and ran toward Jamee. Jamee saw him running and started to climb. Billy had just reached the cut when he heard a racket. He turned and watched the tent and two metal boxes being dragged over the drop-off.

He turned and quickly joined Jamee in her ascent.

He said loud enough for her to hear, "Hurry!" They were twenty feet up when there was a flash of light that turned the night to day. This was followed by an explosion from the valley far below. It was a tremendous blast that rocked the entire mountain. They held on but were nearly knocked loose from the cut.

Billy looked up and saw the wide-eyed look of fear on Jamee's face. The light lasted a few moments and then it was pitch black. Billy shoved Jamee's rear to get her moving and they started climbing blind. They moved slowly until their night vision returned and then increased their speed.

Above the sound of rocks falling Billy could hear shouts and confusion below. He heard a soldier shout that they saw someone climbing up the cliff. Billy and Jamee never stopped and were up to the top of the cliff in only twenty minutes. Billy told Jamee to wait and ran back toward the outcrop.

While Billy was gone, Jamee looked over the side. She could see where a section of roadway had slipped into the valley far below. Billy was only gone for a few minutes and returned with their packs and his bow.

He said, "Where is Flick?"

Flick landed on his shoulder and in a moment Jamee said, "Flick says to head to our right and follow the cliff and hurry!"

They moved off quickly and ran for about thirty minutes.

Jamee said, "There is a hole in the mountain a hundred yards ahead. It is behind a large rock. Go into it and keep moving. Flick says it will take us through to the other side."

Billy didn't hesitate as he ran ahead. He saw a huge boulder close to another cliff face and ran to it. Behind the rock they saw a clump of small bushes. He raced through them and found an opening about three feet high. They plunged into total darkness.

Billy stopped a few feet in and carefully tried to stand. He found the ceiling inside the opening was higher than he could reach. He took off his pack and used the cord he had and tied it around Jamee's waist and then his own.

He said, "I will lead and you hold the cord tight in case I fall into a chasm."

"What was that noise and light back there, Billy?"

"I don't know. We'll talk later, but right now we need to keep moving. I think someone saw us climbing up the cliff."

He moved off with his hands held out in front of him.

It was pitch black and Billy was putting his full trust in Flick and Jamee. They traveled slowly for several hours and then Billy started to notice his surroundings. There was light filtering through cracks in the ceiling. It was daylight outside. The tunnel they traveled through looked man-made. The floor was relatively smooth but with rock debris in places. They sat and rested for a few minutes.

"You were great back there! You did everything I asked and you moved like a cat climbing up that cut. I even had time to admire your beautiful rear."

Jamee smiled and said, "You did pretty well, too. When we have time I'll show you more."

They moved off and walked for what seemed like hours. There were a few small passages leading off the main tunnel that were pitch black and did not look inviting so they continued on. The floor of the tunnel showed no signs of anything passing through for ages. When Billy could see a light ahead he told Jamee to wait. He untied the rope and moved toward the entrance of the tunnel. His view was blocked by a large rock.

Billy moved to the entrance and could see the path made an S-turn to get outside. He carefully moved out into the sunlight and looked around. There was no one in sight. He walked farther out checking the area, turned and looked back towards the entrance. The entrance was completely hidden. He started back for Jamee, but before he had taken a few steps she was stepping out.

"Jamee, I told you to...Oh, never mind."

They started down towards the foothills and Billy looked back several times, marking the position of the tunnel entrance. It was late afternoon. They traveled for another hour and found a cluster of rocks to make camp for the night.

"We'll rest for a few hours and then keep going until we reach the prairie," said Billy.

They ate a trail cake each, drank the last of the water and then settled down to rest. Worn from traveling for two days with very little sleep, they had to rest. Jamee told Billy she would take the first watch and Billy lay down next to her and was asleep in seconds.

Jamee thought about how scared she had been back there and how brave Billy was. She was so glad to be with him and thought about what she would have done if something had happened to him. She didn't like the thought and didn't want to live without Billy. Jamie vowed that she would never leave his side again when danger was around. She would not smother him and would give him time alone if he needed it but not when there was danger. With the staff and her power she could help protect him.

After a couple of hours she woke Billy and lay down to sleep awhile. They rose before daybreak and headed south toward the prairie.

Once they entered the prairie they picked up speed and ran all day with only a few breaks for rest. About an hour before sundown Billy found a large creek with a clear pool of water and filled their containers. They moved out until they found a large clump of rain berry bushes and moved into the center. They drank, ate another trail cake, rain berries, settled down and were both asleep within minutes.

When they woke at dawn, Flick was perched on Billy's chest looking into his eyes. She was royal blue.

"Good morning, beautiful," Billy said, smiling and rubbing the sleep from his eyes. "Thank you again for your help last night."

Jamee stirred but did not wake. Flick's colors changed to royal blue and yellow and moved up and down rhythmically.

Billy smiled and said, "You really shouldn't watch us all the time."

Her colors flashed through the rainbow and then back to royal blue as she perched and watched Billy. Billy laughed but said nothing, knowing it would do no good.

Jamee woke, saw Flick sitting on Billy's chest and laughed. "Good morning, Flick."

Flick looked over at Jamee and asked, "When will you mate again?"

Jamee gave Flick a serious stare and shook her head, saying without speaking aloud, "That's none of your business. Why is that so important to you anyway?"

"I like to see you and Billy happy. You are becoming important to me and it makes me think about mating, too," Flick answered turning bright yellow.

"Are there many other birds like you, Flick?" Jamee asked.

"No, there are only a few of us. The others live far to the south with the Ancient people."

"Who are the Ancient people?"

"They have been here as long as my kind. They have powers like yours, Jamee, but much stronger."

Billy asked, "What are you two talking about?"

Jamee said, "Did you know there are people that live far to the south?"

"Other people? I've never heard of anyone living to the south. My people believe that we were the first to come to this world."

"Flick calls them the Ancient people and say they have powers like mine but stronger."

Billy looked at Flick and asked, "How far south do they live, Flick?"

"She says many days flight from here."

Billy thought about this as they prepared to leave. He would ask the village elders about it when he returned.

As they started off Billy said, "We can slow down now, Jamee. I don't think we are being followed and Green Hiding is only about half a day from here."

Both were tired from the five days of hard traveling so they took their time and enjoyed walking and touching one another as they moved toward Green Hiding. They stopped several times to rest and they arrived at the top of the trail as the sun worked its way toward the western horizon.

Enjoying the view and Billy said, "We can rest here for a few days before we head for my village."

Jamee again wondered how she would be accepted but said nothing and kept the concern from her face.

She said, "I would like to see more of this valley before we leave. It is beautiful and being alone with you these past few days makes me want you more!"

CHAPTER 10

When they entered the cave, May and Nuuna jumped up, ran to them, hugged and kissed both of them.

May exclaimed, "We've been so worried about you two! Are you all right?"

"We're fine, May, just tired," Billy said.

Nuuna had jumped into Billy's arms, kissed him again and leaned over to kiss Jamee and said, "I'm glad you're back."

As they continued to talk, Red and Silver walked in holding hands. When they saw Billy and Jamee they ran over to greet them with handshakes and kisses. Silver clung to Jamee and pulled her over to sit and talk.

Red asked Billy, "How did it go? What did you find?"

"It went well. We caused a lot of problems for the Koros and Volls. I'll tell you all about it in the morning. I brought you and May presents." He handed them each one of the long knives he had taken from the Volls camp.

Red looked at his new weapon and said, "These blades have been partially treated like the Steer blade."

"Right now I need some food and rest."

"Of course, Billy. Come and get some of May's cooking. She has outdone herself while you two were gone."

May beamed and went to get food for them both. Billy noticed new wooden bowls, spoons and other items near the fire.

While Billy talked to Red, Silver asked Jamee many of the same questions. Jamee looked at the smile on Silver's face but also noticed sadness in her eyes.

"What's wrong, Silver?"

"Nothing, Jamee. I'm just so happy you're back." She looked at Jamee and said, "We'll talk tomorrow. Right now let's get you something to eat and then off to bed you go."

Jamee wanted to ask more but let it drop until the next day. Billy and Jamee ate everything put before them as the others watched. As Jamee ate she looked up at Red and saw the big man's smile but also the same sadness in his eyes. After eating, they all went to the river to wash up. No one wanted to let Billy or Jamee out of their sight. It was a little embarrassing for them to bathe with all eyes watching, but everyone acted like it was a normal thing. It was dark by that time and that eased Billy's mind. They dressed, went back to the cave and soon Billy and Jamee were asleep at the back of the cave.

Late the next morning, Billy woke to an empty cave. There was food set out for him. As he ate he looked at the wooden bowl his meal was in. It was beautiful, a golden red with black lines circling all the way down to the base, which flared at the bottom. It was smooth to the touch and had a hard, shiny finish. He had never seen wood that color and the quality of workmanship was excellent.

He went out to find Jamee but after a short walk came upon May working an uteta skin she had staked out. May was scraping and working the skin and it was nearly finished.

"May, where did you get that uteta skin?"

"What do you think we've been eating? I killed it and a few other animals while you were away," pointing towards a small pile of pelts near a tree to her left.

"How did you kill them? All you had was a knife."

May stood, walked to the tree beside the pelts, reached around behind the tree and produced a long, thin shafted spear.

"It ain't much but it works." May said.

Billy took the spear from her and examined it.

The staff was about five feet long, a golden red color and very smooth, with a hardened wooden tip.

Billy flexed the shaft and found it to be strong with little flex in it.

"This is beautiful! Where did you find the wood for it?"

May beamed at the compliment and said, "I found a tree that had fallen not too long ago and made the spear from one of the limbs. I also made a few bowls and spoons too."

"I saw one of the bowls. I have never seen anything like it. The workmanship is great and the color is nothing like I've seen before. How did you make it so smooth?"

May's smile grew even bigger. "It wasn't easy, but I used a knife to shape it and river sand to smooth it. I didn't do anything to the color. Do you really like it, Billy?"

"It's beautiful!"

She reached over and gave him a kiss on the lips, giggling with pleasure.

"Thank you for the gift. The blade is amazing. I don't think I will have to sharpen it for a long time."

"Where is Jamee?"

"She went off with Silver early this morning. I think they have things to talk about."

"Can you show me the tree?"

"Yes. It's only a short walk."

May took Billy's hand and led the way through the trees. He spent an hour with May examining the fallen tree and talking about the things she had done while he and Jamee were gone.

He left May to find Jamee. Billy walked down by the river and found Red bathing. He waved and Red came out of the water, dried himself and dressed. Billy self-consciously looked at Red while he walked from the water. He was a big man and Billy could see no fat on his body. For someone who was forty-two, Red had the body of a young man. Red sat down and Billy saw the sadness in his eyes.

"What is wrong?"

Red blurted out, "It's Silver. I'm afraid to touch her!"

"Why would you be afraid to touch her? Did something happen while we were gone?"

"Nothing happened and I can see the hurt in her eyes. What should I do, Billy?"

"I don't know what you're talking about. What should you do about what?"

Red took a deep breath, looked at the water swirling in the river and said, "I'm afraid I'll hurt her if we... make love."

"I still don't understand. You and Silver looked like you were so happy to be with each other when we left. Silver doesn't want to make love?"

"No, just the opposite; she wants to, but I'm afraid I'll hurt her."

"You're going to have to explain this to me. I still don't understand why you would hurt Silver."

"Billy, I wouldn't do anything to hurt her. I love her...! Okay, here it is." Red took another deep breath. "I'm so big and Silver is so tiny. I'm afraid I would hurt her if we made love, you know... I am big," he said looking down. "I haven't had sex in many years, but the last time I did the woman I was with screamed and made me stop. She said I was tearing her apart. I couldn't do that to Silver. I'm afraid, Billy."

Billy looked at Red, finally understanding what he was saying.

He shook his head and said, "I don't know what to say. Jamee is the first girl I've ever been with so I don't have a lot of experience. I will say this; making love isn't everything that makes me love Jamee but it is important. And I know it's important to Jamee as well. Maybe it's something you and Silver should talk about together. I think Silver would know what to tell you."

"I know about her past," Red replied.

"No, I'm not talking about anything like that. I just know Silver is very smart and a good woman. She befriended Jamee when Jamee had no one and she helped her grow up to be a good, strong woman. I think Silver is smart enough and honest enough to tell you the truth."

Red looked at Billy and said, "I just don't want to hurt her."

"Come on, Red. Let's go back. I'm hungry again. We'll talk more later."

They rose and headed back to the cave.

While Billy and Red had talked, Jamee and Silver sat close to one another in a glade filled with blue violets, white crocus, yellow sunflowers and red poppies.

Silver was saying through her tears, "I don't understand. Red doesn't want to make love to me. I think it's because I was a whore on Ocean. I thought I had finally found the man I've been waiting for and he doesn't want me. I guess the truth is too much for him."

Jamee hugged Silver. "You're wrong. I saw how he looked at you before we left and I still see that look in his eyes. There must be something else. Maybe he's afraid of hurting you. He is a big man and men don't seem to be as smart as women when it comes to knowing what we want-- although Billy is a fast learner. Do you love him?"

"Yes! I love him and I don't want to give him up."

"Then give him a chance. You taught me everything about men and how to please the man I love. If it weren't for you, I wouldn't have known what to do after the first time and now I can please Billy in so many ways, not just when we're making love but in his life as well. I love you, Silver; not as a teacher but as my sister."

"And I love you, not only for being my friend when I had none but as my baby sister." She smiled. "Now it seems you are becoming my teacher."

They hugged, kissed and laughed through their tears.

"Let's bring Billy and Red to this glade to enjoy its beauty one day soon."

Jamee said, "Let's get back to the cave. I must talk to Billy and I am hungry!"

Silver and Jamee entered the cave and Silver caught Red looking at her. She could see the love in his eyes. She walked over, kissed him and sat down. Jamee moved to sit with Billy and took food from his bowl and began eating hungrily. Once her hunger was sated, Jamee told Billy to walk with her.

"But I'm still hungry."

When he saw the look she gave him, he rose and left the cave without further complaint.

May said to Nuuna, "What is going on around here?"

Nuuna looked up at May. "Something important."

May shook her head and said, "Love— when will it be my turn?"

Nuuna whispered, "Soon, May."

Jamee led Billy a little way into the woods, turned and asked, "What did Red say?"

Billy gave Jamee a wide-eyed look. "How do you know I talked to Red?"

"A little bird told me," she said with a laugh.

"Red is afraid he will hurt Silver if they... you know."

"Well, we need to give him a chance to find out, but I'll tell you now he won't hurt her. They're too much in love for that to happen."

"Red thinks he... his ... is too big and she is a small woman."

"You mean his little buddy?" she said with a laugh. "Well, it's time he finds out. Tomorrow morning tell Red you need him and Silver to go to the head of the river to keep watch and they will have to stay all night. I'll take care of the rest."

"Yes, my love."

Jamee laughed, kissed Billy, reached down and squeezed his little buddy. Billy grabbed for her but she slipped away, running back to the cave.

When he entered, he went over to where Red and Silver were sitting and said, "Red, I have decided that I need you to go to the head of the river and keep watch tomorrow and you will need to stay there all night. I also want Silver to go as well because two sets of eyes are better than one."

Red started to argue, but Billy cut him off. "It is important!"

Red said okay and Silver agreed as well. Jamee pulled Silver over and started to prepare a pack for them to take and talked quietly to Silver. Billy saw a smile come to Silver's face and knew he had made the right decision. He told May to make sure there would be enough food for them to take in the morning. May smiled and nodded. Billy finished eating, went to his blanket, lay down and soon was asleep. Sometime later he felt Jamee lie down beside him, reach over and squeeze him.

Billy was up early the next morning and walked outside to enjoy the sunrise. He saw May sitting outside the entrance.

He sat down next to her and asked, "Why are you up so early, May?"

"Oh, I couldn't sleep."

She turned to look at Billy in the growing light. "I know what you're doing. You're sending Red and Silver off so they can be alone. I know Red is worried about being with Silver and I can guess what it is. Red's a big man and Silver a little bitty thing. Men ain't got a clue when it comes to women! She could spin him around her little finger if she wanted to but she won't. Those two are so much in love. He needs to let Silver lead him around a bit and things will be fine."

Billy looked at May and wondered how women seemed to know what it took him a while to figure out.

"I guess you're right."

"You are a good man! I hope I can find someone like you, because Jamee ain't gonna share."

She leaned over and kissed Billy hard on the lips, stood and walked into the cave to prepare the morning meal. She passed Jamee at the entrance and smiled.

"Well, I see you're hard at work this morning," Jamee said.

"I wish she wouldn't do that."

"She is just being friendly," Jamee said laughing. "You watch and see. One day she'll meet someone who will take all that teasing right out of her."

"I hope it's soon and not just for my sake. She is a good woman and needs a good man to try and tame her."

Jamee sat next to Billy and kissed him long and deep.

"I need to have my breath taken away soon," Jamee said.

"We'll find some time later today, my love."

After everyone had eaten, Red and Silver got ready to go.

Red said, "I still don't know where or why we're going."

Billy said, "This is important, Red."

Jamee gave Silver the directions to a place where they could watch the area without being seen. Jamee kissed Silver and whispered something in her ear, and then Silver walked over to Red and Billy.

She stood on her toes and kissed Billy on the mouth and smiled, then turned to Red. "Are you ready, darling?"

Red replied, "Lead the way, honey."

They walked out holding hands.

May said, "I bet you could get used to all this kissing; couldn't you, Billy?"

Billy ignored her and picked Nuuna up and headed for the river.

Jamee started helping May clean up.

"May, you are really something."

May turned with a look of concern on her face. "You know I'm only teasing him, don't you?"

"Yes, I know, but I wasn't talking about that. These bowls, spoons and the things you've made are so beautiful! Do you think you could teach me to make some of these?"

May beamed with pride. "It would be my pleasure but not today. You and Billy need to take it easy today. You need to take away some of that heat that's burning him up."

Jamee's blush was a deep red.

She walked over to May, kissed her on the cheek and said, "I'll try."

"Do more than try, little girl!"

Jamee continued to help May for a while and then walked down toward the river to find Nuuna and Billy.

Billy and Nuuna were playing in the water, splashing and laughing. They had washed their clothes and had hung them in a nearby tree. Jamee stripped out of her clothes and began to wash them.

"Can I join you?"

Nuuna laughed and said, "Yes! Come and have fun, too!"

Jamee hung her clothes and walked out to where they were still playing. Billy watched her walk into the water. Jamee's hips swayed as she walked and her body moved in a beautiful rhythm. She was looking into his eyes with a small smile.

Nuuna said, "Jamee, you are very beautiful. Do you think I will look like you some day?"

"You are already beautiful and someday soon I'll wish I was as beautiful as you."

Jamee reached down, scooped up some water and joined in the water fight. Billy could hardly take his eyes off of her. He moved deeper into the water to hide his excitement and swam out to a large rock in the center of the river. Jamee and Nuuna both squealed as they played. Billy enjoyed watching them both. Jamee was still a young woman and it brought him pleasure to watch her get so much enjoyment from playing with Nuuna. He wondered what would happen to Nuuna once they reached his village.

Jamee and Nuuna walked from the water and dressed, then sat on the bank waiting for Billy.

As he walked out of the water Nuuna smiled. "You're beautiful, too." Billy smiled and quickly dressed. As they sat talking, Flick landed on Billy's shoulder. She was royal blue. She was looking at Nuuna and turned a deep, shining green.

Nuuna clapped her hands in delight. "Oh! What a beautiful bird. Is she yours, Billy?"

"No, Nuuna. Flick belongs to no one. She is my friend."

Flick flew to Nuuna and landed in her outstretched hands. Nuuna carefully brought her close to her face, admiring her. Flick flashed a rainbow of colors for Nuuna and came back to the deep green. Nuuna squealed in delight. Flick flew to Jamee turning a bright yellow.

Flick said, "You must keep a close watch on this little one. She has power, too."

"What kind of power, Flick?"

"I'm not sure. She can't use it now, but when she is older, I think she will be strong with it."

Jamee turned to Nuuna and looked closely at her. She said, "This is Flick and she has given you the color green."

Flicked turn a deep green and dipped her head to Nuuna.

Nuuna asked, "What's your color Jamee... and Billy's?"

Flick turned bright yellow and then flew to Billy, turning royal blue.

"Oh! Just like your eyes, Billy!" She turned to Jamee. "What were you talking about with Flick?"

Jamee's eyes widened and she said, "How do you know we were talking?"

"I'm not sure, but I just know you were."

"We were talking about you. Flick likes you."

Nuuna smiled happily. "I like you, too, Flick. I like my color. Thank you."

Flick turned a very deep green and then disappeared into the trees.

They all got up and walked toward the cave. Billy slipped his hand to Jamee's rear and squeezed. Jamee smiled, nodded and continued walking.

Silver and Red had been walking for an hour or so, talking quietly, when they heard the sound of rushing water. As the column of water came into view they both stopped and stared.

Red looked around and said, "This is beautiful, but what are we supposed to be watching?"

Silver replied without looking at Red, "You'll see."

She led him around behind the column until she found the steep stairway in the cliff face.

She pointed and said, "Up there; that's where we're supposed to go." Remembering Jamee's instruction she started up the stairs ahead of Red.

She moved her hips in a way she knew Red wouldn't be able to ignore. As her left leg moved up a step, she stopped and turned, looking over her left shoulder at Red.

She could see the heat in his eyes and said, "Isn't it beautiful, Red?"

Red nearly missed a step as he turned a deep red. "Yes...I mean, yes, it is beautiful here."

Silver laughed, turned and continued moving seductively as she climbed. They reached the cave and turned and looked out at the top of the water column.

"Oh my, this place is perfect." Silver said.

She turned to Red, reached up high and pulled his head down, kissing him deeply. She released him, turned and started taking their equipment and supplies from the pack. Red was quiet. It was finally dawning on him why they had come but he said nothing.

"Why don't you go down and bathe while I straighten up everything?"

Red left without a word.

Silver watched from the cave until Red was out of sight and then hurried down the steps to wash also. She stripped and stood on a rock that was just below the surface. The water was cold, but as she rubbed her body clean it felt like liquid fire. Her skin was tingling. She could hardly believe how excited she was.

Silver would do everything to show Red he had nothing to fear. She would give him love, something she had never given to any man. She finished washing, hurried back to the cave and waited for Red. She quivered with excitement but forced her body to calm as she heard Red approaching the top of the steps. Red stood at the entrance, his eyes locked on Silver's body.

It was flawless. Her skin was a cream color; her breasts were small and fit her body perfectly; her pink nipples and short black hair above her flower gave an accent of complete beauty to her. His eyes moved to hers and he looked into the large silver pools that seemed to reflect all the light back to him. She was so tiny to him and delicate. She slowly turned so he could see all of her. Her proportions were perfect, her slender shapely legs, the roundness of her rear and the dimples at the base of her back, the arch of her back and long slender neck. Her hair hung below her shoulders and was black as night and shone like obsidian.

As she finished her turn she looked back into his eyes. "Red, I truly love you. You are the first man I have ever loved. I never thought I would have that kind of love and I'm so happy I've found you."

"Silver, you are the most beautiful woman I've ever seen and I love you completely. I don't know what you see in me and I don't deserve you, but I will love you every day of my life."

"You deserve everything I can give to you. I will spend the rest of my life making you happy and satisfied."

Desire filled Red's body. "I would never do anything to hurt you and I'm afraid I will if we make love."

"You don't have to be afraid. You won't hurt me, I promise. Let me be your guide this first time. Let me show you how much I love you, please."

Silver walked over to Red, took his hand and led him to where she had spread the blanket out. She reached up and began unbuttoning his coveralls. Silver pulled them down from his wide shoulders to his waist and then ran her hands through the soft covering of reddish-brown hair on his chest. Her hands felt the strong muscles in his chest as she leaned in and kissed his chest softly.

Silver pulled his coveralls down to his thighs and let them drop. She kneeled down letting her shoulder brush him lightly and then helped him remove his boots and step out of his clothes. Red just stood there, almost afraid to move. She directed him to the blanket like a child and had him lie back.

Silver moved up his body, letting her breasts trace two trails of heat up to his chest. She kissed him and let her tongue slowly move into his mouth and touch his.

She moved to his right ear and whispered, "I love you; never forget that. Just relax and let me be your guide."

Red did not utter a word, but she felt his hand move to caress her side. Their roughness sent shivers through her, but she held herself in check, not letting it show. She wanted Red to understand that her body was for him to enjoy and that he wouldn't hurt her. Silver knew she had to move slowly to take his fears away. He would see the pleasure he gave her and they would have the rest of their lives to enjoy each other.

Once he saw what her body was capable of, his fears would vanish. Silver moved back to his face and kissed his forehead, eyes, cheeks, chin and then to his lips. She kissed him with a long gentle kiss and let her fingertips run across his stomach. She could feel his muscles ripple and she knew a heat was running through his body. She could feel the tingling in her body that came from touching him. She had total control of her body, but it was becoming hard not to let her excitement show. She moved her head down Red's chest kissing and nibbling. Her fingertips moved down his stomach. Then she moved her kisses down his belly and could feel the muscles jump. Her fingers moved down and encircled him.

As she kissed him, she tilted her head back so she could look across his belly and into his eyes.

Red had raised his head to watch what she was doing and as her bright silver eyes locked with his, he felt them burning into him.

She slowly raised her petite body over his and placed one hand on his chest. Silver was burning inside, but she made her face remain calm and smiled down to him. She lowered her body until they were joined. Silver stopped, letting Red see the heat in her eyes and feel the heat of her body. A moan of pleasure slipped from her lips as she slowly lowered her body to his. All the time they moved, Silver never lost contact with his eyes, letting him see her pleasure without any pain. She quickened her movements, letting go of her control. She could feel the buzzing tingle of her body begin and waves of pleasure moved to every part of her. She felt Red shudder and knew his pleasure was complete. She lowered her head onto his chest, letting the warmth spread through her.

She looked back up into his eyes. "That felt so good. I love you so much."

"Are you sure I didn't hurt you? That was incredible."

Silver gave a laugh that sounded like a child's uninhibited gaiety and looked deep into Red's brown eyes. "Does it look like I'm hurt or feel like I'm hurt?"

"I love you. You are so beautiful and your body is perfect."

"Don't ever be afraid to touch me, my darling. Any time you want me I am yours."

Silver moved off of Red, stood and put her hand out to help him stand. "Come; let's go wash and cool off a bit."

He stood with her, then bent down and kissed her.

They went down the steep steps and walked naked to a place where the water ebbed by the bank. Red jumped in, the water coming to his chest and the coolness took his breath for an instant. Silver dove in, swam around Red and then came to him, putting her arms around his neck. They kissed again and let the swirling water clean them.

Silver put her mouth to his ear and softly said, "I want more." She could see the gleam in his eyes, laughed and climbed out of the water letting the water run down her sleek form. Red's breath was taken again. They walked back to the stairs. Again Silver took the lead.

When they reached the cave Red's excitement was obvious. Silver lay down on the blanket, looked into his eyes. "No more fear, Red. I want you now!"

Red sat beside Silver, leaned down and kissed her while moving his strong hands over her body.

He sat back, looked down at Silver and said, "My love, I want to give all the pleasure I can, but to tell the truth, I haven't been with many women and even then I felt like I didn't really know what I was doing."

"Anything you do will please me. You've pleased me since I first truly saw you, darling."

"Yes, you've been my happiness since I first saw you, too, but I want to do this for you. I want you to be my guide again, but this time show me what you need."

Silver gave him a direct look and said, "Do you say this because of what I was before coming to this world?"

"No! Never say that again! Silver, both of our lives have begun again and what we did before has no meaning to me now. I love you. I love you for who you are and nothing in the past will ever change that. You make my heart sing. I only want to give you what you have given me."

Tears flooded Silver's eyes and she jumped up to wrap her arms around Red's neck and kissed him softly.

"I didn't mean to say that. I will never ask again. You've said what my heart wanted so badly to hear you say. I love you and I am yours forever. Yes, I will show you what makes my body and mind breathless, but it will take many times to show you them all."

Red smiled and said, "I will be happy to do this as much as you want."

Silver lay down again. She said, "And I have many things to do for your pleasure, but that too will take time."

She guided Red and it was something neither would ever forget.

They lay together after and Red said, "That was incredible. I never knew making love could be so good. Did I please you, honey?"

She tilted her head back and her eyes glistened. "Yes, my love. You took my breath away."

They lay there for a long moment and Silver said, "I'm hungry."

Laughing, they sat up and enjoyed the food they had brought. Later Red started a fire and they went to bathe. When they returned they lay down, talked for an hour and then fell asleep in each other's arms.

CHAPTER 11

After Billy and Jamee left Nuuna with May at the cave, they walked through the woods hand in hand.

Jamee said, "I wonder how Silver and Red are doing."

Flicked landed on Billy's shoulder, turned red on top and silver on the bottom and let the colors move up and down.

They both laughed and Billy said, "I guess that answers your question."

Jamee looked at Flick. "You seem to know when there is mating going on."

Flick took off and disappeared.

Billy said, "Speaking of mating." He turned Jamee and kissed her. "Let's find a cool place."

They found a shaded glen and enjoyed the afternoon.

Billy said, "I love you with all my heart forever."

"My life was empty until you found me!"

They picked up their clothes and walked and talked as they moved through the forest.

Jamee asked, "When will we have to leave?"

"In a few days. We need to get back to my village but we don't have to hurry. I think the Volls and Koros have enough trouble to keep them busy for a long time."

"What will happen when we get there? I know I've asked before, but I'm afraid there might be trouble when you bring so many strangers into the village. Will there be trouble for you?"

"I don't think it will be a problem, except maybe for Red. My people know whites only as old enemies. I have been thinking about this and need to teach him a few things before we arrive. Silver, May and Nuuna shouldn't have a problem. You have nothing to worry about. Even if the worst happens and they won't accept any of you, I will never let anything happen to you. We will be together."

The answer worried Jamee. She didn't want to be the cause of trouble for Billy, but she would never leave him. She decided to hope for the best and keep her fears from Billy.

As they walked deeper into the forest, the trees were larger, their tops intermingling and cutting off much of the sun's rays. There was little undergrowth making travel easy. Billy caught a movement of something off to his right. He stopped Jamee and they moved behind one of the large tree trunks. Billy peered out around the trunk and he saw a large meta heading their way. Meta's were massive animals that could weigh up to 3 tons. They weren't normally aggressive but the large bear-like creatures were very short-sighted and could be dangerous to encounter. It was heading straight for them.

Billy reached for his knife and realized they were still nude. He reached into his bundle of clothes and pulled his hunting knife free. He held Jamee's arm and they moved around the tree trunk to keep out of sight as the meta passed by and continued on its way. He waited several minutes until he was sure the meta was leaving the area.

He took a breath and said, "That is something you don't want to meet with only a knife and no clothes on. It is a meta and can be dangerous."

They hurried to dressed and started back toward the cave.

Around mid-morning the next day Silver and Red arrived, both wearing big smiles and holding hands.

May looked up and smiled. "You two look like you did more than just look around!"

Neither said anything as May walked up to Red, kissing him on the lips and hugged Silver.

"I'm happy for you, white man."

She went back to her work. Silver went over to where Jamee was checking supplies, sat down and started whispering. They were laughing and hugging and Red could only smile as he went to find something to eat. Billy walked in, saw Red but said nothing. Billy walked around looking the cave over and as he passed Red his leg thumped into him.

He turned with an angry look and said, "Keep out of my way. You're so big you take up too much room."

"Sorry, Billy," Red replied still smiling.

"Sorry. Is that all you have to say!" Billy said with hate in his voice.

Red stood and turned to Billy. "What's the matter, Billy? Have I done something to make you angry?"

Before Billy could answer Jamee ran over to him. "Billy, what has gotten into you?"

Billy looked down at Jamee with a look of pure anger and then looked at Red. "Come with me, white man. Now!" and he started walking out of the cave and then turned and said, "As a matter of fact, everyone follow me!"

Billy stormed out of the cave and they all looked at each other, puzzled. Everyone moved to follow him.

Billy walked through the trees to an open glade, went to the center, removed his knife belt, shirt and stood waiting. When everyone arrived they waited for Billy to explain.

Billy only looked at Red and said, "It's time you were put in your place, white man!"

"Put in my place?"

"That's right, white man."

Billy moved to Red and slapped him hard across the face. Jamee, Silver and May started toward Billy, but the hard stare he gave them brought them up short.

"This is none of your affair— this is between him and me!"

Red looked at Billy and said, "If I've done something to cause this anger... well, we can work it out."

Billy glared at Red. "Are you a coward, afraid not only of women but men as well?"

Billy leaped at Red, slapping him again. Now Red's anger matched Billy's as he removed his knife, placing it on the ground, and advanced on him.

"I don't want to do this. I have you by at least fifty pounds."

Billy only laughed and waited.

Red charged at Billy with his arms open. He wanted to hold Billy until he calmed down. Just before he reached him, Billy leaped in the air, spun over Red's head and hit him in the back of the head hard enough to make him stumble to the ground. Red spun and charged again. Billy side-stepped as Red reached for him and drove a side kick into his ribs. He heard a whoosh of air come from Red, but Red only turned and approached Billy slowly.

Billy stood with his hands at his sides and laughed. Red moved in and punched straight-armed at Billy's face. Before Red could react, Billy tilted his head to the side, letting the punch slip past him, and punched Red in the face three times, then dropped his stance slightly and punched Red in the ribs in a blur. Red spun to grab Billy but only grabbed at air.

Now Red was furious and he moved in on Billy. He threw fast lefts and rights but not getting close. Red closed in again, faked a jab and threw a front kick that caught Billy in the stomach. Billy flew back several feet, landed on his feet and it looked as if the vicious kick had no effect on him. He laughed again and moved in on Red.

Billy passed right through the punches and kicks and lightly slapped Red on the face and moved 10 feet away before Red realized he had moved.

Red advanced on Billy but Billy raised his hands and said, "Peace, Red. I'm sorry I had to treat you this way."

Red stopped, still burning with anger. "You better explain yourself!"

"Red, truly, I'm sorry. I only acted this way to give you an idea of how you may be treated when you arrive at my village. You will be challenged, and I didn't want my brother to go into it blindly. You are my brother! We will work together on the trip to the village and I will teach you some of our fighting techniques. If this were a battle, you could have hurt me, but a challenge is one-on-one and usually without grave injuries." He could see the color of Red's face returning to normal and he walked up to him, hugged him and asked, "Peace?"

"Peace, Billy, but don't do that again."

"I promise not to trick you again. You are my brother and we will work together to protect our family."

Smiling, Red hugged Billy, lifted him off the ground and said, "Yes, we will work together for our family!"

Billy turned to the women and could see anger in all their eyes. Only Nuuna smiled at Billy.

"I did this for all of us so you might have an idea of what is in store for Red when we reach my village. I'm sorry for the way I acted, but I felt it important for everyone to see the fighting skills of my tribe. I hope you will forgive me for fighting my brother."

He saw all the eyes soften except Silver's. She advanced on him. "You're pretty good, Billy, but I want to try you as well. You hit my man and I won't let that happen without a challenge."

Billy blinked and said, "There is no need, Silver. I have apologized to you all."

"Sorry? That's not good enough for me. Besides, I want to see how a little man will stand against a tiny woman like me."

Jamee said, "Uh, oh."

As Billy turned with a questioning look to Jamee, Silver, with lightning speed, moved in and slapped Billy across the face. When Billy's head snapped around, Silver stood in the same spot as before. Red started to say something, but the look in Silver's eyes closed his mouth and he moved to the edge of the clearing.

Billy shrugged his shoulders and moved in on Silver. Silver moved so quick that he hardly saw her. She hit Billy in the head, chest and stomach. Then she slapped his inner thigh, jumped over Billy, kicking him in the head, came down with blows to the back of his neck and landed on the back of his knees, collapsing him to the ground. She let Billy stand and backed off several feet. Billy moved in on Silver with kicks, blows and spinning kicks, never making contact. Silver lashed out with a punch to Billy's back. He felt a blinding pain that spread to his kidneys and fell to the ground.

Silver knelt down and said, "Sorry, Billy. Now lie still and I will make it better."

She touched and rubbed his back and the pain was gone as if he had never had it. He rolled over on his back and looked wide-eyed at Silver. "How did you do that?"

"I've trained with some fighting masters on my world. I will train with you and Red as we travel. Okay?"

Billy nodded his head as she helped him up.

Silver wrapped her arms around Billy's neck and kissed him soundly. "I love you, brother."

May stepped forward and said, "Okay, Billy; now it's my turn!"

Billy raised his hand and said, "No, May. I've seen some of your abilities and don't question your skills."

May beamed at him, walked over, kissed him hard on the mouth. "You called us a family. Thank you for that!"

Nuuna ran to Billy and kissed him and said, "I knew you weren't angry."

Billy moved to Silver and asked, "Can Jamee fight like you do?"

"I trained her for several years when she came to visit me. I wouldn't want to make her angry."

Jamee, Silver, May and Nuuna moved over to Red. Each kissed him and checked to see if he was hurt.

He laughed, wrapped his big arms around all of them and said, "Let's get cleaned up and then eat. I'm hungry!"

Billy and Red led the way to the river, stripped and dove in as the women undressed. When they turned around, their eyes opened wide as all three women walked arm in arm into the water. Billy drew his breath in as he looked at Silver's body and all three sets of hips swaying in perfect time.

"Billy, you're supposed to be looking at me!" said Jamee laughing.

"And what about me?" May said as she jiggled her large breasts.

Both men turned crimson, but no words came out. Nuuna followed them into the water, laughing and splashing. They washed and played for a while and then made their way back to the cave. After eating, Red motioned for Billy to come with him outside. Billy kissed Jamee and followed Red.

They walked a short distance and Red said, "In all the excitement I haven't had a chance to talk to you about your trip to see the Koros."

Billy related all that had happened while Jamee and he were away, including the bright light that made the mountain shake.

"That sounds like an explosion. That's the reason the Volls are so interested in the Verdance. You may have accidentally shown them how to detonate it."

"It won't do them much good if they have to drop it off a cliff every time they want it to explode."

"You're right, but they will think of a way to use it. They have been testing it for a while. You did the right thing by destroying it. If what Jamee said about the road is true, then they are trapped there for a while. The ships they have travel through space but can only land, not fly around through the air. That's why they have to land out in the prairie and walk to where they need to go."

Billy thought about all Red said and asked, "Do you think the Volls will be a problem for the people of this world?"

"Yes, they will. That's another reason they came out here. They want to enslave the people of these outer worlds and take them back to Earth. If they can't do that, then they will try to kill all of us. The Federation is desperate for people to recover all the empty lands on Earth and make them livable. They only want to do that with slave labor. One day I will tell you all I know about the problems on Earth, but for now let's concentrate on teaching me how to fight like you do."

"If it had been a battle, it would not have looked so easy. You have natural fighting skills and great strength. I took you by surprise this time. I don't think it would be so easy next time."

"You beat me and that hasn't happened to me in a long time. I want to learn all you and Silver can teach me."

Red continued, "The long knives you brought back are excellent. They are made similar to the way the Steer blade is made but they are steel, coated with a layering of the material the Steer is made from. They are not as strong as a Steer. I will give mine to Silver, though she doesn't seem to need a lot of help."

Billy laughed and said, "I have never seen anything like that before! She made me feel slow."

"What about me? I have much to learn from you both. She is amazing."

"You are a lucky man and so am I."

Red smiled and said, "We have to help May find a man. She's too much woman to be left alone around you and me."

"Yes, she is, but I don't think she'll need too much help finding someone to love her. I just hope she can find someone who can handle her."

They both laughed as Billy continued, "You understand that I must lead this group for now, but later after you become accustomed to our way who will lead?"

Red said, "You are the leader as long as we're all together. I know I'm much older than you, but I trust you with Silver's and my life. Later, if you want, I will be your advisor in matters I have knowledge of. I will help you all I can, but you are my leader."

While Billy and Red talked, Jamee went to see what May was doing. She hadn't seen much of her and wanted to see if she was all right with everything that had happened. May was coming out of a niche at the back of the cave.

"Can I help you with anything?"

"No. I'm just about done. I'm just going to check on supper."

"I'm sorry I haven't been much help to you and I want to tell you how much I appreciate all that you do. What were you doing back there? Maybe I can help."

May turned and went back to the niche and brought several items into the light. There were packs made from pelts, several more bowls and a number of other wooden objects. Jamee picked up one of the packs and examined it. It was beautifully made, with stitched designs of different colors.

"May, this is beautiful! You made all this yourself?"

"Nuuna helped some, and I have several more things too." May smiled and went back to the niche. She brought out a bow and quiver filled with arrows and several cured pelts. Jamee took the bow from May, admired the texture and pattern of the wood. She pulled an arrow from the quiver and it was of the same type of wood. The tip was cut to a sharp point and had small, thin wooden feathers for guidance. She pulled the bowstring and found the bow to be strong and flexible.

"I've never seen wood like this."

"I found a tree that had fallen not long ago and the wood from it is strong and light. It's the only tree I have seen like it. The limbs near the top were so straight I didn't have to do much to make the arrows or the bow staff. The bowstring is from gut and wood slivers that I wove together. I've made a pack for each of us and I want to put fur around the sheaths of the long knives you and Billy brought so they will look like normal knives."

"I don't know what to say. You have done all of this, taken care of Nuuna and everything else around here while we've been..."

May laughed. "I am happy to do it. It has kept me busy and has taken my mind off of being the only woman without a man. Don't worry; when my time comes it will be your turn to take care of us all."

Jamee laughed. "Deal."

Jamee turned to Silver just as Billy and Red walked in and waved to them to come and see the things May had made. They all walked over and admired May's work. Billy was especially impressed with the bow.

"I will get some steel heads for your arrows when we get to my village."

May went back to the niche and brought out another bow and gave it to Billy. It was shorter than hers but had intricate designs carved into the limbs and with prairie cat fur covering the grip and arrow-rest.

"I made this for you. It is shorter so you can use your arrows."

Billy hugged and kissed May. "I will treasure this bow and think of you every time I see it."

May blushed. They all hugged and kissed May in thanks for her efforts and then went to the fire to eat.

After eating, Jamee and Silver began to clean up. May gathered up the long knives and left. Billy and Red entertained Nuuna. Soon after, they all settled down to sleep. Billy heard May come in during the night and lay down with Nuuna.

The next morning May presented Red with his long knife. "I got the idea from the way Billy covered the staff Jamee carries."

The handle and sheath were covered tightly with prairie cat hide.

"You are amazing. It's beautiful!" He turned to Silver and said, "Silver, you take this. I think the women should have the deadliest weapons to protect our backs. I'll get another one when I get the chance."

Silver took the knife, reached up, kissed Red and then hugged May.

The rest of that day they made preparations to leave. Silver spent several hours with both men instructing them in fighting techniques. She also spent time with Jamee and May, showing them how to improve their skills. Nuuna played with the bo staff May had made for her as she watched the women train.

Later in the afternoon they all went for a swim. All were a little sad and anxious about leaving the valley. After eating, Red and Silver slipped off to be alone. Soon after, Billy and Jamee left.

CHAPTER 12

The next morning they packed all the equipment, including all the things May had made, and prepared to leave Green Hiding.

Billy said, "We will be crossing the prairie and staying in Bookus trees at night. We aren't in a hurry so we'll stop in the afternoons to give us time to train. We must keep our eyes open for danger and if we meet a patrol of Koros or Volls, women to the rear and let Red and me deal with it. I'm saying this knowing that Jamee won't listen and I doubt Silver will either. May, your responsibility will be Nuuna if anything happens."

They headed towards the path leading up to the prairie.

Billy was carrying the new bow May had made for him, leaving his trek bow hidden in the cave. They started off heading southeast at a fast walk, letting the miles pass under their feet. After stopping a few times for rest and food they reached a Bookus grove about mid-afternoon.

Billy took them up to a water cave on the second level and explained about the pools, how to build a fire and the care of the trees. "These trees have always provided for the people of Prairie and Jamee has found a way for them to heal us using matting from the walls of the water caves. Treat them like a part of the family and they will always provide for you."

May and Jamee went off to hunt and gather herbs while Silver, Red and Billy continued their practice. When they returned at sundown Nuuna and May were not there. Jamee said she had told them to go out and explore the tree while she got supper ready. Silver and Red went to have a look around and look for May and Nuuna. Billy went over, hugged and kissed Jamee. Jamee responded, pressing her body against him.

"I need you, my love."

Billy's hand slid down her back and said, "I need you, too."

"Let's find a water cave of our own tonight. I have things I want to tell you," Jamee said with a bright smile.

Silver and Red moved up to the next level and decided to keep climbing. As they came out onto the platform formed by the intertwining limbs, they saw May and Nuuna sitting watching the sunset. Silver gasped at the beauty of the scene as the prairie stretched before them. The sun was just moving below the horizon and the golden-crimson light painted the contours of the prairie in a soft glow.

Nuuna said, "It's so beautiful and you can see so far."

Silver said, "Yes, it is. This is a beautiful world we have come to. It is our home now."

As the sky darkened they made their way back to where Jamee was cooking the hoppers and making a soup with vegetables and herbs they had picked. They all settled down to a delicious meal.

After cleaning up, Jamee looked at Billy and he said, "This cave is a little small for all of us. Jamee and I will stay on the next level up to make more room."

May laughed. "Oh! That's good thinking, Billy. We need the space and it will be quieter. Maybe Silver and Red wouldn't mind finding another cave, too. Nuuna and I need our rest."

Billy smiled at May. "Well, we wouldn't want to disturb you; would we, Jamee?"

Jamee punched Billy and gave May a hug,

"No, we wouldn't. Thank you, May."

Billy gathered up his things and said, "If there are any problems or you need anything, we'll be one level up."

He gave May a big smile, blushed a little and went out of the water cave with Jamee in tow.

As they entered the cave he placed his things by the entrance and then took his knife and cut a large hole in the floor. Jamee laid out a blanket, stripped out of her clothes and jumped into the water. Billy was waiting and grabbed her, pulled her back to him and slid his hand up her stomach. He heard a soft moan pass her lips. Jamee turned and kissed him, letting another moan escape into his mouth. Billy lifted Jamee and sat her on the edge of the pool.

He pulled her hips until she rested on the edge, pushed her torso back, which caused her to move her hands behind her for support. He slowly began kissing her legs and moved to her flower.

Billy savored Jamee's taste and knew she enjoyed his kisses. He felt her feet come to his sides and caress him.

Jamee's body jerked at his soft kisses. She pressed his sides with her feet and lifted her body as her hips jumped at his touch. She felt the heat overwhelm her and vibrations passed through her. She fell back to the floor letting her release ebb.

"Oh, Billy. That was so quick and wonderful. Let me catch my breath, my love."

Billy pulled Jamee into the water and gently held her and whispered into her ear, "I love you so much. I could do this every day and you taste so good."

"Let's get out of the water for a little while, please."

He helped her out and then jumped out beside her. It was pitch black in the cave and everything was done by touch. Jamee pushed Billy until he lay on his back. She gently kissed his lips, moving her tongue to his. They kissed and cuddled and then made slow, tender love. Their hearts and souls were one.

She had never dreamed before being with Billy that loving someone could be that good. Silver had taught her muscular exercises and techniques but never described the pleasure making love would bring her. She had only told her what it would do to the man she was with. She wondered if Silver had ever felt this completeness. She hoped she was finding it with Red. Jamee drifted off to sleep to the caresses of Billy.

Early the next morning Billy and Jamee went to the top level to enjoy the sunrise. When they arrived they found May and Nuuna already there.

May looked around and said, "Good morning. Did you sleep well?"

Billy replied with a smile, "Yes, we did. What about you two?"

"It was very quiet; didn't hear a sound."

As they settled down, Silver and Red arrived as the sun peeked over the horizon. Red was smiling but said nothing as he and Silver found a place to sit.

May looked at Jamee and said, "I'm not even going to ask."

Silver leaned over and kissed May on the cheek. They all watched the sun turn the world from soft pastels to golden green with a dark-blue cloudless sky overhead.

"Will we stay in these kinds of trees every night?" Red asked.

"Yes, unless something happens. It will take about ten days to reach my village and there are Bookus groves along the way. The last night we'll sleep near the village. I want to arrive in the morning.

"I don't expect any trouble between here and there but be ready. The Koros usually stay near the mountains to the north but do send parties out on patrols. I have only seen Volls a few times and never this far south."

"Billy, why don't we post a lookout at night? Aren't we taking a chance?" Red asked.

"I have watched Koro patrols before and for some reason they avoid the Bookus groves. They will go out of their way to circle them so we are safe in the trees. Let's get started. I want to reach another grove early so we can continue our training."

Billy didn't say it but he was still worried about how his tribe would react to the others, especially Red. He knew Red would be challenged by at least one of the hunters and he wanted him to be ready. They moved down to the second level, ate a quick meal and started off to the southwest.

As they walked, May pulled Jamee back to the rear and looked at her self-consciously.

"What is it, May?"

May, not looking at Jamee, said, "I am older than you, but you and Billy are together and you both look so happy. What... what I want to ask you is... well, I'm not sure how to put it."

"You can ask me anything and I will answer you honestly."

"Well, to be honest, I've never been with a man and I've been on my own most of my life and I have no idea how to... oh, I've heard men talking and I know how it works, but if I ever meet the right man, I want to do it right."

Jamee's eyes widened with surprised— not that May had never been with a man but that she was asking her for advice.

"I've only been with Billy, no one else. I did have a good idea of what would happen and even had..."

Jamee thought about all the wrong things she had heard from the women of her group and about the advice and help Silver had given her. Without Silver, she would have been in the same position as May.

"May, will you give me a minute to talk to Silver, please? I'll be right back and we'll talk all you want to."

"Okay," May said with a questioning look.

Jamee hurried to Silver and pulled her aside to talk. They spoke for a short while and then both of them dropped back to walk with May.

Jamee said, "I want to help you and the best help I can give you is for Silver to talk to you. She helped me growing up and the last few years she taught me things that helped me be the best woman I could be when I met the man I loved. Will it be all right if she talks with you?"

"Sure! Silver and Red look like they know how to treat each other. I'd like to put a silly smile on a man's face some day and you seem to know what you are doing," May said with a laugh.

"You'll see. Silver was my only friend and I know she'll give you good advice. I'll leave you two alone to talk."

Jamee walked up to the head of the group to listen to Billy and Red talking.

She glanced back from time to time and saw Silver talking to a wide-eyed May. She laughed and rubbed against Billy.

"What's going on back there?" Billy asked as Red looked on.

"Oh, nothing. Silver and May are getting to know each other better."

They stopped around midday and Silver and May sat away from everyone talking in hushed voices. A few hours later Jamee looked back, saw May straining in concentration and knew Silver was teaching her some muscle control techniques.

Billy took them to a Bookus grove several hours before sundown and Red, Silver and he moved off into the grove to practice.

That night while they ate supper Jamee burst out laughing as she looked at May's face. She had beads of sweat on her brow and a strained look.

Billy looked at May and asked, "May, are you okay? You're not catching a cold or anything, are you?"

May blushed and a deep red mixed with her dark skin. "I'm fine! Mind your own business."

She got up and walked out.

"Jamee, what's going on?" Billy asked.

It was then that Jamee remembered that she had not told Billy about the help and exercises Silver had taught her.

She said, "It's nothing, my love. I will tell you tonight."

Billy looked at Red and could see he was wondering the same thing, but they both let it drop. Later that night both Jamee and Silver told them, in their separate caves, about what Silver had done for Jamee and what she was now doing for May. Both were sworn to secrecy and both laughed until they cried at May's dilemma.

The next morning as they prepared to leave Billy went over to Silver and kissed her softly on the lips. "Thank you, sister. You are a good teacher."

Silver slapped him playfully and told him to be quiet. As they walked along the trail, Billy and Red would look back at Silver and May talking and smile because May was walking a little stiffly.

The group was moving through the tall grass, walking at an easy pace, when Flick spoke to Jamee. "There are men just in front of you! They were sitting down and I didn't see them."

Just as Jamee started to warn Billy a patrol of Volls appeared in front of them. Billy and Red attacked immediately and three Volls were down in an instant. Two other Volls charged in with long knives drawn trying to stop their attack. As Billy and Red were engaging the two Volls, several more came at them from the sides. One of the Volls moving in took an arrow in the neck and the other two were cut down before they reached Billy or Red. The two others were brought down, one dying from a knife wound and the other was smashed to the ground by Red's powerful fist. They wheeled around looking for more and saw Jamee, Silver and May, with Nuuna by her side, standing behind them, guarding their rear.

They saw no one else and Billy and Red went through the equipment of the dead Volls.

Red took a long knife and sheath strapped to the side of one of the Volls. He examined the last one and said, "This one is still alive. What should we do with him?"

Billy said, "Leave him. He can find his way back to his people, maybe."

"I would like to take him with us and question him. He's not very big and I can carry him to the next camp."

"I don't think it's a good idea to take him to a Bookus grove. If we let him go after you talk to him, he can tell the others."

Red said, "You're right, but it might be important to find out why they are so far out in the prairie."

"Okay. Follow me and no talking," Billy said.

They set off towards the north following Billy's lead. Red had the soldier draped across his shoulder, walking as if he weighed nothing. He had tied his hands and blindfolded the captive with a piece of fur.

About an hour before sunset Billy stopped. They could see a Bookus grove about three hundred yards ahead. Billy pointed to Red to take the Voll away from them so he would not hear what was said.

Billy said, "Red and I will set up a false camp over there in the rain berry bushes. Jamee, you take everyone else to the Bookus grove and go into one of the trees. Mark the transit limb with a strip of leather. We will find you later tonight."

Jamee wanted to argue but trusted Billy's judgment and nodded. She led the others off toward the grove.

Red and Billy set up a small camp deep in the clump of rain berry bushes. Red said, "I may have made a mistake. I don't know if this one got a good look at me, but if he did and he reports back, then they will be after us for sure. They will want to get me back and question me. Then they'll kill me."

"It's too late now. The information may be important. You stay out of sight until we know for sure but don't go too far away. There are animals around that hunt at night."

Billy waited until the man started to move around and then he built a small fire. He sat the man up, took off the blindfold and gave him some water. The man looked to be in his late twenties. The soldier blinked, looked around and gave Billy a frightened look. Billy was wearing animal skins and leather, with long black hair, a muscular body and had a serious look on his face.

Billy asked, "What is your name?"

The man answered, "Bert."

"Okay, Bert. What are you doing out here?"

Bert looked around and asked, "Where is the other guy? I thought I saw a white man."

"You are the only white man alive out here. My brother is keeping watch and he's not white. Now, answer my questions or you are of no use to me." Billy pulled out his big hunting knife.

Bert said quickly, "We were sent out to look for the place where the people who live here are located."

"Why do you want to find them?"

Bert looked into the fire. "I don't know. We were just told to look for them and report back."

Bert started to say more but Billy held up his hands and moved to the edge of the firelight. Bert could hear the deep rumble of one of the giant cats he had been warned about. He didn't want to meet one with his hands tied.

Billy crouched silently for a moment and the rumble of the cat came closer. Bert saw Billy take a deep breath and let out a scream—imitating the prairie cat— that sent chills through him. It was so loud Bert fell back in fear. After another few minutes Billy returned to the small fire and helped Bert sit up.

Billy continued as if there had been no interruption. "I don't believe you. If you don't answer me truthfully, I can promise that you won't like it!"

Bert stared at him in wonder for just a moment and then blurted out, "Our commander has orders to capture or kill everyone on this planet. It's not my idea and that's the truth!"

"Why do you want to kill us?"

"I think they want to take you back to Earth to work for them. Really, I'm just doing what I was ordered to do. I don't want to be here fighting at all."

Billy said, "You tried to kill me today. You might not make it back to your home unless you tell me more."

"I'm sorry. I'm just one of the regular troops. As far as I know, the main reason we are here is because of the stuff we get from those lizards. We're trying to make explosives with it. Now the lizards are asking for more and more weapons and command is fed up with them. I think there is a plan to kill them and mine the green rocks, using colored people as workers. It's too much trouble to bring in a lot of people so they are trying to capture the ones that live here."

"Colored? You mean people like me— ones who aren't white?"

"Yes, but even the lizards don't know where you live and the captives in the mine won't answer any questions no matter what they do to them."

"How do you communicate with the other Volls?" Billy asked.

"We don't! We only have short-range radios so we didn't bring anything with us. We were told to head south for one week and return if we didn't see anything."

"Why is this rock you get from *the lizards* so important to you?"

"We are not trained to fight with knives and spears. We want our modern weapons and the rocks might help us develop something with more power to clean up the outer worlds. Are you going to kill me?"

Billy looked at Bert and after a moment he said, "Not this time, but believe me, Bert, if you come back, we will fight and you will die."

"I believe you. They are bringing in trackers from Forest. Those guys are very good at finding whatever they are sent out to find. They are also bringing two large troop transports, which hold around five hundred troops each. The commanders are very serious about capturing or killing the people on this world. I heard something happened at the mine and they suspect your people had something to do with it. I heard it will take a couple of months to build a new road and they are upset. Are you an Indian?"

"I have heard that was a word used to describe all the different tribes where we came from."

"What is your name? I only want to know for myself. I won't give it to my commander."

"You can call me Running Wolf. Tell this commander that we want only to be left alone. We will fight if he comes against us and he will lose. We will not be his slaves. If he sends trackers, they will not return. We are few and he will gain little by trying to capture us. Tell him all of this."

"I will tell him, Running Wolf. Boy, I really like that name. I used to read forbidden books when I was younger and I loved to read about Indians most of all. Could a white man join your people, Running Wolf?"

"It has never happened before and for anyone who fights against us it would be difficult. If you truly want to help us, go back and tell your friends we are good people and not afraid to fight but we want only to be left alone."

"Running Wolf, after I do all this... would it be possible for me to return and live with your people? I'm sick about what my people are doing to the people of the outer worlds and want no more to do with it. The truth is life on Earth is terrible and this is a beautiful world! I used to daydream about living in a world where a man could be free and make a life for himself."

Billy looked into Bert's eyes and could see the truth in them.

"Bert, I do not speak for my people, but if ever you do return, speak my name, Billy Running Wolf, and ask to be brought to me. I can't promise you will not be hurt or even killed, but if you come in peace and only for yourself, there is a chance you can live here in peace. Say my name and speak the truth."

Bert smiled and tried to shake Billy's hand but his hands were still tied. Billy reached out with his knife and cut his bonds and then he shook Bert's hand.

Bert said, "I believe you! Your people must be very tough. The lizards refuse to go against you. They say your people kill all who come against them."

"We only fight when we are attacked. I will leave you now, but my brother will keep watch until first light. You will head north and travel only during the day. It will take at least three days for you to find the Volls. I will give you food and water but no weapons. Do not fight us again, Bert. I think I could like you and don't want to kill you. Good luck to you."

Billy stood and shook Bert's hand again. He opened his pack, left a few supplies with Bert and moved out of the light of the small fire. He passed Red and motioned for him to follow.

Billy and Red entered the Bookus grove and something small hit Billy in the back. He spun and saw Jamee standing nearby looking at him.

She ran to him and kissed him. "I stood guard waiting for you."

Billy looked down at her in the darkness and said, "You don't listen..." He laughed and finished, "I love you, too."

It was late as they entered the large water cave. Everyone was awake, waiting for their return. Silver moved to Red and kissed him. "Did you learn anything?"

"Yes. Running Wolf did very well."

"Who?"

Red looked at Billy and asked, "Is that your real name, Billy?"

"Yes, my name is Billy Running Wolf, but Billy is enough for us."

"Well, Billy Running Wolf, my name is Jim Travis, but no one has called me that in years."

They shook hands and smiled.

"Let's get some sleep. We'll leave after first light." They all bedded down in the cave and were soon asleep.

At first light Billy and Jamee were at the top of the tree to watch. As the morning brightened they watched Bert make his way north.

"Where was Flick yesterday?"

Jamee said, "She was there and gave me the warning, but before I could warn you everything happened."

Flick landed on Billy's shoulder, walked to his neck and lightly pecked him on the cheek.

"Try and give us more warning next time, Flick," Billy said with a smile.

Flick flashed through the colors of a rainbow and launched into the air. They moved down to the ground with the others and headed south.

An hour later Billy changed direction to the southwest, Billy and Red in the lead, Jamee and Nuuna close behind and Silver and May bringing up the rear whispering together.

"Red, you did well yesterday. You moved quickly!"

"The training is paying off."

They stopped at midday, rested a few minutes and then continued on. Early in the afternoon they stopped in a Bookus grove for the night.

Billy gathered everyone around and told them what took place the night before. May said, "I'm from that place the Voll talked about. I never knew it was called Forest but I guess that's a good name for it. It's covered with large forests and very little water above ground. It does come up into small springs, but the lakes are small. The trackers the

Voll talked about are as good as he said. If they come near us, you let me deal with them. There is no way to hide your tracks from them and they don't give up 'til they find what they are looking for. They are never to be trusted!"

Billy, Silver and Red went to practice and Jamee and May went to gather food. Nuuna went to explore the tree. Later Billy took Jamee into the grove to be alone and talk.

"You should use other birds to keep an eye on us to help Flick. That was a close call yesterday. Everyone handled themselves well, but more warning would be better."

"Flick talks to me often while we travel, but I will use other birds to help. Are you going to tell the others about what I can do?"

Billy laughed. "I guess the only one that doesn't know is May. When we travel tomorrow you can tell her if you can get her to think about something besides what she and Silver are talking about."

Jamee laughed. "She is taking those talks seriously. She's sore from using muscles she's never used before. I hope the man she finds is ready for her."

They walked until dark, stopping to kiss and caress often.

After eating, Red motioned for Billy to follow him. He led the way to the top of the tree.

Both moons were high in the sky. The giant white and the smaller red cast a soft glow over the expanse of the prairie. Red said, "What Bert told you is true about the Volls wanting people, but I think it's time to tell you some of the reasons why.

"Six hundred years ago on Earth there was a great mix of people, but the white nations and people felt threatened and many people had a great hate for anyone not white. The white factions banded together into a Federation and began an aggressive fight to control the world.

"A weapon was developed that could destroy animals and humans but not cause damage to vegetation or structures. The whites, through a leader gifted with the ability to make great speeches, filled the white nations with hate. One day in November the weapons were used in large areas of the world. Much of the world became void of life. The white armies found pockets of non-whites and killed everyone.

"At the same time there were groups of scientists, mostly Christians, who had developed a space drive that would move ships faster than light. They kept their discovery hidden from the rest of the world and sent out probes to other galaxies. These probes never returned until the scientists finally equipped them with very old technology that didn't use microchips and then they started to return with data. They discovered four planets many light years away that would support life."

Billy said, "These must be the people who brought us to Prairie."

"You're right. I see now what a great thing they did.

"Their base was hidden in the far north, a placed called Canada. They hid many of the non-white people there and began to transport them to these outer worlds. Your world was the last and the farthest from Earth and the final place they brought people.

"All of this was unknown to the Federation until a few hundred years ago. The groups helping the non-whites were discovered and all killed for their crimes, but before they died they destroyed most of the information about the Stardrive.

"The Federation scientists finally discovered the secret to light speed travel about seventy-five years ago and somehow discovered the location of these outer worlds.

"The Earth is a terrible place to live. The people are crowded into small areas. There are vast areas where no one lives because the weapons they used did much more damage than was expected. The plant life changed in those areas and it was a dangerous place to go.

"Slowly these areas are becoming livable again, but people are afraid to go there. That's why the government of Earth wants your people. They want to put the people they capture in these areas to make them livable for the whites. They will kill all the non-whites when they have completed their work or keep them as slaves."

Red looked over at Billy but could not see his expression in the dark.

He said, "Billy, I didn't tell you everything before because I was ashamed and I didn't think it would help us with what we are doing. I'm sorry."

Billy had listened to every word and wouldn't have believed it as truth if he did not trust Red as a brother.

He took a moment before he spoke. "Red, you have nothing to be sorry for. I believe what you have said, only because it is you who said it. I don't understand all of what you have told me or this hate the white nations have for us. We have never been taught to hate others, especially because of their skin. We have a fear of white people because of the old stories, but as a people we don't hate them. We fight to protect ourselves, but we don't go out and kill others because of who they are... What do you think we should do?"

Red said, "I don't know what to tell you. I don't think peace is possible. If you could take their reason for being here away or hurt them badly, they might leave."

"I will think on this. I must tell the elders, but maybe we can come up with a plan to give them also."

They left the grove at dawn heading southwest. Billy and Red walked in silence. Both had much on their minds. Jamee practiced with her staff. May and Silver continued talking.

On the tenth day from Green Hiding near mid-morning a mountain range came into view in the distance.

Billy told everyone, "That is where we are heading. My village is in the foothills."

A little while later Jamee said, "Billy, there is a herd of bovals up ahead. I don't see any signs of people anywhere around."

As the group walked up a rise they could see a great herd moving through the prairie.

May exclaimed, "Look at that! What are they, Billy?"

"They are bovals. They travel the prairie eating as they go. They are a source of food for all the people here. Let's wait here and let them pass. They are not usually dangerous, but you don't want to be close if they get excited."

Red said, "I would never have believed there could be so many animals. This world is so beautiful."

They sat down to wait for the bovals to pass. Red said, "They look a little like the pictures of buffalo I have seen but their horns are massive and they are bigger. Why don't you call them buffalo?"

Billy said, "It was decided that on this new world we would use new names for most of the animals. Perhaps my people didn't want to be reminded of the old place."

Jamee went over to Silver and May and asked, "How is your training going?"

"I'm ready to find me a man and try it out, but like Silver keeps telling me, it's only for the man I want to stay with. But I'm ready!"

Jamee laughed. "Don't grab the first man you see. I waited for a long time for Billy to come to me. You will meet the right man someday and he will be lucky to find you."

Silver said, "I've missed talking to you, Jamee. I hope when we get to Billy's village we can stay for a while."

"So do I. How is the training going?"

Silver smiled and said, "There's not much for me to show Billy. I taught him some pressure points and how to move a little quicker. Red is a good student and picking up what Billy and I show him quickly. He will be ready when we get to the village. I've even had time to teach May a few things. I just hope she doesn't confuse her lessons when she meets her man."

They all laughed at that.

"What will become of Nuuna when we get there? She's a wonderful child," Silver said, looking over at Nuuna sitting in Billy's lap.

May answered, "She can stay with me, but what I would really like is for all of us to stay together as a family."

"I would like that too," Jamee said.

Silver looked at them both with a tear sliding down her cheek and nodded.

Billy motioned for everyone to get started again and Jamee stayed close to May as they walked. She told her everything about her powers and about Flick.

May was amazed at what Jamee told her and in the end she said, "Jamee, I wish I could do that. You are so lucky!"

Jamee hugged and kissed May and said, "On my old world it frightened people and I was alone all the time until I met Silver."

"Well, you'll never be alone again!" May said taking Jamee's hand as they walked. "Do you think I could meet your bird?"

"She is not my bird and her name is Flick. I'll ask her."

Flick landed on Jamee's shoulder and looked at May and then turned a shiny dark cream color.

Jamee said, "Flick says hello. She has given you this color. She also said you are warm inside and need to mate."

May blushed and said, "Hello, Flick. You are beautiful! Why does she say I need to mate?"

Jamee laughed. "She likes to watch. I'm not sure why, but I think it makes her happy."

"She likes to watch...well, if she helps find me a man, I guess it will be...okay." Flick turned a brilliant yellow and flew off.

"She said she will keep an eye out for a mate you will like."

"Jamee, does she talk to you about other people... making love?"

"Not in words, but she lets Billy and me know what's happening with everyone. Don't worry, May. It's not our idea and Flick has a mind of her own."

They reached a Bookus grove early in the afternoon. Billy had Red help him gather dead limbs from a stand of trees not far from the grove and they carried them into the center. They drove the limbs into the ground making a large circle. One limb was about six inches in diameter and they placed it in the center. Billy went to the water cave the women had chosen and asked them to join him. He told May to bring her bow.

When everyone was gathered he said, "Today we will have a little entertainment and a demonstration of skill from May and Jamee. May, walk back about seventy-five yards and shoot all your arrows into the center post."

May moved into position as the group moved to the side and sat down.

Billy said, "Watch closely."

May looked at Billy and he nodded. May nocked an arrow, pulled and released. Before the first hit the target she had another in the air and continued in a near blur until all twenty arrows were released. May had made four groups of five arrows down the center of the post. They all clapped and got up to admire what May had done.

Silver said, "I have never seen anyone shoot so fast! That was great. I have seen contests on Ocean and you would have won them all easily."

Everyone gave praise to May and she smiled happily as she removed the arrows.

Then Billy said, "Now, Jamee, I think it's time to show us what you can do with your staff."

Everyone moved back to take a seat farther away from the circle. Jamee moved to the center, smiled and gave a bow. As she straightened, the staff whirled, striking the center post six times. Jamee moved in a great leap to the outer ring of smaller limbs. As she came down the top two inches of the first post fell away. She twirled and two-inch sections vanished until only a small piece was left standing.

She leaped across the circle, moving, spinning and jumping around the circle. The staff was a blur. She never stopped at a post, but as she passed it seemed to disappear in tiny pieces. As she passed the last one, she released the staff and it buried itself into the center post. Jamee followed the throw quickly and grabbed the staff, moving it to the ground, splitting the post. She spun again. The post disappeared into a cloud of chips.

Before all the chips hit the ground they all heard a snap as the blade retracted, and Jamee faced them and took another bow.

They howled with delight, especially Nuuna, clapping and running to hug Jamee.

Red said, "Jamee, I know what this staff is, but I have never seen anything like that. You are a one-woman army!"

Billy said, "Well, at least we have plenty of firewood, even if it is kind of small." They all laughed, hugged and kissed Jamee and May.

Billy said, "I wanted everyone to see what anyone who comes against our family is in for. Now it's time for practice."

As Billy led Silver and Red off, Jamee, May and Nuuna gathered up enough wood for the fire.

May said, "As long as I have my bow, I think I will go and find a small uteta for us to eat tonight. Jamee, you were really something!"

Jamee smiled and said, "You too. While you're out Nuuna and I will gather some herbs and vegetables."

That night they had a feast, filled with laughter and happy talk. After cleaning up, Silver and Red left to find a cave of their own. Red carried a firestone with him and made a small fire as Silver cut a hole in the floor at the back of the cave.

Red asked, "What are you teaching May?"

"Well, I've shown her some exercises to strengthen her muscles and talked to her about being with the man she loves. May had no one to talk to about those kinds of things before.

Everything I've taught her and talked to her about are ways to make the man she decides to spend her life with happy."

"What kind of exercises? I didn't really understand what you told me the other day."

Silver looked at Red and smiled. "I guess I'll have to show you, my love."

She took his hand and led him to the pool. They both jumped in and cleaned the day's toil off of each other. Red couldn't take his eyes off of her.

"You are the most beautiful woman I've ever seen and I love you with all my heart. I still don't know how I was so lucky to have found you."

Silver smiled. "We both had to travel a very long way to end up in the same place and I am the lucky one. I found a man who loves only me and shows me every day how much he loves me. I love you more every day."

She moved into his arms and kissed him deeply, letting her tongue explore his. Her hands moved across his body as his did the same to her. They kissed, massaged and touched each other until both were excited and wanting more. They got out of the water and lay down with Silver resting her chest on Red's. She then explained what she had taught May— with her body. Red was astounded and completely satisfied with what Silver showed him. He then spent a long time bringing Silver to her release, using his lips and fingertips. They both went to sleep with smiles on their faces and completely fulfilled.

The next morning as they were getting ready to leave Billy asked Red, "Are you okay? You look a little tired."

Red answered, looking over at May, "I'm fine. I was learning some muscle control last night."

May laughed happily and looked at Silver, who was blushing but smiling.

"I can't wait to try!" May said.

Red laughed and said, "You're going to make someone a very happy man."

May blushed and walked out of the cave.

As they started walking Billy suddenly stopped and looked back at May and said, "Oh."

May picked up a stick and threw it at Billy. Jamee laughed and pushed Billy forward toward the mountains ahead.

Billy changed direction, more towards the south but still headed for the mountains.

Jamee could see more details of the mountains as the group drew closer. They were sloped upwards towards the sky and had so many different shades of green. She thought about the barren, rock strewn Slave Mountains of the north and how lifeless they seemed.

These were beautiful and covered in forest. The closer she got the more the mountains revealed. She could make out very tall trees and open grassland on their slopes.

"What is the name of this range?"

"They are called The Nations. Many of the mountains have the names of all the tribes that were brought here."

"We are only a day's journey from my village but we will stop at the last Bookus grove before we reach the foothills."

A little after midday they stopped for the night.

Billy, Red and Silver practiced an hour or so and Billy said, "That's enough. Red, you need to relax and prepare your mind for tomorrow. I don't really know what will happen, but I expect you to be challenged by at least one of the young hunters. I will protect you if it gets out of hand, but until that happens, the best thing I can do is stay out of the way. You are ready and I am proud of how you have adjusted to these new techniques. I think you should relax tonight and get a good night's rest." He smiled at Silver as he said the last part.

Silver smiled and said, "And I am proud of you both in how quickly you picked up the things I have shown you."

Billy and Jamee spent the rest of the day walking and talking together. Silver and Red asked May to show them how to use her bow so she spent a few hours working with them. Silver was amazing. She listened to May and after the third shot hit anything May picked out as a target. Red learned also, but it took him a number of tries to get the feel of the bow.

They walked out onto the prairie to a clump of rain berry bushes and Red quickly brought down two large hoppers. Silver picked a pack full of berries and they headed back to prepare supper. That night they ate the hopper that had been soaked in rain berry juice. It was delicious.

As they were finishing up, Billy said, "Tomorrow, we arrive in my village. When we get there everyone walk behind me in single file. I want Red behind me and then the rest of you follow. We have few customs that will cause you problems. Answer questions when asked; ask when you're not sure of what to do and hold your heads up.

"Remember, we are a family and I will handle any problems. Be polite and don't look for trouble. If Red is challenged, don't interfere. I will help if needed. We will first find the elders and I will present you to them and then we'll see. People will stare at you because you are three beautiful women and a beautiful child. I want you all to know that I will be with you no matter the outcome. I have grown to love you all and Jamee and I will make a home with you."

The women came to Billy, hugged and kissed him and then did the same to Red.

"Oh! One more thing. May, don't go grabbing the first guy you see and try to drag him off," Billy said with a laugh.

May blushed but said nothing.

"I almost forgot. Don't bathe nude near the village. My people don't do that and I don't want them fainting."

They decided to sleep together that night and sat around talking and joking for a few hours before lying down.

CHAPTER 13

Everyone was up early the next morning and packing. They were all nervous. When they started out, it was a quiet group that walked out onto the last of the prairie. Billy led them into a valley at the foothills and they were soon walking on a wide, well-used trail. The valley was beautiful, with a variety of tall trees and open expanses. They began passing farmland with tidy houses and beautiful gardens and crops that thrived in cultivated fields.

As they came closer to the village Red was surprised to see the quality of the houses. They were small but expertly built. Each house had a flower garden filled with color. The village had neat, orderly roads with shops selling many products.

Red hadn't expected to see such order and beauty. He had read of the stoic, fearsome and nomadic people, wearing buckskin and with feathers in their hair. What was before him was a tidy, simple and well-kept village. He could see the love of nature in everything that he looked upon. He felt a tinge of embarrassment as he looked at the gentle, proud and brave man who walked ahead of him, leading this group into a world Red wanted to know.

They walked through the village receiving many stares from the people they passed. Not many looked happy to see the strangers, especially the big white man. All the men were armed with hunting knives and several had bows.

They reached the village square and Billy headed towards a group of men sitting in front of a large wooden building. Billy approached and they all stood and faced him.

"I see you, Red Eagle. I have returned from my trek with important news," Billy said to the tallest man.

Red Eagle said, "I see you. You have brought more than news with you, Running Wolf! Is this white a prisoner?"

"No; he comes with me as my brother. I will tell you all that has taken place."

"Who are these women and the child? They do not have the look of the People."

Billy turned and motioned for Jamee to come forward and he said, "Red Eagle, this is the woman I love and she will be my wife. Her name is Jamee."

He motioned for Silver to come forward. "This is Jamee's sister and is to be this man's wife. Her name is Silver."

Then he motioned for May and Nuuna to come forward. "This woman and child come as part of my family. Their names are May and Nuuna."

Billy spoke to the group and said, "These men are the elders of this village. They make the decisions for the village with great care and responsibility."

Nuuna smiled up at them and said, "Hello. I am very pleased to meet you."

Red Eagle looked down at Nuuna, smiled and said, "Welcome, child. I too am happy to meet you."

He then focused on Red with a hard stare and said, "You are the first white man I have ever seen. What is your name?"

"My name is Jim Travis, sir. I too am very glad to meet you. I come to you in peace and friendship."

"We shall see."

He turned with the other elders and walked away several feet and began talking. While they talked, several young men came and stood in front of Red staring up at him.

One said, "We have no need for whites in our village! You should return quickly to where you came from."

Red answered in a calm voice, "I have nowhere to return to. I will stay with my brother, Running Wolf."

The one who had spoken looked at Billy and said, "Why have you brought these strangers here and how can you call this one your brother?"

Billy said, "Little Dog. Do you question the words I have said to the elders?"

Little Dog smiled but not with his eyes and said, "It is good you bring these women. Maybe I will take one as a mate and show her what one of the People can do for her."

He turned and walked away. The other hunters stared at Red and then turned away to follow Little Dog.

Billy turned to Red and smiled. "That went well, didn't it?"

Red didn't reply.

After about twenty minutes the elders returned to the group.

Red Eagle said, "These people can stay for now until we decide what should be done. Running Wolf, you are responsible for them until that time. As for the white man, he must not cause trouble and if he is challenged he will have to accept or leave."

Billy said, "I understand. They will stay in my care until you decide."

"There will be a meeting tonight. You will come and report your news and answer questions about these people."

He moved forward and hugged Billy. "I'm glad you are home, Billy. You were gone longer than we expected."

"It is good to be home."

Billy turned and motioned the group to follow and led them out of the village heading south.

They walked for about fifteen minutes and came to a small farm and he led them to the house.

May saw a man and woman come out and Billy ran to them, hugging and kissing the woman. The man looked to be about fifty years old, tall with a strong body and a handsome face. The woman was as small as Silver and almost as beautiful. She had a youthful face, with light reddish-brown, smooth skin.

"Billy, we were worried about you! You've been gone so long. We were worried," the woman said.

The man shook hands, gripping Billy's forearm, then hugged him. "I'm glad you are back, son."

Looking behind Billy at the group standing watching the welcome, he said, "You have found more than Koros out on the prairie."

He looked them over one at a time and gave Red an even look. He smiled down at Nuuna, gave May and Silver small smiles.

When he looked at Jamee his eyes widened and he smiled and said, "I see you have brought someone very important with you. My son goes on a trek and returns with a woman of power who is to be his wife."

He walked over to Jamee, kissed her cheek and hugged her. "Welcome, daughter. It is good to meet you at last."

Jamee smiled with tears in her eyes. "Thank you! It is good to be here. My name is Jamee."

"My name is Sam Walking Bear and your mother over there is called Little Dove. I call her Honeybee but you can call her Honey. Go and meet your mother, Jamee."

Sam turned to meet each of the others, welcoming them. He picked up Nuuna and carried her with him as he approached Red. Red held out his hand and Sam took it in a firm grip.

"My name is Jim Travis but most people call me Red. I am honored to meet the father of Billy."

Sam was a tall man but still had to look up a bit. "You are a big man. I hope you are as strong as you look. You will have many tests here but not in this house. Here you are welcome."

"Thank you, Walking Bear."

"If you are to be a member of my family, call me Sam. All of you call me Sam because you are now with your family."

May and Silver came over to him with tears flowing down their cheeks, hugged and kissed Sam. Nuuna leaned over, smiled and kissed Sam as well.

While Sam was making his greetings, Jamee walked shyly over to Little Dove and was about to speak when Little Dove wrapped her arms around her neck and kissed her lips softly and said, "Welcome, Jamee, my new daughter. We have waited a long time to meet you and I am pleased with you."

Jamee had no words but with tears flowing hugged Little Dove and looked up at Billy. Billy was trying hard not to show his tears but finally just put his forehead to the two women and hugged them. Each of the others presented themselves to Little Dove and received a hug and kiss from her.

Red had to lean down to receive his kiss and he said, "Thank you, Mother."

Little Dove took Nuuna from Sam and motioned for the women to come with her into the house. Sam, Billy and Red walked over to a large spreading tree and sat down on a bench beneath it.

"Billy, I have always been proud of you, but watching you arrive today with this group has made me know you as a good man. Many of the young hunters would not have taken on such a responsibility. I want to hear all about how you came to meet these people, but first I want Red to know this: you will have a hard time here for a while because you are white. In this house you will be a part of this family, but are you prepared to fight for the right to live here?"

Red said, "I don't want to fight anyone except to protect my new family, but I will do whatever I must to be accepted."

Sam said to Billy, "I can see he is strong and has a good heart. Can he meet the challenge of the young men?"

"Yes, Father. Red was a warrior and Silver and I have been training him every day to make him better. He will stand up to the challenge."

"Silver helped train him? She is a small woman like your mother. What could she have taught him?" Sam asked.

"She is amazing! She beat me in a challenge. I have learned much from her as well."

"She beat you! Billy, you have only been beaten once since you were a small child. I would like to see her fight if she is good enough to beat you," Sam said.

"If anyone tries to harm Red, then you will see. Red and Silver want to get married and Jamee and I would like to be married at the same time."

Red spoke up, "I would like that as well. I doubt if Billy will tell you all that he and Jamee have done for us, so let me be the one who tells the last part of this tale. You go first, Billy, because I have heard only a little of how you and Jamee met."

Billy told about how he had rescued Jamee and how they fell in love from the start. As he told about coming upon Red and the others, Red stopped him and told the story to Sam, leaving very little out. He did not mention Silver's past or the training she gave May, but everything else was told.

Red said, "I could see right away that Billy was a good man with a kind heart and now I can see where he gets that from. It will take me some time to get used to the openness of the People. It is not the same with my people."

Sam smiled and said, "Let's get something to eat. Billy will have to tell all of this to the elders and what he has learned about the Volls and Koros. He will go with me, but all of you will stay here. Little Dove will be with you. And let me say now what is ours is yours. I now have three sons and four daughters. I will walk proudly into the meeting."

After they ate, Billy and Sam left for the meeting. Little Dove and the women sat in the front room talking. This gave Red a chance to have a look around. He walked through the house admiring the beautiful woodwork. The floors were made from a dark wood with a red blush and had been sanded and polished to a soft shine. The walls were made of a blond wood with a brilliant finish. The cabinet and tables looked hand made by a professional woodworker.

There was a door that led to the eating and kitchen area, attached to the back of the house. The kitchen had a polished stone floor and a sink and counter made of dark dense wood.

In the bedrooms there were large post beds, curtains and closets. Oil lamps were throughout the house and they gave a warm smokeless glow. The handmade artwork had a foreign look with beautiful intricate designs of every color and hung on the walls all through the house.

Red was surprised at the workmanship of everything. Embarrassed, he hadn't expected such quality. He had expected to see basic living from an aggressive people. Their life was much simpler than that of the people of Earth: no electronics or even electricity, but it wasn't a Spartan lifestyle. He sat down in a large chair and enjoyed the murmur of the women's voices.

Jamee asked Little Dove, "Mother, how did you know that Billy had picked me to be his wife?"

Little Dove smiled and replied, "Billy is a handsome man and many of the young women have tried to gain his interest. He is always polite and kind to everyone but showed no interest in the girls. It worried his father some, but I knew he was waiting for the right woman to find him. When you all arrived I saw right away the brown of your eyes in Billy's. Silver and May are beautiful also, but it was you who had his heart. I also saw the way Silver looked at Red and knew that she too had chosen." She laughed and said, "May has a hungry look but has not found the one searching for her."

May blurted out, "I wish he would hurry up and find me!"

They all laughed as May blushed.

Little Dove said, "Do not worry, May. You are too beautiful for him to wait a long time. Silver, I see an old sadness being replaced by true happiness in your eyes. It is good to see."

Silver said, "You are right, Little Dove..."

Little Dove looked at all of them and said, "Call me Mother."

Silver continued, "Mother, I have found a love in Red I never thought someone like me would find. And I want to tell you that all of us here, including Red, haven't been part of a family for a very long time and it gives me a warm feeling."

May said with tears flowing down her cheeks, "I could never have hoped for a better mother or father! I already feel a part of something good and it makes me whole inside."

Little Dove hugged and kissed her.

Nuuna asked, "Do you have more children, Mother?"

Little Dove said, "Yes. We have another son, who is ten years older than Billy. His name is Luke. He is a long hunter, which means he is gone for weeks at a time exploring new areas. He should be returning in about a week."

May asked, "Is he married?"

Little Dove laughed. "No. It seems his interest is in traveling far and not many women want to be left alone for long periods."

"Does he have eyes like Billy?"

They all laughed as Little Dove answered, "No. Billy is the only one who has eyes of blue. Almost all the People have dark eyes. No one can explain how Billy came to have his eyes, but I know it is because he has been chosen to be someone of greatness. I can also see that Jamee has a power in her that no one else has."

She was looking at Nuuna as she spoke and then looked directly at Jamee, giving her a knowing look.

"That's enough talk for tonight. Let me show you the bathhouse and then the girls will sleep in Billy's room. Red and Billy can sleep here in the front room." She saw a flicker of disappointment in Silver and Jamee's eyes and laughed.

Little Dove rose, picked up a lamp and led them to the bathhouse. Red followed along to see where they were going. Near the back of the house were two room separated by a wooden walkway. In one was a wooden toilet made of a dark dense wood and a sink. In the other was a large stone-tiled tub filled with water. They could see the wisp of steam lacing the top of the water.

Little Dove pointed to a stone bowl near the tub and said, "Wash yourself here before you get in the tub. That keeps the water in the tub clean. It is heated from below. It will relax you and you will sleep well. There are a few cloth nightdresses on the shelf but I will bring more in a few minutes. Tomorrow I will find clothes for all of you, except Red. You are so big; I will have to make you something."

Silver, May, Jamee and Nuuna stayed behind as Little Dove and Red went back to the house.

They removed their clothes, took a bucket of water and began to wash each other with soap. Once they rinsed their hair and bodies they all got into the large tub.

May said, "This water is hot!"

It took a short while to get used to the hot water, but the warmth soon soaked into them and they began to relax. Little Dove came in carrying extra nightclothes and they all sat up, a little worried about what Billy had said about being nude.

Little Dove saw their concern and said, "In the bathhouse it is proper to be naked." She began to undress and removed a pin from her hair, letting it fall to below her waist. Everyone admired her firm, petite body, which showed very little age. Her breasts were small but pert, stomach flat and her rear and legs firm. She washed and stepped into the water with a smile.

Jamee said and they all agreed, "Little Dove, you are beautiful. It is hard to believe you have two grown boys."

"Thank you."

They all relaxed for about fifteen minutes and then dressed in the nightclothes.

As they walked sleepily into the house, they each kissed Red goodnight and went to their room.

As Little Dove opened the door to her bedroom she turned and looked at Red, pointing to the room where he stood and said, "You sleep here tonight."

She closed the door leaving Red alone. Not knowing what to do, he went out to the bathhouse and was soon relaxing in the hot water. After drying and putting his clothes back on he headed for the house. Silver waited outside the door.

"I can't wait until we can bathe together."

She kissed him deeply and said goodnight. Red went to the front room, found a place in the corner and was soon asleep. Later that night he heard Billy and Sam come in but went quickly back to sleep.

Red woke early, seeing Billy still sleeping nearby. He quietly rose, went into the kitchen and found all the women busy preparing the morning meal.

"Good morning. I have never seen so many beautiful women in one room!" Red said. Nuuna rushed into his arms and said, "Red, we are making breakfast! That's the morning meal."

Little Dove said, "Good morning, Red. Take Silver outside for a walk. It will be a short while before the meal is ready."

Red and Silver walked out into the backyard, looking around at the fields of crops growing. They walked to what looked like a barn with a fenced-off corral.

"I missed you last night. I don't want to spend many nights without you next to me. "

"Isn't this place beautiful? Little Dove is so kind. I can see where Billy gets his easy-going nature from. Oh! I missed being with you last night too but I had three beautiful girls to keep me warm," Silver said with a laugh. "I think until we are married we will not get to sleep together, but we can find some time to be alone." They walked to the corral and looked at the large oxen-like beasts there. They had large flat horns, broad shoulders and strong legs.

"They must use these to plow the fields," Red said.

"Do you know how to farm?"

"No, but I would like to learn. It seems a very gratifying way of life."

"I would make a good wife to a farmer," Silver laughed.

Nuuna ran out to be with them and said, "The food will be ready in a few minutes." She jumped into Red's arms and kissed him on the cheek.

"I like it here!"

"So do I, Nuuna."

After eating, Billy gathered everyone outside under a large tree with benches built around its trunk.

"The meeting went well last night. It was agreed that Jamee, Silver, May and Nuuna can stay as part of the village. The elders are still undecided about Red. There were a few angry voices at the meeting and a few in support of letting Red stay. Most wait for the elders to decide. As for now, Red, you have the freedom of the village, but they asked that you not carry any weapons. I think that their decision waits on how you do at the challenge. It was decided to be held in three days, so that gives us more time to practice, but you are ready now. Jamee and I are to be married in one week and I have requested that Red and Silver be wed at the same time. The elders said that would depend on the outcome of the challenge. The elders are still deciding what to do about the threat of the Volls and Koros, but in the meantime they have sent out more scouts and will have patrols closer in on the prairie. Let's spend the day seeing the village and meeting people. Red, you stay close to me."

Little Dove called the women into the house, leaving Sam, Red and Billy outside.

Red said, "I'm still a little unclear about these challenges. I don't want to hurt anyone."

Sam said, "You will have no choice and must fight. There will be some pain, but try not to hurt anyone too seriously. That is how the others will fight, or at least how they are supposed to fight. Go with Billy today and get some idea of how it will be. For now let Billy show you your new home, because I am sure you will stand up to what you must do."

The front door opened. May and Nuuna stepped out and moved to the side. They still wore their syncotton coveralls but had beautiful arm bands on and Nuuna had a green ribbon in her hair. Jamee walked out wearing one of Billy's shirts and leggings with a yellow ribbon in her hair and then Silver stepped out. She wore a dress of thin tan leather with fringe and beautiful designs stitched along the sleeves and down her chest. She also wore a silver bracelet on each upper arm and a silver hairpin held up her hair.

All three men stared at her as she walked up to Red and asked, "How do I look?"

"You... You're the most beautiful woman I have ever seen."

She smiled up at him and said, "Thank you, my love. Little Dove and I are the same size and she has let me wear this. It feels so soft, it makes my skin tingle."

"Mine too!" Billy and Sam answered at the same time.

Everyone laughed and Little Dove said, "Sam, don't I make your skin tingle?"

"Every time I see you, Honeybee"

Little Dove continued with a laugh, "I will have clothes for everyone in a few hours. Go and see our village and meet the people."

As they walked off toward the village Billy said to Red, "You must not show anger today, no matter what is said or done. I will be your anger if it is needed, brother."

They met a group of women walking out of the village carrying bundles under their arms and they stopped to introduce themselves. The women were polite and gay, but they looked over the group with sharp stares, especially Red.

In town they visited some shops filled with beautiful blankets, bolts of cloth and many other types of dry goods. They went to the blacksmith. The smithy was a big man with arms as large as Red's. His name was George Quiet Bird and he and Red got along well.

As they left Red said, "I hope George isn't one of the people who will challenge me."

Billy laughed, "Not this first time, but he will one of these days for fun."

The village was neat and clean and so far everyone they met was friendly, except for a few hard stares at Red and a lot of interest from the young men given to the girls. May was enjoying the attention and she looked at every young man with interest. The young women they met gave Billy and Red coy looks and were polite to the women.

The people were dressed in buckskin pants or skirts and some wore cloth shirts-- all with beautiful designs. They rounded a corner near the square and several young men stepped out to block their path. Billy stopped and tried to introduce everyone. The one he had called Little Dog stepped past him, ignored Red, and stood in front of Silver.

"I think this one interests me. Why don't you come with me and we can get to know each other better."

He reached for her as the other young men laughed.

"Don't touch her, Little Dog! She has no need to talk with a man with no manners," Billy said.

"Does she belong to someone?"

Silver answered, "Yes. I am Red's woman."

Little Dog sneered, "You have no need for a White. Let me show you what one of the People can do for you."

He reached out and grabbed her arm and before anyone could react Silver put her hand over his, stepped back with her right leg turning to the right and stepped across with her left. Little Dog came over her arm and landed on his back in the dirt.

Silver said, "Oh! I am sorry. I slipped. Are you all right, Little Puppy? I mean Dog."

He jumped up and made a move toward Silver, but Billy stepped in front of him. Little Dog took a step back, glared at Billy and turned to Red.

"You are not welcome here and in two days you will be beat from this village." Red said nothing; he only smiled down at Little Dog. Little Dog and his friends turned and walked away.

Red said, "I think I'm going to enjoy meeting him again."

They all laughed and continued into the square and sat down on a bench under a tree.

Several other young men came, introduced themselves and began talking to May. She smiled, talked and enjoyed herself immensely.

One of the elders walked over and said, "I am Walter Blue Cloud. I want to welcome you to our village. We will have a contest of skills tomorrow with bows, knives and fighting styles. Billy has told us of your skills and I would like to invite you to join in."

They looked to Billy and he nodded. Everyone agreed to join in except Red.

Walter said with a laugh, "I agree that you should wait until the next day to show your skills."

An older woman came over while they spoke and invited everyone to her house to eat lunch.

Walter said, "This is my wife, Walks Far, and it would give us great pleasure for you to join us for lunch."

They all agreed and went to a house not far from the square and had a delicious meal of venison, fresh vegetables and sweet cakes.

They left the house and a young man stopped May and asked her to walk with him to see more of the village. She agreed to meet them in the square in two hours and off she went.

Jamee said, "I think May is going to like it here."

"I hope you all will."

"I will be happy wherever you are, Billy," said Jamee taking his arm.

Red picked up Nuuna and put her on his shoulder. They walked east, out of the village and soon came to a slow-moving river.

Billy said, "If you like to fish, I know some great places to try your luck."

They walked for an hour, making their way back to the village. May was sitting with three young men talking and laughing.

Silver asked, "May, are you ready to go or would you rather stay here a while longer?"

May jumped up, waved to the young men and took Silver's hand as they walked away.

It was late afternoon when they arrived back at Billy's house. The group of women they had passed earlier that morning sat on the porch talking but when they saw Billy and the others they stood and waited for them.

Little Dove said, "May, Nuuna and Jamee, please come in the house. Silver, Red and Billy, wait out here."

The women led the girls into the house. Billy took Silver and Red over to sit on a bench under the tree.

Billy said, "Silver, I forgot to tell you how beautiful you look in your dress."

"Thank you, but what is going on?"

"You'll soon see."

Sam walked up and joined them and they told him about their tour of the village. The front door opened and Nuuna came out smiling, ran to them and jumped in Sam's lap. She was dressed in a soft tan leather skirt with leather fringe along the bottom and a white cotton blouse with beautiful designs in green stitching.

"You look beautiful, Nuuna."

Nuuna giggled and said, "Thank you, Red."

Next out the door came May. She stood on the porch with a big smile and slowly turned for them to see. She wore a narrow cream-colored headband with beadwork designs in the colors of a rainbow. Her dress was soft dark-cream leather fringed down her left side. It was sleeveless and the front and back curved down to show her strong muscles and the swell of her breasts. May wore a belt of beadwork, pulled tight to show her small waist and flaring hips. She had on a pair of soft leather boots to match her dress.

As she walked towards them, Sam stood and said, "I guess I'm going to have to get a big stick to chase all the young men away. You are a very beautiful woman."

She laughed, ran to him and kissed him on the lips, then did the same to Red. "This is the first dress I ever had! It's so wonderful. Billy, what do you think?"

"I am proud to call such a beautiful woman my sister."

Billy had his back to the door and May kissed him, then grabbed his shoulders and turned him around.

Jamee stood looking at him through her big brown eyes. Billy's mouth dropped open and May backed him up and sat him down on the bench. Jamee had on a headband with bright yellow and royal blue designs entwined around it. Her hair hung over her shoulders in two braids with the yellow and royal blue ribbon tied near the ends. Around her neck was a yellow collar with a many-colored design around it. Her blouse was white cotton with a low neckline that showed the swell of her breasts. Along the collar line were the same yellow and royal blue designs but in needlework. Jamee's skirt was soft cream-colored leather so thin it folded to the form of her legs. As she turned they could see two fringe lines about eight inches apart going down the back of the skirt. As she walked down, not a man said a word.

Silver finally jumped up and hugged and kissed Jamee. "I don't believe it. You have made them speechless! Billy, what do you think of Jamee's clothes?"

Billy finally blinked and said, "My love, you make my heart sing. You are beautiful."

She walked over and kissed Billy, then turned to Sam and Red. She laughed at the look on their faces as they quickly stood. She gave them each a good long kiss on the lips that sat them back down.

Then she said, "Okay, Red. It's your turn. I think all the women have waited for this moment. Go on and see what they have for you."

Red got up and slowly moved into the house.

They heard giggles from inside and then a few loud, "Oh My's!" Silver laughed but said nothing. Several minutes later Red stepped out, along with all the women. He wore a long-sleeved leather shirt that had long leather fringe down the outside of both arms. It was a tan color and had simple red and silver designs intertwining around the neck opening. The shirttail was long and hung to his upper thighs. He had a loincloth and leggings of the same color with fringe down the outside of both legs and soft leather boots.

As Red walked down, his face was flushed as he said, "They made me strip down in front of everyone."

Sam laughed and said, "This may be their only chance to see what a white man is made of. From the sounds that came out of the house, they may even make a song of it."

Jamee said, "You look very handsome. Don't worry. If they make a song, it will be a long one."

Jamee had to sit down she was laughing so hard and everyone but Red joined her.

"That's very funny."

Silver, May, Jamee and Nuuna gave Red kisses and hugs to ease his embarrassment.

The women of the village came down to the newly dressed people.

An older woman said, "We hope you like your new clothes. The leather is called buckskin and we have also made a set of everyday clothes for you to wear. We do this to welcome you to our village and because of the love we have for Little Dove and Sam." The new arrivals came and hugged each of the women and thanked them for the gifts. As Red hugged the women, each one giggled and hugged him back firmly. The women then said good-byes and hurried away chatting and laughing.

Billy moved over close to Red and said in a soft voice, "Red, looks like you will be well known and looked up to."

"I just wish I would be looked up to for something else." Then he looked at Billy and they both laughed.

Billy took Jamee's hand and led her off to the barn. He kissed her softly and then said, "Jamee, you are the most beautiful woman I have ever seen. I don't want to sleep alone. I need you."

Jamee kissed his lips softly. "I love you more every day. I don't want to be away from you either, but we must follow the customs of our parents' house. We cannot be together for a few days anyway. It is my moon time now and waiting will make our loving better."

Billy looked at her and thought about what she had said and then he realized what she was talking about. "Oh!"

They walked back to join everyone for supper.

Early the next morning Billy and Red went off to an isolated spot to train and talk about the coming challenge. It was late afternoon when they returned and they saw the family walking back from the village. Jamee and Silver wore the second outfit they had been given, soft leather blouses with leggings and short skirts. May wore her dress. Everyone was talking excitedly. Even Sam was smiling proudly as they came into the yard.

Sam exclaimed, "Billy, you didn't tell me that my new family is a group of deadly fighters! I have never seen such a display. May won the bow competition and she was presented with a bag full of the finest arrowheads we make. She also had

almost every young hunter following her around
like a bunch of puppies."

Billy laughed and said, "I bet she hated that
part. What about Jamee and Silver?"

Sam puffed his chest out and said, "All my
daughters were something to behold! I have never
seen anyone move like Silver, and Jamee and that
staff could take on a whole war party and win. This
will be a day remembered by many!"

Billy gave Jamee a questioning look and
wondered if she used the blade of her staff. Jamee
looked back and shook her head no.

Sam turned to look at the women and said, "I
am proud to walk among you all. And I think Nuuna
will soon be as good with teachers like this around
her."

That night the meal was special as they all sat
around and talked excitedly and enjoyed the feel of
being a part of a family. The girls asked Little Dove
to give them cooking lessons and she promised to
do just that. Red ate sparingly, too nervous about
the next day's events. After supper Sam took Billy
and Red for a walk to help settle the food and Red's
nerves.

"Red, we will take a long bath and you will get
a good night's sleep. Billy has told me of your skill
as a fighter and you have nothing to worry about.
You will also make me proud, my son."

Red laughed and said, "What do you think of
having such a big family?"

"I couldn't be happier. Little Dove and I
always wanted a big family, but as much as we tried,
we were blessed with only two good sons. Now our
wishes have come true. I only wish you would have
come sooner."

"I am nearly as old as you, but my father you are. I have wanted to be a part of something that is good and now my wish has come true."

They went to the bathhouse and relaxed in the hot water and let their minds drift on the steam that rose from the water. After everyone was asleep, Red woke during the night, feeling someone lay down beside him.

Silver whispered in his ear, "I love you with all my heart. My spirit will be with you tomorrow and nothing will stop you, my love. You are the finest man I have ever met. Soon I will be your wife and our love will only grow."

She kissed him softly and slipped away back to her bed.

CHAPTER 14

Red was up early and felt worn from the long night. He had dressed in the other outfit the village women had made for him. It was sleeveless and with less finery but fit perfectly, giving him freedom of movement. Red noticed everyone else wore their best outfits. Around noon they left for the village.

Little Dove said, "There is not a more handsome family in the whole village. I wish Luke was here to be with us."

They entered the square and many people smiled and waved, but others stared at Red. He smiled back but didn't think it helped.

Red Eagle met them and said, "Are you ready, Jim Travis?"

"I have no wish to fight anyone, but if I must to be accepted, then I am ready."

"Many of the People already like you and I do as well. I wish you good luck today. Follow me."

Red Eagle led Red off to the west side of the village where there was a large cleared area. A large crowd had gathered and more followed Red Eagle and Sam's family. Red Eagle waited, with Red by his side, until everyone found a place to sit or stand.

He said in a loud voice, "Today we have a man who wishes to join our village. Several of the People have spoken for this man and it has been agreed that he should meet the challenge of any who step forward. Are there any here who wish to challenge this man?"

Four young men stepped forward. One was Little Dog. One young man was tall with a large, strong body. The others were smaller but looked to be strong and ready.

Red Eagle said, "This is a contest of skill and strength. It is not to cause grave injury. Remember my words. Jim Travis, are you ready?"

"Yes,"

"Then step to the center and be prepared."

The first young man stepped forward. Red did not recognize him as one of Little Dog's friends.

He said, "My name is Jason Bear Killer! I believe that it should be difficult to join our village so I challenge you to prove your worth."

Red nodded to him. Jason advanced on Red and then leaped in low and kicked Red in the stomach with both feet. Red took a step back but showed no sign of pain. Jason leaped high to kick Red in the head, but Red took a half step to the left, bent his knees and with the back of his hands lifted Jason over his head and he landed on his back. Jason was up and attacking with hands and feet, but Red moved with each punch and kick, blocking and stepping to the side. Red punched Jason with his palms open in the chest and sent him flying into the dirt.

Jason stood, dusted himself off and moved in on Red. He swung with his right hand and as Red moved to block it, spun and kicked Red hard across his right cheek. Red spun, sweeping Jason's feet, but Jason leaped into the air and hit Red hard on the chin. They both backed off and Red looked at Jason and smiled.

Red moved in so quickly, Jason didn't have time to react. Red punched Jason in the stomach and followed through, punching him in the back. Jason dropped in pain and was unable to rise. Red walked over to Jason, bent down and massaged a spot on his back and the pain disappeared. Jason stood, looked at Red and then extended his hand. Red took it and nodded to him. Jason walked off the field.

The next man to step forward was the big man Red thought looked familiar but couldn't remember meeting.

"My name is Daniel Quiet Badger, son of George Quiet Bird. My father spoke to me about the big man who was polite and friendly to him. I am here to test this man's strength." Red, remembering the blacksmith, knew this would be a hard-fought contest and nodded to Daniel.

Daniel smiled as he moved in on Red. He swung a big fist at Red's face and Red easily ducked it. Daniel swung several more times and each time Red moved out of his path. Daniel, still smiling, moved in with another swing but stopped before it made contact and kicked out with his right leg, catching Red in the chest and knocking him to the ground. Red leaped up, rubbed his chest and smiled.

He moved in on Daniel, swinging with a left and right, then spinning with a back kick, catching Daniel in the stomach and knocking him to the ground. As Daniel rose, Red leaped over his head, catching Daniel under his chin with both hands and pulled him back. They landed on the ground with Red wrapping his left arm under Daniel's chin in a chokehold.

Daniel's face turned red and he reached up, grabbed Red's left wrist and with tremendous strength pulled free of Red's grasp. They came to their feet at the same time and grappled in a contest of strength. Both men strained and it looked to be even, but then Red dropped his left knee, raised his right shoulder, lifting Daniel off the ground and heaving him away. Daniel hit hard, with the wind knocked out of him.

Red walked over, grabbed his belt, lifted his stomach and let it settle back. He did this several times until Daniel was breathing normally. Daniel stood, looked around and then smiled, taking Red's hand in his. He walked off the field still smiling and tapped Little Dog on the shoulder.

Little Dog looked at Red. Little Dog did not look happy. Red was smiling.

He took a deep breath, stepped out onto the field and said, "I am Johnny Little Dog! I did not want this white man in our village, but I have seen him fight and he is brave. I challenge him man to man, not because of color."

Red, still smiling, nodded to Little Dog. Little Dog walked slowly, as if to talk, to where Red was standing. Just as he reached Red he threw two vicious blows to Red's face and kicked him hard in the stomach. Red staggered back a few steps as Little Dog danced around Red and smiled.

Little Dog leaped at Red and Red took a half a step right, grabbed Little Dog's legs and swung him twice in a circle, released him, sending him flying twenty feet away. Little Dog rolled as he hit the ground, standing quickly. Red moved in on him, raised his right arm to smash him, but dropped to the ground just as Little Dog brought up his guard and swept his feet out from under him. Little Dog hit the ground and Red grabbed him with a choke-hold and squeezed. After a few seconds, Little Dog tapped Red's arm, indicating that he had had enough. Red released him and they both stood facing each other.

Little Dog extended his hand and as Red took it Little Dog said, "I have been rude to you, Jim Travis, and for that I apologize."

Red said, "Call me Red and I will call you friend, Johnny."

Little Dog walked off the field in the direction of Sam's family. He stood in front of Silver.

"I acted very badly to you the other day and I want to tell you I am sorry and ask your forgiveness."

Silver gave him a stern look and said, "I too spoke rudely to you, Johnny, and for that I am sorry." She gave him a hug and a soft kiss on the lips. "Friend."

Little Dog's grin looked like it might split his face as he walked back to the other side of the field.

The next man stepped forward and said, "My name is Arthur Sitting Bird and I have come to challenge this man, Jim Travis, today! I have seen his skill, bravery and honor and it is enough for me."

He walked out onto the field, held out his hand and Red took it.

"Please call me, Red, Arthur." Arthur walked off the field smiling.

Red Eagle stepped forward and asked, "Is there anyone else who wishes to challenge Jim Travis on this day?"

No one spoke up.

"Is there anyone who does not wish for Jim Travis to be a part of this village?"

No one spoke.

He turned to Red and said, "Welcome to our village, Red. You may call me William except when you come before the elders."

He extended his hand with a smile and Red took it happily. Then the whole crowd let out whoops and cheers and moved in to congratulate Red.

That day there were more challenges but only for sport and many people brought out food to eat. Red moved among the people, sampling many different foods with Silver by his side. He thought that this day would be added to his memories as one of his best days. Only meeting Silver and becoming a part of Sam's family would surpass it.

Sam's family went home in the late afternoon— all except May. She stayed behind surrounded by young men vying for her attention. As they walked, Little Dove, Jamee and Silver followed behind and talked quietly.

Sam remarked, "We better watch out. They are planning something. I only hope it is a good something."

That night Red slept like the dead, so relieved to have the worries of recent days off him. May had returned home early, bubbling with happiness.

Little Dove asked her if she had met anyone who interested her.

"They all interest me, but no one has stopped my breath. I think I will wait to meet Luke! If he is anything like Billy, then he may have a chance."

Little Dove only smiled.

Later that night May decided to soak in the hot bath and went out to the bathhouse. She opened the door and she saw Sam and Little Dove making love beside the pool. She couldn't take her eyes off of them as they moved together on the floor. When Little Dove turned her head and looked at May, May jumped back, shut the door and ran to bed. Her sleep was restless that night.

After breakfast, Little Dove asked her to help carry some wash out to a nearby pool of water.

While they walked May blurted out, "Mother, I am sorry for looking last night. It was an accident!"

Little Dove laughed. "Daughter, do not be sorry. I know you weren't spying on us. Your father is very vigorous, isn't he?"

May giggled and said, "I hope I will find someone as vigorous after so long in marriage."

"I am a lucky woman and I think you will be as well."

Several times that day Sam asked May to do something and each time she blushed when she looked at him.

He asked Little Dove, "What is wrong with May?"

"Nothing. I think being around all the young men has put thoughts in her head."

"That is not any kind of answer."

Little Dove looked at him and said, "It is the only answer you will get."

Sam knew when to let well enough alone and went off to do his work.

The next several days were very peaceful and everyone had time to relax. The women constantly talked and made plans but would not reveal what the plans were to the men.

One day Sam, Billy and Red set up targets of packed prairie grass. Thick posts were driven into the ground and square boards were laid out nearby. Sam sent Billy to the neighbor women who had helped make clothes for the new arrivals to ask them to come to the house. When all was ready, Sam called May, Jamee and Silver to bring their weapons and see what had been done.

When everyone arrived, Billy stepped forward and said, "Mother, you did not attend the competition where May, Silver and Jamee showed their fighting skills so we have arranged for them to give you and our neighbors a demonstration."

Billy brought May out and showed her five packed straw targets arranged at different places about 40 yards away. Three were supported by limbs on the ground and two were hung from poles about six feet in the air. He set the two targets hung from the poles in motion and stepped back to join the others.

May turned to Little Dove and bowed. "I hope you enjoy this, Mother."

She turned back to the targets and drew and released one arrow after another until all twenty arrows had been sent on their way. It had taken only seconds for all of this to happen. She placed two arrows in each of the targets and then two more, one at a time, in each target. She turned and bowed again to yells of delight and clapping.

May rose from her bow and she looked into the green eyes of a man she had not seen before.

Their eyes locked for a moment. Then she walked back to join the others. She kept glancing over and saw those eyes looking back at her.

As Silver moved out to take her place, Billy stepped out and motioned for Red and Sam to come out. It was then that he saw his brother, Luke.

"Luke! You're just in time to help us. Come on out here."

Luke looked around at Billy and said, "What?"

Little Dove hugged and kissed Luke and then shoved him towards Billy. Silver positioned the men in a semi-circle around her, about ten feet apart. Everyone but Luke picked up the one-inch thick board near their feet.

Silver walked over to Luke, picked up the board and handed it to him and said, "Don't move."

"What?"

He looked at her and Silver said, "Don't move!"

She moved back and looked at Little Dove and smiled. She began to move in a smooth, fluid motion, slowly passing each man. Her hands moved in intricate waves and her feet slowly kicked into the air as she spun around the men. Sam, Billy, Red and Luke held the boards straight out in front of them watching Silver.

She moved back close to Little Dove and stopped. Then she was moving full speed. She was a blur as she whirled passed each man, fists and feet coming within a fraction of an inch of their bodies. She spun back and leaped into the air, breaking the one-inch board Billy held, then Red's board, then Sam's and Luke's last of all. She leaped away and landed beside Little Dove.

Again whoops and claps followed. Little Dove hugged her and smiled. Billy and Red cleaned up the broken boards and everyone moved back to the gathering. Billy had to push Luke back toward the others.

Billy smiled at Jamee and nodded. Jamee moved out to the center, her staff in her right hand. She turned and bowed to Little Dove saying, "I hope you enjoy this, Mother."

She turned to the three thick posts that had been driven into the ground and began to twirl the staff slowly. She increased its speed until it was a blur and in quick leaps went to each post, battering them with her staff.

As she backed away the staff was still a blur. She stopped for an instant and then moved in again. As she passed each of the posts, they disappeared in a cloud of wood chips. When she passed the last post, she leaped into the air, flipped and landed beside Little Dove. There was silence for a moment, the villagers not believing their eyes, and then the clapping and yells began.

Little Dove stood and faced her new daughters. "If I had not seen this with my own eyes, I would not believe it! My daughters are as wondrous as they are beautiful. Wouldn't you agree, Luke?"

Luke looked at his mother and said, "What?"

Little Dove laughed and said, "I'll take that as a yes. Come here and meet your new sisters and brother."

Luke looked around, gained control, walked over and kissed his mother.

Little Dove said, "This is your sister, Jamee. She is to be Billy's wife."

Jamee hugged and kissed Luke.

"This is your sister and brother, Silver and Red."

Red shook hands and hugged Luke and then Silver kissed him warmly.

"This is Nuuna."

Nuuna jumped into Luke's arms and kissed him. "Hello, Luke."

He put Nuuna down and Little Dove said, "And this is May. I don't think she will be your sister but she is a part of our family."

May stood staring at Luke and finally said, "Hello."

Luke said nothing, just stood there staring back.

Luke looked just like Billy with some age on him. His hair was long and tied back and he had forest green eyes.

Silver said, "Uh, oh!"

And they were all soon laughing so hard tears began to roll.

Sam looked at everyone, including the neighbor women, and said, "What is going on?"

He looked at Little Dove, but she was laughing so hard she could only hug Sam.

May looked around and said, "Oh, no... that's not true," and then stormed off, causing more laughter.

After things settled down and the neighbors had left for their homes, Little Dove went to look for May. She found her sitting under a tree by the corner of a planted field in back.

"There you are, May. Is everything all right?" She sat down next to May.

"Is everyone finished laughing at me?"

"No one was laughing at you; they were laughing at the situation, honey."

"You didn't introduce me as your daughter. I thought I was a part of your family."

Little Dove turned May so she could see her face and saw tears in her eyes.

Little Dove said, "Oh, my beautiful daughter, I am sorry! I didn't mean it to sound like that. I am your mother now, but I also knew that when you met Luke it could be that you would find the one you've been looking for. I was teasing him. Luke has never looked at any of the women in the village the way he looked at you. He has been on his own for more than ten years now and I thought he might never meet anyone to love. That is, until the day I first saw you."

May looked at Little Dove and asked, "How could you know what kind of person I was at first sight and how could you know I would be the right one for your son?"

"I have always been able to see things others cannot. I saw in an instant that Jamee and Billy belonged together. I'm not trying to push you, May, and I won't push Luke, but I can see his eyes in yours and your eyes in his. It won't be easy for him, but I think it is what will be."

"I won't throw myself at anyone, but Luke is like no one I've ever seen before. I will not throw myself at him; he must come to me. I will give him a chance, but... You told me no one had eyes like Billy's!"

Little Dove hugged and kissed May. "You shouldn't chase after anyone, but don't run away either. What I said was 'no one in our village has blue eyes.' Now let's go get something to eat and we'll take a nice long bath after."

They rose and walked to the house. When they arrived everyone came and hugged May and apologized for being rude to her.

Silver said, "We love you and no one will hurt you as long as we are around."

"I love you, too. Now let's eat."

Billy looked around and asked, "Where is Luke?"

Sam said, "He took off like an arrow a little while ago and I still don't know what is going on."

Little Dove said, "I will explain later, honey."

The next morning Little Dove, Jamee, Silver, Nuuna and May were up early and left the house without saying a word. Billy left to find Luke, so Sam and Red decided to go visit George, the blacksmith.

Billy went to Luke's small house, several miles into the forest on the south side of the village near a stream that came down from the mountains. Billy looked around the house but didn't see Luke, so he walked down to the stream and found Luke sitting under a willow tree.

"Luke, what are you doing? You left last night before anyone got a chance to talk to you."

"I talked with Mom, but the rest of you were laughing like a bunch of crazy people so I left. What's all this about? A new brother and sisters and that other girl?"

Billy sat down and took his time retelling the story of how they had met and what had taken place up to now. When he finished the two men sat quietly while Luke thought about everything Billy told him.

He finally said, "You're a good man. Not many young men would have bothered with people lost on the prairie. I'm happy for you too, finally meeting a girl you want for a wife. You're lucky."

"What about the others? What do you think about them?"

Luke said, "I had heard about the white man before I arrived. Word has spread about the big man and the beautiful women who had arrived at the village. To be honest, I don't remember much about them, except for the young girl with the bow. I've never seen anyone shoot like that. What was her name?"

"Her name is May and she isn't a girl; she is a woman. She seems taken by you, too."

"Billy, I must be ten years older than her! To me she is a girl."

Billy grinned and said, "Come on, Luke. I saw the way you looked at her."

"Well, it doesn't matter how I looked at her; she's still a young girl. She must have every young hunter in the village following her around."

"There are many who have come to visit, but she hasn't shown any real interest in anyone, until yesterday."

"I'm a long-hunter and have no time for girls or women right now."

"Okay, Luke, but will you at least come back and spend a few days with your family and get to know the others, even if you have no time for women? I want you to know Jamee, Silver, Red, little Nuuna and May. They are all good people and Mother and Father have accepted them into our family. Will you do this for me, brother?"

After a moment Luke looked up at Billy and said, "Yes, but I don't want that girl chasing me around."

"Do you mean Nuuna?"

"You know who I mean."

Billy laughed and said, "Okay. I will tell May that she is not to chase you around."

"Very funny, younger brother."

They rose and started walking back toward the village. They approached the blacksmith's shop and saw Sam and Red.

Red was stripped to the waist, hammering on a piece of red hot iron.

George said, "That's it. Now you're getting the hang of it." He looked up and said, "Luke, Billy, your brother would make a good blacksmith. I might keep him here for a while."

Red laughed. "No. I think a few lessons will do me fine. This work is too hot."

Luke walked over to Red and held out his hand, and as Red took it, he said, "Billy has told me many things about you and I have heard much from the other hunters about your fighting skills. I welcome you as my brother."

"Thank you, Luke. I am proud to be your brother. I have to tell you that much of my fighting skills have been taught to me by Billy and Silver."

"Silver? She can fight, too?"

Sam said, "You were there yesterday. Didn't you pay any attention to what was going on?"

Billy smiled and said, "He saw the girl shooting the bow."

Luke gave him a hard stare but said nothing.

Billy continued, "Luke is coming with me to meet his new family and has agreed to stay for a few days."

"Well, that's good. Let's head back to the house and find something to eat. All this work Red's been doing has given me an appetite," Sam said with a laugh.

It was midday when they arrived and found no one there.

"Where is everyone? The women have been acting strange the last few days. I guess we'll have to find our own food," Sam said.

Luke was looking around and seemed relieved that no one was there. When they entered the kitchen they found a large meal laid out for them. They ate and then Sam suggested they go fishing for a few hours.

As they walked to the river he asked Red, "When you get married, who do you want to stand with you?"

Red thought about it and said, "I guess I would ask Daniel, George's son."

"He's a good man and I think that is a good choice."

They fished for several hours and then headed back with several large fish.

Billy said, "These will be good for tonight's supper."

When they arrived, all the women were busy in Little Dove's bedroom. They heard the men arrive and came out, closing the door behind them.

Sam said, "Look what we caught for supper."

Little Dove said, "Take them out back and clean them. Luke, come over here and meet your sisters again. I want you to remember them this time."

Luke came forward and received hugs and kisses from each one, except May, who had disappeared.

As Nuuna jumped into Luke's arms, Jamee asked, "Now, where did May get to?"

Nuuna looked closely at Luke and said, "You look just like Billy except for your eyes. If I were older I would like to marry you."

Luke grinned and said, "Maybe I'll just wait 'til you grow up."

"Oh, no; I don't think you can wait that long."

They all laughed.

Little Dove took Luke out the front door and told him about the next morning's plan. After talking with Little Dove, Luke walked around the yard while waiting for supper, not wanting to go into the house and run into May. As he walked, he thought about seeing her for the first time yesterday. She was the most beautiful girl he had ever seen. No, she was a woman and denying the fact wouldn't make it true. He enjoyed his solitary life and hadn't given any thought to having a wife, until he saw May.

He shook his head. *Now where did that come from?* He continued walking, rounded the back of the barn and nearly tripped over May sitting on the ground. May jumped up and looked into those green eyes.

Luke said, "I'm...I'm sorry. I didn't see you."

Their eyes were locked together, but finally May looked down at the ground and said, "No, it was my fault. I shouldn't have been sitting here."

She turned to leave and Luke said, "May. We haven't really met yet. My name is Billy ... I mean Luke!"

May smiled and held out her hand.

Luke gently took it and said, "I am happy to meet you and welcome you to our family."

"Thank you. It's been a very long time since I was a part of anything and I couldn't have picked a better family."

Luke realized they were still holding hands and gently released hers.

Their eyes were still locked together and Luke said, "I think supper is about ready. Would you like to walk back with me?"

"Yes."

They came around the barn and saw Sam, Red, Silver and Jamee looking at them. No one said a word, but they both blushed.

They had a delicious meal of fried fish, vegetables and cornbread. The conversation was lively, but everyone held their teasing of May to a minimum. After supper the women cleaned up and the men went out to sit on the benches under the tree in front of the house. Silver and Jamee came out and took Red and Billy off for a walk. May finally came out with Nuuna and Little Dove. May sat near Sam but did not talk. Nuuna sat in Luke's lap and busily asked questions.

"Mother says you are a long-hunter. What is that?"

"I travel far away exploring the land, usually to the south. I am gone for weeks at a time and see many wonderful things."

"Why do you do that? Don't you like people?"

Luke laughed and said, "I like people fine, but I really enjoy seeing new places and being by myself isn't so bad. I'll have to come around more often, now that you are here."

Nuuna laughed and said, "Maybe you could take me with you and May, too! Did you know that May was a forest guide on her world?"

"Really? I didn't know that."

He said, looking over at May, "Nuuna, would you like to go hunting with me one day? And maybe May would like to go with us."

Nuuna smiled and looked at May and asked, "Could we do that?"

May smiled at Nuuna and said, "Yes, I think I would like that, one day."

Sam said, "Well, not tomorrow! That's a big day for all of us."

Little Dove smiled and said, "I'm so excited! Billy and Red are in for a big surprise. I don't think they have a clue."

Luke smiled, "It's a big day for us all. I bet the whole village will be there. May, would you and Nuuna like to take a walk with me?"

Nuuna jumped up and pulled May to her feet. "Yes, we would."

They walked off and Sam asked, "Honeybee, how long before there's another marriage?"

"I don't know. Luke has a lot to work out. He thinks he is too old for May, but he will change his mind and when he does we won't be able to wipe the smile off his face."

"How do you know so much, my love? I wouldn't have picked Luke and May, but now I see them looking at each other and I know you are right."

"Some things stand out to me long before others see it."

That night Red and Billy were the only two that had a good night's sleep.

CHAPTER 15

Before the sun was up Little Dove woke Billy and Red. "Time to get dressed. People are waiting."

Billy rose and asked, "Waiting for what?"

He looked over and saw Daniel Quiet Badger sitting in a nearby chair.

"What are you doing here, Daniel?"

Daniel said, "I am waiting to take my friend to see the dawn."

Billy looked around and saw Luke dressed in his finest clothes and then noticed that Daniel was also well dressed.

It finally dawned on him and he said to Red, "Hurry up, big brother! We don't want to be late for this."

Sam hurried them both into the bedroom, where they found new clothes. They dressed and looked at each other. Red wore a buckskin shirt that was a soft tan color, with stitching and beadwork in beautiful patterns of silver and red. His loincloth and leggings were the same color, with long leather fringe down the outside of the leggings. He put a beautifully beaded armband on his right arm. It fit his big arm perfectly. Billy was dressed the same except the colors stitched in his shirt were royal blue and bright yellow. His armband matched Red's.

Red said, "This must be something very special we're going to."

Billy laughed and said, "Yes, it is. It's a day we'll never forget."

Sam came in, dressed in his finest cloths and said, "Let's get going. Don't want to miss the dawn."

Luke and Daniel led Billy and Red toward the river, with Sam following close behind.

They approached a large glen by the river and saw all the villagers, many holding torches, gathered in a semi-circle with the opening toward the east. The crowd parted to let the men pass through and Billy and Red stopped and stared at the center of the glen.

Nuuna, May and Little Dove stood off to one side dressed in beautiful blouses and skirts, but what Billy and Red were looking at was Jamee and Silver in the very center. They were both dressed in white soft buckskin dresses with beautiful intricate designs. Silver's dress had red and silver designs and Jamee's dress had royal blue and yellow designs. They had white feathers and flowers woven into their hair and headbands of red beadwork for Silver and royal blue for Jamee. Daniel and Luke took Billy and Red's arms and led them to stand beside Silver and Jamee and then they took their places with the family.

Luke stood beside May and said, "You are beautiful."

May looked up at Luke, smiled but said nothing.

Billy was speechless, even though he had finally realized what was happening. Red could only stare at Silver, looking down at her beautiful face.

Red Eagle stepped from the gathering and moved in front of the two couples. As he took his place, the torches were extinguished and the soft glow of a new day filtered into the glen. The sun had begun its journey, peeking above the eastern foothills.

Red Eagle said in a loud voice, "As this new day begins, so does a new life for these four members of the People standing here. Jim Travis and Silver Dove, do you accept this new life, which will last for the rest of your lives?"

Silver looked up at Red and said, "I accept this new life with Jim Travis with all my heart."

Red looked down at her with tears in his eyes. "I accept this new life with Silver Dove with all of my heart."

Red Eagle then said, "Billy Running Wolf and Jamee Soft Dove, do you accept this new life, which will last for the rest of your lives?"

Jamee looked up at Billy and said, "I accept this new life with Billy Running Wolf with all my heart."

Billy answered, tears also running down his cheeks. "I accept this new life with Jamee Soft Dove with all my heart."

The sun rose above the hills filling the world with the light of a new day. Red Eagle said, "Then it is done! You are man and wife and no one can take this away. Kiss your wives, Billy and Red, to seal this for all to see."

The couples kissed softly and a great cry of joy rose up from those gathered to witness the event. Everyone rushed in to kiss the women and shake the hands of the men.

The couples were led off to the village square and were seated in the place of honor. Each member of the village came by to present the couples with gifts of blankets and handmade items to get them started in their new lives. Little Dog came to Red and Silver and presented them with two beautifully crafted knives. One was small and delicate and the other was a large hunting knife that he handed to Red.

"It is good to have you here, Red and Silver."

Silver hugged and kissed him on the lips and Red shook his hand. "Johnny, I will treasure this knife and your friendship."

The celebration lasted into the night. There was singing and dancing in the style of the People. Food, and a great joy spread through the village. Later in the evening the two women were taken off by the other women, leaving Red and Billy to sit and listen to many hunting tails and stories from the men.

While the men laughed and joked with the two newly married men, Red could hear the singing of the women. He could not understand the words, but the melody was pleasing, yet strange to his ear. It was sometimes shrill and with a wavering that caused his heart to beat faster. Then he heard melodies that were soft and flowed with sweet soft sounds of women's voices. He couldn't hear the words but knew they were songs of love and happiness.

Red said to Sam, "The sounds of the women singing are so pleasing. I am surprised they don't sing all the time. The sounds fill me with pride and love for the people of the village."

Sam said, "Yes. They sing songs of duty, love and family. There is a sadness here that keeps us from singing often. We have lost men and women to the Koros and cannot find a way to get them back. This sorrow is felt in all our hearts. But tonight our hearts are filled with joy. You have made me a proud man and my heart is light tonight. Thank you, my son, for coming into our lives."

When at last Sam said it was time to take them away, both men were worn out.

Red asked Sam, "Are we going home now?"

Sam laughed and said, "No! There is more celebrating to do!"

All the men laughed and pushed the two along. They walked out of the village for several miles, laughing and joking all the way. They came to two small, newly built cabins near the river. They were about 20 yards apart.

Sam turned around and in a loud voice said, "Make sure we get them in the right cabin!"

Another roar of laughter erupted as Billy and Red were shoved toward separate cabins. They stood on the porches looking back at the men.

Someone in the crowd yelled, "This is as far as we go. We can't show you what to do next!"

Another roar went up as they all turned and started back to the village.

Billy turned and opened the door. He stepped into the soft glow of a lamp and his breath caught as he looked at Jamee lying on the bed completely naked.

"I hope you sent everyone home, my love. Little Dove said we have to stay here three days. I hope you will be up to the jobs I have for you to do."

"I will give it my best, my love."

Billy undressed and stood by the bed and looked down on his beautiful wife. His heart was full of love and contentment, his body full of heat for her. Jamee reached out to caress him. Billy closed his eyes in pleasure. He felt something on his shoulder and he looked over to find Flick staring at him.

Flick had a feather in her beak and she flew down to Jamee, placed it on her chest and flew back to Billy. "This is my wedding gift to you, Jamee. Tell Billy that I too am a part of your family and I will watch over you both. Now, I must hurry to give Silver her feather," Flick said with a little laugh in her voice.

She took off and disappeared. Jamee told Billy what Flick said as she turned the feather in her hand. It changed colors from bright yellow to royal blue. Jamee had continued to caress him the whole time and Billy now leaned over her and kissed her softly and then with more urgency. Jamee laid the feather on a stand next to the bed and turned her attention to Billy's ministrations. Billy moved his mouth to hers and kissed her again while his hands massaged her body. Jamee moaned and reached for Billy's hips, pulling him on top of her.

"Husband, make me feel good!"

Billy moved to her. Their movements were in concert, their kisses and caresses firm and their love complete. Jamee felt her body building to release, feeling Billy's every touch. She wanted the feelings to last forever, but her body demanded more than she could control. The humming waves swept through her and she cried out as she felt Billy shudder in release and heard his deep moan.

As they lay in each other's arms, he raised his head and looked into her beautiful almond-shaped brown eyes and asked, "Did I make you feel good, wife?"

"Yes, my husband, you pleased me completely."

Jamee ran her hands through his long shining hair and soon heard the even breathing of sleep. She rolled him onto his back, letting him slip from her. She reached over, turning the lamp out, snuggled close and was asleep in moments.

As dawn broke the next morning Billy was having a wonderful dream of making love with Jamee. She was on top of him, placing her creamy breast to his lips. His mouth drew her in and he suckled and then he felt her draw him in and very slowly begin to move.

Oh, what a fine dream.

He came fully awake and opened his eyes he looked up into Jamee's smiling face and knew that this was no dream. She kissed his lips and arched her back, lowering her lips to his chest and kissed him softly. All the time she never stopped moving. She raised her head, looking down at his blue eyes, letting her stomach brush across his as she moved. Billy began to move with her and soon they both cried out in release.

Billy looked up at Jamee and said, "I love you so much! I could wake up like this every day."

"I love you with all my heart and I could wake up to your warmth every morning." She smiled and then laughed. "I have to pee!"

"Me, too."

So they got up, wrapped in a blanket and stepped outside.

They were looking around, not sure if there was a bathroom or if they would have to go to the trees, when Red and Silver walked around their cabin and said, "It's around the back. We'll meet you down by the river."

After their visit to the bathroom, Jamee and Billy walked together down to the river's edge and found Red and Silver in the water kissing. Billy threw off the blanket and they rushed into the water, splashing the other couple.

"Good morning, brother and sister. Did you sleep well?" Billy asked.

"Only a little," Red said with a big grin.

For the next two days they enjoyed each other's company but spent much of their time in their cabins making love and talking.

Billy said, "If we keep this up, you will be with child very soon."

"No, Billy, I have an herb that prevents that for now, but if you are ready I will stop taking it."

"What do you think, Jamee?"

"I think we should wait for a while. I am still very young and we don't know what will happen with the Volls. I will go with you, whatever my condition."

"I think that's a good idea for now. I do very much want to have children with you but we can wait. We have a whole lifetime together."

While the two couples were enjoying their new married life, May and Luke were getting to know each other. Nuuna was always with them and found many opportunities to put them close together.

The family and a number of villagers built two small houses about fifty yards to the west of the main house, near a large spreading oak tree. The houses were for the two couples. May worked hard and seemed always close to Luke. He admired her stamina and told her so several times. On the second day after the wedding Luke invited her to go for a swim.

May asked Nuuna to go, but she said with a smile, "No. I'm going to stay with Mother and help cook supper."

Instead of heading for the river, Luke took her through the woods to the west. They walked for about thirty minutes and came to a stream with several large deep, clear pools.

Luke said, "I liked to come here when I was young; the water is cool and there is never anyone around."

"You like to be alone, don't you, Luke?"

"No, not really. It's just that I never met anyone who I wanted to be with. I like going into the deep woods and most people don't like that."

May watched as Luke stripped down to his loincloth and dove into the water. He had a strong, muscular body and looking at it gave her a warm feeling she had never felt before. She began to undress with her back to him.

She thought to herself, *Well, it's now or never to show him I'm not a little girl.*

May took a deep breath and removed all her clothes. Slowly turning, she could see Luke staring at her with a look of more than friendship in his eyes. She walked to the edge of the pool and looked at him, but his eyes were not on her face. She dove in and swam to him.

She said, "Luke, I'm not a little girl."

"Yes... I can see that. You are the most beautiful girl I've ever seen."

"I am not a girl."

"Yes... you are beautiful."

"What am I?"

"May, you are... a woman, but I'm so much older than you."

"You are not that much older than me. I'm twenty-two and if you want me to leave I will."

May stood in the waist-deep water facing Luke.

She started to turn and he said, "No! I mean... No, May, I don't want you to leave. Please stay and... well... stay."

She lowered her body into the water up to her neck.

"I'm going to say something I have never said to any man. From the first time I saw you, I knew I wanted to be with you. I'm not trying to trap you or trick you or chase after you and if you don't feel the same I will leave you alone and you will be my brother, nothing more."

There were tears in her eyes as she spoke and she splashed water into her eyes to cover them.

Luke stared at May for a long moment and said, "May, from the first moment I saw you I have thought of nothing else. I tried to tell myself that I was too old and I wanted a life that didn't include someone else, but it hasn't worked. I don't believe that now. I think of going off alone, without you, and it hurts my heart. I've never felt like this toward any girl... woman before. I want to know more about you. I don't want you to leave me alone. I guess what I'm trying to say is... I don't know what else to say."

May moved over to Luke, put her arms around his neck and kissed him for the first time. "You don't have to say anything more, Luke, because I've known from the moment I saw you that I don't want you to go away without me."

They came together, kissed and held each other, and both felt a giant weight lift off their chests. May took his hand and brought it up to her breast. The warm feeling in her turned to heat that ran all through her body. She kissed him harder and a soft moan escaped from her lips into his. His hands slipped around her and drew her close.

He stopped and looked into her dark, beautiful eyes and said, "I've never done this before and if you want to stop I will. I don't want to hurt you."

"I've never done this before either, but I know whatever you do, it won't hurt me. I need you, Luke. Please don't stop."

He took her hand and they swam across the pool and got out. Luke laid his clothes out for May to lie on. His eyes were full of her strong, shapely body as she lay down. He stood and took off his loincloth, never moving his eyes from her body.

May said, "Jamee gave me some advice for the first time we made love so lay down and let me do this."

"Jamee told you what to do. You mean she knew we would be making love?"

May laughed. "I think everyone knew we would be doing this except you and me."

Luke lay down on his back and smiled. "I think you are right, now that I think about all the looks and comments the family has made to me."

"It's time to stop thinking."

Luke kissed May. His hands moved to her body, massaging and stroking her gently. Another moan moved from May to Luke.

May had never felt a heat like this and could feel it building. She wanted to linger at his mouth, but her body demanded more so she moved down, kissing his chest and stomach and then moistening him.

She could hear him gasp for breath and she moved her body over him, letting her weight do the rest. She felt a sharp, quick pain and then only need for him. The humming started in her loins and spread across her body. A loud groan escaped her lips and she thought her mind would explode. May felt Luke shudder, but he continued to move.

He massaged and kissed her and as her mind began to clear again she felt the need for him build. Luke moved in slow movements until he looked into her eyes and then he couldn't control his thoughts.

Luke gasped, "May, I never knew it would feel this good."

May collapsed onto his chest, trying to catch her breath.

She whispered, "Oh, Luke! That was so good." She jumped up, pulling Luke to his feet and ran with him into the cool water.

She came close to him, looking into his eyes, and asked, "Luke, do you love me? I mean, maybe you just needed to be with a woman and now..."

"May, I love you. I would never lie to have sex with someone, especially not you. Until this moment I never realized how empty my life has been. I've waited for you all my life and I want you for the rest of my life. What would make you ask a question like that?"

"Look at me. My skin is dark. My hair is not smooth like everyone else's and my breasts and butt are too big. I see how beautiful Jamee and many of the young women of this village are and Silver is the most beautiful woman I've ever seen. With their light skin and long beautiful hair, I don't know why you would pick me, except maybe just to..." May turned away and looked at the far bank.

Luke took May by the shoulders and turned her to face him and he saw the tears flowing down her face.

"May, stop this crying. Your words hurt me as much as they hurt you. Come here."

He pulled her onto the bank of the stream. When the water settled he pointed to the surface and said, "Look. Your face is so beautiful. Your big dark eyes that look as if they are smiling all the time and your high cheekbones, pretty nose and chin, that is the most beautiful face I have ever seen. You hair is short and fits your head perfectly, but if you want to let it grow, I know you will be beautiful with curly hair. Now, look at your body. Your face takes my breath away, but your body does this to me." He looked down and May giggled.

"You complain about being too big. Every man should have that problem with his woman," he laughed.

"Am I your woman?"

"If you'll have me, then I'm your man."

He reached and gently kissed her.

"Your flat stomach and the hair of your...your— what do you call this wonderful place that gives me so much pleasure?"

"Jamee and Silver call their woman's place *a flower*. That is the word used on their world. Where I come from it is called many things by men but they weren't very nice."

"Flower. I like that and it's a good way to describe it. The hair of your flower is soft and silky with its tight curls."

He turned her around and told her to look into the water at her reflection again.

"May, you have beautiful legs, back, shoulders, and as for your rear, it is strong and smooth and your skin is so sleek and soft. The color is like dark cream and it's the second thing I saw that made me want you."

"What was the first?"

"Your eyes. But after I got to know you a little, your heart is what captured me completely. I would have loved you even if you weren't so beautiful, but I'm glad you are. I will love you forever. Even if you walk away right now, I couldn't change my heart."

May threw her arms around Luke and this time tears of joy flowed down her cheeks as she kissed his face.

"What Nuuna said about you looking like Billy is true, but Luke, I love you for you and the way you look at me makes me warm and happy."

She kissed him, laughed and pushed him into the water and then dove in after. They swam to the other bank and May got out and stood facing Luke.

She said in a soft voice, "Luke, I love the way you look at me."

She went to her clothes and started to dress. Luke was still in the water staring at May and then he shook his head as if to clear it and smiled as he got out of the water.

As they walked back, Luke said, "I think we should wait to tell everyone, since this is Silver and Jamee's time right now."

"Okay. But that doesn't mean we have to wait for everything, does it?" May said, smiling up at Luke.

"No. We'll find time to be alone."

Jamee, Billy, Silver and Red were sitting by the river when Flick flew in and landed on Billy's shoulder.

She said to Jamee, "This has been the best few days I've had in many years."

While she spoke her colors changed from silver and red to royal blue and yellow and then to creamy-brown and light green. Each set of colors moved up and down in unison.

Jamee laughed and said out loud, "Flick, I don't know what to think of you. You watch us making love and enjoy it almost as much as we do. What are the cream and green colors?"

"May and Luke." Then she flew over to Red's shoulder, pecked him on the cheek and flew off.

Jamee laughed and clapped in delight.

"What is it?" Silver asked.

"Luke and May have been busy while we've been here."

Billy asked, "What do you mean busy?"

Jamee gave him a look and then punched him.

"Oh, I don't believe it. Luke was so sure May was just a girl and too young for him."

Silver laughed and said, "Men! I wonder how May's exercises worked out."

They all broke into loud, happy laughter.

As Luke and May walked into the yard they separated a little and tried to look as if nothing had happened.

Nuuna ran and jumped into May's arms and kissed her and said, "Did you have a good swim?"

May blushed and said, "Yes, we did."

"Well, it's about time!" Nuuna jumped down and ran back to the house.

They rounded the back of the house. Sam and Little Dove sat relaxing on a bench. The look Little Dove gave May left no doubt that she knew what had happened. May blushed. Little Dove smiled and said, "There you two are! We've been holding supper for you. You both look very hungry."

Luke said, "I'm starving," and then headed for the kitchen with Sam.

Little Dove hugged and kissed May and whispered, "I'm so happy for you both." May looked at her and said, "Thank you, Mother. I'm happy, too."

After supper, Sam and Luke sat on the porch with Little Dove and Nuuna. May was in her room.

Sam was looking at Luke and finally asked, "Luke, I have never seen you look so content. What are you thinking about?"

"Nothing, Papa, but I am happy with all that has happened. The new family fits very well."

"When will you be off on one of your long trips?"

Luke looked at Sam and said, "I... I'm not sure. I may stay around for a while."

"Well, if that's what you want, you can help me with a lot of things around here. I'll keep you busy."

Little Dove said, "Luke has plenty to do without you thinking up things. I'm sure he has more on his mind than working with you."

She looked at Luke and saw him blush. She leaned over and kissed him on the cheek. May walked out with a large pack.

Sam said, "You're not leaving, are you, May?"

"I found my pack and I have some things I forgot to give you and Mother." She pulled out five bowls, forks, spoons and a few other items.

She handed Little Dove a bowl, large spoon and fork, saying, "I made this while we were in Green Hiding. I want you to have it."

Little Dove turned the bowl in her hands and saw the careful craftsmanship that had gone into making it. "This is beautiful! I have never seen wood like this. The craftsmanship is so perfect. I couldn't take it."

"Please, Mother. It would make me so happy. I have four other sets. I want to give Jamee and Silver one each and I have one for Nuuna when she gets married. I also will keep one for myself for when I get married." She looked up at Luke.

Nuuna said, "I hope that will be soon."

May blushed and said, "I found a tree that had fallen and used almost all the wood to make things. The wood is so strong it was hard to cut. I've made Billy's and my bows from it. The limbs near the top were so straight that they made perfect arrows."

Luke took the bowl from Little Dove and said, "I think I have seen one of the trees you talk about. It was very far away to the west. It doesn't have a name as far as I know."

"Well, it's time to name it. I think Luke should pick, so it will be known to the People," Sam said.

Luke held it up to the lamplight and turned it in his hand.

"I can think of only one name. We will call it a May Tree."

Sam, Little Dove and Nuuna clapped with delight.

Sam said, "I couldn't have thought of a better name. May Tree it will be from now on."

May hugged Little Dove, putting her head in the crook of her neck and cried.

"Now, May, it is a good name. Don't you like it?" Sam asked.

"Yes, I do, Father. You are all too good to me."

After a moment she reached in her pack, pulled out a knife sheath of the same wood and handed it to Sam.

"This is for you, Papa. I love you very much."

Sam looked at the prize and said, "I love you too, daughter."

She moved to Sam, kissed and hugged him and then kissed Nuuna, and turning to Luke, kissed him softly on the lips. She turned and ran to her room.

Little Dove stood and said, "Nuuna, you and Papa come with me. We are going to the bathhouse." They all left, leaving Luke to sit by himself.

May came outside to sit beside Luke and hold his hand.

Luke said, "I want to be alone with you. Will you go with me on a short trip to the prairie?"

"Yes! All I've thought about is being with you. I think a trip would be the right thing to do and you could show me some of this world. It will give you a chance to get to know me and be sure."

"There is nothing to think about. I've never been surer about anything. It will give us a chance to really get to know each other, and from what I've heard, you'll be teaching me a few things as well."

May felt the heat of anger rise within her and she asked, "What do you mean by that?"

"Billy told me you were a forest guide on your old world and very good at tracking and hunting. I would like to learn from you."

"Oh..." May's heat turned to embarrassment. "We can both learn from one another. Will we be staying in the Bookus groves?"

"They are the safest places to stay at night."

A new heat came to May, but she only kissed Luke and didn't speak.

"We'll leave right after Billy and Red get back."

The next day around noon Billy, Jamee, Red and Silver walked down the road toward the house.

Everyone was in the yard, just having finished the last touches to the new houses. When Jamee and Silver saw May they ran to her, hugged and kissed her and told her how happy they were.

May asked, "Happy about what?"

They laughed and both said, "About you and Luke."

May was stunned. "How do you know about that?"

Jamee said, "Flick told us all about what happened at the pool."

"Flick? You mean she was watching?"

"She loves to watch us *mate* so get used to it. And remember she is there to help you and warn you of danger, too."

Silver smiled and asked, "Did you try the things I taught you?"

May looked down at her boots but smiled and said, "Not until the very end. I forgot."

They all laughed as they walked into the yard. Everyone came to greet them and then led them to their new homes.

Sam announced, "These are for you until you decide to build your own places, which I hope won't be for a long time."

The family and neighbors gave them a tour of both houses and the sound of laughter filled the new homes.

"How can we ever repay you?" Red asked.

Sam smiled and said, "There will be times when you help do this for others."

Silver and Jamee both saw the beautiful bowls May had made sitting in the small kitchens and kissed her again. Everyone walked back out in the yard. Luke walked up to May with two packs and his bow.

"I want to show May some of the country around here."

Sam said, "What? She just crossed the Great Prairie! Let the girl rest before you drag her off."

May slung the pack onto her shoulders, kissed Luke hard on the lips and started off down the road with him.

"Oh... No one tells me anything," Sam said to the laughter of everyone.

Book II

CHAPTER 16

Luke and May traveled for three days, making their way slowly into the prairie. Luke showed May many different kinds of animals and plants that lived in the prairie. They stalked a prairie cat and watched as it made a kill. It was an exciting, nervous time for May. She was growing used to the vast openness of the prairie, but she worried that Luke would change his mind about her.

At night they stayed in rain berry clumps. Luke was reluctant to stop in the Bookus groves. He too was nervous about making love. He was so inexperienced and spent much of his time alone before he met May. He didn't want to lose her. Luke also didn't want May to think he only wanted her for her body.

Neither one wanted to disappoint the other. It turned out to be a content time filled with tension for them both as they talked and got to know each other.

May told of her life on Forest and Luke talked of growing up on Prairie. They grew closer and shared many things they would tell no one else.

One night May asked, "Luke, everyone in the village has a name relating to animals, many I've never heard of. Why is that?"

"The names are taken from the world the People were brought from. We have lost many of our customs, but these names were handed down from the first generation of the People who came here. We call many of the animals here by these names, but some we give new names because we want this world to be our own and not memories from the past."

"Why do you call yourselves the People? I heard the Volls call you Indians and Billy didn't seem offended by that."

"From our history we've learned that many people called us Indians, but the truth is that we were many different tribes and nations, not just one people. When our ancestors were brought here, we were of many different tribes, but no tribe was strong enough to live apart from the others. As the groups separated into different villages, it was decided we would all be called the People.

The word came from several of the plains people who were among the groups. The word Indian has no bad meaning to us but we prefer the People. That is also why we speak the same language as you do. We were so many different tribes it was decided that the language of the whites would be accepted."

"What do you call other kinds of people?"

"I only knew of two other kinds of people, the whites and blacks, before I met you, Nuuna, Jamee and Silver. I have met only a few black people. We call them the Black Nation.

"When we were first brought here there were as many Blacks as Indians, but it was decided by both groups that we would remain separate. The Blacks moved far to the east and we have little contact with them."

"Are they dark like me? Is that why they are called Black?"

"The few I have met are darker than you. They made it clear to me that they want to be left alone. They are a proud people and have some very different views on the way they live their life. They don't marry but they...

Someday you will meet them and can judge for yourself. You are similar in color but not in manner. You are much like Jamee, Silver and Nuuna and that pleases me."

May thought about this and said, "My eyes and face are close to theirs, but on my old world many people looked down on me because of my dark skin. I'm so happy the people of your village don't look at me like that. I feel so at home here."

"May, my love, it is not my village; it is our village. You are now one of the People." He took her in his arms and kissed her softly. "I love you. Tomorrow we will go to a Bookus grove."

"Oh, Luke, I have been so nervous about this, but I need you. I want to do the right things to make you happy. You called me my love."

The next morning they were up and moving at dawn. They hurried to be in a safe place where they could be alone. Traveling all morning they headed north and stopped briefly for a meal around midday. An hour later they saw a Bookus grove several miles ahead. They stopped long enough to shoot two large hoppers and gather herbs for their supper.

May was tense with excitement. As they walked she did the exercises Silver taught her. She ran all the things through her mind she could remember that they had talked about, not wanting to forget anything. May was trembling when they finally reached the grove.

Luke held her hand as he led her to a transit limb but turned and looked at her.

"What's the matter, May? You're trembling."

May looked shyly into his eyes and said, "I have a great need for you and I want to give you as much pleasure as I can."

Luke held her in his arms and said, "There is no need to worry about that. My need is as great as yours and just being near you gives me great pleasure."

May hugged him tightly and squeezed the tears from her eyes.

She took a deep breath and said, "I am the luckiest woman on this world! Let me go first."

She started to climb and heard Luke suck in his breath. She smiled, knowing he was looking at her as her hips swayed as she climbed. They climbed to the third level and entered the water cave. Luke dropped the firestone he had picked up on the ground and moved quickly to the back of the cave and jerked out his knife and rushed to cut a hole in the floor.

May said as she was tearing at her clothes, "Slow down, Luke. Don't hurt yourself!"

He finished, turned and saw May standing there nude. Wide-eyed, he stepped back and fell into the pool, fully clothed.

May laughed so hard she had to sit down. Luke, red-faced, climbed out of the pool and started to pull his wet clothes off.

"So you thought that was funny?"

He couldn't stop laughing as he went to May, picked her up and dumped her into the pool. He jumped in and they held each other while they laughed, but the laughter died as May felt Luke's hands massaging her body. She reached around and rubbed his back. Their lips came together in a heated kiss. They each took a piece of matting and began to clean each other.

They moved out of the pool and Luke lay May down on her back. He kissed her and moved beside her. His lips moved to the top of her head, kissing her short, soft hair and then moved down to her ear. As he kissed, his hot breath sounded in her ear and Luke felt her shiver. His hands felt the heat of her body. Luke kissed her forehead, eyes, cheeks and neck, his lips nibbling as he moved.

He kissed her softly, lingering in places he knew she would enjoy. Luke slowly moved down to her belly, tasting her and feeling her muscles ripple under his touch. Her taste was locked into his memory and a new aroma filled him with need.

May was almost mad with feelings. She tried to calm herself and was only just successful. Her mind filled with lights and sparks. She let go of her control. A surge passed through her body and it felt as if she were on fire as her release came. It lasted and lasted and then began to ebb and she finally released Luke's head.

"Oh! Oh, Luke, that felt so good!"

"You didn't let me finish, my love," Luke said with a chuckle. "Now relax and let me give you more pleasure."

He moved up and kissed her and turned her onto her back.

"Luke, let me... let me have a turn, please!"

"You will, my darling, but after me."

He started at the back of her neck, tasting her sweat and savoring it. He gently bit her neck and made a low growl that sent shivers through her. Luke nibbled her shoulders and kissed his way down to the small of her back, kissing the dimples there. His lips nibbled down the backs of her legs and sent more shivers through her as he kissed the back of her knees. He turned her over and moved to her. His need was almost more than he could control. They moved together in warm concert and Luke's release came quickly. As they looked into each other's eyes, they both felt the love and completeness of finding each other.

"Luke, my love, you are my first and the last man I'll ever want. I love you. How did you know to do all of that?"

"I just felt your body respond to what I was doing. And I got a few tips from Billy."

"I owe Billy a big kiss when we get back," May said with a laugh. They made love again and this time May took the lead.

They rose slowly and got back in the pool of cool, clear water.

Later, while the hopper was cooking they went up to the platform to watch the sunset. May felt so content and happy. She had no idea life could be this good.

Luke had a look of peace on his face and she asked, "What are you thinking about?"

He laughed and said, "I was just thinking that I have to give Silver a big kiss for teaching you those things. I never knew loving could feel so good."

As the sun set below the western hills, they both smiled at the life that put them together.

After eating they bathed again and May laid out a blanket for them to sleep on.

"Luke, there's something that has bothered me for a while. Our village is so peaceful, but there have been people taken from there to be made slaves of the Koros. I never heard anyone speak of that. Doesn't anyone care about those people or want to get them back?"

Luke sat down beside May and said, "Yes, we want them back and we have tried several times. People don't talk much about it because... well, I guess we are ashamed of our failures. We send out scouts often, trying to find a way to help them escape. That is what Billy was doing when he met you. The scouts usually spend a few days looking for a weakness or opportunity, but so far none has been found. The Koros keep the people in the main cave and no one can get past the entrance. There are people of the other tribes and a few blacks there as well and we would like to help them."

"I'm so glad you tell me all these things. You make me happy."

"I will do anything to make you happy. You make my heart sing." They lay down in each other's arms and were soon asleep.

The next day they moved to another water cave and relaxed. They made love, slept and ate Bookus nuts.

A few hours before sunset Luke said, "I'll go and get another hopper and herbs and vegetables. I won't be gone long."

May replied, "Okay. While you are gone, I'll tidy up and get some more Bookus nuts. Don't be gone long." Luke rose grabbing his bow and started out of the cave. "Luke, don't you think it would be better to put some clothes on? The rain berries have some big thorns."

Luke looked down and laughed.

It was dark and Luke had not returned. May had gone to the platform just after sunset but didn't see any sign of him. She waited for another hour, went to the water cave, dressed in her shirt and loincloth and then strapped on her long knife. As she reached the ground the first moon was rising, giving her just enough light to see where Luke had entered the tall grass. She could sense danger and there was something familiar about it. She moved through the grass opening all her senses. May approached a rain berry clump and a smell touched her that jerked her to a stop.

Trackers!

Now she moved ahead with all the skill she had learned on her old world.

Trackers were from Forest and now she remembered Billy saying that the Volls were bringing some here to find his people. Trackers lived by their own code and had no mercy. She had encountered them in the giant forest before. Two of them tried to rape her and only by playing along was she able to kill them and escape.

She did not enter the clump but circled about ten feet out. She found another trail barely noticeable leading in and a few feet away she found a clearer trail leading out. They were dragging something or someone. She could smell the scent of blood mixed with the foul smell of the trackers. There were at least two of them.

She had to put Luke out of her mind so she could bring herself down to a level of a hunting animal, but Luke was the love of her life. She stopped for a moment and forced her thoughts from him. She knew it was the only way to save him if he were still alive. No! He is alive! They wouldn't have dragged him away if he weren't. Trackers want information.

She took grass and surface dirt and rubbed her body with it. Taking another small clump of grass, she twisted it to bring out the oils and rubbed her inner thighs to mask her scent and then took some of Luke's blood and marked her face. Her mind was now that of a hunter. Taking her prey was her only unquenchable need. She moved with stealth, becoming a part of the prairie; only the whites of her eyes and the dull glint of her long knife gave any sign of her passing. She had traveled for perhaps a mile when she stopped, hearing the hiss of whispers.

Back in the village Little Dove was preparing for bed when a sense of fear coursed through her. She had goose-bumps all over her skin and knew something had happened.

"Luke!"

Then she heard a scream come from Nuuna's room. Sam was first in the room with his large hunting knife drawn. Little Dove was right behind him and she brushed past him and took Nuuna in her arms.

Sam put his knife away and asked, "What is it, honey?"

Nuuna said, "May needs help! She's in danger."

Sam started to rub her back in comfort and said, "It's only a bad dream, baby..."

Little Dove cut him off. "No! Luke is in trouble, too. We have to send help, now."

Sam had seen Little Dove's feelings turn out to be true, so he jumped up and ran to his bedroom.

He was throwing a few things into his pack and yelled at Little Dove, "Go get Billy and tell him to be ready to travel in five minutes."

When he finished dressing and strapping on his knives, Billy and Jamee came rushing in with their gear.

Sam looked up and said, "No, Jamee. This is something for Billy and me to do."

"Father, Jamee is going. She will help find them much quicker than either of us can."

Red and Silver came in with their packs.

Sam started to protest, but Little Dove put her hand to his lips and said, "Jamee and Silver are going."

Billy looked down at Nuuna and asked, "Little sister, do you know where May is?"

"She is somewhere in the prairie. I felt her moving through the tall grass like a dangerous, wild animal hunting something. She only had one thought and that was to kill."

Little Dove said, "Luke is hurt, but I don't know what happened. I don't know where he is."

Sam looked at her and said, "Go to Red Eagle and tell him to send out patrols. We may be in danger as well. We won't come back without them."

It was midnight when the five left the house at a run and headed north toward the prairie.

Jamee called out to Flick, "Flick, I need you to help find May and Luke."

Flick answered, "They were in a Bookus tree about two days run to the north, but I left them yesterday about midday. I will find them."

"What were you doing with them?"

"Watching them mate. May enjoys mating very much," Flick said as she flew off. In spite of the situation, Jamee smiled as she ran.

She ran beside Sam and Billy and said, "They were two days due north yesterday at noon."

Sam asked, "How do you know this?"

Billy answered, "Just trust her for now. We will explain when there is time."

May had moved to within twenty feet of the voices. In the moonlight she could see two trackers, but she could sense another one far off to her left. Her body was tense with the need to kill, but she had to know where Luke was. She could smell him and knew he was close.

One of the trackers whispered, "Jot, let's kill this one and finish what we were sent here for."

The other tracker, Jot, said, "We were sent for information and to find where these *Indeeans* live. This one will give me information."

"We questioned several at that big cave of the lizards and none would talk, even when we killed a few of them. Let's kill this one and be on our way."

Jot said, "I'll try once more. Go tell Jet to head back to the Volls and report we are close. The whites can bring up their army."

The tracker left and Jot moved to a figure lying crumpled in the grass. He grabbed the body by the hair and lifted him to a sitting position.

"Now, tell me what I want to know! Where is your village, red man?"

"I will tell you nothing," Luke said with a weak groan.

"Tell me or die. I want to know..."

Jot's head jerked up and he sniffed the air and swiveled his head around, looking. Something was out there. It was an animal drawn by the smell of blood.

He turned back to Luke and said, "You are of no use to me. I will find where you come from. It will only be a short delay, but you need not worry."

He drew his long knife, but before he could swing, a blade appeared out the front of his chest. He started to grunt, but it was cut off before all but a quick sound could escape. The blade traveled up his chest, cutting his windpipe, taking the warning from his lips. He was dead as he slumped to the ground.

May crouched down beside Luke and whispered, "Quiet now. I have come for you."

Luke looked up and said, "May?"

She put her hand over his mouth but knew it was too late. She dropped him and silently moved into the grass.

Jet followed the other tracker ten yards back. The tracker came into the area of flattened grass, searching the area with all his senses. He could smell blood and saw two bodies in the grass. As he turned to warn Jet his head separated from his shoulders. Jet had his bow ready and fired at the darkness that separated from the night. He then turned and ran. His job was to report back to his employers.

May grabbed the bow and quiver dropped by the other tracker, ran to a small rise and with the moon at her back, scanned the prairie. She could see the other tracker running full speed about fifty yards away. She pulled and released an arrow and sent a second arrow right behind the first. A third and fourth were sent slightly to the left and right of her running target. The first arrow took him high in the back. The second missed. The tracker jumped to the right when the first arrow hit him and the third arrow entered his back and passed through his heart.

May ran to where the third man went down and cautiously approached. He was dead. She listened for others that might be in the area and then felt the pain in her side. She looked down at the arrow shaft that protruded from her body just below her ribcage on her left side. It took her a moment to realize she had been hit.

She reached around behind her, grabbed the head of the shaft that protruded out of her back and broke it off. The pain shot through her and her knees buckled.

She grabbed the feathered end of the shaft and pulled straight away from her body, freeing the arrow. She cut clumps of long grass and wrapped it around the wounds trying to stop the flow of blood. She got to her feet and moved as quickly as she could back to where Luke was.

Luke lay with his hands and feet bound trying to clear his head. His right arm shot jolts of light and pain to his brain every time he tried to move. He raised his head and looked into the eyes of one of the men who had captured him. As he looked, he realized there was no body with the head. He heard a noise behind him and tried to rise, but strong hands held his shoulders and pushed him down to the ground.

"It's all right, Luke. It's May. I've come for you."

"May! Is it really you? How did you find me? What happened?"

May kissed his lips softly and said, "Yes, it's me. Now lie still and let me cut you free."

May cut his bonds and helped him sit up. He cried out softly, holding his right arm. May felt Luke's body, checking for injuries, and found that there was blood covering his back and left leg. She pulled off her shirt and quickly cut it into strips. The first strip she tied around her chest to hold the grass bandage and then went to work on Luke.

She bound his wounds as best she could and said, "Luke, we have to leave this place. Can you walk?"

Luke rose to his feet with May's help. He leaned against her and they started off towards the Bookus grove. About halfway there Luke collapsed.

May stood him up again, put him over her shoulder and lifted. The pain and his weight were almost more than she could bear, but all she could think about was Luke needed help and she had to get him someplace safe.

After what seemed like hours, Luke began to stir and weakly whispered, "Let me stand."

She put him down and he looked around and saw the Bookus grove about a hundred yards away. He supported May and began to walk. May started to collapse. He held her up and moved her to his back. She dropped her arms across his shoulders. He dropped down a bit, wrapped his left arm around her arms and lifted her off the ground. He walked slowly to the grove.

Luke reached the transit limb and sat her down. "May, I can't carry you up. Do you think you can climb?"

"Yes. I have to take care of your wounds."

She was totally spent, but she began to climb and Luke gave her what aid he could. They finally made it to the cave as the early morning sun shone in. They rested a moment, but both knew they had to clean and treat their wounds. Luke took May's hunting knife, cut her clothes off and began to do the same to himself.

May laughed weakly, "Luke, I think we better rest awhile before we make love."

He moved her to the pool and dipped water out of it to clean the two holes in her body. She had stopped bleeding, but the wounds were an angry red. He pulled matting from the wall, placed it over her wounds and wrapped it with a strip from their clothes.

After a few moments she sat up and began to clean and dress his wounds. His right arm was broken and she moved to her quiver and removed two arrows. She bound the arm using the cut arrows as splints. She reached into the pool, cupped water with her hands and gave it to Luke. He drank several handfuls and then passed out. She drank some water and lay down beside him; she too passed out.

May's dreams were terrible. Trackers were chasing her. They were naked and had great erections, yelling at her to stop so they could use her. She ran and ran but they stayed right behind her. Each tree she passed, she could see Luke cut nearly in half, draped across a limb. She wanted to stop, but she had to get away from the trackers. Then a softer darkness came and she felt coolness pass through her and knew she was safe. She slept a deep and peaceful sleep.

When she opened her eyes she saw Jamee and Sam looking down at her. Thinking she was still dreaming, she smiled and closed her eyes again. She could hear voices, but her sleep was so peaceful she ignored them.

Jamee looked at Sam and said, "She will be all right, Father. She just needs to rest."

Sam looked at Jamee with wet eyes and asked, "Are you sure? She looks so weak."

"Yes, Papa. She is strong and we got to them in time."

The next time May opened her eyes she saw Billy looking at her.

She said weakly, "Billy? Is that you? I thought I saw Jamee and Father."

Billy smiled down at her. "I see you. We're all here, May. You've had a bad time, but you're going to be fine now."

She tried to sit up, but Billy held her down. "Lie still, May. You've been hurt badly and you still have to rest."

She looked around frantically and cried out, "Luke! Luke! Where is Luke?"

Jamee ran to her and said, "Luke is fine. He's okay, May. Sam took him out to sit in the sun. He'll be back in a moment."

"You're sure he's okay? He was hurt."

"He is okay, May, I promise. Your wound was worse. The arrow must have been tipped in some kind of poison. You nearly died, but you are fine now."

From behind her she heard Luke say, "May? You're awake! Oh, my love, it is so good to see your beautiful eyes. I love you!"

"I see you. Kiss me, please."

Luke leaned over her, moving his still splinted right arm out of the way, and kissed her softly on the lips. May's right arm came around his neck and she pulled him close and returned the kiss.

"Okay. That's enough of that. I don't want you two hurting yourselves. There will be plenty of time for that later," Sam said laughing and dropped down beside May. "We were so worried about you, daughter."

May looked up into the tear-filled eyes of Sam and reached for him. Luke sat up as May pulled Sam down to kiss him hard on the lips.

"I love you, Papa."

Sam hugged her tight and said, "I love you too, girl."

"I'm not a girl, Papa."

Sam sat back and laughed. "Well, that's for sure. I got to see more of you than you know. When we found you two, you were both naked and holding each other, even though both of you were passed out. I thought you were... were... Never mind. When I saw you move my heart jumped in my chest!"

May smiled and said, "So your heart jumped when you saw me naked."

"Go ahead and make a joke, but just seeing you now with your eyes open is worth it."

"How long has it been since you found us?"

Billy said, "Four days and we didn't get here for at least a day after you were wounded."

May asked, "How did you know we were hurt and how to find us?"

"Mother and Nuuna woke us up in the middle of the night and said you were in trouble. We left right away and Flick led us to you."

"How did Flick know where we were?"

Jamee answered with a smile, "You know about Flick. She cares about all of us and she likes to watch us..." She looked over at Sam and he was listening intently to her.

He asked, "Watch you what?"

Jamee blushed and said, "Flick likes to watch us mate."

Sam's face turned red. "What? That bird watches you..."

Jamee said, "She watches you too, Papa."

"What? And then she tells you all about it?"

"Sometimes."

Sam got up and walked out of the cave as they all began to laugh.

Luke, never leaving May's side, said, "My love, it's so good to see you laugh. I was so worried, but I never gave up hope. That stuff Jamee used is amazing. I can't believe we've lived here all this time and didn't know this secret about the Bookus trees."

"How are you, Luke? Your wounds were bad."

"I'm fine, May. I've been up for two days and almost completely healed. I think I'll be ready to take this splint off tomorrow."

Red and Silver came in and Red said, "We've made a complete circuit around the grove and... May! You're awake."

They ran over to her, knelt, kissed and touched her.

Silver said, "May, you had us worried, but to see your eyes open..."

Red turned to Billy and said, "We didn't see any signs of anyone in the area."

May said, "I killed all three of them. They were trackers from my world and they were sent out to find where we live and get information. That's why they didn't... kill Luke right away. They were working for the Volls, but I think they are a long way to the north."

Luke said, "I can't believe they took me so easy. I never heard them until they stabbed me in the leg and knocked me out."

May said, "You've never met anyone like them. They are trained from the time they are small children to track and kill. It's all they know. I only got close because they were busy with you."

Billy said, "May, I have seen you hunt. I've never seen anyone move the way you do."

"I had a reason for finding them," she said looking at Luke.

Jamee brought her a bowl of broth and May drank it down.

Jamee said, "May will be ready to travel tomorrow, but we'll have to take it slow."

Sam came back in looking around. "Where is that bird? I have a few things to say to her."

Jamee said, "Father, her name is Flick and you must remember that she saved Luke and May's life. No matter what her bad habits are, she cares about us."

Sam glared at Jamee for a moment, then looked at the floor. "I guess you're right, but I don't like the idea of her watching me and Little Dove."

Silver gave Jamee a questioning look and Jamee explained what had happened.

Silver laughed. "Father, don't let it bother you. There is nothing you can do to stop her, unless you stop doing that."

Sam gave Silver a hard stare and then said, "I'm hungry."

By the next morning May was up and looking much better. They packed up and headed south at a slow pace. It took them three days to make it back to the village. Little Dove and Nuuna were waiting at the edge of the prairie.

When they saw the group approaching they ran to meet them.

Little Dove hugged and kissed May and Luke, examining them carefully and then exclaimed, "You're not hurt! I saw you both in my mind and you were terribly injured."

Sam said, "They were wounded, but they are okay now. Let's go to the house and Luke can tell you as we walk."

After Luke explained, Little Dove moved to Jamee and asked many questions.

They reached the house and Little Dove took Jamee aside and said, "This thing you have discovered about the Bookus trees must be told to the elders. We will go tomorrow and talk with them."

Jamee nodded her agreement.

After everyone had cleaned up and eaten, the men went out on the front porch to talk.

Billy said, "I think we will have to go after these trackers. Never before has anyone gotten this close to our lands. The Koros leave us alone because they fear us. The Volls have just started coming in numbers and it will take them a long time to find us without the help of the trackers. I think these trackers are our greatest danger."

Red said, "Billy, there is something else. As long as there is Verdance, the Volls will continue to come, and once they find a way to use it as explosives we will be in great danger."

Luke said, "There is another matter as well. May asked me questions about the captives at the mine, and the more I think about it, the more ashamed I am. We must find a way to free them."

Sam spoke up. "We've been watching for a way to get our people back and there seems to be no way to do it safely."

"I agree, but maybe it's time we took some chances. The more I think about it, the angrier I get. How can we allow our people or any of the others to be held as slaves?"

Red finally spoke up. "I have to agree with Luke. I've seen people on the other worlds treated like slaves and I have never understood why the people put up with that kind of treatment. Yes, the Volls are a trained fighting force, but they are always outnumbered. It's only through intimidation and brute force that they control people. It sounds much the same with the Koros. How many people are at this mine?"

Sam replied, "We don't know. Over the years a hundred or so from all three of the People's villages have been taken, but there is no way to know how many there are from these other worlds."

Red said, "From what I heard, there may be as many as three hundred sent from the other worlds."

Billy said, "That's as many as our village. We should bring this to the elders and start trying to come up with a plan, even if it means taking risks."

The next morning Sam, Little Dove and Jamee went to see the elders. Sam spoke to them of a need to meet and discuss what the village might be facing. It was agreed that a meeting would be held that night. He left and then Little Dove and Jamee presented this new discovery of the healing powers of the Bookus trees.

After listening to Jamee and hearing the words of Little Dove, Red Eagle said, "You have found something that can help the whole village! You must talk to the healer and help him decide how best to present this new medicine. We must keep in mind that the Bookus groves are important to all the people of Prairie and we must not harm the trees. They have always provided a place of safety and nourishment for our people."

Little Dove and Jamee agreed and went off to find the healer.

That night as the elders and many of the hunters gathered, the men of Sam's family presented their ideas. The elders talked among themselves for a while and then came back to the group.

Red Eagle said, "There is much to think about, but we have agreed that these trackers are a great danger to us. Luke, do you have a plan for these people?"

"I have a few ideas, but May is the one who can help us with a way to deal with them. Let me talk to her and then I will give you an answer."

The elders nodded and Red Eagle said, "Take a few days to think about this and when you are ready come back to us. As for the people captured by the Koros and the ones brought here by the Volls, there is no easy answer, but I too think we have let this go on for too long. We sit in our village, thinking we are safe and we shouldn't do anything to endanger that. I think the time has come to take action. We will think on this as well. If any of the hunters have thoughts on this, come and speak to us. For now the meeting is over."

As Sam, Luke and Billy walked back to the house, Luke said, "Father, there is something I want to tell you. I want to marry May."

"Have you asked her? You don't need my approval, but if you seek it, you most certainly have it! May is a part of this family and will always be, but for you to take her as your wife would please your mother and me."

Luke smiled and said, "I haven't asked her but I am sure she will say yes. We want to be together as man and wife."

Billy said, as he clapped Luke on the shoulder, "You better hurry and ask. There are a lot of hunters who have had their eyes on her."

That night Luke took May to a quiet spot. He took her hands in his and kissed her. "May, I don't want to be away from you. I have loved you since I first looked into your eyes. Will you marry me and make me the happiest man on Prairie?"

"Are you sure, Luke?"

"I can't imagine my life without you. I need you and love you with all my heart."

May's heart was so full the words would only come in a whisper. "Yes, Luke, I will marry you. I will love you forever."

The next afternoon May was still recovering from her wounds and needed to relax, so the women and Nuuna went to the bathhouse. They were all excited for Luke and May and the thought of another wedding soon.

Little Dove examined May's arrow wounds. "You will have small scars but they won't take away from your beauty. Your skin is so soft and the color is so rich."

"Mother, I hope I will have a body like yours after I've had children. You are so beautiful."

They moved to the tub and Nuuna sat in May's lap. "When I saw you in my dream you were very scary. You were like a big cat. Even your mind was like an animal's. Were you frightened when you went after those men?"

"No, Nuuna. When I saw Luke's blood and the trail left by the trackers dragging him off, I knew the only way to get him back was to go after them. I had to take everything from my mind except the need to get what was mine. I was trained to clear my mind, but this was different. They took the one I love and I wasn't going to let that happen. I'm sorry if I frightened you."

"Oh, I wasn't afraid for me. It made me feel safe thinking that you would do the same for me."

Jamee said, "I'm so happy you are getting married soon. Flick said you enjoyed being with Luke very much. Did you have any trouble with the exercises?"

May blushed and looked over at Little Dove bashfully.

Little Dove said, "There is no reason to be shy. When love comes to two people, you must express it in many ways. I am happy for you and Luke."

May said, "I never really got a chance to try them. My mind was filled with so much pleasure, it would kind of shut down. Luke didn't seem to mind, though. I will use them soon, I hope."

Little Dove asked, "What exercises are you talking about? Do you think it is something an old woman could learn?"

Silver said, "Mother, I don't think you need any help. I see the way Father looks at you. He loves you completely."

After bathing, Jamee hurried off to see the healer. They were to go to the nearest Bookus grove and collect some of the matting. The healer was concerned that taking too much of the matting might harm the trees. Billy and another hunter would go with them for protection.

Little Dove and Silver lay May on a table in the bathhouse and began to massage her to help get her strength back. Little Dove sent Nuuna out to play. She applied aromatic oil to May's skin and began to knead her legs and feet. Silver worked on her neck and shoulders.

As they worked, Little Dove said, "I want to know about these exercises. I have seen the looks on Billy and Red's faces after you have made love and I would like to see that look on Sam."

Silver began to explain about muscle control and the exercises that would make the muscles stronger.

"The more you practice, the stronger you get and the longer you control it. Give me your hand, Mother."

She took Little Dove's hand and placed it just above her flower and began to contract her muscles. Little Dove could feel the movement inside Silver's body. She moved her hand down and covered Silver's flower and her eyes widened.

"I want to know this! I want to add something to Sam's pleasure, and mine."

Silver said, "If you do this to Father, you will put a big smile on his face."

They all laughed and then, as they continued to massage May, Silver explained the technique.

At supper that night Red was looking at Little Dove's face, wondering where he saw that look before. It leaped out at him and he jumped back, causing his chair to bang to the floor. His head jerked around to look at Silver and he could see the smile on her face.

Sam said, "What's the matter, Red? Why is your face so red?"

Red calmed himself and looked into the hard stare of Little Dove and said, "Nothing. I...I just bit my tongue."

He continued to look at Little Dove. He saw the concentration come back to her face and he started to laugh. Soon Little Dove, Silver, May and Red were caught up in the laughter and couldn't control it. They all got up and went outside to try and calm down.

Sam said. "Now what's going on? Why am I always the last one to know anything? Hey! What's so funny?"

Luke looked as bewildered as Sam and said, "I know how you feel, Father. It's like they have their own language and we can't speak it."

Soon the four came back in, a little calmer, and continued eating. Red refused to look at Little Dove and concentrated on eating. The women all smiled but said nothing.

Sam looked at Nuuna and asked, "Do you know what's going on?"

Nuuna replied, "Yes, but I can't explain it."

This brought more laughter and finally Sam rose in disgust and walked out.

That evening Luke talked to May about going after the trackers. "I will take a few hunters and go to the camp of the Volls. We should be able to find these trackers and deal with them."

May said, "The only way to deal with them is to kill them. There is no other way, and you are not going anywhere without me! You need to understand. In this thing I am the only one with experience and you will have to listen to me. You are my man and in almost everything I will not go against you, but in this you will listen to me." Luke looked into her big, dark eyes and saw no room for argument.

He said with a smile, "You are my woman, and you will do as I say!"

He saw the heat rise to her face and quickly said, "You will always give me your opinion and we will work together. I love you with all my heart and we will protect each other."

As quickly as the heat appeared it vanished and she was in his arms kissing him.

Luke asked, "What was so funny at supper?"

She smiled up at him and said, "I'll show you in a few days, my love."

The next morning Luke and May went to Red Eagle and told him about their plan to go after the trackers.

Red Eagle said, "It is a good plan and it is something I have thought about. I think we should go out with two parties. One will deal with these trackers and also hurt the Volls if they can. The other party will go to the mine and try to free the people and perhaps deal with this Verdance as well. Decide who you would like to go with you, Luke. You have at least four more days."

"I have already thought about two hunters I would like with us. I will be in charge until we get close, but then May will take over."

Red Eagle looked at May and smiled. "There has never been a woman on a raid like this, but that has changed. I will talk to the other elders, but I agree with this. May has proven herself with bravery and trust. Go and talk to the hunters you have picked."

Around midday Billy and Jamee returned from the prairie. They walked into the kitchen and stopped short, looking at the concentration on Little Dove's face.

Jamee smiled and Billy said, "Mother!"

Little Dove looked sharply at Billy and said, "Hush. This is none of your concern."

Billy blushed but said nothing.

Little Dove asked Jamee, "How did it go with the healer?"

"He is a good man and knows quite a bit about the Bookus trees. We tested several trees, pulling down a lot of matting, and each time after we took several bags full the walls would harden. After that happened we could remove no more matting, even when we went to the other water caves on the same level.

"The healer took the matting with him and will study how long it will stay fresh and aid in healing. He will go back every few days and check to see if the tree repairs itself."

Billy said, "Jamee and I will be leaving soon to go back to the Koro mine."

Little Dove looked at them but said nothing. She knew how dangerous it would be to go into that territory, but she also knew that it needed to be done. It was hard to think of losing one or both of them, but she was proud of them.

After supper Little Dog came to the house to talk to Red.

When Red and Little Dog were sitting outside he said, "Red, are you going to free the people at the mine?"

"Yes, I will go."

"I want to go with you. A few of us have been talking about this and we think we can help. We've all been to the mines before and we also have an idea for you to think about. I think we should..."

"Wait. I want to get the others. They will want to hear this."

Red went to the house and soon returned with Billy, Jamee, Silver and Sam.

Red said, "Johnny has an idea about freeing the people at the mine and I think we should all hear what he has to say."

Billy stood in front of Little Dog.

They had never been friends and he wondered why he had come to offer help.

"Little Dog, I am surprised to see you here. Have you come to challenge Red again or show us how much you dislike my family? What trouble have you brought with you?"

Johnny stood and gave Billy a hard stare, but then he nodded his head. Before he could speak, Silver said, "Billy, we should give Johnny a chance to speak. He is a friend and I would like to hear what he has to say."

Billy looked at Silver and Red and then turned to Johnny. "You're right. I apologize, Little Dog. We have never been friends, but you are a good hunter and I have no right to speak as I did. I would like to hear what you have to say."

Johnny smiled and sat back down. "You're right, Billy. I have behaved badly in the past and I was wrong, but now, after hearing your words at the meeting and becoming friends with Red and Silver, I want to help. Several of the hunters want to go with you and help free the people at the mine. We've talked about this and I wanted to tell Red what we know."

They sat down as Johnny began.

"We have all traveled to the mine on several treks and what we've found is there may be a way to get a large group of people away and into the mountains quickly. I had thought that would be the main problem after they are free. We will have to move them away from the mine by an easy path because I think they'll be in very poor condition.

"Along the road to the mine about a mile away there is a narrow bridge that leads south across a steep chasm. On the other side of the bridge there is a trail that is not too steep and leads into some old caves. Bear Killer has been in several of the caves and in one he found a tunnel that leads through the mountains and comes out near the foothills far to the west."

Billy said, "This is good information."

Johnny continued, "When Bear Killer was there he saw no signs of anyone passing that way. We can make our way to Green Hiding and rest before we bring them here."

Jamee asked, "What about getting into the mine? Do you have any thoughts on that?"

"No one has ever gotten close to the entrance except to watch it from higher up on the mountain. Once we are there we can come up with an idea."

Sam spoke for the first time, "You understand this raid will be dangerous and some may not return from it."

"Yes, Walking Bear, I understand, but it is in my heart to help get the people away from the slavery they have been put under. Jason Bear Killer, Tommy Uteta and I want to go with this raiding party."

Billy again spoke, "Little Dog, I want you to know that Jamee and Silver will be going and because of some special skills they have they will be telling us what to do at times. Do you have a problem with that?"

Johnny smiled at Jamee and Silver. "I have been witness to a little of what Silver can do and we've all heard of Jamee's way of chopping wood. No. I will do whatever they say."

Red said, "Their abilities are greater than what you have heard. I trust them both with my life and it may come that you must do that as well."

"Red, my friend, your word is all I need. I will not cause trouble on this raid. I know I have been a problem in the past, but that time is gone. If I am allowed to go, you won't be sorry, I promise."

Billy stepped up to Little Dog, put out his hand and said, "Johnny, I welcome you as a friend and hunter. It will be good to have you with us."

Johnny said with a smile, "That is the first time you have called me by my first name. This is a day I will never forget."

Jamee and Silver stepped to Johnny and both kissed him on the lips. "Welcome, Johnny."

Johnny laughed and said, "It won't be hard to tell me what to do with kisses from beautiful women."

They laughed and agreed to gather everyone together to talk over the plans.

At dawn the next morning Luke and May were married in the same manner as the other two couples. The celebration was a happy time for the village. There was a great deal of tension about the coming events and the people let their joy dispel it for that day and night. As the men deposited Luke at the cabin by the river, they all joked and laughed.

Daniel called out, "Hey, old man! We'll check on you in two days to see if you are still alive."

Someone yelled, "If you need any help, just call out to one of us young men!" They left Luke on the porch of the cabin and laughed and whooped as they walked away.

Luke entered the cabin to the glow of soft light from a single lamp. His breath caught in his throat as he looked at May lying nude on the bed. She had rubbed aromatic oils on and her skin shown like polished obsidian in the light.

"I need you to rub my back and legs with this oil, husband. There were a few places I couldn't reach."

She rolled over, lifting her hips seductively and looked back at Luke. Luke stood transfixed at the sight before him. Her body was covered in the soft glow, with darkened shadows along her contours.

Her big, almond-shaped eyes, the curve of her neck and the lines of her strong back were a sight to behold. Long muscled legs led up to the beautiful mounds of her rear and reminded him of a valley running out to the golden mounds of the prairie hills.

"You are the most beautiful woman I have ever seen. I still can't believe you are my wife. I will love you forever."

"And I love you with all my heart. You are the only man I have ever wanted and the only man I will ever need. Now come and do as you are told," she said with a laugh.

He started to walk over to her, but she said, "The clothes go outside. We won't need any for a few days."

Luke tore at his clothes, opened the door and dropped them on the porch. He rushed to the bed, turning May over, kissing her and caressing her.

May broke the kiss, looking into his green eyes and in a husky voice said, "Oil, darling."

She turned back over and Luke looked down at her. His hand shook as he picked up the small bottle of oil. He tried desperately to calm his mind and was only partially successful.

Luke poured a few drops and began to rub the oil on the soft skin of her neck and back. It brought out a golden tone to her skin. He put oil in the palms of his hands and moved to her feet and then her ankles, calves and the back of her knees. Luke's hands gripped and kneaded her rear and then parted her cheeks and applied oil in the soft crease. It was almost more than he could stand as he watched May put her head onto the pillow and let out a soft sigh, enjoying the sensation his touch gave her.

Their loving was soft and gentle, pressing, urgent and so very complete. May showed Luke the exercises she had been practicing just for him.

"I never dreamed something like that was possible! We didn't move but it was... it was so good."

"Now you know the secret that we were laughing about."

Luke, through his hazy mind, thought about what May just said. His eyes popped open and he looked at her. "You mean my mother is going to..."

May laughed and said, "Yes. Papa is going to be a happy man very soon."

The next two days were filled with love and lovemaking for Luke and May. Sometimes during the day Billy would stop by to let them know about the planned raids, but he stayed for only a few minutes, not wanting to disturb their wedding days. Luke and May talked about the coming events and knew there would be danger. It made their short time together all the more intense.

Around midmorning of the fourth day they returned to their family's house. There was a great deal of preparation going on. Everyone was busy packing materials into backpacks.

Luke asked, "When do we leave?"

Billy said, "Not for a few days, but we want to make sure we take enough to help anyone we free. You will travel much lighter and with a small group. Two hunters have requested to go with you, but the final decision is yours and May's. The two who have asked to go are Daniel Quiet Badger and a long-hunter called Apache Joe."

Luke said, "Daniel will be a good man to have with us, but I must talk to Joe first. He is a dangerous man and if he is willing to listen to May, he will be a great help to us. We'll go and talk with him."

Before they left Little Dove came out, smiling with satisfaction and telling everyone lunch was ready.

She ran down the steps and hugged and kissed Luke and May. "I am so happy for you both. How was your time together, Luke?"

Luke looked at her, blushing, and said, "It...was... a happy time, Mother."

They all sat down to eat just as Sam entered the kitchen. He was smiling so big, he looked a little odd. As he sat down, Luke chuckled and then began to laugh. Everyone looked at him and then at Sam's face and they too began to laugh.

Sam looked around and said, "What is the matter? Haven't you ever seen a happy man before?"

This caused them to laugh even harder until everyone except Little Dove got up and went outside.

Sam looked at Little Dove and said, "Where is that damn bird? Has she been talking?" Little Dove came around the table and kissed Sam tenderly. "No, honey, Flick hasn't said a word. It's your smile that gave it away."

"Well... well...I don't care, Honeybee. Last night was so good, I don't care who knows, but they better not talk about it!"

After everyone calmed down and came in to eat, nothing more was said, but Sam ate his entire meal while blushing.

Luke and May approached Apache Joe's cabin cautiously. Luke had warned May that Joe was one of the best woodsmen he knew but was unpredictable. As they approached through a clump of bushes Joe dropped from a limb with a scream right above May. He grabbed for her and she lunged to the side, grabbed his shirt and had him on his back, with a small dagger she carried penetrating the skin of his neck a fraction of an inch. Joe looked up into the deadly stare of May and released the knife in his hand.

Luke touched May's shoulder and pushed her back slightly and said, "May, I would like you to meet Apache Joe. Joe, this is my wife, May."

Joe sat up holding his hands palms out and said, "Hello, May. I guess everything I heard about you is true."

"What have you heard?"

"I talked to Sam and a little girl called Nuuna. She told me not to test you because I wouldn't like it. She also said you had the heart of a great cat when you needed it. I believe her now."

He stood and offered his hand to her.

May put the dagger away, took his hand and finally smiled. "Did I pass your test?"

"Yes, ma'am, you did and I won't ever do that again, except maybe when you teach me how you did it."

They followed Joe to his cabin and sat outside. Joe offered them a drink made from an odd-looking fruit.

May said, "This is delicious. What kind of fruit is it?"

"It comes from an Apache tree. I found it far to the west of here."

Luke smiled and said, "I guess you gave it its name."

"Yes, I did. The fruit is hard with a green skin and it keeps for a long time."

Luke said, "Someday I'll have to show you a May Tree; no fruit but the best wood I've ever seen."

They discussed what they were going to do and Luke asked, "Joe, will you have any problems doing what May tells you when we go after these trackers?"

Joe looked at May and with an awkward smile. "No. I would like the first time I ever let anyone tell me what to do to come from a beautiful woman. Are these trackers as good as you?"

"They are better. They have spent their whole life doing this one thing and they never give up."

"This sounds like it will be interesting. Who else is going?"

Luke replied, "Only Daniel Quiet Badger will come with us."

Joe said, "I know Daniel and his father. They are good people, but do you think he will kill without question?"

"I don't know, but after May talks to him, I think he will know the dangers."

Joe looked at May and said, "I'll be ready to go whenever you say."

Red Eagle called a meeting of the entire village the next day. When everyone had gathered he stepped forward and said, "It has been decided that we will send out two small parties. One will go to the Koros' mine and free the captives; the other will go to find these trackers. The party going after the trackers will also cause as much trouble for the Volls as they can and then return.

"It is also decided that we will send out runners to the other villages and ask for their aid. If they agree with what we are doing, they will join two large parties that will follow the first two. Our parties will follow four or five days behind and will support the first two parties. We will leave enough hunters behind to protect the village and the women will make ready to take care of any people we bring back.

"The group that goes to the mine will be led by Billy Running Wolf and Jamee Soft Dove. Jim Travis, Silver Dove, Johnny Little Dog, Jason Bear Killer and Tommy Uteta will go with them. The group that will go after the trackers will be led by Luke Deer Catcher and May Golden Dove. Daniel Quiet Badger and Apache Joe will go with them. Let all our prayers go with them and bring them safely home again."

The next morning May went with Luke, Joe and Daniel into the forest. She spent the day talking to them about how to deal with the trackers. They discussed all the things they thought might happen.

Near the end of the day May said, "Today we have all learned much. We must be ready to use this knowledge when we go." She looked directly at Daniel and spoke, "Daniel, I know you are a good, strong man who knows more about the prairie than I do, but you must understand and not question the fact that these trackers must die. We will not try to capture them. They will give us no information. Their whole way of life is based on secrets and nothing we can do to them will make them talk. We will not try to injure them because if they recover they will come after us and will not stop until we are dead or they are. We must kill them. At a distance would be better, but if you have to fight close up, give them no quarter. Do you agree with what I've told you?"

Daniel looked around at the others and said, "I have never met a man I could not reason with, but I won't disagree with you. I will do as you tell me, May."

Joe said, "I will keep Daniel close to me. We can watch each other's back."

Luke stood and said, "We will travel light, only taking dried meat, blankets, weapons and matting from the Bookus tree. If you are injured, use the matting and get away quickly. The trackers' weapons may be tipped with a poison so get as far away as you can if you are wounded. We will find you. After we find them we will decide what to do, but we will not leave these trackers alive."

Billy and his group also spent the day preparing and talking about what they would do.

"We know where the captives are but not how many. I am thinking one of us might have to go into the mine. I would like to find a way to keep the Koros from mining the Verdance. If we can do that, then maybe the

Volls will have no more use for this world and they will leave."

Johnny said, "Once we reach Green Hiding, I will go ahead of you and look for a way to enter the mine and a way to get out. I will find you when you arrive."

Jamee said, "That won't be necessary, Johnny. We will find you."

She looked at Billy and he spoke for her. "Jamee has a special way with birds. They let her know what is around us and one little bird can find things Jamee asks her to find. You must all trust Jamee's judgment. You must also trust Silver's judgment and abilities. We will work together on this because I want us all to come out of it alive."

The other hunters agreed, without questions.

It was a good group. Billy continued, "We will travel fast, but we will each have a heavy load to carry. We will leave our supplies at Green Hiding and rest for a day. Johnny will continue on to the mine without rest."

As they rose to leave, Billy asked Johnny to stay behind. "Jamee will show you something to help you, but I would like your promise to keep what she shows you a secret."

"I promise."

Jamee stepped up to Johnny and said, "I want you to meet a friend of mine. This is Flick." Flick appeared out of nowhere sitting on Jamee's shoulder. She was bright yellow and she was looking at Johnny. Jamee continued, "Flick can talk to you through colors. If you are in danger, she will look like this."

Flick turned a shocking red. Johnny's eyes widened but he showed only interest. Jamee continued to explain what different colors meant and soon Johnny felt he could follow everything Flick had to say.

Jamee said, "You will have to trust Flick. She won't let you down. She will understand everything you say to her, so ask questions until you understand what she is telling you."

"I will listen and trust this beautiful bird— I mean Flick. How can she stay hidden? Her colors are so bright they will be seen from far away."

Flick flew to Johnny's shoulder, turned a light blue, nodded to Johnny and then seemed to disappear, still sitting on his shoulder. She then reappeared and flew to Billy's shoulder, pecked him on the cheek and flew off.

Jamee said. "Flick likes you. She has given you the light blue color you saw. That color will be only for you."

Johnny smiled with pride and nodded.

The next day was spent finishing the packing and preparing their weapons, but it was also a time for the family to be close. Sam double-checked everything and touched his children often. Little Dove hovered close and they would often catch her looking at them. At one point Red picked her up in his arms and sat her in his lap, away from the others, talking quietly to her. Little Dove put her forehead on Red's neck and listened.

As night fell, they had a good supper and went into the front room to continue talking and just to be close. Sam got Billy and Luke to help move the furniture outside to give them room to lie down together. Little Dove brought padding and blankets. Jamee, Silver, May and Nuuna cuddled around Sam and the brothers around Little Dove. They talked late into the night. Nuuna's eyes never left Red.

May asked, "What is it, Nuuna?"

Nuuna would not answer but only snuggle close to her.

CHAPTER 17

The new day began and the first wash of color appeared as the other members of both groups met at Sam's house and waited. The family came out on the porch, said their goodbyes and they turned to go.

Sam said, "You have already made us proud! Do what you are sent to do and return to your family. Little Dove and I love you all very much." And then he raised his voice so the others could hear. "We are proud of you all! Our prayers go with you my brothers and with my children."

Tears shone from Little Dove and Sam's eyes as they stood watching until the group was out of sight. Nuuna had her face buried in Little Dove's skirt. The two groups walked out of the valley and many young hunters stood on the hilltops; they whooped and raised their bows, watching the parties head into danger.

The groups separated as they entered the prairie, with waves and complete silence. Billy's party headed northwest and Luke's due north. Jamee sought out a Great Eagle and through its eyes checked the prairie for danger. She then had the great bird fly low over the heads of Luke's party and then brought it back to their party and did the same. Billy looked at her and smiled.

Jason Bear Killer said, "This is a great sign! Our success is promised to us by the Great Eagle!"

Jamee smiled back at Billy. Billy's party moved as quickly as it could with the stores they carried on their backs, stopping each night at a Bookus Grove.

On the tenth day they were close to Green Hiding. Johnny separated from the party about midday, giving his large pack to the others.

He said, "I will look for you in two or three days' time. Rest well. We will need all our strength to bring the people out. I will be near the mouth of the mine."

He left them at a run. They struggled with the extra weight, but near sundown they found the trail leading down into Green Hiding. It was exciting to return to the beautiful valley and Jamee wanted to be alone with Billy.

That night after they ate Billy said, "Jamee and I will travel into the valley tonight and in the morning look for another way down the cliffs. It may be that we will come out of the mountains further west of here and if we can find an easy way down it will be better for the people. We should return before sundown tomorrow."

Jason said, "Be careful. There is a big meta bear that lives in this valley. I have met him once before."

Billy and Jamee nodded, picked up two packs and left.

They traveled for a few hours and then found a small cave in the cliff face and lay together, holding each other. Each drifted to sleep in each other's arms and woke the same way the next morning. They moved along the cliff face for several hours.

Billy said, "There is a cut in the cliff a few hundred yards ahead. It may be what we are looking for."

The cut was soon in sight. It had an easy climb almost all the way to the top of the cliff. The trail was about three feet wide and turned back upon itself several times. About twenty feet from the top the trail narrowed, turned left and ended. Billy made the easy climb up the cliff face and then motioned for Jamee to follow. When she stood on top of the cliff she looked down.

The trail was invisible where it turned to the left. It looked like a dead end.

Billy said, "If we had come on this from the top, we would have never seen a way down. I think it will do well to get a large group of people down into the valley."

"We can bring ropes here tomorrow and secure them for our return. We can hide them here behind these boulders. Can you find this spot if we come at night?"

Billy looked around and mentally marked the area. "Yes, my love. Let's get back to the others and tell them about this."

They climbed down and made their way to the valley floor.

While they walked back through the valley, Jamee pulled Billy toward the river.

"There's something I need at the river."

When they came to the bank of the river, Jamee started removing her clothes and said, "I thought I could wait until this is over, but I need you now!"

Billy hastily pulled his clothes off and pulled Jamee into his arms. "I have been holding back because I thought you wanted to wait but I need you, too."

They made quick, hurried love and then swam in the river. Jamee pressed herself against him and whispered in his ear, "Billy, don't ever think you have to wait. I am yours any time you want me."

He kissed her and smiled. "That might be embarrassing if I made love to you any time I wanted you. Every time I look at you I want you."

They dressed and headed back to the cave.

When they arrived they told the others about the cut they had discovered.

Jason said, "That will be much better than bringing them all the way around. While you were gone I drew a map of this area and where we are going. Show us where the cut is." Jason had used a piece of soft red rock and drawn a detailed map.

"Tommy told me about the area where he has been around the mine and I added it to my knowledge."

"You did a good job drawing this."

Billy looked over the area of Green Hiding and pointed to where the cut was located. Jason added it to the map.

Jamee looked at it and pointed to the road leading to the mine. "I don't know what we will find, but I saw a big section of the road fall into the valley as we were leaving."

Billy said, "When we meet up with Johnny, he'll know more and then we can decide what to do. We will leave early tomorrow, so everyone get some rest tonight."

Red and Silver went out but returned just as everyone was eating.

Red asked, "Why don't the Koros come down into this valley? It seems like the perfect place to live."

Tommy replied, "I'm not sure why they don't come here, but no one has ever seen a Koro close to this place. I think it might have to do with the trees. I have watched Koro patrols out on the prairie walk all the way around the Bookus groves even when it would have been much quicker to pass through."

Jason added, "Tommy's right. I've seen several patrols avoid going into the groves. I didn't give it much thought at the time. We have always stopped at the Bookus groves and I have never heard of any hunter seeing Koros near them."

Red said, "That is good to know, but we must remember; if there are Volls after us, I don't think the trees will worry them."

Billy said, "I plan on keeping the people here in the valley for three or four days and hopefully by then we will meet up with the larger party Red Eagle is sending out. If we do meet any Volls, we will have to fight. A few of us will have to try and lead them away from the main body of people."

Silver asked, "How many people do you think there are in the mine?"

Billy said, "When Jamee and I were there we only saw about fifty, but there may be as many as three hundred. If we stay here for three days with them, then we can make weapons for the people that are strong enough to use them."

That night as they lay down together Jamee quietly said to Billy, "Luke and May are close to the Volls camp but that's all I can tell. They are not moving around."

CHAPTER 18

Apache Joe had led the way across the prairie. They made good time and stopped in Bookus groves to rest and eat. Daniel proved to be quick and lithe for a man his size. He moved leaving a trail that was all but invisible. Joe took them on a winding route, changing directions often but always making for a point far out in the prairie. He had told them during one of the rests that there was a rise on the northern side of the prairie that would give them a long view of the area.

On the tenth day they topped the rise about an hour before sunset. Luke picked out the Volls' campsite to the east of where they stood. They were about five hundred yards from the camp.

May looked it over and said, "After dark, Joe and I will move down to the camp and take a look. I don't think the trackers would camp among the soldiers but we need to make sure. Luke, you and Daniel find us a place to hold up for a day or two. Remember all I've told you about the trackers. We don't want them finding us before we find them."

Luke and Daniel moved toward a nearby creek bed that led off toward the north.

Joe and May settled down to watch the camp. They saw Voll patrols coming in and from the number of tents and men milling around, they guessed their numbers to be around one hundred.

Joe whispered, "Why are there so many camped here? It looks like they have been here for several weeks, too."

May pointed at a group of about forty people trudging toward the camp carrying carcasses of animals and several packs.

May said, "Those aren't Volls; they look like captives."

Just before they reached the camp two men came out of the tall grass and moved to the captives. May stiffened and Joe could see intensity of her look.

She said, "Trackers!"

As they watched, the two trackers spoke to a guard and then took two small women captives and dragged them off east of the camp.

Joe said, "Their camp must be away from the Volls."

"Maybe, but I don't think they would leave a trail leading right to their camp. Tonight you and I will go to the Voll camp and get information."

Joe smiled and said, "Yes, ma'am."

May gave him a withering stare but said nothing. They waited until it was completely dark and just before they moved out May heard a soft noise behind them.

They settled into the grass ready to kill. Daniel moved to within a few feet of them, stopped and raised a hand. Joe and May rose up beside him and he jumped back with his knife drawn.

He let out a breath and said, "We have found a place to stay. It is about thirty yards southwest of rocks that are to the north of here. Follow the creek bed to the rocks."

May nodded and said, "You and Luke stay there and keep watch. We should be back in a few hours."

Daniel nodded and moved off.

Joe and May made their way down the slope toward the camp. They made a wide circle to the west around the camp and approached from the north. When they were within fifty yards of the camp they could see two large tents with a wooden corral around them and people in ragged syncotton coveralls milling around inside. Joe held a closed fist in front of him, indicating captives.

They could see four guards outside the corral. There was a large fire to the east of the captives giving off enough light to see the entire camp. The Voll tents were east of the fire and a number of soldiers sat on benches drinking and laughing. To the north, very close to May and Joe, were two large storage tents. There were also two small tents about twenty yards east of the storage tents. They appeared to be empty.

May and Joe moved east, circling the camp. They had moved about seventy yards around the outside of the camp when May froze. Joe felt May stop and he readied himself for whatever was to come. Some scent had touched May's senses and she remained still, reaching back in her memory. It was a smell of...It took her mind over and the urge to kill leaped into her being. It was the smell of something the trackers chewed when they had tried to rape her.

The smell was on the breath of the one who held her to the ground with his legs and one of his hands holding both of hers. His other hand had ripped her shirt open and he was groping her breasts. It was a smell that brought instant hate. Whatever it was that he chewed dulled his mind and probably saved her life. As he had reached down into her pants, she freed her right hand, pulled his hunting knife from its sheath and plunged it into his side, killing him.

She felt a light touch on her arm and looked to see a questioning look on Joe's face. She calmed herself and made a walking motion with her fingers and then moved her hand up to her nose several times. Joe nodded. They turned east and silently moved like smoke on a breeze in the direction of the smell. About ten minutes later they froze. Twenty yards away they could see the flickering glow of a small fire. Soft whimpers came to them on the breeze.

They crawled forward, up a slight rise and stopped ten yards from the fire. Joe raised his head. Only his eyes were above the level of the grass. He saw two men. One was holding something down and the other, stripped from the waist down was making a humping motion into the small clump on the ground. He heard the whimper again and realized that the clump was a small woman or girl being held down with her face pushed into her knees. The man was raping her and the other one had a big grin on his face.

"Hurry up, Blu! I want to have some of that sweet meat."

"Shut up, Tre! You'll get your turn."

Joe's mind turned red with hate and just as he started to rise he felt a strong hand pull him back from the edge. May had moved up beside Joe and saw what was happening, but she also saw the other girl in front of the small tent.

She looked like a bundle of rags carelessly thrown down. May pointed at her and Joe finally saw her too, but what caused him to freeze was that she was looking directly at them with big, wide frightened eyes. May raised her head just enough for the girl to see her and put a finger to her lips. The girl by the tent blinked but did not move.

May lowered her head and moved her face close to Joe's. The great cat from her soul looked at him and she pointed to her bow. With a grim look of death, Joe nodded. May touched her bow and then touched her left arm and nodded. They readied their bows and turned to look at the terrible scene before them.

Blu gave a grunt and pumped hard a few more times and as he rose said, "Okay, Tre, see if you can do any better. This one is better than the other one. She doesn't stink as bad."

Tre released her arms and head, then stood and said, "Blu, I'll show you how to get a squeal out of this one. I'm going to..."

The last thing either of them heard was the low buzz of arrows in flight. Both arrows found their mark, nearly passing completely through their bodies. The trackers hit the ground without a sound. Joe moved in to the small campsite as May readied another arrow, checking the surrounding area. Joe went to the girl by the tent and touched her forehead and then touched his own. He held his finger to his lips and she nodded. He helped her stand and was shocked to see that she was just a child, maybe twelve years old.

He took her hand and led her to the other girl. She still lay in the dirt. He reached down and was about to pick her up but she started to scream. His hand was across her mouth just as the first of the scream passed her lips. She began to struggle and he turned her to face the other child. The little girl put her hands on the other's face and forced her to look into her eyes. When the struggling girl's eyes made contact with the other child she stopped. The child smiled and pointed at Joe and put her finger to her lips and then to Joe's hand, which was still clamped over the other's mouth. The frightened girl nodded and tried to look up at Joe. He slowly released his hand and she remained quiet, turning to look into Joe's face. The other girl rushed to her and they held each other tightly.

May appeared before their eyes and they both jumped but made no noise. May moved to the trackers and one let out a gurgling moan. May stabbed him in the heart and twisted the blade out. She turned to look at the two girls.

The look in May's eyes frightened them, but the smile on her face reassured them she meant no harm.

May motioned to Joe that they had to leave quickly. Joe removed the arrows from the bodies and then motioned for May to take the girls on ahead. He indicated he would remain behind for just a moment. He carefully removed the torn syncotton coveralls from the girl who had been by the tent and had her put on his light vest. She did everything he indicated, without the look of fear that had covered her face when she had first seen him. The child put on his vest and smiled up at him.

May led the children off into the grass and Joe turned to the dead men. He removed their hunting knives and slashed each of the bodies, making sure to plunge the knives into the holes left by the arrows. He laid them across one another, letting the knives drop, and put the syncotton coveralls in one of their fists. He ran east into the tall grass, making an obvious trail, until he found a creek bed about forty yards away. He carefully backtracked to the camp and then made his way out of camp without leaving any trace.

He caught up to May behind the storage tents. When he appeared the girl who had first seen them rushed to him, clinging to his legs. Joe looked at May for help, but she only smiled and pointed at him and then the child. They moved off with the girl holding Joe's hand. Heading back to the rise where they had first spotted the camp, May was in the lead.

She started up the rise and a man stood up, looking around for the source of the small noise he heard. May was on him, raising her knife to kill him when he whispered,

"Billy Running Wolf...Billy Running Wolf... Please."

She stopped the blade but brought it down to his neck, just under his chin. She held the knife in place as she studied him and he remained frozen, his eyes wide in fear. Joe came forward and indicated for her to kill him. May shook her head no and continued to study him.

She put her mouth close to his ear and whispered, "How do you know that name? Answer me or you are dead!"

He said, "I'm Bert! Don't you remember? Billy captured me and then let me go. I asked him if there was a way I could join his group and he told me if I ever decided to leave the Volls I was to walk south and speak his name if I met anyone. I saw four of you on top of this rise before sundown and decided it was time to leave. I've been waiting here ever since. I left my homing tag back in camp."

May looked at his face, remembering the time they had been attacked by the Voll patrol. She also remembered Billy talking about Bert.

"Running Wolf; is he dark-eyed and very tall?"

"No. He is a young man, not quite six feet tall. He has very blue eyes."

May removed the knife from his neck but stayed on guard.

"What do you want?"

"I want to come with you, and if you need my help I will give it to you. I want to live here and I don't want to see all these captives treated the way they are. I want them to be free."

The little girl holding Joe's hand pulled him down so she could whisper in his ear.

Joe went close to May and said, "The little one says she knows this man. She says he was always nice to them and gave the others extra food when he could. I say we can't take any chances. Kill him now or I will!"

May turned and looked at Joe and said, "No. We will take him with us and then we will decide."

Joe's eyes blazed in anger but he said, "Yes, ma'am."

May checked Bert's uniform to make sure there were no tags on him. Bert allowed her to roll him over and check everywhere, giving no protest. When she was satisfied she indicated for him to stand and put her finger to her lips. She motioned for Joe to lead off in search of Luke and Daniel.

CHAPTER 19

Billy led the group away from the cut after concealing the ropes. After storing most of the provisions in the cave, they now carried weapons and small packs on their backs. Heading due north the party rested twice and each time he checked with Jamee about the terrain and dangers.

Jamee told him after the second break, "Flick is here and keeping me informed, but I still use other birds to see for myself."

When they neared the foothills, Billy told Jason to take the lead and head for the tunnel entrance he knew. Jason led them off to the northeast. They had just entered the foothills and Billy stopped the party again.

He took Jamee off a short distance and said, "Is it possible for Flick or another bird to pass through this tunnel and check it for danger?"

Jamee looked toward the mountains and became quiet.

After a few moments she looked at Billy and smiled. "Flick says she can do that if you will trust her. I think she's a little upset that you might not trust her after our last visit here."

"Where is she?"

A flash of color flicked before his eyes and there sat Flick on his shoulder.

He turned his head and kissed her on the head. "I trust you with my life, my beautiful friend."

Flicked turned a soft pink and flew away.

Tommy asked, "What was that all about, Billy? I've never seen a bird like that."

"I'll tell you when we reach the tunnel."

He indicated that Jason should start off again.

They reached the entrance of the tunnel around mid-afternoon. It was concealed much like the tunnel Jamee and he had passed through. It was invisible until you approached at just the right angle. Billy had everyone sit down, take a break and eat. While they rested he told Jason and Tommy some of the things Jamee could do.

Jason asked, "Jamee, you can talk to birds?"

"Only this one bird and her name is Flick. She can be trusted completely and she is our friend," indicating Red, Silver, Billy and herself.

Tommy and Jason nodded but said nothing.

It was a few hours after sunset when Flick returned.

She spoke to Jamee, "The tunnel is clear and doesn't appear to have been used in a long time. It will take you four or five hours to pass through if you don't stop. I found Johnny as well. He is near the entrance of the cave that you used when you were here before. It is a few miles away from where this tunnel comes out. There are people on both sides of the new bridge that has been built. The lizards are guarding the entrance to the mine."

Jamee turned to the others and told them what Flick had said. They had made torches in the valley and made ready to enter the tunnel.

They walked through the tunnel, only using one torch at a time. The visibility was low, but all could see that the tunnel was not natural.

Billy said, "Jamee and I went through another cave like this one and it looked like someone had made it."

Jason said, "I have been through one further east and it was the same. I saw some strange markings carved in the wall in a few places. I wonder who made these tunnels and why."

Jamee said, "Flick once told me about people who lived far to the south. She called them the Ancients but said no more about them."

Tommy said, "My grandfather was a long-hunter and I remember him telling me about stone houses he found far to the south. I was just a kid and I thought he was trying to frighten me, but maybe there is something to what he said."

They had walked for about three hours when they came on the markings like the ones Jason had talked about. Billy called a short halt and they crowded around the single torch.

Red said, "It looks like writing but none I have ever seen. There used to be many languages on Earth and I have seen some of the books written in other languages but they don't compare to this."

Silver spoke up. "I have seen ancient books from our ancestors that came from the East, on Earth. The writing was like tiny drawings but I never met anyone who could read it. These markings seem to flow."

They looked at the writing a few more minutes and Billy said, "Maybe we can send someone back here one day to make a copy of it, but now we must go on."

There were other tunnels leading off the main one, but they passed them by as they hurried through. Before they reached the end, Flick flew in and landed on Billy's shoulder. Her royal blue sparkled in the firelight. She turned her head to look at the others, changing to their colors as she looked. When she looked at Jason and Tommy, they backed away, eyeing her warily. She flashed through a rainbow of colors and dipped her head.

Jamee said to them with a smile, "Flick says not to be frightened; she will not eat you. She also asked if you are married."

They both said no and Jason asked, "Why does she want to know if we are married?"

Jamee chuckled and said, "She just wants to know." Silver smiled and looked at Red. Jamee continued, "She says that the exit is just ahead and there is no one around. We will be safe when we go outside. She also says there is a cut in the rocks we can climb to a wide ridge that will lead us to the mine."

Billy smiled at Flick and nodded to her in thanks.

When they exited the tunnel it was still dark but they could see a drop-off and a small bridge about fifty yards away.

Billy said, "Tommy, stay here and find a way for the people to get up here. If you can, find a way to rig that bridge to fall after we cross; it may help us escape. Be careful."

Tommy said, "I will be waiting for you and all will be ready."

The party found the cut and quickly climbed up to the top of the ridge. They moved as quickly as they could, being careful not to make any noise.

After about an hour Jamee stopped.

She brought everyone close and whispered, "Flick says there are two Volls above us, about a hundred yards ahead. She says if we move quietly we can pass beneath them and be around some rocks fifty yards past them without being seen."

They moved out and soon saw the Volls twenty feet above them. They had piles of rocks on the edge of a short drop-off to push down on anyone who passed below them.

The party moved beneath the Volls and they heard one of them say, "William, look at that! It's a little bird. That's the first animal I've seen in these stinking mountains. Look at its color and it doesn't seem to be afraid of us."

William said, "Come here, little bird. I won't hurt you. I'd like to take you back to my tent and keep you. Come here."

The party continued on until they were out of sight of the Volls and they heard one of them shout, "Come on, bird. Don't fly away."

The sun was just beginning to turn the dark gray world to a soft pink when they arrived at the other tunnel.

Billy asked Jamee, "Where is Johnny?"

Jamee answered after only a moment, "He's further around the cliff, about five hundred yards."

They carefully made their way along the top of the cliff, staying away from the edge. They saw Flick sitting on a rock. She was black and hard to see, but as they approached Johnny's head popped up above the rock and he smiled. He motioned for them to follow and led them back toward a jumble of boulders and into a cave-like depression. It was full daylight now, but under the boulders it was still dim and the six of them gathered close.

Johnny smiled and said, "It's good to see all of you. Where is Tommy?"

"He will wait at the tunnel entrance and try to weaken the small bridge nearby."

Johnny nodded and continued, "There hasn't been a lot of activity, but once a day the Koros bring the captives out to work on the new bridge and cut a road into the cliff face. I don't know how you and Jamee did it, but almost two hundred yards of roadway is missing. It looks like it just slid into the valley below."

Red asked, "How many captives have you seen, Johnny?"

"They only bring around seventy-five out at a time. I have watched and it seems to be the same people each time. I counted fifty young men, twelve young women, ten older men and three older women. All of them look weak and in poor health, but they are forced to work hard."

Billy asked, "Have you seen any of them killed or tortured?"

"I saw one captive, a man, working when a large rock shifted and rolled onto him. When the others moved the rock and pulled him out, he looked to be injured badly. The Koros forced three of the people to throw him over the cliff and then go back to work. Billy, it is hard for me to watch these people; they seem to have lost all hope."

Jason said, "Well, now we will give them hope and freedom."

There was a murmur of agreement. Jamee asked, "What else did you find?"

Johnny said, "The entrance is always guarded and the Volls have patrols going down the road at least three times a day and several times at night. I think they have people stationed along the cliff as well. What I have found that might help us are several air shafts that come up from the mine. You wouldn't believe the smell that comes from down there! There are two small shafts that come out on the sides of the peak above the mine and one larger one higher up. There is a flat area around the big one and a trench to take away rain water. There are also several large boulders leaning over the opening so that it's nearly impossible to see. While I was looking around, Flick kept landing on my shoulder and then flying off in the same direction, so I followed her and found it."

Red asked, "Have you seen anyone up above the mine?"

"Only once. Two Koros were up there but not for long. I don't think the Volls go up there because of the smell."

Billy asked, "Can we get up there in the daylight without being seen?"

"Yes. I can lead you around to a ridge several miles away and we can cross over."

"Then let's have a look at the mine entrance first and then we'll move around to the air shafts."

Johnny led them to a depression at the edge of the cliff that provided good cover. Peering over the side Billy could see the long wooden bridge about one hundred yards from the mine entrance. Captives were working on the cliff face trying to cut a roadbed into it. The Volls had moved their camp and were now set up against the rock face on the other side of the road near the mine. There were about one hundred Volls working and standing around their camp. The party watched for an hour and went back to the boulders.

Billy said, "Johnny, how many Koros have you seen?"

"I've only seen ten at the entrance of the mine. I have never seen more than twenty of them at a time but usually only about ten. I don't think there are as many of them as we have always thought. Some may live down in the mine, but I think they probably have a village somewhere else."

"Okay. Let's go look at the air shafts."

"You better eat something now because you won't be able to eat once you smell the air up there."

They settled down and ate a quick meal and relaxed for a few minutes.

The party moved along the ridge at the top of the cliff and then crossed over to the peak above the mine. The foul smell came to them as they approached the main air shaft. The air was filled with the smell of rotten eggs and decaying flesh.

As they approached the shaft Billy could barely make it out. There was a flat area, with large, smooth rocks leaning in all directions but no evidence of a tunnel. Johnny led them around to a small gap between the leaning rocks and the slope of the mountain. They squeezed through the gap and the smell was almost unbearable.

Red looked down the shaft and saw that it was almost a perfect circle about three feet in diameter. It also looked to be absolutely vertical. The wall of the shaft wasn't smooth, but seemed to have handholds that went out of sight. He could see a hint of light far below, maybe two hundred feet down. He asked for a length of rope and tied a round rock to the end. He lowered the rope down as far as he could see and stopped. As it stopped its slight swinging he could see that the shaft was indeed vertical.

As he pulled the rope up, Silver asked, "What are you thinking?"

"Wait a moment, my love. Let me check a few more things and think for a moment." He moved around the shaft, laying the rope along its edge, being careful not to drop any debris down the shaft. When he completed the circle he gathered the rope. He tied a small knot to mark the circumference of the shaft.

He turned and looked at the long, slender boulders that were leaning to make a kind of roof over the air shaft. He selected several and measured their circumference. Most were too small or too big, but one was twelve inches shorter than the shaft's circumference. He stepped back and looked around and then sat down thinking.

He was quiet for almost ten minutes and then he stood and said, "Let's get some fresh air," and then led them back out to the windward side of the shaft.

He motioned for everyone to sit, but Jason moved off to keep watch. Red looked over at Billy and nodded toward Jason with a smile. Jason had taken it upon himself to guard the area without being asked. He was a good man to have around.

"Seeing this shaft started me thinking about what happened the last time you were here. You pushed the boxes of Verdance over the cliff and when they hit a thousand feet below they exploded. What if we could do the same thing again but cause the explosion inside the mine? One of the reasons we came here was to try and find a way to take the Verdance away from the Volls."

"That's right, but what has that got to do with what you were doing back there?"

Red held up his hands and said, "Let me finish and I think you will see where I'm going with this. Okay. I've measured the shaft and the long, slender, very heavy boulder and it will fit inside the shaft. If we could get some of the Verdance and place it at the bottom of this shaft and drop the boulder down onto it, I think that might cause an explosion and seal the mine entrance."

"Red!" Billy exclaimed, "That would work. Now we have to find a way to get the Verdance."

Jamee said, "We also have to figure out a way to get the captives out of there and away before the explosion."

Red said, "Someone needs to go down the shaft and take measurements to make sure it doesn't get any smaller. I don't think I will fit."

Johnny spoke up, "I'm the smallest one here. I will go."

Silver stood up and said, "No, you're not, Johnny. I am the smallest and the climb up and down would be easy for me. You will be needed up here to help prepare the boulder. I am going."

Red wanted very much to say something, but he knew she was right. The thought of her going down that shaft gripped his heart like steel bands, but he said nothing, just reached out and took her hand.

Silver prepared to climb down the shaft. She removed her leggings and shirt and then put on a small vest to cover her chest. She bent down to tighten the lacing on her boots when she became aware of eyes watching her. She straightened, turned and faced Jason and Johnny. Their faces turned as red as the second moon as she walked over to them.

She looked up into their eyes and said with a stern look on her face, "Did you enjoy that? Do you know what Red would say if he caught you two looking at my body like that?"

Johnny lowered his head as Jason sputtered, "I...I'm sorry... Silver. I didn't mean to stare at your..." He stopped and lowered his head.

Johnny looked into her eyes with a sad, embarrassed look and said, "I'm sorry. You are very beautiful and you are my friend. I'm really sorry."

Silver gave a laugh that sounded like tiny bells in the wind. "Jason, Johnny, I'm not angry and I'm sorry I teased you. Young men look at women and there is nothing wrong with that, but don't let Red see you. He might not understand."

"Understand what?" Red asked as he squeezed through the boulders.

"Nothing, my love. I was just giving these two hunters some advice on finding a wife."

Jason and Johnny were still blushing and Red said, "Oh, well, you better listen to her."

They both nodded.

"I'm ready," Silver said as she picked up the length of rope she would use to measure the shaft.

She kissed Jason and Johnny on the lips and walked over to Red and kissed him hard.

"Please be careful."

"I will, honey. I'll be back soon."

She went to the edge of the shaft, stepped out and was gone.

"Johnny, keep an eye on her. Jason, you start moving the debris out of here so we can prepare this boulder."

"I'll help, Jason," said Jamee as she stepped through the opening.

She removed her leggings to use as a basket for the small rocks. She turned towards the boulders and started working. Jamee bent over the debris and her rear wiggled as she reached out to sweep the rock into her leggings and her shirt fell open at the bottom, revealing two beautiful creamy brown breasts. Both Jason and Johnny gave out slight groans but turned away to do their jobs.

Johnny muttered to Jason, "I've got to get me a wife."

While Silver was still down measuring the shaft, Billy and Red looked over the boulder they intended to drop down the air shaft. It was about ten feet tall, almost three feet in diameter and had to weigh many tons, but it was leaning against the peak in a good position for it to slide into the shaft. All they had to do was think of a way to move it two and a half feet.

Jamee walked over, took a long look at the boulder and said, "If we could brace it by placing rocks underneath it, then it would slide right in the shaft. We might have to lift it just a bit to get it moving. Maybe we could make a slight channel to guide the bottom of it as it moved."

Red and Billy looked at each other and smiled.

Billy said, "Now, why didn't we think of that?"

Jamee moved close to him and put her lips to his ear and whispered. Billy blushed and even Red blushed when he guessed what Jamee said.

Billy said, "Yes...Well, how are we going to make a channel in this? It is solid rock."

Jamee pulled her staff from its sheath on her back and looked at Billy.

Red said, "I think that will work."

A few minutes later Silver emerged from the air shaft and walked out into the fresh air.

They all followed her out and waited until she had breathed the fresh air for a few minutes

She said, "I don't know how anyone could live down there with that smell. The air shaft is the same size all the way down until it reaches the mine shaft. Then it widens a few feet. When I was near the bottom I could hear voices that sounded like the captives. I stuck my head out for just a second and could see the cages they have them in. I could also see a brighter light in the other direction. I think the entrance is about fifty yards away."

Billy said, "We know where the captives are and we think we know how to seal the mine. Now we need to figure out a way to get some Verdance and a way to get the captives out and across that bridge."

Jamee motioned for Silver to follow her and she went back between the boulders to the air shaft.

Jamee held and kissed her. "I'm so glad you are safe. I was worried about you."

Silver smiled, hugged Jamee and said, "What do we do now, sister?"

"I am going to dig a channel to slide the boulder into the air shaft. You keep any debris from falling into it."

She moved the lever on the staff and the blade sprang out with a *snick*. She put the blade into the rock floor and with only a little effort cut a channel to the rim of the air shaft. She left a two-inch section at the edge of the boulder to hold it in place until they were ready to move it. Red, Johnny and Jason came in and moved large rocks under the incline of the boulder to help keep it upright when it started to move. When all was ready, except for the last section of channel at the base of the boulder, they went outside.

Billy said, "I have a plan but we need to rest for a while. Tonight we will get the people out of there and seal the mine."

CHAPTER 20

Joe led the party down the creek bed, the two girls close behind him, followed by Bert. May lagged behind several feet, watching the rear for any danger and keeping an eye on Bert. It was just beginning to turn light and the sun would bring the world into sharper focus in a short time.

Joe rounded a turn in the creek and saw a cluster of boulders off to his left. He stopped and looked around carefully. He saw a slight movement to his right and then a bow rose above the grass for an instant. He motioned for the others to wait. He looked at May and then at Bert. May nodded. He moved off toward the spot where he had seen the bow disappearing into the grass. Before May could do anything the little girl with the vest moved quietly after him.

Joe moved forward about forty feet when he saw another movement to his left and then the grass moved aside and Luke's face appeared. Joe moved to Luke, but before he could say anything they heard a noise. Both whirled with knives ready and the little girl stepped out and went directly to Joe. Luke gave Joe a questioning look, but Joe shrugged and said nothing.

Luke whispered, "We have found a small hollow in a boval wallow about thirty yards ahead. You and your child go ahead. I will go get May."

Joe gave him a hard look and whispered, "There are two others with her and one is a Voll. Don't kill him or you'll make your wife mad."

Luke's eyes widened, but Joe just turned, with the girl holding his hand, and moved off.

The wallow was a large depression and in places very steep. Under the rim of one of the steep sections was a hollow that went back under the prairie for about eight feet. They all gathered and watched the two little girls eat anything that was passed to them.

May was washing a cut on one of the child's very dirty legs and said, "Your skin is black."

The child smiled and said, "Not just my leg; I'm black everywhere and so is my friend, Belle."

Joe looked at her leg and then up into her large, dark shining eyes and asked, "What is your name, little one?"

"My name is Jasmine, but you can call me Little One if you want and I am going to call you Papa."

"What? I'm not your papa!"

"You are my papa now. You saved my life and I am going to be your daughter."

She said it with such conviction and gravity that she left no room for argument, but Joe shook his head no.

May spoke up as everyone else smiled. "Joe, let it go for now. Wait until we get back before we say any more about this, Papa."

Joe spun on everyone and said, "You think this is very funny, don't you?"

Luke said, "Yes, it is, Papa."

Joe whipped his knife out and said, "The next person who calls me Papa will not live to say another word! And I'm not your papa."

Jasmine looked up at him and smiled. "Yes, Papa."

Joe went to the edge of the hollow and looked out at the wallow. Soon Jasmine moved over to him and then they were holding hands. Daniel was about to say something, but May gave him a warning look and he remained quiet.

Belle hadn't said a word since she had been rescued. She looked around with tears in her eyes but refused to talk. May took her hand and moved to the other side of the hollow, away from everyone else.

"Are you okay, Belle? You don't have to be afraid now. We'll take care of you."

Belle looked up at May with tears rolling down her face and whispered, "You saw what that man was doing to me. Both of them did it a lot. They always picked Jasmine and me. You and Joe saw and now you won't want me."

May lifted Belle's face with her hand, kissed her and said, "Belle, what those men did was very wrong, but it wasn't your fault. No one here or in the village where we will take you will think anything bad about you or Jasmine. I won't let them. I have a sister about your age. Her name is Nuuna and she is going to love having some friends to play with."

"Not when she hears about what they did to us," said Belle.

"Wait until you meet her; you'll see that she will love you and know that you didn't do anything wrong."

Belle smiled up at May. "Do you really think so?"

"Yes, I know so. Now, dry your eyes and get some sleep. I know you must be tired from all the walking we did."

The children slept as the others questioned Bert about the camp.

May asked, "How many trackers are there in camp?"

"Four, but two of them left for the mine just before sunset yesterday."

"They left for the mine! Are you sure?"

"Yes. I heard the commander order two of them to check the area around the mine for anyone trying to sneak in there and then report to the commander at the mine."

She looked at Luke and said, "I've got to go! I have to warn Billy and kill the trackers."

Joe answered before Luke could open his mouth. "No, May. You don't know the way or the location of the tunnel they will use. I do. I will leave now and be there in two or three days. I will kill these trackers. They won't hurt any more little ones."

The look of a death bringer was in his eyes and no one doubted his words.

Luke said, "Joe is right, my love. You don't know the way and you have seen Joe hunt. He is the only one I would trust, besides you, with my brother and sister's life against these trackers."

May finally nodded and put her arms around Joe's neck and kissed him softly. "Be careful, Joe, and kill them."

Joe smiled, "Yes, ma'am, I promise, if you give me another kiss when I see you again."

"I will."

Joe said to May, "Watch over the little ones."

"With my life." May hugged him again.

Joe woke Jasmine, took her hand and moved to the edge of the hollow and spoke to her for several minutes. They watched her nod and saw the tears in her eyes, but finally she stood and kissed him on the lips and hugged him hard. When they came back to the group Joe's eyes were wet as he checked his pack and readied to leave. He shook hands with everyone, including Bert, and turned to leave.

Jasmine called softly after him and said, "Be careful, Papa."

He turned his head and said, "I will, Little One," and then he was gone.

After Joe left, the girls clung together and talked quietly. Luke continued to question Bert and came to believe his claim that he wanted to help and live on this world. Luke brought May, Daniel and Bert together to come up with a plan.

"I think we must free the captives, cause as much confusion as we can and then make our way back to the village. If we meet the party Red Eagle is sending out, we will turn over Belle, Jasmine and Bert, then make our way to Billy and help if we can. We should move late tonight. Bert, can you warn the captives to be ready when we come?"

"I think so, and I can start fires in the supply tents. That will keep the soldiers busy while we make our escape."

Daniel said, "So far I haven't been much help on this raid. I will take care of any guards and lead the captives straight south. May and Luke, you help Bert destroy the supplies. I don't think they will follow us too far into the prairie without supplies."

Bert said, "They will send out a patrol, no matter what. These are the last of the captives to offer the lizards. The commander has been ordered to get more Verdance, even if he has to kill the lizards to do it. There are eight hundred men almost ready to move out to the mine. They may be only a few days behind us."

May asked, "How many Volls are left behind to guard the ships?" Bert said, "Maybe a hundred or even less. We were told the natives would never think of attacking the ships."

Luke said, "They may be in for a surprise." He looked at Daniel and said, "When you reach Red Eagle's party, tell them what you have heard and ask them to head this way to pick up the trail of the large group of Volls that are heading for the mine. May and I will join you after you free the captives, if we can, but then we are going to find Billy."

Daniel said, "I will do all you ask, but I will join the party going after the Volls. Someone else can lead the freed captives back to the village."

Luke nodded and said, "Bert, it's time for you to go back to the camp. We will meet you near the supply tents around three in the morning. Do all you said you would do."

Bert stood and said, "I give you my word and I will not fail. The captives will be warned and I will be ready to fire the tents and fight with you."

They shook hands and Bert left.

"Daniel, follow him and see what happens when he enters the camp." Daniel picked up his pack and left.

May went over to the two girls, who were still awake, clinging to each other.

Jasmine asked, "Are you going to give us to other people?"

May smiled down and said, "I'll make you both a promise. We will not give you away, but we are sending you to our mother. You will love her and she will love you both. We will see you again soon and I promise you will be happy."

Jasmine said, "Will my papa come there soon, too?"

May looked at her and asked, "Why do you want Joe to be your papa?"

"He saved my life and I can see he is a good man. He needs someone to help him be happy. He is my papa."

May smiled and said, "You are right; he is a good man and needs to be happy. I think you are just the little girl who can do that. I think Joe is very lucky to have found you. And Belle, don't you worry either. There are many people who will love you, too. We will look after you."

Belle asked, "Will I be a slave in this place I am going?"

"No! There will be no more slaves on this world. You will be a part of our family."

Belle smiled and slowly closed her eyes and went to sleep. Jasmine lay beside her, already asleep.

Daniel returned just after sunset and said, "I watched him until they lit the big fire. Bert helped feed the captives and I saw him talking to several of them. I think we can trust him."

Luke said, "I just wanted to be sure. Let's get a few hours rest. We have a long night ahead of us."

At around two in the morning Daniel took Jasmine and Belle to within a few hundred yards south of the Volls' camp. He found a small clump of bushes and sat them down.

He pulled their heads very close to his lips and said, "You two wait here. When you hear a lot of noise get ready to run, but don't go anywhere until you see me and then run as fast as you can to me. We are going to take all the people you were with and run away back to my village. Do you understand?"

They both nodded yes and Belle whispered, "Don't leave us, Daniel."

Daniel kissed them both on the cheeks and whispered back, "I promise you both that I won't go anywhere without you."

They hugged and kissed him and sat huddled together as he made his way toward the camp.

Daniel worked his way around to the west side of the camp where the captives were being held. The big fire in the middle of the camp gave enough light to see four guards around the enclosure. He worked his way to within about ten feet of one of the guards and waited. One of the other guards walked over and began talking and joking with the guard Daniel was near.

They heard a *Whoosh* and spun around to see the supply tents on fire. Before they could shout a warning, Daniel took them both down and clubbed them with his big fist. He was up and running around the fence and smashed the third guard in the head without stopping. He was then running to bring down the last guard. The man was looking at the fire but spun as Daniel ran toward him. He raised his spear, but Daniel blocked it aside, plowed through him and smashed his head to the ground.

Daniel ran to the gate. He pulled his knife and cut the straps holding it closed. He wrenched the gate open and motioned for the people inside to hurry. As the first man staggered past, Daniel grabbed him by the arm and said, "Run in that direction," pointing south. "Don't stop but help the others. Keep your right shoulder pointed at the moon."

Not looking at the fire, he searched the area for people left behind. He turned and was heading out of camp when he heard the screams of women. He spun around and saw two small tents near the supply tents but away from everything else.

Two naked women were struggling to break free of the grasp of two Volls. He also saw that men were waking in the large tents just off to his left and trying to get dressed. Daniel had no time to think. He just ran towards the big tents with his hunting knife in his right hand. One man turned toward Daniel as he ran up but never had a chance to shout as Daniel hit him with his fist. He dropped like a rock.

Daniel passed between the tents and slowed, cutting all the stays supporting the tents as he passed. The tents collapsed to the shout of angry men just waking up. He passed between two more large tents and cut their stays as well as he ran toward the two small tents. He reached a smaller, much better quality tent as a man came out shouting orders to get the fire out. Daniel lashed out with his left hand, hitting the man in the jaw. He collapsed without even a grunt.

Daniel was now thirty yards from the two small tents where two men were struggling with the naked women. They paid no attention to the fire. One man was dragging a woman back into the tent and the other was hitting the other woman in the face, trying to get control of her.

As Daniel closed the distance between them, the man finally looked up and shouted, "What do you...?"

Daniel plunged the knife into his chest. He moved to the other tent, ripping it from the ground and smashing the second man in the head with the heel of his knife. Towering over the two women, they could only stare with their big, wide eyes at the big copper-skinned man in buckskin looking down at them.

Daniel said in a calm voice, "Grab your clothes and follow me." He started off but turned around, seeing the women just staring at him. "Now! If you want to be free," and he turned away again and moved off.

They quickly grabbed up their coveralls and ran naked behind him. Daniel had turned back south and ran around the big collapsed tents, heading for the prairie, looking for the clump of bushes where Belle and Jasmine waited.

As Luke and May approached the back of the supply tents, someone stepped out and said, "Billy Running Wolf."

It was Bert. He motioned them forward, bent down and lifted two bundles that clinked as he stood.

Luke said, "Bert, we don't need supplies. We have to hurry."

"I think you'll want these. They're the special long knives we give to the lizards, very sharp. I have everything ready when you tell me to light the tents."

May and Luke lifted the bundles to their shoulders and May said, "Go ahead." Bert motioned for them to step back with him and then he bent and struck flint and steel and the torch he laid by his side burst into flames. He picked it up and tossed it into the opening in the back of the tent he had cut earlier. There was a whoosh and blast of heat as the fire leaped up to consume the tent. The other tent burst into flames a few seconds later. Luke and May turned and ran, but Bert pulled something from his shirt front and threw it into the fire and then he turned and ran to catch up.

They ran for about forty yards, stopped and turned.

Luke said, "I want to make sure the captives get away."

They looked over at the area where the captives were kept and saw a long line of people running and staggering toward the prairie.

Luke and Bert turned, but May said, "Look, there's Daniel. What is he doing?"

They watched Daniel cutting the stays on the tents and then hitting a man standing outside another tent without stopping. He was headed for the supply area, where Volls were starting to run toward.

"What is he doing?"

May said, "Look."

Daniel had reached the naked women and killed one Voll and probably the other one that they could see. He shouted something, ran a few feet and turned and shouted again. He then turned, heading back toward the tents and didn't look back. The women had gathered up their coveralls and ran naked after him.

Luke laughed and said, "There will be many stories about how Daniel ran all the way through an enemy camp with two naked women chasing him."

Turning, they ran and circled around the camp to head south.

Following the well-marked trail of the captives for about five hundred yards Luke could see the stragglers just ahead so he stopped.

He took the two bundles and laid them on the ground and then removed his buckskin shirt. "Bert, take off your jacket and throw it away. Put this on so no one kills you by mistake. Run up and let Daniel know we are watching the rear. Take these bundles with you and do whatever Daniel says."

Bert tore off his uniform jacket and pulled Luke's leather shirt on, lifted the two bundles and ran off toward the front of the column of captives. Luke and May pulled their bows from their backs, readied them and they slowly made their way south. They traveled for over an hour and the dawn slowly opened the area around them.

May spotted a column of men moving quickly toward them.

She reached out and pulled Luke to her and said, "I love you, Luke. You make my heart sing."

He said, "I love you, Golden Dove, with all my heart," and they kissed.

May said, "Move off to the right and hide until they are within your range. Fire three arrows and move back fifty yards and fire again if they keep coming. Keep doing that until you're out of arrows."

Luke smiled, giving her a quick kiss and said, "Yes, ma'am." He turned and moved off to the right before she could swing at him. He heard soft laughter as May moved to the left.

The Volls were moving quickly in disciplined lines. They could tell by the tracks they were getting close. The leader turned his head to check that his men were formed up properly. He saw three men to his left drop with arrows sticking from their chest. He heard a noise to his right, but before he could turn his head an arrow struck him in the chest and he went down.

The column stopped and the next in command checked the bodies and said, "They're all dead. All right. Move forward but stay alert."

A man in the second column said, "Keep alert for what? I didn't see anything until the arrows hit. We don't even know how many there are out there!"

The new commander said, "Shut your trap, soldier! Do as I say."

There were still over fifty Volls in the patrol and everyone started forward but looking all around. They traveled about fifty yards when six more men died in the front ranks, including the soldier in charge.

No one would take charge and someone said, "There must be at least ten of them out there. I saw five myself."

Another soldier said, "Ten against forty, we can take them."

Another said, "We were over fifty just a moment ago!"

Six more arrows sprang from the chest of the men in front, killing them. That started the stampede. The soldiers turned and in a jumbled mass ran back to the north, never looking to the rear.

Luke and May waited a few moments and moved to the dead men. They retrieved their arrows and Luke ran back fifty yards and soon returned with six more arrows.

"That should stop them for a while, but they may be back. We'll lag behind and keep an eye out."

They traveled another hour and moved up to the group of people who had stopped in a creek bed and were drinking from a pool of water.

Daniel came over when he saw them and asked, "Are they following us?"

Luke said, "They were, but May and I turned them back, for now."

Luke grinned and looked behind Daniel and said, "Daniel, don't you think your women should put some clothes on?"

Daniel said, "My women? What are you...?" He turned to see the two naked women standing close to him. "Oh. You two; you can put your clothes on now. Go get some water and stay with the others."

They looked at him with big, beautiful brown eyes and said in sweet melody, "Yes, Daniel."

They dressed and walked toward the pool, looking back at him smiling.

May laughed and asked Luke, "Are two wives allowed in our village?"

"I don't think it has ever been done, but I don't know of any law against it."

Daniel's eye opened wide. "What? That's not funny. I just helped them get away and that's all."

May walked over to Daniel and kissed him on the cheek and smiled up at him. "Daniel, you saved their lives last night. They won't forget that."

Daniel blushed and said, "Should we keep heading due south or turn toward a Bookus grove?"

Luke asked, "What condition are they in?"

"They are tired but, except for a few, they are in good shape. We can get some of the stronger ones to help the weaker ones."

Luke said, "Tell them we will head south but change course several times and then at sundown we'll get them to backtrack and head west to a grove. As you walk with them, explain about moving through the prairie without disturbing the grass, but tell them not to try it until we are ready to turn west. We want a big trail for the Volls to follow."

"Me? You tell them. You and May are in charge."

May said, "No, Daniel, you are in charge of these people now. They trust you and will look to you for answers. Besides, you might pick up a few more girlfriends if you are nice to them."

Daniel gave her a hard stare and said, as Luke and May laughed, "Funny, very funny." He turned and walked to the pool getting everyone started again.

Luke and May waited until the party was about a hundred yards ahead and then followed behind them.

May said, "There are around fifty or sixty people that Daniel brought out. If Billy's party brings a big group out, they will fill the village."

Luke smiled, "Yes, but we will make room. The People have been sad for a long time, thinking about the captives taken from our village. This will put a happy peace back in them."

An hour before sunset Daniel stopped the group, turned them around and walked back about a mile. Luke and May helped him organize the people into long lines, facing west, about ten feet apart. They passed along the line telling everyone to be very careful not to disturb the grass as they moved out. They also told them to walk for at least thirty minutes like that and then Daniel would bring them back together.

Luke, May and Daniel stayed behind to repair any signs of their movement. Luke smiled as Daniel had to point angrily toward the group moving off to get the two young women he had rescued to move away from him. They carefully walked away and waved at Daniel.

He looked at May and asked, "What am I going to do about those two? They stay right beside me everywhere I go."

May smiled and said, "At least they don't call you Papa."

They all chuckled quietly and went back to work. When they finished they ran east, leaving a clear, small trail, hoping the Volls would think it was another trap. After running out about four hundred yards they slowly turned and circled back to the freed people. Daniel got them moving as a group again and headed southwest to where he knew a Bookus grove was located.

The freed captives entered the grove and they all looked frightened as they stared at the giant trees.

Daniel gathered them around and said, "This grove of trees are called Bookus trees. They are very important to my people. Do not mistreat them or cut limbs and don't try to start any fires. We will explain how to make a fire without hurting them and also how to get cleaned up."

Someone asked, "You mean we are going up in these trees and get cleaned up?"

"Yes. There are water caves at each branch of these trees and they will hold around ten people in each."

An older black man stepped forward and said, "We haven't had time to thank you for what you did for us. You are a very brave man."

They all murmured agreement.

Daniel said, "It wasn't just me and we were doing what we thought was right so no thanks are necessary. Now we need to show you where you will sleep and get you something to eat."

May and Luke came walking in with ten large hoppers and May said, "This should be enough meat for tonight and in the morning. Who knows how to cook?"

Several women stepped forward.

"Luke, get some men to find some fire stones and bring them up. Also gather some rain berry limbs to hold these over the fire. Come, ladies. Let's clean these hoppers." May moved off towards the prairie and she called back, "Daniel, get the rest of the people into the cave and show them how to bathe."

Luke and Daniel said together, "Yes, ma'am."

Daniel, with a gloomy look, asked Luke, "Do you think Billy is having this much fun?"

CHAPTER 21

Just before sunset Red, Billy and Jason waited for the small outpost to change guards. Watching from behind a small outcrop they saw two Volls making their way along the ridge towards the outpost.

They were making a lot of noise and one of the men from above said, "You two couldn't sneak up on an old woman!"

One of the men climbing said, "We don't want you idiots rolling rocks down on top of us." When they arrived all four stood and talked and joked.

One said, "We've been here for a month and I haven't seen anyone around here, except those lizards."

Another asked, "When are we going to stop playing with these lizards and just take the stuff the commander is after?"

"Well, if we do fight them, you better kill them quick! I saw one fight with one of the slaves and he didn't stop until the slave was dead, and then the lizard dragged the slave off like he was going to have a big supper that night."

"You mean they eat them?"

"Think about it. Have you ever seen those lizards bring in anything to eat? We've given them over a hundred slaves and my buddy said when he first got here a year ago they had almost two hundred slaves. Now I bet there are only a hundred working in the mine. What do you think happened to the others?"

Another Voll said, "I heard the captain saying that they always keep five or six caged up on the next level down from the entrance. It scares me just to think what they do with them down there."

As the two going off duty were leaving, one said, "Just don't get caught alone with them or you might get invited to supper!"

They all laughed at that. "See you after sunrise." The two soldiers made their way down to the path along the cliff and headed back towards their camp.

Jason asked Red, "Do you think that's true?"

"I don't know."

"They're not going to eat any more people," said Jason and then and he fell silent.

They waited for an hour and then Billy led the way to the path that led up to the outpost. He moved silently and when he peered over the edge of the stacked rock he saw both of the Volls were asleep. He motioned for Red and Jason to follow. They were over the side and had the Volls subdued with almost no struggle. One of the Volls was as big as Red and Red told him to strip. He started to protest and Red smashed him in the mouth and told him again to strip. He removed his uniform and then was tied and gagged like the other one.

Red stripped off his clothes and began putting on the uniform. He looked down at the two Volls and said, "If you two huddle together you can stay warm. The young man here," pointing at Jason, "will keep watch on you from up above. If you break free, he will get to do what he has wanted to do."

The Volls looked at Jason, who sat close by with his big hunting knife out sharpening it. Jason had a look of pure hate in his eyes and he was staring at the two Volls. The blade made a metallic ringing as it ran along the sharpening stone. The Volls groaned and looked away.

Red said, "Your buddies will be back at sunrise and they will free you. Let me give you some advice that you can pass on. Don't go up against the Red Indians that live here. They will kill you before you ever see them."

Red and Billy moved down the path to the ridge and waited. Jason made his way down and had a big grin on his face. They headed along the ridge towards the mine entrance and stopped when they found the cut they would use to climb down to the road. Billy took two ropes and secured them to a small outcrop and let the ropes down slowly. He turned his head and whispered to the two men kneeling beside him, "Remember, we don't need a very big piece of Verdance. Be careful and don't get caught." He handed a short piece of rope to Jason, who put it in his pocket. Jason had rubbed dirt all over his face and clothing and made several tears in his shirt.

Billy said, "I will wait here until you return. We can't do this without the Verdance." Red went over the side first with Jason right behind him.

It took about twenty minutes to make their way to the bottom of the cut. When they were down, Jason took dirt and pebbles and rubbed it in his hair. He wrapped the short rope around his wrists so that he looked to be tied securely and then nodded to Red. Red pulled the hat down on his head. He pushed as much of his growing hair under the hat as he could. He grabbed Jason by the back of his collar and started walking toward the supply tents.

As they came to the tents, the lone guard stood up with his spear ready.

Red said in a low but friendly voice, "Look what I caught trying to cross the bridge!" He lifted Jason off the ground and shook him by the collar. Jason opened his mouth and Red slapped him hard across the face. "Keep your mouth shut, redskin."

The guard lowered his weapon and stepped up to look at Jason and said, "I ain't never seen an Indian up close. He don't look like much."

Red said, "He put up a good fight for such a little guy. Hey, you wouldn't happen to have a smoke on you, would you?"

The guard said, "Sure," and pulled out a bag of tobacco with papers.

Red took it and said, "Let's walk over behind the tents. I don't want to get you into trouble for smoking on guard duty."

The guard asked, "Aren't you going to turn him in now?"

"I'll do it in a minute. I'll just give him to the lizards at the entrance, but there's no hurry."

He dragged Jason roughly over to the front of the tent and pretended to tie him to the main support of the tent.

"That will hold him for a couple of minutes."

He laughed, put his arm over the guard's shoulder and guided him around to the back of the tent.

Red told a few jokes and then the rumor about the Koros eating their slaves.

As soon as they were out of site, Jason slipped into the tent. Billy had told him what to look for and he went straight to the boxes he had described. Red was making enough noise to cover him lifting the top of a box and removing a five pound piece of Verdance. He strapped it to the inside of his leg just above his ankle and moved back to take his position in front of the tent. A few minutes later Red and the guard came around the corner still talking.

The guard asked, "What's your name? I haven't seen you around before."

Red smiled big and stuck out his hand. "My name's Shorty Call. I just got here a few days ago and they put me out on patrol right away."

The guard took his hand and said, "I'm Lamar Gull. It's good to meet you, Shorty."

Red laughed and said, "Well, I guess I better deliver the lizards some supper," and he bent to untie Jason and tied his hands back behind him.

He lifted him by the collar and walked him out into the dark. He kept the act up until they were close to the cut and then released Jason and patted him on the back. Jason took the rope from his hands and smiled up at Red. They made the climb up the cut and Billy was waiting at the top. Red quickly changed clothes and hid the uniform in some nearby rocks.

Jason handed Billy the Verdance and asked, "Is that enough?"

"Yes, this should be enough."

They gathered up the ropes and started back to the air vent.

When they had all gathered round, Billy said, "We are just about ready. Silver, Jason, Johnny and I will go down the air shaft, place the Verdance on the floor of the mine, free the captives and then make a rush through the entrance and onto the bridge."

Jamee said, "Johnny and I have a better idea for the Verdance."

She took the rock from him, and then Johnny and she tied it to the nose of the boulder with leather straps. She had cut furrows in the rock to hold the straps in place.

Billy examined what they had done and smiled. "This will work better than laying it on the floor. There is no way the rock can miss now."

Jason said, "Billy, I want to go first and try to free the captives on the second level. Give me five minutes before you climb down."

"Jason, if you're caught, it might cause our whole plan to fall apart."

Jamee asked, "What are you talking about? What captives on the second level?" Billy told her and Johnny about the conversation between the Volls they had heard.

Jamee gasped, "Do you think they really eat them?"

"I don't know, Jamee, but it would explain why there aren't as many captives as we had thought."

Jamee took him by the arm and went outside.

When they were alone she said, "Let Jason try. If we left anyone behind to be eaten, I could never forgive myself."

"You're right. We came here to free all the captives and not leave anyone behind."

He kissed her and they walked back inside the rocks.

"Okay, Jason, we'll give you ten minutes to get back to the vent and then we're coming down." He turned to Red. "You wait ten minutes after we leave to move the rock into the shaft and then run as fast as you can and meet us at the entrance to the mountain tunnel."

Red agreed.

Silver took off her long knife and handed it to Jason saying, "You may need this if there are steel locks on the cages."

Jason took it and smiled up at Red. "I'm glad you are on our side, Red. You scared me when I was your prisoner."

Red laughed and gave Jason a big hug.

Jamee and Silver hugged Jason, kissed him on the lips and Silver said, "I'll give you another kiss when you bring the people to the tunnel."

Jason blushed but had a big grin on his face. He shook hands with Billy and Johnny and then went over the side of the shaft.

Jason went down the shaft quickly, knowing that time was not on his side. He had to move and not be seen. He reached the bottom of the air shaft and stuck his head out and looked around. There were no Koros but he could hear noise toward the entrance. He dropped to the floor and saw several captives looking wide-eyed at him from a cage twenty feet away. He put his finger to his lips and saw them nod. He whispered, "I'll be back," and then moved past them and headed deeper into the mine.

The mine shaft was large with the ceiling about ten feet high and the walls were about fifteen feet apart. There was light glowing from cutouts in the rock wall but he didn't have time to examine the source.

The smell was so strong that Jason cut a strip of leather from the bottom of his shirt and tied it around his head, covering his nose. The further he went into the mountain the more he could see that the mine was very similar to the tunnels he had passed through. He was looking for a way down and he didn't have much time. He thought if he had to spend much time there he might pass out from the smell. He moved toward openings in the tunnel wall and carefully approached each, looking for a passage to the next level. Each passage was dimly lit, but he didn't hear or see anything.

Jason moved towards one opening and he heard what sounded like shuffling. There was no place to hide so he flattened himself against the wall a few feet from the opening. The noise grew louder and it sounded like someone walking. Jason had Silver's long knife in his hand and thought he was ready, but what he saw was a total shock to him.

A Koro stepped into the tunnel with a human forearm gripped in his hand and he was eating from it. The Koro pulled a strip of meat from the arm and saw Jason. He grunted and reached for a long knife in his belt. Jason leaped forward and swung so hard he cut through the Koro's neck and the blade dug into the wall of the tunnel. The body and forearm dropped at his feet and he had to fight not to be sick. He stepped around the dead Koro and looked into the tunnel where the Koro had appeared. He could see stairs that led down.

There was nowhere to hide the body so he left it and moved cautiously down the steps. The smell grew more intense. The stairs wound down about thirty feet to another opening. Jason stuck his head out and what he saw made him violently sick. There was a large, open room and in one corner there was a pile of glistening bones and skulls up to the ten-foot ceiling. The skulls were human and were cleaned of hair and meat, as if they had been boiled clean.

About twenty feet away was a large pot with a low fire beneath it and a bubbling vapor coming from it. The pot seemed to be one of the sources for the foul smells in the mine. He wiped his mouth and spat trying to get the taste out of his mouth. Jason continued to look around.

At the back of the room he saw a door with a metal lock. The door had a small opening about four feet up from the floor. Jason ran for the door, listening for any noises. When he reached the door, he looked in the opening, but it was pitch black and all he could hear was water trickling down from somewhere inside.

He whispered, "Is anyone in there?" He heard some shuffling but no other noise. "Is anyone in there? I've come to free you."

He heard a moan, but it was quickly cut short. Jason was running out of time so he made a decision, stepped back and cut into the lock that held the door closed. The lock dropped away and Jason flung the door open, ready for what was inside, or so he thought.

What Jason saw made him drop his sword arm and stare. There, inside, was a small huddle of people, all completely naked, but more startling than that was a white girl huddled alone in the other corner. She had almost pure white skin and golden blonde hair. She looked at him with big frightened light-blue eyes. Jason tried to speak, but nothing would come out.

He took a deep breath and said, "I'm here to rescue you. Come with me, because I want you to live."

The girl or, more accurately, the woman continued to stare at him.

Jason stepped to her and said, "Please, come with me. I'm going to take you out of here." He then took her hand gently and guided her out of the cell.

"What about us?" someone called from the cell.

Jason turned his head and said, "Yes. Everyone come with me. Help each other if it is needed. We are going up to set the other captives free."

The four naked people came out of the cell and huddled around Jason and the girl.

"Stay close, but give me room if we meet any Koros. I will kill any I see."

He started off for the stairwell holding the hand of the white woman and the others crowded around his back. It would have been comical if not for the situation. Jason thought, *I wonder what kind of teasing I'll get for showing up with five naked people.* He glanced at the girl again just as they reached the stairs. Her blue eyes stared back, but some of the fright was gone. He smiled at her but she only stared back.

Just as they started up, Jason saw a door open about ten feet to the left of the stairs. The captives froze and backed against the wall. There was stark terror in their eyes. Two large Koros stepped out into the room. They saw the door hanging open where the captives were held.

The Koros pulled their knives and Jason leaped at them. He cut into the first Koro and ducked as a knife sliced the air where his head had been. Jason brought his long knife around in an arc and cut the belly of the other Koro open. He continued his swing and cut deep into the neck of the first one. He then brought the long knife over his head and finished the second Koro.

It had taken him just a few seconds to kill both Koros. Jason motioned to the captives and they all moved up the stairs to the first level and found the dead Koro where Jason had left him. They all stepped around it and like a clutch of chicks around their mother, they stayed close to Jason.

Jason approached the air shaft opening as Silver dropped to the floor with a knife ready. She took a step toward Jason to let the others get down but stared at the comical scene. She looked at the beautiful, naked white girl staring at Jason and holding his hand.

Silver smiled and said, "I guess I won't be giving you that kiss later." She turned toward the entrance to guard for the others.

As each member of the party dropped into the mine shaft they stared at the beautiful white woman and then grinned at Jason. He was turning a bright red but could say nothing.

They all moved off toward the cages, where many eyes were staring out at them.

Billy whispered, "We have come here to free you, but you must be very quiet." He saw many nods. "When I open this door, you will have to run with us. We are going out of the mine, across the bridge and down the road. You will have to keep up. If you can't, someone will help you. We want everyone free."

Someone whispered from the cage, "Even that white girl?"

Billy stepped to the side of the cage and said, "Everyone! If you want trouble, there are plenty of Volls out there you can loosen your anger on. Does everyone understand?" There were nods and several soft yesses. Billy stepped out of the way and Jason moved forward and with one swing of his long knife cut the lock away from the cage door and opened it. Billy held up his hands and the captives stopped.

"You will follow us quietly. We are going to kill the Koros at the entrance as quietly as we can. If there isn't a lot of noise, we will all walk quickly to the bridge. Once we're past the guards on this side we will have to run and deal with the guards on the other side of the bridge. Then we have a few miles to run to the escape tunnel. We have to hurry across the bridge because we are going to destroy the mine and it will be very dangerous to stay here. Do you understand?"

The captives nodded.

While Billy talked, Johnny took up a position near the entrance. Silver looked around and saw Jason looking at the naked girl's body as she clung to his hand.

"Jason! Pay attention!"

Jason jumped at the sound of Silver's voice and blushed even deeper as he looked at her.

"Give her your shirt to wear so you will be able to help."

Jason quickly removed his shirt and helped her put it on.

She reached up and pulled the wrapping from around his nose and looked into his eyes and whispered, "Thank you." Jason gave Silver her long knife back and pulled out his hunting knife.

Billy motioned for all his people to move to the front and started off toward the entrance. The white girl followed close behind Jason, as did the others he had saved.

They came to where Johnny was and he put his lips to Billy's ear. "There are six Koros at the entrance. Let Silver and Jason deal with them and then you and I can kill any of them outside."

Billy motioned for Silver and Jason to move close and then told them what to do. Without a word Silver and Jason moved to the front. Billy put his hand on the white woman's shoulder to hold her back. As one, Silver and Jason moved forward and sprang on the six Koros. Jason killed two quickly, but Silver had the other four down and dead before he finished.

Billy and Johnny rushed past to kill any who were outside but found the area empty. It was around four in the morning and everything was quiet. Billy ran back into the mine and the captives emerged and followed silently. The woman was once again close behind Jason, holding on to his belt.

They walked toward the bridge and when they were about twenty feet away Jason reached back and removed her hand.

A guard said in a loud voice, "Halt! Who goes there?"

The group continued forward and Billy said, "Slaves going out on a work party."

As he finished his words he sprang forward and cut the man down. Two more Volls rushed out of the darkness and Johnny jumped at them, killing one and wounding the other. Jason was there to finish him.

Red and Jamee were looking down the air shaft but could only make out movements. They couldn't tell what was happening. Then all the movement was gone and the ten-minute wait was over.

"It is time, Jamee."

She looked at him with a determined look and said, "I just hope they are out of there."

Red braced himself under the boulder and nodded to Jamee. She extended the blade of her staff and made the final cut in the channel for the boulder to slide into the shaft. Red tried to lift the stone but nothing happened. Jamee ran under the stone to add her strength to Red's and still nothing happened.

She ran back around to the front of the boulder and with her staff she hacked at the back of the base of the boulder, but it did not move. Red groaned, putting all his great strength into the effort, and just before his strength gave out he heard the scraping of rock as the boulder moved slightly.

Jamee ran back around and screamed with effort as she and Red heaved. The boulder began to slide and dropped slightly onto the big rocks that were placed under it to give support. At this slight drop the boulder picked up speed and the base dropped into the shaft. Red and Jamee continued to push with all their might and the boulder tipped forward and vanished down the shaft.

Red grabbed Jamee and pulled her out of the enclosure and then they ran for their lives. At a cut near the mine entrance, Red started down.

Jamee said, "Red, we're supposed to take the ridge to the tunnel."

Red paid no attention and continued down. Jamee quickly followed. They were down in a matter of seconds and only a short distance from the bridge.

Red ran on the bridge, pushing through the crowd of captives, with Jamee right behind him.

The large party moved onto the bridge and walked quickly. The bridge was about two hundred feet long and built very strong. They were about forty feet from a large group of Volls with spears and swords at the ready when a blinding light leaped from the entrance of the mine and then they heard the explosion. Everyone was temporarily blinded and the party stopped. Billy started forward, still unable to see when something big brushed past him and he heard a roar come from the beast and then he heard a higher-pitched scream as another beast pushed past him.

All he could think was, *That's Jamee!*

Red crashed into the still blinded Volls, smashing them to the ground as Jamee flew through them, cutting them to pieces. Soon Billy and the others were fighting through as well. In a matter of seconds twenty Volls lay dead and the party was running as fast as they could down the road. The ground shook violently and threw everyone down, but they were back up and running as the earth continued its deadly dance.

Billy said, "Everyone spread out and help the stragglers but stay ready for more enemy."

It was growing light when they were about a mile away from the tunnel and they stopped for a moment to catch their breath. The small party of rescuers went to the edge of the drop-off and looked back. The bridge was gone. Smoke and clouds of dust were pouring out of the entrance to the mine.

Johnny said, "The waterfall has stopped! Where is all the water?"

"I don't know, but maybe it is filling the mine. If that happens, no one will ever go in there again."

They got everyone to their feet and started running again for the entrance of the escape tunnel.

When the boulder flew out of the air shaft it hit the floor of the mine with such force, it drove itself several feet into the rock below. The Verdance exploded, causing a large section of rock to shift down, sealing the underground river's path, forcing the huge volume of water up and into the cave. The mine was huge and it would take several weeks to fill, but eventually the water would exit out the entrance and the air vent and pour back into the valley a thousand feet below.

CHAPTER 22

Daniel slept on the platform of one of the Bookus trees, trying to keep away from the two beautiful women who would not leave his side. After they had bathed in the pool of a water cave, he got his first real look at them. He stood just outside the cave wondering what he must do to get away from them, but his eyes kept straying to them as they dried their bodies. They were about Jamee's height. Both had large almond-shaped eyes that tilted upward, giving their eyes a permanent smile. Their skin was the color of honey and they had strong, shapely bodies. They were beautiful! They also were identical in every way that Daniel could see.

He tried to avoid them, but he would have had to run out in the prairie and hide to get away. He finally pleaded with May to make them sleep with the other women in one of the caves. He moved up to the platform to have some peace and get some much needed rest. In his dreams they were there dancing around him naked, teasing him, trying to get him to lay down with them. He tried to run but his feet had grown into the Bookus tree and he couldn't move. Everywhere he looked their breasts seemed to be pointing at him.

Daniel woke with a start and was sweating. It was just before dawn and he decided to find an empty cave and wash up. He moved down to the fifth level and worked his way around the great trunk and found a water cave no one was in. He quickly cut a hole in the floor, stripped off his clothes and eased himself into the water. He took a piece of matting and began to scrub himself clean. He ducked his head under the water and held his breath, trying to get the girls from his mind.

When he came up for air and his eyes focused, they were standing there, watching him. He started to rise but remembered he was nude so instead he turned his head away and said, "What are you doing here? Get out and leave me alone."

One of the women said, "Daniel, don't be afraid. You saved our lives and, even more, you saved us from those men. You have no idea what that means to us... to me. We want to thank you."

Daniel spoke without looking, "Okay, you've thanked me and I was glad to help you. Now please leave."

He heard them moving around and when he looked they were slipping into the water with him. His eyes were wide with fear and he moved back against the opening. He wanted to jump and run, but he couldn't let them see what they were doing to him.

One of the girls, not trying to move close to him, said, "Daniel, please. We don't want to hurt you or make you hate us; we just want to stay close to you. We... I feel safe when I'm near you. Won't you at least talk to us and get to know us a little? You'll see we aren't bad and we didn't want to go with those men. They forced us into the tent. We have been hiding in the group ever since we got here. We didn't want anything like that to happen to us."

Daniel turned and looked from one to the other and said, "I don't hate you. I know you didn't want to be in that tent. I heard you screaming and that's what made me run back for you. I wanted to help you, but...well... you don't owe me anything."

The girls moved a little closer to him and one said, "It's easy for a man like you to live in the world. You are so big and strong and confident, never afraid to walk around. You're handsome and maybe you're married already."

Daniel looked at the two girls and could now see their faces were identical.

He thought, *So they are twins.* And then he said, "Why are you afraid? No one is going to hurt you now. I won't let them. But girls, you can't follow me around everywhere I go. It's making me nervous. When we get back to my village there will be a lot of young hunters who will be very interested in you, and if you want husbands, they will be easy to find for two beautiful girls like you."

Now the two girls turned and looked at each other and then back at Daniel and said at the same time, "You think I'm beautiful?"

The sounds of their two voices were sweet harmony. Daniel's breath caught in his throat. "Yes, I do."

Now they moved up against Daniel and he felt their breasts brush his arms and chest. They looked down in the clear water and could see his excitement and they both smiled.

"Don't you even want to know our names?"

"Yes, I...I do. What is your name?" Daniel asked looking at the girl on his right.

"Sawaan," she said and moved just a little and her body left a trail of fire across his chest.

He looked at the other girl and asked, "What is your name?"

"My name is Sirilak."

Her teeth were so white, they shone in the morning light. Daniel felt two small hands touch him, grasp and then release. Sirilak and Sawaan jumped from the pool.

They were holding hands and looking down at him.

Sawaan said— or he thought it was Sawaan— "Daniel, we have talked about finding a husband already and my sister and I choose you. We want to show you something no man has ever seen before."

They turned their backs to him, reached behind their heads and each pulled a long, shiny pin from her hair. Their hair whispered as it fell down their backs all the way to their calves. Turning towards him their beautiful, honey-colored bodies were curtained in black silk and again Daniel's breath caught in his throat. They were the most beautiful girls he had ever seen and their bodies were perfect.

They dressed quickly and as they turned to leave, Sirilak said, "We will give you time to think about what you have seen and heard, but you are ours, Daniel."

They walked from the water cave with their hair swaying down their bodies like black water flowing over smooth rocks and then they were gone. It was only then that Daniel realized what she had said.

"Both of them?" he said out loud.

When Daniel got to the ground he found May helping some of the men shape spears from long thin branches.

He ran over to her and said, "May, I need to talk to you."

May looked at the concern in his eyes and motioned him to follow a short distance away from the others.

She turned and Daniel blurted out, "They both want to marry me! What am I going to do?"

May's eyes crinkled in a smile, but she tried to keep a serious look on her face.

She moved to Daniel, lifted up on her tiptoes and kissed him on the lips. "Well, if you love them, marry them both or pick one or neither. There are plenty of men who would call you lucky. You're a good man and I wish I could help you, but this is your choice. Sawaan and Sirilak have talked to me and told me they want to stay together and that they have both fallen in love with you. I told them to let you know how they feel but then give you some time to think about it."

Daniel looked at her like a bear that had been struck in the head by a falling tree.

"Both of them; I don't think that's allowed in our village."

"Luke said it would be something for the elders to decide, but he couldn't think of any rules or customs against it. If it's something you know you don't want, pick one of them or neither, but I don't think that will work. Think about it for a while. They are both very sweet and they are serious about what they want.

"Come and help me. We must make weapons for the people. It might take your mind off your problems," she said with a smile. "When I came down this morning, there were limbs lying all over the ground. It's like the Bookus trees just dropped them last night."

Daniel moved in a daze but picked up a limb and started sharpening the tip.

Luke came out of the prairie with two young men and a young woman, walked over to May and Daniel and said, "We've been about five miles north and didn't see any sign of pursuit. I think we can wait until noon before we head out again. I want to make sure there are strong, armed people with the weaker ones. Daniel, since those women aren't going to leave your side take them and stay behind the main group about a mile and keep watch to the north."

Daniel started to protest but realized Luke was right about the girls. They weren't going to leave him alone. He just nodded and picked up two short limbs and began to cut sharp points on them.

Bert came up to them with one of the sacks he had taken from the supply tent. He opened it and dumped its contents on the ground. There were eight long knives and several hunting knives. Two of the long knives were the specially coated ones.

May picked up one and handed it to Daniel. "Take this. It will come in handy if you run into any trouble."

Daniel picked up two hunting knives as well and stuck them in his belt with a sour look on his face.

Luke laughed and said, "Daniel, you look like you ate some bad meat. Are you okay?"

"You would look like this too if you had two girls who wanted to marry you."

Bert said, "Not me; that would make my day!" He would have continued, but the look Daniel gave him closed his mouth.

May said, "Luke, I think you should lead the group and I will stay on one side and Bert on the other. That way, if we run into trouble, we can help organize a fight."

"Good. We will make the next grove around sundown if everything goes well."

They started out at noon and made good time to the next grove and prepared for the night. After eating, Daniel went up to the platform and got ready to sleep.

"Daniel? Please come and sleep in the water cave. We're afraid and need you to help us sleep," Sawaan said.

"No!"

"Please, Daniel. I promise we won't make you angry and we'll be good girls. Sirilak is crying because she's afraid to be alone. Please."

Daniel growled and then followed Sawaan to the cave. Sirilak really was crying and Daniel's heart dropped when he heard her quiet sobs.

"Sirilak, don't cry. There is nothing to be afraid of."

"Nothing. What about all those Volls who want to kill us or even worse?"

Daniel took a deep breath and said, "Okay, I'll sleep here tonight, but you have to promise that you won't try anything while I'm asleep."

Sawaan asked, "What would we try, Daniel?"

"You know what I'm talking about. Now promise."

Both women said in their beautiful harmonic voices, "I promise, Daniel."

He lay down near them but made sure they weren't touching. Daniel tried to stay awake but was quickly asleep and woke just before dawn and felt their warm bodies curled up next to him. The warmth felt good and he lay there enjoying the feeling. He was thinking about having two wives and smiled at the thought of waking every morning to this warmth. How would they make love? His excitement rose and the girl in front snuggled closer and settled back down. Daniel didn't know if it was Sawaan or Sirilak, but she felt good. He rolled her on her stomach and let his big hand slide down her body and then he rose and left the cave.

They started out around midmorning still heading south.

About three hours later Sirilak said, "Look over there." She was pointing off to the east and Daniel could see movement and dust being kicked up. Whatever it was, it was slightly ahead of their position.

He said, "I'm going to go over there and take a look. Stay here."

He started off at a lope and after ten minutes he stopped on a small rise. Daniel could see a large group of Volls marching at a quick pace heading south. There were at least seventy of them and they carried shields, swords and some had bows.

He felt a movement close behind him, whirled and saw a Voll raising his spear to throw. As Daniel moved to the side he saw the Voll drop, with a wooden spear sticking out of his back. Sawaan stepped forward and put her foot on the Voll's back and pulled, retrieving her spear. She looked up at Daniel with a dazzling smile, so proud of what she had done.

Daniel ran over to her and said, "I told you to stay..." And then Sirilak stepped out beside Sawaan, smiling as well. "Never mind. Come on. We have to warn the others."

Sawaan and Sirilak grabbed up the spear, knife and shield the Voll had dropped. They ran down the rise and Daniel was surprised to see that both girls kept up with him with little effort.

They reached their large group a few minutes later and Daniel called out to May. "There is a large party of Volls off to our left and they are getting ahead of us. They are armed with shields, swords, spears and bows."

They ran to warn Luke.

After Luke heard, he quickly looked around and saw a hill that rose out of the prairie a half mile away. He said, pointing to the nearby hill, "There! Let's get everyone up there and prepare to fight them if we are found."

Bert came running in and said, "Luke, there are soldiers off to our left and they have seen us."

Luke pointed at the hilltop and ran to the group, hurrying them to change direction and move as quickly as they could.

The people were formed with the weak behind the strong. There was only one shield to protect them from arrows. The Volls had turned toward them and were advancing in an orderly formation.

Bert said, "Let me take a small group and flank them. We will attack from the side. It will confuse them."

May said, "Pick five strong people and do it!"

Bert turned and quickly chose five people, including Sirilak, and then moved off to the north. Daniel watched as Sirilak was leaving, wishing she wasn't going. She turned and blew him a kiss and gave him a beautiful smile and then was gone.

Sawaan stepped close to him and took his hand and said, "Don't worry. She will be back."

He could see the worry in her eyes and put his arm around her, then bent down and kissed her softly.

The Volls were moving to within arrow-range as Luke told everyone, "Keep your eyes on the flight of the arrows and try to dodge them as they fall. Daniel, May and I will return fire. When they charge us, use your spears and kill them, because they will kill you if you don't fight back. If you are injured and can't fight, try and move to the rear. Are you ready?"

With a great roar that Luke hadn't expected, they all cried out, "YES!"

May looked at Luke and smiled, then pulled him to her and kissed him hard on the mouth. "I love you!"

"I love you, May!"

They turned to meet their enemy.

CHAPTER 23

Billy's party arrived at the small bridge to find Tommy waiting.

"Did the green rock make that light and noise, Billy?"

"Yes. Now show us how to get to the tunnel."

Tommy led them across and then under the bridge, up a stone path to the entrance of the cave.

He said, "I'll go and bring the bridge down. I have it set to fall."

"There's no need, Tommy. The big bridge at the mine is gone. They won't be coming after us from that direction."

Tommy looked disappointed but then smiled and started handing out torches. He had made a number of new ones from the wood he had removed from the small bridge. Billy turned to the people gathered at the entrance to the tunnel. He saw many eyes filled with fear at the thought of going back into the mountain.

He said in a voice loud enough to carry to all, "We have to go through this tunnel to reach the other side of the mountain. It will take many hours to pass through, but it will be safe. The floor is flat and walking will be easy. There are a number of other tunnels leading off this main one but do not go into them. Stay on the main path. Do not be afraid. This tunnel will lead to your freedom."

To give them something to look forward to he said, "After we are out of the tunnel we will go to a beautiful valley where you can rest. We will hunt and you will have food to eat and you will be safe."

Billy motioned for Johnny to lead off into the tunnel and the large party started in.

He counted as the people passed by. One hundred and five captives had been freed and none of his party had been hurt. Red and Silver were in front with Johnny. Jason and Tommy were about midway and Billy and Jamee brought up the rear.

After only an hour Red called a halt and let the tired people rest for thirty minutes. He started them up again and walked for two hours and then rested for an hour. They had only a little water and a few pieces of dried beef. Once out of the tunnel they would get water from creeks on the prairie and hunt to provide food on their way to Green Hiding.

Red stopped a number of times to let the people rest. A few were in relatively good shape, but most were thin from the hard work and poor living conditions and constant fear. Very few had any major injuries. Billy was told by a young man near the rear that injured people were either thrown into the valley or taken to the next level down.

As Jason walked along, he saw that the four people he had freed from the second level were all close by, watching him.

"Why are you watching me?"

One of the young men said, "You saved our lives from something worse than death. We will follow you wherever you go."

Jason asked, "How long were you down there?"

"We were there just a few days, to fatten us up, except for the white woman. I have never seen her before. So she must have been there for a long time."

Jason looked at the young woman with the blue eyes and asked, "How long were you down there, um... What's your name?"

"My name is Sarah and I don't know how long I was there. It seemed like forever, but it must have been at least a month. They were keeping me hidden from the Volls."

"How did you come to be here, Sarah?"

"My father was an official on QB-45 and he was caught changing the records and diverting money to help the people of Ocean. That's what we call QB-45. His punishment was to see me raped by three black slaves and then he was murdered right in front of me. The people who did it sent me here as a prize for the Koros, but I had to be smuggled in so the soldiers wouldn't see."

Sarah knew Jason could see her tears in the torch light. She turned and looked to see his tears and she smiled for the first time.

Sarah said, "I have seen things that I never thought possible, but I have also seen a man risk his life for me and that is something I will never forget. Thank you.... What is your name?"

"My name is Jason."

"Is that your whole name? I would like to know the full name of the man who saved me."

"I am called Jason Bear Killer."

She looked at him in surprise and asked, "Have you really killed a bear?"

Jason smiled and said, "I am a hunter of the Eagle Tribe and I have hunted many things, but there are no bears here. Many of our names come from stories of our people when they lived far away, in another place."

"Are you an Indian?"

"We accept that name now since all the tribes were put together. So, yes, I am an Indian."

Sarah moved close to him and looked at him for a long time as they walked. He was not tall but several inches taller than her. His hair was black and silky and fell down to his shoulders. His skin was dark and smooth and his face, with high cheekbones and a prominent nose, gave him a strange beauty.

She leaned over and kissed his cheek and asked, "How old are you?"

"I will be nineteen in two months. Thank you for that kiss; it felt good."

Sarah asked, "Do you have a woman?"

Jason's eyes widened and he said, "No, I don't have a wife. Why do you ask?"

Sarah looked down at the floor of the tunnel and said, "I just wanted to know. By the way, I am twenty years old."

They were about thirty minutes from the exit of the tunnel when Flick landed on Billy's shoulder and looked at Jamee.

Jamee's eyes widened in fear. "Three people have entered the tunnel from this end. One is Apache Joe and he is following the others. The two in front look dangerous and Flick hasn't seen them before."

Billy said, "It'll be hard to get past all these people. Flick, go warn Tommy and Jason and then Red, Silver and Johnny. Hurry!"

Flick took off and Billy and Jamee started to work their way forward through the people.

Flick flew in front of Jason and then Tommy's face, flashing bright red and silver. She flew toward the front a few feet and returned and hovered in front of their faces for an instant longer and flew away, heading for the front of the line.

Jason said, "Come on, Tommy. I think Red and Silver are in trouble."

He gave Sarah a quick kiss and hurried toward the front of the line of people. Tommy followed close behind.

Flick was in front of Silver's face flashing red and black colors, then flew a few feet forward and came back. She did this several times and finally flew toward the exit of the cave.

Silver grabbed Red's arm and whispered, "There is danger ahead of us."

Red didn't question Silver's words. He raised his big hands and everyone stopped. He told Johnny what was happening and all three started forward. They had gone about forty feet and could hear people hurrying through the crowd behind them. Johnny had an arrow nocked in his bow and moved next to Silver as Red advanced in front and to the left of them.

They heard someone ahead scream, "Trackers!" and heard the thrum of a bow string.

Silver tried to leap forward but Johnny jumped in front of her and let an arrow fly. Both arrows found their mark. The tracker's arrow pierced Johnny's chest, cutting into his heart, and passed through him, entering Silver's chest above her right breast. Johnny fell to the ground holding his chest and Silver slumped to the floor beside him.

Jason and Tommy ran past them looking only briefly as they ran towards the intruders. Red was already there lifting the body of one of the trackers.

A voice called out ahead of them, "I am Apache Joe and I'm coming in." Joe appeared out of the darkness and said, "I killed the other one. There were only two."

Red clapped him on the shoulder and smiled, but Jason stopped close to Red and said, "Red, you better go back. Silver and Johnny were hit."

Red spun and said, "Silver!" and he ran back to the torch light.

When he arrived Jamee was kneeling over Silver and there was a lot of blood on the front of her shirt. Billy was kneeling and was cutting Johnny's vest off of him. There was a large hole in his left breast and blood was flowing onto the floor. Red's heart nearly stopped as he kneeled down next to Jamee as she opened Silver's shirt. Jamee pulled a large piece of matting from her pack and handed half to Billy. She was looking at Silver's face, which was very pale in the glow of the burning torches.

"You're going to be all right, Silver! The arrow missed your heart, but it pierced your right lung. Try not to talk. Breathe slowly. I have to pull the arrow out and seal the wound with the matting."

Silver looked up at Red and tried to smile and then asked in a whispered voice, "How is Johnny?"

Jamee turned Silver's head and looked into her eyes and said, "Not good. I think the arrow cut into his heart and hit his spine as it came out."

Tears came to Silver's eyes as she whispered, "He saved my life. Now take the arrow out and let me see him."

Jamee asked Jason to help hold Silver down, but Red moved in and took hold of her shoulders.

He said, "I love you, Silver Dove."

Jamee stood over Silver, placing her hand on Silver's chest close to the wound and held the arrow shaft in her other. With a quick steady pull the arrow came out. Silver never uttered a word and waited for Jamee to put the matting into the wound and wrap her chest. She then demanded to see Johnny.

They helped slide her beside Johnny and she raised her head and looked into the deathly pale face of the man who had saved her life. His eyes flickered opened and he smiled up to her.

He said, "You are the most beautiful woman I have ever seen and I am glad to be your friend."

Silver, with tears running down her face, whispered to Johnny, "I am lucky to have a friend such as you, Johnny Little Dog."

She leaned down and kissed him softly on the lips.

Johnny smiled weakly and looked up at Billy and said, "Don't forget me, Billy."

Billy let his voice rise strong and proud and said, "Johnny Little Dog will be a name never forgotten by the People! It will live on and the story of your bravery will never die. I am proud to be your friend."

Johnny smiled and then closed his eyes and a restful look came upon his face.

Billy looked up and said, "He is gone."

They dragged the trackers' bodies out to the edge of the foothills and left them on a nearby boulder to rot in the sun. They carried Johnny and Silver back to Green

Hiding with all the freed people taking turns carrying them. Silver wanted to walk, but Jamee forced her to lie on the stretcher they had made from the shirts of the men of her tribe until they were back at the cave. They went to the main trail leading into Green Hiding.

It was near sunset when they arrived and Jamee helped the women prepare a fire while Billy and Tommy went to hunt. Red never left Silver's side, except to help carry Johnny's body. They put him outside the cave and guarded his body all night and then at dawn they buried Johnny in a glade near the river.

Few words were spoken, but with Red's help, Silver stood and said. "Johnny Little Dog will live on in our hearts and in the hearts of our children. I would like everyone here to know he was my friend. I shall call this place Little Dog Glen. Know you all that he is one of the People and we are proud of him!"

There were tears and a few picked flowers and laid them on the grave. There was no marker except the glade in which he rested.

As they walked back to the cave, Sarah took Jason's hand and walked with him.

She was silent for a long time and then said, "I'm sorry I never got to talk to Johnny, but I will get to know his people better if they will let me."

Jason smiled. "I don't think that will be a problem. I will introduce you to my village and will let no one speak against you."

She said, "Will you walk with me by the river?"

He guided her to the river bank and they walked hand in hand for a while. Jason had found another shirt to wear. Sarah wore his other shirt and a loincloth Jamee had given her. Her white skin was already turning bronze from the sun. Her blonde hair was clean and sparkled. They sat on a rock at the edge of the river and watched the flow pass swiftly by.

She took a deep breath and asked, "Jason, do you think you could ever like someone like me?"

"What do you mean, Sarah? I like you very much."

She kept her eyes on the flowing water and said, "I mean someone who is not a... not a virgin, and I am white. The white people have done so much wrong to your people and the people of the other worlds. I would have expected you to hate us."

Jason touched her chin with his hand and turned her head so she would look at him. Those beautiful blue eyes looked at him with a sadness that touched his heart.

"We have never been taught to hate other people. Look at Red. He is white, but he is also one of the People of my tribe. Sarah, what was done to you was not something you could stop and when I think of the terrible things you have seen, I want to find a way to take those memories away from you. But even if I can't, I will be your friend and protect you."

"Do you think you could ever be more than a friend? I know I am older than you and I am not beautiful like Jamee or Silver, but I can't seem to take my eyes off of you. When you came into that room and freed me I thought you were the most handsome man I had ever seen."

Jason blushed at her words and then he said, "Thank you for saying that, but there are many hunters in my village who look better than me. You have a beauty I have never seen before. Your face, hair, skin and, more importantly, your heart are more than any man could hope to find in a woman. Yes, I could be more than a friend, but I don't want to take advantage of you. I'm not very good around girls. They frighten me sometimes because I don't know what to say or how to act."

Sarah smiled, put her arms around Jason's neck and pulled him to her, kissing him softly. She leaned back and said, "For someone who doesn't know what to say, you say all the right things. Do I frighten you?"

Jason kissed her and wrapped his arms around her. "Yes, you do." They laughed and kissed again.

Billy and Apache Joe sat outside talking about how Joe happened to be in the tunnel.

Billy smiled and said, "I had a feeling we would see Bert again. I'm just glad I was right about him. What are you going to do about this girl, Jasmine?"

Joe looked up from his whittling and said, "I'm not sure, Billy. I think she would have tried to follow me here if Luke hadn't watched her. She's so pretty and brave. You know me: I have never had many friends and since I was fifteen I've been a long-hunter. Being around crowds makes me nervous, but there is something about Jasmine that really touched my heart, maybe for the first time."

Billy said, "Joe, don't take this the wrong way. Are you attracted to her in a... a womanly way?"

Joe's eyes became steely black and his hand moved toward the knife at his belt, but then he relaxed and smiled. "No, Billy. She is just a little girl and needs someone's help. She picked me and no one has ever depended on me to protect them before. I have started to depend on her too to put some happiness in my life, but what am I going to do with a child?"

Billy smiled. "Joe, I didn't mean anything by my question. I know you well enough to know you are a good man and there are many people who depend on you and trust you. It sounds to me like your decision has been made, Papa."

Joe laughed and said, "I guess I'm going to have to get used to that name since everyone who hears it calls me papa. I do need someone in my life. I just wasn't expecting it to be a daughter."

"When people find out what a good heart you have the women will start looking to help you raise your daughter."

"I'll be leaving early in the morning to get back to Luke and May and give them a hand getting all the people to the village."

Jamee and Silver swam in a quiet pool of back currents off the main flow. Silver was still weak but nearly recovered from her wound.

Jamee said, "I will make you a broth of Bookus matting when we get back. I think your lung is still not healed.

"Stop fussing over me. I'm fine. I'm still recovering from Johnny's death. I thought the matting could repair anything."

Jamee looked across to the other bank and said with sadness in her voice, "When your heart is injured, there isn't much anyone or anything can do to help. What do you think happens to your spirit when you die?"

Silver said, "I don't know. I never really thought about it until Johnny died. I hope there is more. I remember a man who came to my house a few years ago just to talk to me. He told me about a life better than this one after death for those who lived a good life and gave themselves to a Spirit Son of a greater Spirit. I laughed at him because of the life I was living at the time, but he told me all that could change just for the asking. I still don't understand, but my life has changed so much in these last few months. Maybe there is something to what he said."

Jamee said, "It is something to think about. Sister, do you plan on having children?"

"Yes, I do. Red would be a good father and I think he wants children, but he doesn't talk about it. What about you?"

"I know Billy is ready and I am too, but this world is so uncertain right now. Maybe we should wait until the Volls are gone."

"The Volls may be here for a long time."

There was a huge splash right beside the two women and they jumped, but when the water settled there was Red, grinning big.

Jamee said, "Red! I thought a great bear had come to eat us," and she splashed water in his face.

Red laughed and said, "Maybe not to eat you, but I do need some kisses from my wife."

"What have you been doing all day?"

"I've been helping the people make spears while Jason and Tommy have been making bows and arrows so we can defend ourselves if we run into any Volls."

"Do you think there is a chance of that?"

"There are almost a thousand Volls around here somewhere and I'm sure they are looking for us so it's best to be ready. We have set up watches out on the prairie, but I don't think they will come here."

Jason walked up to the bank of the river and with his head turned away shyly asked, "Jamee, could I talk to you?"

"Yes, Jason. Come on in and swim with us. We can talk here."

"But... but you're not wearing..."

Red laughed and said, "If you're going to be around these women, you might as well get used to seeing more than you thought you had a right to see. Come on in."

Silver laughed. "You've already seen more of me than you thought you would."

Jason turned a bright red and smiled.

"What are you talking about?" Red asked, looking at Silver.

"Nothing, my love. Come on in, Jason."

Jason took a deep breath and then hurriedly removed his clothes and plunged into the water. He looked at Silver's wound where the arrow had gone in just above her right breast. It looked completely healed over.

He said, "It looks very good... the wound I mean."

Jamee had moved to his side and touched his arm. Jason jumped at her touch.

"Calm down, Jason. I'm not going to bite you. We are just enjoying the water. Now, what do you want to talk about, besides Sarah?"

Jason turned to look at Jamee and his eyes locked on her breasts for a moment. When he looked up at Jamee's face, she was smiling.

He blushed again and said, "How do you know about Sarah?"

Jamee and Silver laughed and Jamee said, "It's hard not to notice the way she follows you around and the way you look at her."

"I do really like her, but I'm afraid that she likes me only because I got her out of that cage. I don't want her to feel like she owes me something."

"You sound just like Billy. After he found me on the prairie he was so worried that I thought I owed him something for rescuing me. Well, he was right in a way, but I fell in love with him because of him, not because I thought I owed him. Women are a lot smarter than most men think."

Red laughed. "That's the truth!"

Silver punched him in the shoulder and said, "Be quiet. I want to hear my sister explain the facts of life to Jason."

"I don't think Jason needs a lesson in that. This is between you and Sarah to make sure your feelings for each other are real and not because of the situation you were in, but I can tell you I've seen the looks she gives you and they are real. Now you must decide if you have the same feelings, because love is for the rest of your life."

Jason said, "My feelings are real. I've never seen anyone so beautiful and I can feel her goodness when I'm around her."

Jamee smiled and then nodded to someone behind Jason. When he turned, Sarah was there looking at him.

She was blushing at his words, but there was something more in her look.

Jamee said, "Come in and join us, Sarah. The water feels so good."

Sarah's blush deepened and Red said, "Look, she is part Indian. I've never seen anyone with such pretty red skin."

Jamee and Silver splashed water at him and told him to shut up. Sarah turned around and began to remove Jason's shirt and hung it on a limb. Then she untied the loincloth, stepped out of it and hung it on the tree. She stood for a moment with her back to them and Jason looked at the smooth lines of her body and the dimples in the small of her back. Her legs were long and well-shaped. Her skin was so white, it shone like a first moon.

Finally she turned and started into the water.

Everyone gasped a little and she stopped and looked down at her body and then up into their eyes. "What's the matter? Is something wrong with me?"

Silver said, "No, Sarah. You are beautiful, but I have never seen hair that color above a flower before."

"A flower... what does that mean?"

Jason had broken his stare to look at Silver, too.

"That is a word from my old world that means your femaleness."

Jason said, "Oh," and then blushed.

Sarah's flower was covered with a soft cloud of short golden hair that sparkled in the sunlight. As she walked she was looking down at the water.

The effort of walking through the water caused her hips to sway more than normal and Jason could not take his eyes off of her. Her white breasts with pink nipples moved with the effort.

When she got close to Jason she dropped down until the water was over her shoulders and then she raised her eyes and smiled.

Silver punched Red as he stared at Sarah and said, "Did you enjoy that, husband?"

"What? I mean, she is very pretty, my love, but you are the most beautiful woman I have ever seen."

Silver laughed and said, "Good answer."

"By the way what do you called the male part?"

Silver said, "It has many names."

Jamee jumped in without thinking and said, "Billy calls his *Little Buddy.*"

And then with a blush continued, "But don't tell Billy I told you!"

They all laughed and began to talk happily. Jason and Sarah moved off a bit to hold hands and talk. Jamee got together with Red and Silver and decided it was time for them to send someone to the lookout point at the water tower beside the cliff.

When Jamee got back to the cave she pulled Billy outside and told him what they had decided.

He laughed and said, "I have noticed the way they look at each other. Are you sure, my love?"

"Yes. I see love in their eyes."

Billy turned and called to Jason and Sarah. When they arrived he said, "Jason, I need you to go to the head of the valley and keep watch tonight and during the day tomorrow, but be back here by sunset. We will be leaving early the next morning. Sarah, since you are new to Prairie, I want you to go with Jason and start to learn about living here. It can be a dangerous place without the right guide. You can help Jason keep watch. Jason, pack enough for tonight and be sure to take a few blankets. Jamee will tell Sarah where to go while you pack."

Jason nodded, turned and went inside. Billy walked away towards the trees and Jamee began to tell Sarah how to get to the water tower. She also explained the real reason for sending them there.

Sarah hugged and kissed Jamee and said, "Thank you. I never expected such kindness and friendship from everyone."

"Just be sure Jason is the one you love, because it is a commitment for life."

Sarah's smile was so bright that Jamee knew the choice had been made. She walked to find Billy and saw Joe leaving with his weapons and pack, knowing he was heading back to Luke and May.

CHAPTER 24

Bert whispered to the small group battle tactics they would use against the Volls. He said, "Rush in, stab and cut for fifteen seconds, then back away quickly into the tall grass and then run to your left and come back at them from the rear. Stay together. After that follow me or if I go down, just keep moving and hitting them two more times and then fall back into the grass and catch your breath. Keep it up until they run or you're dead. If I am still with you, there might be a change in the plan so keep careful watch. Do not be afraid. You are fighting for survival and a life more than slavery. Kill, kill, kill."

Just as the Volls came to a halt to launch arrows at the escaped captives, Bert, three men and two women attacked their right flank. The soldiers were caught completely off guard, expecting little resistance. The group cut down at least ten Volls before backing away.

They moved quickly, keeping low in the tall grass. They came back at the Volls near the same spot as their first attack. Bert's party came out of the grass at full speed, slashing, stabbing and screaming, and then they were gone. Bert heard the yells of confusion and the shouts of the officers trying to restore order. He led them toward the rear of the formation, knowing they would be expecting an attack on their left flank.

He rushed out of the grass and saw the soldiers' heads turned toward the left of the formation. They made contact with a roar which turned the heads of the closest Volls just as they were cut down. They backed away into the tall grass and several Volls followed, now enraged at the surprise attacks. These soldiers were cut down as well. Bert led the group further into the grass and stopped to catch his breath. He looked into the faces of the *warriors* with him. He was startled by the calm animal intensity as they stared back. Sirilak had a small wound on her left arm, but she pushed him away when he tried to examine it.

He said, "Now comes the hard part. They still outnumber us and without shields many of our people will be killed. We will circle around to the head of the formation and then run along the entire front, chopping bows and killing. We do this for our people!"

He didn't bother asking if anyone wanted to stay behind. He saw the looks in their eyes. As he started to move off, Sirilak grabbed and kissed him hard and then pushed him forward. They ran, staying low, around the side of the Voll formation.

Luke and May watched from the hilltop and saw the confusion in the rear of the formation of Volls. They heard the roar of their people and the screams of the soldiers.

Luke said, "We must attack. They will kill our people."

May said, "No! Not yet. Bert is confusing them and when he puts his group in real danger we will attack."

The first volley of arrows was in the air as Luke shouted to watch the sky. The arrows came to ground and several people were hit, but no one tried to run. They only had a few bows to return fire, but Daniel, Luke and May stepped forward and released their arrows. May picked her targets well, as Luke and Daniel fired at the archer just behind the front rank of shields.

May found the leaders shouting orders to their soldiers, and every shot was true, causing more confusion in the ranks of Volls. After each volley, Luke's small group would move along the front ranks so the Voll archers had to change their targets at the last second, making their shots less accurate.

There were only a few true weapons among the captives, but everyone knew their freedom and lives were at stake. The Volls were in great confusion now and their arrow supply was nearly gone, but Luke could see more archers at the rear being called to the front. Luke knew now was the time. As he released his last arrow he called for them to advance. They were moving at a fast walk with weapons drawn. The new Voll archers were arriving at the front and preparing to fire.

Then the party heard the roar of the small group again and saw Bert leading them directly in front of the formation, hacking and stabbing.

Luke yelled, "Let's go!" And they increased their speed to a run.

May yelled, "Kill, kill, kill!" and the shout was taken up by the charging people.

Bert was staggered by a blow from a swinging shield but kept moving. One of the men went down from a sword cut to his chest and then Sirilak went down. Daniel was at the head of the charge when he saw Sirilak fall. He roared and doubled his efforts to get to the Volls. He brushed a spear aside and crashed into the locked shields and drove them to the ground. He had a long knife in his right hand and his other hand was empty but almost as deadly as he smashed and cut his way through the soldiers. The others had followed close behind and there was a great clash as the front rank came against the shields.

The Volls were not prepared for the viciousness of the escaped captives, thinking they would be weak and weaponless. As a Voll went down, the men and women of the party would pick up their weapons and turn them against the other soldiers. Within a few minutes the Volls were only trying to escape.

Luke roared, "Throw down your weapons and live!"

Some Volls did just that, but small pockets continued to fight. These were quickly killed and the people looked around for more. Luke and May yelled at them not to kill unarmed soldiers and had to restrain a few from doing just that. A handful of Volls were escaping to the north and Luke yelled at a small group that had started to pursue them. They stopped and returned with a look of disappointment on their faces.

As soon as the Volls broke and ran, Daniel spun and ran to where Sirilak had fallen. Sawaan was already tearing at her sister's shirt to check the wound from which blood flowed. Bert and Daniel reached her at the same time and knelt beside Sawaan, staring at the deep wound in Sirilak's stomach. May ran up and told Daniel to get her pack from the hilltop. He didn't seem to hear her and just stared down at Sirilak.

May grabbed him, spun him around and said, "Daniel, go get my pack! It will save her life. Now go." Her voice softened and said, "Daniel, she will be all right. Now hurry, please."

Daniel leaped up and ran as fast as he could toward the hilltop.

Bert touched Sirilak's hand and said, "You are the bravest woman I have ever seen. What did you say your name is?"

Sawaan answered, "Sirilak; she is my sister."

Bert turned to look at her close for the first time and was startled to see Sirilak looking back at him with a smile. They looked exactly alike. He turned to look down at Sirilak and found her eyes on him. She smiled tiredly but squeezed his hand.

Many Volls died that day, but their wounded were treated just as the parties' wounded were. Only three members of their party were killed, including two in Bert's patrol. Luke moved everyone to a large cluster of rain berry bushes with giant pampas grass nearby. He did not want to take the Volls into the Bookus grove and give away one of their secrets. He had some of the worst wounded of the group moved secretly to a Bookus grove about a mile away and treated there. The next day a large party from the village found them.

Luke spoke to the leader, William Jumping Horse, and he brought Bert to meet him. After the story of Bert's help and bravery was told, a loincloth and leggings were found for him to wear. Bert didn't wait but threw off his syncotton uniform and proudly put on his new clothes. He drew a few laughs at his very white skin that had been covered all this time, but he only smiled. Luke told Jumping Horse about the large group of Volls that were to head for the mine.

Jumping Horse thought about all that was said and announced, "There is a party moving toward the mine of the Koros so we shall move north and pick up the trail of these Volls just as Luke has suggested. Luke, you are to continue with your party back to the village. If we need you, we will send a runner. Now, what shall we do with these prisoners of yours?"

Luke told William that Daniel, May and himself would be going to meet up with Billy's party and not going back to the village.

He said, "That is a promise we have made. May and I have two brothers and two sisters in that group and Daniel is their friend as well. We will go."

Jumping Horse agreed and assigned four hunters to stay with the freed people.

He said in a loud voice, "The man Bert, who has white skin but a red heart, will go to our village as one of the leaders of the group of freed people. He has shown his bravery today and his desire to join our people. I think the elders will make it so."

May had already sent people to the battle area to gather arrows and to make sure she got her May Wood arrows back. She spoke to several women and told them to watch over Belle and Jasmine like they were their own children.

"You will give them to my mother when you arrive at the village." Then she knelt beside the children and said, "We are going to help our brothers and sisters, but we will come to the village for you. You are going to stay with my mother, Little Dove, and my father, Sam Walking Bear, until we return. My young sister is there and she will be happy to see you two."

Jasmine asked, "Will you please bring my papa back, too? Please tell him that I love him and miss him."

May hugged and kissed them and then rose to leave.

Belle called out to her, "I love you, May."

Daniel was with Sawaan and Sirilak, telling them he was leaving but would see them in the village. Sirilak was still recovering and resting in the shade of the rain berry bushes.

Sawaan and Sirilak looked at Daniel with tears in their eyes and Sawaan said for them both, "You will return, but you will not want us."

"Why do you say that, Sawaan?"

"Because it is always the same with us; we meet a good person and they leave and forget about us."

Daniel smiled and said, "No one could forget two beautiful women like you. I will not forget. We will be together as friends very soon."

Sirilak said, "You called us beautiful."

Sawaan said, "You called us women."

And together they looked at him and said in their singing voices, "We want more than friendship, Daniel."

Daniel leaned down and kissed Sirilak softly on the lips and then Sawaan.

He rose and said, "We'll see."

As he walked off Sawaan called to him, "Daniel, I... I... Come back to us soon."

The main party headed north and Daniel, Luke and May northwest. Both groups were moving quickly and were soon out of sight. Luke thought it would take two days of hard traveling to reach Green Hiding. He hoped Billy's party would be there. He wondered how things had gone at the mine.

CHAPTER 25

A small group of soldiers staggered into the large camp at dawn and guards from the outpost helped them to the commander's tent. The commander's name was Harry King and he was a veteran of the Earth wars. The killing of people only trying to have a better way of life had caused him many problems on Earth. He had found more and more ways to avoid the slaughter and command had become angry with his tactics.

He was ordered to the outer worlds. Command thought that killing colored people instead of whites would bring the brilliance of the past back to him. They were wrong, but with the overall commander so zealous in his pursuit of the people of the outer worlds, it left him little room to make any changes. He now commanded the rear guard of one hundred and fifty men.

The guard reported to his tent and told him about the soldiers that were waiting outside. He stepped out of his tent and looked at the five soldiers in dirty, torn, and blood-stained uniforms.

"What has happened? Make a report!"

One of the soldiers straightened and said, "I'm Sergeant Broche. We were transporting slaves to the mine for delivery to the lizards. The slaves escaped, with the help of Indians, who set fire to our supplies and killed two trackers. They also captured several of the special long knives we were to deliver to the lizards. We sent a patrol of fifty men after them at daylight and they were turned back with twelve men killed."

The commander asked, "How were they killed?"

"They were killed with arrows. I was with them, sir, and there must have been at least six or seven men who ambushed us. We had several wounded also so we turned back."

"Go on with your report, Broche."

Sergeant Broche continued, "Commander Werner took our entire complement, one hundred and two men, and pursued the slaves. We pursued them for two days and caught up with them three days ago. They gathered on a small rise and were mostly without real weapons. Most carried sharpened sticks. We advanced on them with archers in the second rank and just before we were in range, we were hit with a flanking charge of at least ten big men. As they retreated another group hit us in the rear, killing a number of men. We were hit with a third charge in the same spot as the first attack. We turned to face them, but they were gone."

He never looked King in the eye but continued, "Commander Werner ordered the archers to fire at the escaped captives. The Indians returned fire with only a few bows, but Commander Werner was killed along with all the other officers. I ordered the men to advance and the slaves charged at the same time. I ordered the archers to fire, but before they were ready another large group hit us all along the front ranks causing confusion.

We killed all of the ones who charged the front ranks but we were overwhelmed by the main force. Only a few of us managed to escape and I believe all the rest were slaughtered. We made our way north until we found you."

The Commander said, "How many of the enemy were there, Sergeant? The truth!"

He looked at his boot and then up into the commander's face. "I would estimate fifty or sixty men and women, sir."

The commander looked over at the guard that had brought them to his tent and said, "Take these men to see the medic and give them new uniforms and food. We will be moving out in one hour. Have someone call for my officers to my tent immediately!"

"Yes, sir."

Commander Harry King returned to his tent. He was sick of killing and especially killing men and women who had made a life here on these outer worlds. He had no hatred toward them because they weren't white. In fact, he found most of the people he had met to be good, honest people. He never had the opportunity to meet an American Indian and wasn't looking forward to battling them.

On Earth he had read many illegal books, some in pursuit of his training and some because of the great interest the first books he had read brought him. His special interest was the American Indian tribes. They were all extinct on earth, but here they were on Prairie. From his reading he learned they were a proud people made up of many different tribes and nations.

They could not organize to fight off the white people who moved in to settle the land hundreds of years ago. They were finally forced into a peace with the white men, but several hundred years later they were exterminated during the *Great Cleansing Wars*.

He thanked God that there was one group with vision and without hate in their hearts who had the technology to save many different races of people by taking them to these outer worlds. Now here they were again to finish what they had started, except now the Earth needed slaves. Those idiots that claimed the neutron bombs were perfectly safe for vegetation and structures but would kill all animal life, including the non-whites, had no idea what the real effects would be.

The officers entered the tent and stood at attention.

He said, "I have just received a report that one hundred soldiers escorting slaves to the mine have engaged in a battle with escaped slaves and a few Indians and were defeated. According to the report, all but six men were killed in this battle. The report claims there were only sixty slaves and Indians in the force that opposed Commander Werner."

There was some grumbling but no one said anything. "We will pull out in forty-five minutes and overtake the battalion, make a report and await further orders. Let's get the men ready to move!"

The officers hurried from the tent. Commander King called his orderly and told him to find Sergeant Smith and have him report to him.

In a few minutes an older, weather-beaten sergeant stepped into the tent and stood waiting.

"Jimmy, do you remember the talks we had on QB-45 about this planet?"

Sergeant Smith looked around and then directly at the commander and said, "Yes sir, I do."

"Do you still feel the same way as I do?"

Jimmy replied, "Yes, I do, Harry. I'm tired of the killing of innocent people and want to find a place to finish my life in peace."

"Well, Jimmy, I think it's now or never. We're in for a fight with Indians."

"Indians! I've always admired the Indians I've read about."

"If you are willing to go, I want you to pick four or five men who may feel the same as we do and I'm going to send you on patrol. I want you to find the Indians to the south of us and try and make a deal with them. Tell them there are soldiers who do not want to fight and wish to stay on this world and live in peace with everyone. Tell them we will do anything they ask of us but we would prefer not to fight the other white soldiers. Make arrangements for us to join them and then get back to me."

"Harry, what if they say we have to fight with them?"

"Then we do what we have to so we can live in peace. If you don't find them, return in five days."

"Yes sir! I'll leave right away."

CHAPTER 26

Bert gave supplies and a few packs to the Volls, who had now all recovered from their wounds.

He said, "Head north until you see the trail you made coming here and follow it back to your camp. Then, if I were you, I would turn east and head for the launch site. Don't move too fast, because if you meet the party that left yesterday, they won't be happy to see you."

One of the soldiers asked, "Aren't you going to give us any weapons?"

"No."

"So you turned traitor and now you're sending us out there with nothing to defend ourselves!"

"Think what you like. I'm tired of killing innocent people and I just want to live my life without being around so many people who hate. These people are returning your lives to you."

The one who had asked the questions said, "You mean those slaves and red men aren't going to hate you?"

Bert looked at the man and said, "These people don't hate you! They are just defending their land and way of life."

"You're a stupid traitor and I hope I get a chance to see you again."

Bert walked up to the soldier, hit him in the mouth and stood over him. "I will be looking for you too and if I ever see you again I will kill you."

One of the younger men spoke up. "Can I talk to you alone for a minute? Please."

Bert motioned for the young man to come with him and walked off twenty yards and turned. He was surprised to see three young men coming toward him.

The one that spoke before said, "Bert... Yes, I know your name, but I won't tell anyone. I'm Leo Flint and we," pointing to the others, "we want to stay here, too. We have all talked it over and we don't want to fight these people anymore. I've been here for four months and this is beautiful land. My parents are gone now, but they taught me not to hate people because they are different. These people have treated us with kindness and I would like to return that kindness. If they will let us stay here on the planet, I will do whatever they ask me to do. I want to be a free man and not treat people like slaves just because they aren't white. Do you think they would let us stay with you?"

Bert looked at them all and asked, "Do you all feel that way?"

He went to each one and listened to their answers. They each said it a little differently, but all felt as Leo did.

Bert said, "Go back to the others and don't tell them what you talked about. Lie if you need to, but wait there until I come back."

Bert went to Two Fists, who was leader of the party now, and told him what the young men had asked of him.

Bert said, "I know you might not trust me, but I believe the three men who talked to me. What do you think?"

Two Fists looked at Bert and asked, "Why would I not trust you, Bert? Luke and Daniel have spoken for you and Running Horse spoke of your bravery. This is something I cannot decide, but we will take them to our village and let the elders decide."

Bert smiled at Two Fists and said, "Thank you. It will take me a while to get used to being trusted so quickly. I will not let you down and I will keep a close watch on them."

Two Fists said, "You deal with sending the others away any way that you think is right. We will leave tomorrow and while we walk I will think of your new name. I will also think about the challenge you will face."

He laughed and walked away.

Bert went to the Volls and said, "The leader has said three of you must stand trial for what you all have done." He pointed at the three young men and said, "You three will stay. The rest of you are free to go now. My advice is to stay out of the big trees you'll see but find rain berry clumps to stay in at night to keep the big cats from getting you. Now go quickly, before the leader changes his mind. Don't fight us again or you will die."

All but the three young men gathered up the packs and headed off to the north.

Leo asked Bert, "You're joking about the trial, right?"

Bert said, "I don't know. The elders of the village will decide all our fates, but the men I have talked with say they are fair. Don't worry about it, unless you've been lying to me."

They started out early the next morning, making their way south toward the village. The four hunters were not happy to be left out of the coming fight but took their responsibilities seriously. Two Fists sent one hunter far ahead and one on each side of the party as it moved. He told Bert to take the other white men and guard the rear.

As they walked, one of the young men asked Bert, "What about these women? Can we be friendly with them?"

"If you mean have your way with them, no! These are good people and if you want to talk to them and find out what we have put them through, then yes, you can get to know them."

Another said, "Did you see those twins? Man, they are beautiful."

Bert stopped and turned on all of them and said, "Get your heads on straight right now. These people marry for life and they don't play around with anyone but the ones they pick for husbands or wives. If I hear of anyone getting hurt or molested, I will hunt you down and so will the hunters of this village."

"I didn't mean anything, Bert, really. I just said they are beautiful."

Bert turned and began to walk and said, "Yes, they are."

Jasmine, Belle and a woman watching over them walked back to Bert. Jasmine held her hands up to him. He picked her up, kissed her on the cheek and continued walking.

"You look very nice in your new clothes, Bert. Are these your friends?"

Bert smiled and said. "I like my new clothes and, yes, these are men I know and I think they will be all our friends."

Jasmine looked over Bert's shoulder and said, "Hello. My name is Jasmine and I will be your friend, too. I want my papa to meet you."

All the young men said hello and tried to shake hands, but Jasmine insisted that they kiss her on the cheek. Belle looked up at them shyly as they walked.

She walked over to a slender young man and asked, "Are you going to hurt me?"

The questioned surprised the young man and he replied, "I would never hurt a pretty little girl, especially you."

She held out her arms. The man picked her up and, copying Bert's action, he kissed her on the cheek and said, "My name is Herman. What's your name, little bit?"

"My name is Belle, but you can call me Little Bit."

He laughed and settled her into his arms.

It was mid-afternoon and everyone was tired. Two Fists could see a Bookus Grove about a mile ahead. He was about to signal the hunters to head in the direction of the trees when the scout that was out in front ran towards him, bleeding badly.

"Koros! Koros!" and he collapsed at Two Fists' feet.

A woman in the group rushed forward to help the injured hunter.

Two Fists let out a loud, screaming yell that rippled with sound. Two hunters ran in and one pointed to the other side of the group. Three Koros loped in with spears held high. Two Fists had his bow off his shoulder and sent one arrow and then another at them. The hunter closest to the Koros ran at them with his hunting knife ready. The arrows hit their mark, but only one Koro went down. The hunter charged in and stabbed the uninjured Koro and then turned on the last one standing. He dodged the spear thrust at him and slashed the Koro across the face. He side-stepped another thrust and stabbed the Koro in the chest. All three were dead.

Two Fists and the uninjured hunters kept their positions and saw five more Koros coming from straight ahead. Bert, hearing the warning, handed Jasmine to the woman and drew his long knife.

As he looked around he saw five Koros coming at them from the rear and he yelled, "Koros!"

He turned to face them and the three young men stood by his side, without weapons. The Koros came straight at them and Bert blocked a spear thrust, stabbed and turned toward the others. The soldiers each grabbed a Koro and tried to take their weapons away, but the Koros were too strong. Bert fought off the fifth Koro as men and women from the group ran in with weapons and killed the three Koros that the soldiers were fighting. Bert killed the last one by slashing his throat and nearly removing his head.

The five Koros Two Fists and the other hunter fought were now three. Two Fists' arrows had killed the first two. As the other hunter fought, trying to keep the three from getting past him, men and women ran to him and attacked the Koros.

The hunters, Bert and the soldiers held their positions, watching and waiting. One of the young soldiers had a deep wound in his shoulder from a Koro spear and a woman tried to help him, but he pushed her away in case more Koros came at them.

Two Fists ran back to Bert and said, "I think that is all of them. I have sent men out each side to look for more."

He told two men standing nearby to run and check the rear. He saw the young soldier bleeding and motioned for the woman to look at his wound.

He said to Bert, "We will move slowly toward the Bookus grove ahead. Keep watch for any trouble," and then he ran toward the front.

CHAPTER 27

About midday May, Luke and Daniel arrived at the cave, tired, dirty and looking around at all the people that crowded the cave. Billy, Jamee, Red and Silver rushed to hug and kiss them.

May said, "What about the trackers?"

Jamee told her, "They are dead. Joe killed one and Johnny killed the other."

May smiled and said, "That is good news!" but as she looked at Silver, she could see the sadness in her eyes. "What has happened?"

Red said, "Johnny Little Dog was killed. He saved Silver's life by moving in front of an arrow shot by one of the trackers. He killed the tracker before he died."

Luke walked over to Silver and put his arms around her. "I have much to thank Johnny for. I'm sorry he is not here to hear my words."

Silver said, "He will not be forgotten."

Luke asked, "Where is Joe?"

Billy replied, "He left heading back to your party. You must have passed him on the way here. Papa was in a hurry to get back to that little girl."

Everyone laughed and Daniel said, "It's hard to believe a man as tough as Apache Joe could be tamed by a little girl, but she's as strong as Joe in what she wants. They will make a good pair. The next thing you know Joe will be getting married and settling down."

Billy told everyone to get some rest because they would be leaving early in the morning.

Billy's party left Green Hiding early the next morning and had been walking for three hours. He was amazed at how fast the people were recovering.

With the food, rest and peace of mind, their bodies quickly healed. The broth of Bookus matting which Jamee had made also helped a great deal. He saw Jason and Sarah walking together smiling and talking. He smiled and knew they would make a good couple. Silver was completely healed, but Red still watched her closely. She looked up, seeing Billy watching her, and waved.

Jamee, also looking over the group and said, "There will be a lot of new people in the village. Do you think there will be room for everyone?"

"There is room to build new homes and plenty of land for farming, but these new people may want to start their own village or move to one of the others. It will be a while before they are all healthy and strong enough to make it on their own. There are only three men from our village and I hardly know them. They must have been taken a long time ago and they don't want to talk about what happened to them.

"I think they have been through something that will be hard to explain to people who never went in that mine. I don't see how they lived with that smell and knowing what had happened to the others. Sarah was down in that place where they... but she is strong and Jason is making her happy. They are a good match."

Billy said, "She is happy and healthy, but you should keep talking to her. I think she's still very afraid of what will happen to her. This is something completely new to her and she will need help adjusting. Many of the others will need help as well. From what I can find out, we have people from four different worlds in this group. From what Red told me, each world is very different from the others. We'll be at a Bookus grove in three or four hours and we will have to show them how to treat the trees."

Jamee walked close to Billy and let her hand stray down his rear. With her eyes tilted up and a look of sadness in them she asked, "Don't you want me anymore,

Billy?" There was a slight smile on her lips, but Billy missed it.

He looked at her in surprise and said, "Yes. I want you all the time." He looked around and whispered, "but we never seem to be alone."

Then he saw the smile grow on her face and knew she was teasing. He looked around at the people nearby and then down at the beautiful woman and her teasing smile. He grabbed her up, his hands gripping her rear, and kissed her. She pressed herself to him and returned the kiss.

He put her down with a look of desire. "Tonight I will have my way with you, woman."

She laughed and said, "It looks like little buddy doesn't want to wait."

Billy looked down and saw his excitement trying to free itself from his loincloth. He looked up and saw several men and women smiling at him and watching his predicament.

He quickly turned his back to them and adjusted himself so he didn't look like he was trying to point the way. He heard several chuckles and turned back around blushing. When he looked at the people around him, they were all smiling.

Jamee said, "See, you do know how to take their minds off their hardships."

He grabbed for her again but she skipped away, laughing as she went and said in a loud voice, "Not until tonight."

It was so funny, seeing her skip like a little girl, Billy let out a heartfelt laugh. It seemed he hadn't laughed in days and with his laughter the tension he felt melted away and he continued to walk with a new spring in his steps.

Silver and Red walked together near another group and Silver had been watching a young woman talking to Tommy. He looked at her several times, wide-eyed, and moved away. She then turned her attentions on several other men walking nearby, who also seemed not to want to talk to her. One even gave her a shove to send her on her way. The young woman turned her gaze on Red and openly let her body take on a seductive walk, but when she saw Silver's hard stare she quickly moved off.

Silver said, "I think I will have a talk with that one tonight."

"Which one?" Red asked.

"Never mind."

She knew the signs. The girl was a prostitute on her old world, probably ever since she was a young girl and she didn't know any other way of life. The new freedom on this world would be hard on her if she didn't learn that offering herself for payment was something not accepted. Yes, she would talk to her tonight and perhaps get Jamee to help.

She told Red, "I'm going to talk with Jamee," and walked off toward where she saw Jamee walking alone and smiling.

Around mid-afternoon they reached the Bookus grove. Billy gathered everyone around and talked to them about how to treat the big trees and then asked Jamee and Silver to take the people up to the water caves and show them how to get to the water. He motioned for Red, Jason and Tommy to follow him. He dropped his pack at the base of a giant tree and carried only his bow. The others quickly followed. Two of the freed men ran to him and asked to go along on the hunt.

One said, "We were hunters and guides on our old world and haven't been hunting in a long time."

Billy asked, "Are you from Forest?"

"Yes."

"There is a woman that joined our group who was from that world. She is now my sister, but she was a forest guide. Her name is May."

They both looked at him with wide eyes and one asked, "Is she dark skinned with short hair and very beautiful?"

"That sounds like my sister."

The man replied excitedly, "May is the best guide on our world. I never met her but saw her passing through a village one time. She always kept to herself but the stories told about her are legends among the other guides. It is said she killed two trackers!"

Billy said, "She has already killed two on this world."

"Your people killed two of them and I wouldn't have believed it if I hadn't seen their bodies."

"Yes, but we lost a good man doing it."

There was a good meal and happy talk that night.

They left the next morning and would reach another Bookus grove about mid-afternoon. Just before the party arrived at the Bookus grove a scout on their left ran in and said a large group of people were heading their way.

Flick landed on Billy's shoulder and Jamee said, "It's the hunters from our village!" They stopped and waited until the hunters arrived. Red Eagle headed the group and came to Billy with his hand extended.

Billy took his hand and said, "I see you, Red Eagle."

Red Eagle smiled and looking around at all the people said, "I see you, Billy. It is good to see that you did what you came to do. How are the people?"

"They are still weak but getting stronger. They have been through some very bad times and they are happy to finally be free again. We are heading for that Bookus grove to rest tonight."

"Good. Let's talk as we walk."

Billy told him all that had happened and when he spoke about Johnny, Red Eagle said, "Little Dog was a good man but had few real friends. I am pleased that he was in good company at the end. What he has done will be remembered by our village. I will have you tell the story of his bravery."

"I will do that, but I think Silver would be a better one to tell of Johnny's gift to her." Red Eagle nodded.

That night Red Eagle sat and talked with Billy, Jamee, Red, Silver, May, Luke and Daniel. He said, "We will leave in the morning to track these other Volls. You may continue on to the village or come with us."

Luke said, "I think we would like to go back to the village with these people and make sure everything is safe there. Then we will come back and find you."

They all nodded and looked at Red Eagle. He said, "Good. We have enough men and I am expecting parties from the other villages to join us in several days. You have all done more than I had hoped for. I am proud of you all. Now let's get some rest and I will speak with you again before we leave in the morning."

Billy stood, took Jamee's hand and whispered, "I need more than rest, my love."

They said good night and hurried to the ground and went to a tree near the edge of the grove. They practically ran up the transit limbs to the third level and into the waiting water cave. Jamee had put their packs in it almost as soon as they arrived at the grove.

Billy had a small fire going as Jamee cut a hole in the floor.

When she finished she turned and walked to Billy. "I want you so much!" and then jumped into his arms.

They kissed and helped each other remove their clothes, trying to go slow but not succeeding. They jumped into the pool and washed, kissed and touched. Billy ducked his head underwater, moving his lips to Jamee's thighs and then kissed down and back up her legs. When his breath was almost gone he surfaced and before he could grab her, she was underwater and kissed him the same way. She came up gasping for breath and laughing. They came out of the water, dried each other and then lay down on a blanket. In the firelight Jamee was a painting of golden light and dark shadows. Billy leaned back to look at her closely.

"Have I changed since we first met?"

"You've only become more beautiful. When I look at you I still find it hard to believe that you love me, but my heart is so happy that you do. I see you walking on the prairie or lying here and I want you, knowing I am a lucky man. I love everything about you."

"Do you love me truly?"

"Yes, my love."

"Then show me how much."

Billy lowered his head, kissed her tenderly and his hands moved over her body. He heard her moan of pleasure come from deep inside. He moved his mouth down the smooth skin of her belly, feeling her muscles ripple in anticipation and the softness of her skin. As he came to the hair above her flower he was surprised to find it cut short but still silky.

He looked up and she said, "Silver helped me. She said you might like it that way. Do you like it?"

Billy kissed through her hair and answered, "Yes, I do."

"I think I like it, too. Oh, that feels so good."

He moved over her and lowered his body to hers. Their feelings mingled and moved together.

This time it was like a small explosion in Jamee's brain that swept down into her body growing more intense. Sensation radiated from her flower as her release engulfed her and took her to a place she had not been before. Just for an instant she passed out, flooded with so much pleasure her mind couldn't contain it.

Billy enjoyed her release, knowing he had brought it about. The feeling of giving filled him with warmth and love for Jamee. He was complete and content.

They lay together for a long time before she spoke. "Was that good?"

"It was more than good."

They went to the pool and cleaned each other, then moved to the blanket and were asleep in moments.

The next morning Red Eagle led his party north and Billy's party headed southwest. They traveled all day and rested once again in a Bookus grove. The people were tired, but each day they showed improvement. Jason, Tommy and May would range ahead, scouting and hunting near the next stop for the night. There was always plenty of game and the women would gather plants and roots to make a delicious meal. Late afternoon of that day they met with a party from another village heading north to help Red Eagle.

The leader's name was Great Bear and he fit his name. He was a giant of a man, even bigger than Red. Billy greeted him and told him they were taking the group to his village.

Great Bear said, "We will consider taking some of the people to our village."

As he looked around he saw Red walking over.

"What is this white man doing with you? Why is he dressed like one of the People?"

Billy said as Red walked up, "This is my brother, Jim Travis, and he is now a member of my village." He motioned for Silver and Jamee to come over and said, "This is my wife, Jamee Soft Dove, and this is my brother's wife, Silver Dove."

The three held out their hands to Great Bear and he took them but kept a wary eye on Red.

He said, "So both women have taken the name of your mother. Your village is changing very quickly, Running Wolf, but you do live closer to the prairie. This white one will be an interesting person at the next gathering. He's big enough, but can he fight?"

"Red has already proven himself many times and was challenged in our village."

Great Bear said, "It is good to know that he has met the challenge, but he has not met the men of my village."

Red smiled and said in a pleasant voice, "I look forward to meeting the men of your village. It is always good to know the strength of others."

Great Bear smiled and nodded. "Well said, Jim Travis. Now, we shall camp here tonight. We still have several days of travel before we find Red Eagle."

That night Billy, Jamee, Red, Silver, Jason and Sarah were sitting on a platform talking when a great light made the night like day. They all stared off to the northeast but had to shield their eyes from the brightness. The light lasted for almost a minute; then darkness came again and they were blinded for several minutes.

Billy looked at Jamee and asked, "What was that?"

"I don't know, but I will try to find out."

She looked off into the distance and Sarah asked, "How will she find out? I don't understand. Does this happen often on this world?"

Billy replied, "This has never happened as far as I know. Jamee sometimes can see things but not all the time."

He didn't know if he should reveal the truth of Jamee's powers now but knew at some point Jamee would have to let the others know that she could see through the eyes of birds.

Jamee said, "I don't know what that was. Maybe we should all get some rest."

Billy could see she had something to say but was reluctant to speak in front of Jason and Sarah.

He said, "Jason, you and Sarah keep watch for a while, but if nothing else happens get some rest. We will leave early in the morning."

As the others left with Billy and Jamee, he motioned them to follow.

When they were gathered in the water cave, Luke and May stepped in as well and Luke asked, "What was that? I have never seen anything light up the night like that."

Billy motioned for them to sit down and then he turned to Jamee and waited.

Jamee said, "There was an explosion or something like that. I think it was where the Volls' spaceships were sitting. The only thing there now is a great hole in the ground and pieces of what I think were their ships. I saw no people around the area, but there were Koros moving away toward the northwest."

Billy turned to Red and asked, "What do you think? Could the Koros have blown up the Volls' ships?"

"The Koros have no explosives, as far as I know. If they managed to damage the light-speed drives, then it is possible that could have caused the damage Jamee described. But why would they do that? It would trap the Volls on this world."

Billy said, "I must go to Great Bear and tell him what we know and we must send runners to the parties from our village.

Billy returned from talking to Great Bear and those resting sat up and listened to what he had to say.

"Red, Silver, Daniel, Luke and May will go to Jumping Horse's party and then, if Jumping Horse agrees, take a party to the place where the Volls' ships are and try to find out what has happened. Jamee and I will continue to the village and then return and find Red Eagle."

The next morning the three groups separated. Billy led his party southwest toward the village, walking as fast as the people could travel. It took them four days to reach the village. Everyone was tired and in need of rest. People were waiting to take care of the freed people and Sam and Little Dove took Billy and Jamee to their house.

Billy spoke to Sam, "Father, we must leave right away. We have to get back to Red Eagle and help where we can."

Sam said, "You will rest for two days. You can't do everything, Billy, and Red Eagle is the best leader we have. Little Dove and I will not let you leave until you have rested." Billy nodded, nearly falling asleep on his feet. He had slept very little, trying to help everyone and keep watch during the night. If it weren't for Jamee, Jason and Tommy, he didn't think he could have kept everyone moving so fast.

Little Dove sent Billy and Jamee off to the bathhouse to clean up. When supper was ready, she went to get them and found them both asleep by the tub.

She woke them up. "Come and eat and then off to bed. Tomorrow you will be in the care of Nuuna and she will make sure you rest."

Late the next morning after they had eaten Nuuna took them to the bathhouse and they bathed together for two hours and then she took them to the river to lie in the shade.

In the late afternoon Nuuna said, "I have missed you so much. Why don't you stay here with me and rest for a few more days."

Jamee said, "We have missed you, too. We must go out again, but when this is over we will sit and play with you for many days."

Nuuna looked at Jamee and said, "I haven't told anyone, except Mother, but I can sometimes talk to Flick. She told me not to tell anyone because it might make trouble for me, but I wanted you to know. I can only speak a few words to her and I have to concentrate hard."

"That's good news. Now we can talk to each other through Flick and if you need help all you have to do is tell her. I think Flick is right. You shouldn't tell anyone else for now. People might expect too much of you if they knew. Where is Flick anyway? I haven't talked to her in several days."

"She's been very busy watching everyone mate. She says she really likes being around all of us."

"Nuuna, do you know what she is talking about?"

"Of course I do... but I don't see what all the excitement is about. It seems like a lot of work to me, but I guess when I get married I'll have to do it, too."

Jamee looked closely at Nuuna but decided to let it drop for now. She would speak to Little Dove later.

Two Fists and his party had arrived in the village several days before, but Bert and the other hunters had left after resting for only a day. They were returning to join Jumping Horse. The elders had allowed Bert to become a member of the village but had told everyone Bert would have to meet the challenge upon his return.

Billy and Jamee left the next morning. Jamee had talked to Little Dove about Nuuna's knowledge. She also asked her to watch and speak to the young woman she had seen openly offering her services on the prairie. Little Dove said she would deal with both problems. She also said she would care for Jasmine and Belle until everyone returned.

CHAPTER 28

Luke, May, Daniel, Red and Silver were hurrying to join up with Jumping Horse. They had stopped only a few times during the day and slept in the Bookus groves at night. The previous night Red and Silver had stayed in a water cave alone. They had talked long into the night.

They spoke of their love and Red told Silver, "My love, you have brought the one thing to my life that I had

searched for and was never able to find. I have finally
found a love that makes me a whole man. I want you to
have my child and I want him to know that he will be
loved all his life. I know this is not the right time to talk
of this, but I feel I need to tell you how much you mean
to me. If anything ever happens to me, I want to know
that you will take another and complete your life with
joy. That is important to me. You are too good to live
alone and I would be sad if I thought you would do that."

Silver looked at Red and wondered what this was
about, but she said, "If something happened to you, I
would not want to live in this world but hurry to you in
the next. I don't want you to talk about things like that.
Nothing will happen to us and we will have a good life
together filled with the laughter of our children."

She did not want to tell him she was already with
child and give him more to worry about. His words
frightened her, but she kept it from her smile.

"Promise me, my love. I want to know that you will
not close your heart to another if something happens to
me. I want to hear you say it."

"I can't make that promise. If I lost you, nothing in
this world would have meaning, and I don't want to live
without you, but I would try to live and perhaps love
again, if only to bring you peace in the next life. Now no
more talk about this. I need you to make love to me and
feel your warmth and strength. Please make love to me."

They made slow tender love until the end. Red
seemed almost frantic as his release came and his
passion and desire helped her reach her release.

Bert and three hunters met them just before they
left the trees early the next morning. Red seemed very
happy to see Bert again and they talked until everyone
was ready to leave. They moved out and were only two
hundred yards from the Bookus grove when they came

under attack from fifty Volls that had lain in ambush waiting for them.

Red and Bert struck them in the center of their strength, while Daniel and Luke came at them from the left. May was firing arrows at the Volls in rapid fire. Silver and the other three hunters went into their right side and with hands, feet and long knives they cut into the enemy with a deadly force. The three warriors went down in a hail of arrows from the Volls. Ten Volls broke off from the center attack when they saw Silver standing alone. They rushed toward her, but Red had seen them moving toward Silver. He let out a vicious cry and cut them off, using his great hands and long knife to cut into them. He alone stopped them from getting to Silver who was still engaged with other Volls. He was mortally wounded and fell to the ground as the last of the ten died. It only took a few minutes to send the few remaining Volls running.

Daniel looked around and saw Silver had an arrow deep in her side, but she was still standing looking around desperately. Bert ran up and stood looking down at Red. Red had two arrows in his chest; one had cut into his heart. Silver ran to him, tearing the arrow from her side, dropping to her knees beside Red. When Daniel and May ran up and saw what had happened, they then ran off pursuing the fleeing Volls. Luke was trying to look at Silver's wound, but she pushed him away and cradled Red's head in her lap.

She yelled at Luke, "Do something! Don't let this happen!"

Luke ripped his pack open and started applying some matting to Red's wounds.

Red said, "It's too late, Luke. Let me be so I can look at the woman I love."

Silver cried, "No, Red! It will be okay! You will be fine, my love."

Red smiled up at her. "Yes, you will be fine, Silver Dove, but I must leave you now. Remember our talk last night. You promised me."

He was getting weaker and his eyes began to close.

Silver cried, "Red, please don't leave me. Red, I have something to tell you! Look at me, my love."

He opened his eyes again, still smiling up at her.

"Red, I am having your baby. I wanted to tell you last night, but I didn't want you to worry. Your baby, Red! Now you can't leave!"

Bert had kneeled beside them and was helping Luke apply the matting.

Red turned his head to Bert and said, "Bert, will you look after her? She will need your help and kindness."

"I will, Red. You have my promise. I will be Silver's friend."

"Protect her, Bert." Red turned to Silver, still smiling and said softly, "My beautiful Silver, I must leave now, but I will watch over you and our child. I have loved you long before I met you and will love you forever. Hold me and let me feel your strength one more time. I love you, Silver Dove."

He closed his eyes as Silver took his head in her arms. He passed from this life knowing he was loved and knowing his child was growing inside the woman he loved. It was a good death. Silver held Red for a long time, rocking back and forth in her sorrow.

May and Daniel returned and Daniel spoke to Silver saying, with tears in his eyes, "They are all dead, Silver. Not one escaped."

She took her knife and cut locks from Red's hair. She gave some hair to May and then a little to Luke but kept most of it for herself. May asked for a little more and Silver numbly handed her the pouch.

She took what she needed and then handed the pouch back to Silver, kissed her and said, "I love you, sister. Come back to us for the child that grows in you."

Silver would allow no one to help her wash the body and dress him in clean buckskin. She took the silver feather from her hair and tied it around Red's neck, using strands of her own hair as a necklace. They placed Red's body in the ground and the silver left her eyes with only a dull gray left behind. She had the look of death. It wasn't only her death but the death she would bring to others.

Silver moved towards Jumping Horse's party after burying Red on the prairie with cold detachment. She would only allow a small amount of matting to be placed on her wound. She moved, hoping it was to her death, but Bert was by her side every step of the way trying to give her some comfort. He said little to her but refused to move away from her side even when she told him to leave her alone.

May stayed close as well, speaking softly to her sister about those who loved her and needed her, but Silver heard no words of comfort. She knew she was being punished for all the years she had spent in a life she considered degrading. Everyone she touched died. She would bring honor to the name Dove with her death.

Bert spoke to Silver and said, "You must use more matting, Silver. If we are to die, I want to see you take many lives before we go."

She looked at him and for the first time really noticed him and said, "Why would you die with me? You must get away from me. I don't need your help doing what will be done. Get away."

"I made a promise to Red and I will see it through to the end. If I cannot protect you, then I will fight by your side and go to the same fate that you seek. I didn't know Red well, but I have heard the others speak of him and his love for you. He picked me to look after you and to look after your child and that is what I will do."

She looked at him for a long moment and finally accepted more matting for her wound but would say no more to him.

Luke led their party and joined Jumping Horse near the Volls' camp. Jumping Horse had made his main camp four miles south of the Volls but had come forward to see if the Volls would talk to them. They found a large group of Volls formed up in defensive positions. The People were outnumbered at least three to one, but they made preparations for war. Never on Prairie had the People gone to war, but now they painted their faces with their death masks and grimly waited for it to begin. A party of Volls walked out onto the prairie to talk. Jumping Horse, Luke, May and Daniel walked out to meet them.

The two groups stopped ten feet apart and the members of the Eagle tribe waited for the Volls to speak.

A man who carried a staff like the one Jamee carried spoke first. "I am Major Vickers! We ask you to surrender and you will not be killed. You will be taken prisoner and moved to a location to await transportation to Earth. Do this quickly and you need not die."

Jumping Horse spoke. "My name is not important to you, Voll, but your men may call me Death because that is what we bring to you. We will never be slaves to any man. If you come against us you will die. We know your ships have been destroyed."

The major said, "I ordered my ships destroyed! We are here to stay and every soldier under me knows it. What you don't know is I have more men than you think. Right now a detachment is entering the villages of the Indians on this world and taking prisoners. If they refuse to be captured, they will be killed and then my soldiers will come at you from the south. Lay down your arms now and surrender or you will be destroyed."

Jumping Horse looked at Luke and for a moment their eyes locked. Jumping Horse nodded for Luke to speak.

He stepped forward and said in a loud voice, "I am Luke Deer Catcher but you also may call me Death. You have killed my brother and I will not stop until I have killed you. If what you say is true about our village, then no Voll will be left alive. This is our home and you are not welcome here. What your people did on the old world will not be done here. I will have your staff and give it to my sister."

He turned and walked away, followed by the other three. The Volls also turned and headed back to their camp.

Jumping Horse sent scouts out east and west as well as sending a party around to the other side of the Volls' camp.

Luke said, "You have cut our numbers by sending the party to the other side. What is your plan?"

Jumping Horse talked to all the hunters and said, "We cannot defeat them with our few hunters. We will harass them if they attack until more parties arrive. I will not send anyone back to the village. Billy is there and he will have to protect the women and children. For now we will watch and wait."

No one argued with him, but many were unhappy about waiting. Many wanted to return to the village to check on their families, but their leader had spoken and they would not go against him.

Late that night a party of fifty hunters from another village joined their group.

Little Wolf, the leader of the arriving party, spoke to Jumping Horse. "Most of our hunters have gone west to join Red Eagle. We were sent to help you."

Jumping Horse said, "You are most welcome. We will need every hunter for the coming fight. Get some rest. We will keep all the watches tonight."

The next morning May was walking through the camp when she saw Billy and Jamee and she ran to them and exclaimed, "Billy! What are you doing here? You should be at the village!"

Billy could see the agitation on her face and said, "What's wrong, May? We have come to help."

Luke and Daniel ran up to him, looking as worried as May.

She said, "The Volls say they have a large group going to the villages to capture the people there. They say if they don't surrender they will kill them!"

Billy asked, "When did you speak with the Volls?"

Luke said, "We met with them yesterday. They demanded we surrender and they said they would be in the village soon."

Billy turned to Jamee and said, "Send Flick to warn them!"

Jamee turned her head and Flick landed on her shoulder but soon leaped into the air and was gone.

Jamee looked around and asked, "Where are Silver and Red?"

From the look on May's face she knew something grave had happened. May pulled her away and walked to where Silver sat on the ground.

Luke looked at Billy and softly said, "Red was killed in an ambush while we were moving to join Jumping Horse."

Billy looked at Luke as if he hadn't heard him correctly. "What, Luke? Red is dead? No, that can't be true." But when he saw the tears in Luke and Daniel's eyes he knew it was.

He sank to the ground and looked off into space as tears filled his eyes.

He looked up at them and asked, "What about Silver?"

Daniel said, "She was wounded but will be all right, except she... I think she wants to die, too."

Luke knelt down beside Billy and spoke in a whisper of sadness. "Billy, she is pregnant. She told Red just before he died, but I don't think that matters to her now. She only wants to die fighting the Volls. Bert has been talking to her, but she doesn't seem to hear. We've all talked to her."

Billy looked up at Luke and asked, "Bert? What has Bert got to do with this?"

"Before Red died he asked Bert to look after Silver and his child and Bert gave his promise that he would."

Daniel said, "Red died saving Silver's life and ours as well. He killed ten Volls trying to reach Silver. He died smiling, knowing that Silver was safe and that he would be a father."

Jamee and May walked up to Silver, who was sitting on the bare ground. Jamee saw Bert sitting nearby but gave him no thought as she dropped next to Silver, taking her in her arms.

"Silver, I'm so sorry. It was too soon for Red to leave. He loved you so much and it's not right."

She put her head in the crook of Silver's neck and cried with great sobs. Silver put her hand on Jamee's head but said nothing. After several minutes Jamee looked up and saw no tears in her flat gray eyes. This frightened her and she looked at May, but she only shook her head. Jamee forced Silver to look at her.

Silver turned her dead stare at her. She said, "I'm pregnant."

Jamee's eyes flooded with tears again and she pulled Silver to her and whispered in her ear, "We will take care of this baby together and I will take care of you, sister."

Silver said in a voice void of emotion, "That's Bert's job now. Red told him to do that, but soon it won't matter."

May kneeled down and put a red bracelet on Silver's left wrist. "I made this from Red's hair, Silver. It will make you strong."

Silver looked at the bracelet and said, "Thank you."

One of the hunters came to speak softly to Silver and then Billy came and said, "Red was a good man, maybe the best of us all and I will miss him. If anyone is to blame it's me. I'm the one who sent all of you here. Now, sister, it is time to wake up and show him you are the woman he loved. You know he is watching you and how it must hurt him to think you do not care for his child you carry inside. You would kill Red's future in this world he wanted to make his own just because you want to be with him. Someday you will be, but if you go to him with a dead child in your belly, do you think he will accept you? I think he made a mistake in loving you and I think I made a mistake in choosing a sister as weak as you."

Jamee jumped up with fire in her eyes, but May pulled her away and put her finger to her lips. Everyone except May was looking at Billy as if he was crazy to say something like that to Silver, but no one spoke.

Billy saw the bracelet on Silver's arm and spoke as he bent down to take it, "You don't deserve to wear a part of Red. Any woman who would kill her own child doesn't deserve such a precious gift."

As he touched Silver's arm, she stood, slapping Billy hard across the face and yelled, "You have no idea what it is like to lose someone you love more than life. If you touch this bracelet, I will kill you. You know how much I loved him!"

Billy closed in on her, put his arms around her, locking her close to his body and whispered in her ear, "He was my brother and I loved him too, just as much as I love you. I would tear out my own heart if it would bring him back to us. You are carrying our child, Silver; yours, Red's, mine, Jamee's, Luke's and May's. Don't take him away from us. We will help you, but you must live. I love you, Silver Dove, and now it's time for you to love yourself as much as Red loved you. You are my true sister. You have done nothing to deserve this."

As he finished his words he released his hold on Silver and looked into her eyes.

Tears flooded her silver eyes and the lost look faded, replaced by grief. He kissed her. Jamee, May and Luke rushed in to take his place. Bert had found a blanket for her to lie on and all three helped her lie down, kissing and speaking softly to her.

Jamee moved to Billy and put her arms around him. "I love you so much! Thank you, my love."

Billy, with tears in his eyes, looked at Bert and said, "Come with me, Bert. We need your help in planning how to deal with these Volls."

Bert hesitated, looking down at Silver, but he saw May and Jamee caressing and crooning to her as she fell asleep at last.

He nodded and in an unusual move hugged Billy. "Thank you, Billy."

"Why do you thank me?"

"For the words you said to Silver to bring her back."

The hunters gathered around a fire to discuss their first move against the Volls.

Jumping Horse said, "Bert has been taken into our village as a member because of his bravery and he knows something of how the Volls fight. We will now listen to his advice on ways to defeat them."

Bert stepped forward and said, "I was not a leader of the soldiers, but I was trained in fighting tactics. They do not know I'm here so they should use planned movements to trap us. The Volls will not wait for more soldiers so we must be ready. They outnumber us more than three to one and they will move on us without fear. They have not fought trained groups on the outer worlds, but on Earth they fought large battles against trained armies.

"The advantage we have is on Earth they had modern weapons and here they must use the same type of weapons we use. I think they will come at us late tonight with half their forces and try to end this quickly. We must not be here when they arrive and we should hit their camp at the same time they think they are hitting us. We can't go at them in a large force but with several small hit-and-run groups I think we can defeat them.

"If we go in and slash them and then move out for a few minutes and then hit them in a different place, it will confuse them and they may surrender. If they don't surrender, then they must be destroyed... I don't think they will surrender, because they have destroyed their ships. Something very big must have happened back on Earth for them to do that. It may have been Earth Command that destroyed the ships. We may never know unless we capture one of their leaders."

Luke stepped forward and said, "We should believe what Bert has said. I saw him take a few freed captives and confuse a much larger group than we were. Then we attacked and there were only eight Volls left standing and three of them have come over to our side. We released the others but sent them in the direction of a Voll party to the east of here."

Jumping Horse talked to Billy and turned to Luke saying, "Since you have fought these Volls already I will turn the party over to you."

Luke said, "No, Jumping Horse. I will give you advice, but I will be among those that go into the camp. I have my brother to avenge."

It was midnight when their plan was put into action. Five groups moved out. Three groups of ten moved to hit them from the north, northwest and northeast. One group of twenty would hit them from the south and one group of twenty-two would move southeast and wait in reserve. Three men would stay at the original camp to keep small fires burning and then join the reserves as the Volls approach the old camp. Luke and May would take three men and join the five scouts to the north of the camp. Billy and Jamee would take a group to the northeast and Bert and Daniel would take a group to the northwest. Jumping Horse would lead the twenty men attacking from the south.

Silver went with Bert's party.

She went to Billy before they left and said, "Thank you, brother, for opening my eyes again. I will fight, but I will live as well so that I may raise my child in freedom with the help of my brothers, sisters and Bert. I love you, Billy."

"Be careful, sister. Your family needs you."

A few minutes later the groups separated. Luke would start the attack and that would signal the other two on the north side to attack. Once they were all in the enemy camp, Jumping Horse would bring the larger group straight in from the south.

They would wait for thirty minutes after the Volls moved out to attack their old camp before their own attack would begin.

CHAPTER 29

It was midday when Flick landed on Nuuna's shoulder. Flick was a beautiful shining green. Nuuna was sitting with Sarah talking and she turned her head and said, "Hello, Flick."

Sarah said, "Oh, what a beautiful bird. Is she yours, Nuuna?" Nuuna held up her hand for Sarah to wait and tried to concentrate on Flick.

Flick opened her mind and sent a strong pulse into Nuuna's mind saying, "Open your mind, Nuuna."

Nuuna felt the jolt and it startled her, but then she concentrated on Flick and slowly her mind unlocked.

Flick said, "Nuuna, just relax and let your mind open to me. You are young and I shouldn't be doing this now, but I have something very important to tell you. I know we have spoken a few times before, but I have much to tell you and it might be difficult. Will you trust me?"

Nuuna spoke, "Yes, Flick. I trust you."

"Are you talking to the bird, Nuuna?" Sarah asked.

Nuuna looked at Sarah and said, "Please, Sarah, don't speak for a few moments. This is very important," and she turned back to Flick.

Flick said, "You do not have to speak with your voice. Just say the words in your mind. Now listen, my beautiful child. Jamee sent me to warn you that the white people are sending soldiers to hurt the people of this village. I have looked and they will be here in three hours from the southeast. There are eighty men with weapons. They have already been to the other villages and have over two hundred prisoners. Walk to find Little Dove and Sam while I talk."

Nuuna stood, took Sarah's hand and began to walk to find Little Dove. Nuuna knew she had taken the girl who was trying to be friendly with all the men down by the river to talk.

Flick, sitting on her shoulder, continued, "The soldiers will try to take everyone prisoner or kill them. You must run and hide before they get here. There will be a big fight tonight where the other soldiers are. Billy and everyone are there and I need to get back and tell them you are okay so they won't worry. Now you must tell Little Dove because she will believe you. Can you remember all I have said?"

Nuuna said in her mind, "Yes, Flick, I will do everything you told me."

Flick hopped to Nuuna's cheek and kissed her with a peck. She looked at Sarah and said, "She's very pretty and has a golden flower."

Flick flew off heading back to Jamee.

Nuuna pulled at Sarah's hand and said, "We have to find Little Dove. I have something important to tell her."

As they hurried along Sarah, said, "That was a beautiful bird, Nuuna. It looked almost as if you were talking to it."

"I was, Sarah. Her name is Flick and she thinks you are very pretty and she likes your golden flower."

Sarah blushed and asked, "How do you know that? Did someone tell you?"

"Flick just told me. Now hurry."

They found Little Dove sitting with the girl by the river. The girl was crying, but Little Dove was holding her hand, leaning over and kissing her cheek as Nuuna and Sarah rushed up.

Little Dove turned and spoke to Nuuna. "I want you to meet Jinda. She is a good friend of mine. She will be coming to live with us. Jinda, this is my daughter Nuuna. She comes from Forest, too."

Nuuna could see that Jinda was very upset so she walked over, hugged her around the neck and kissed her. "Hello, Jinda. I'm glad you will live with us and we will be good friends."

Jinda smiled but continued to cry.

Nuuna turn to her mother and said, "I have something very important to speak with you about. I have a message from Jamee."

Little Dove's eyes widened and she stood saying, "Sarah, will you take Jinda to the house, let her bathe and find some new clothes for her?"

Sarah smiled and said, "Of course. Jinda, come along. You are going to love the bath. I've never seen one like it before and it feels so good."

She took Jinda's hand and walked off toward Little Dove's house.

Nuuna told Little Dove everything Flick had said and was so happy and proud when Little Dove didn't hesitate to believe her.

Little Dove said, "Come, we must hurry to find Father and the elders."

They found the elders in the village square and Little Dove told them everything Nuuna had said.

Little Bull said, "How do you know all of this? If this is true, we have to move now and get everyone out of the village."

Sam stepped forward and said, "Little Bull, if Little Dove says this is a message from Jamee, then it is true. I won't explain now, but Nuuna and Jamee are sometimes able to talk to each other even when they are far away. We cannot let these Volls take our people prisoner. They will make slaves of them and we just risked so many lives to free the slaves of the Koros and Volls."

"What would you have us do? There are only ten men in the village and three of them are whites who have joined us from the Volls."

Little Dove spoke in a strong voice, "Do you think only men can fight? Every woman here can shoot a bow or handle a knife to protect their family. We will do our part in this, but we must hurry and prepare."

Little Bull looked at the other elders and said, "You are right. This will be our battle." He turned to Sitting Bird and Long Runner, two very old elders, and said, "You will gather the old people and the children and take them to the mountain cave and protect them. Little Dove, gather the women in the square after they have collected all the extra weapons. Sam, find the rest of the hunters and bring them here."

Everyone hurried off. Little Dove told Nuuna to rush home and bring Sarah and Jinda to the square.

Sarah took Jinda into the bathhouse and washed her hair and began to wash her own. She was looking at the body of this young woman and admired the beautiful lines. She was tall for a woman, around five feet six inches, had black hair down past her shoulders. Her breasts weren't large but firm and rounded and her belly was flat, with hips flaring out from her narrow waist. She had a firm rear that joined long, shapely legs and her skin was a golden brown.

As they stepped into the warm water Sarah said, "Jinda, you are very beautiful."

Jinda looked suspiciously at her but saw no hidden meaning. "Thank you, but you are the most beautiful woman I've ever seen. I've never seen golden hair down there."

Sarah smiled and said, "It's just different; it doesn't mean I have your beauty. I wish my skin was as smooth as the women with your color. I feel like a dry-skinned old lady around women like you. Even the older women have the softest looking skin."

"I will show you some secrets on how to take care of your skin if you like."

"Oh, yes! I think you and I will be good friends."

"Maybe not after you know what I am."

Before Sarah could reply Nuuna burst in and said, "We must hurry to the village. There are Volls headed this way. Hurry and get dressed. Jinda, come to the house and I will find clothes for you. Hurry!"

Jinda stepped from the water and dried as she walked toward the house but turned when she realized Nuuna wasn't following.

"Nuuna, you said we must hurry."

Nuuna stood watching Sarah, who still sat in the pool.

Nuuna said, "I have to see something first," and waited for Sarah to stand.

Sarah blushed and stood, letting Nuuna see what she was waiting for.

Nuuna gasped and clapped and said, "It is golden! Sarah, you're so beautiful!"

Sarah said, "Okay. Now hurry, Nuuna."

The Volls came openly into the village and pushed a group of twenty prisoners ahead of them. Two smaller patrols of ten men were sent around the edges of the village with torches. Their orders were to fire all the structures and kill anyone they saw.

The Voll commander said, "This will be easier than the other villages. Look, nothing but old ladies sitting outside their houses. Kill the old people; they are of no use to us."

The villagers and freed people were spread throughout the main part of the village hiding and waiting. There were over one hundred, all with weapons. The others would wait until they could rush in, remove weapons from the dead Volls and then attack as well.

One old woman stood and spoke in a loud voice, "You are not welcome here. Turn back and leave us in peace."

The commander laughed and said, "There will be no peace today, old woman. Tell everyone to come out or we will kill them."

He turned to the soldier on his left and said, "Kill her."

The soldier raised his bow and fired, but the old woman nimbly stepped aside, threw off her blanket, raised her bow and released an arrow, striking the soldier in the throat. As the commander started to yell for his men to fire, two arrows seemed to grow from his chest. From both sides of the street a hail of arrows went into the group of Volls. Many tried to run or take cover but arrows found them as well. Several groups of soldiers broke free, trained to move as small units. They attacked the women firing the arrows, but before the first group reached them, Jason and the three white men who had joined them blocked their path. The hand-to-hand fighting was furious. Jason received a deep cut on his left arm. He felt someone bump into him; he spun to find Sarah standing with her back to him and a dead Voll at her feet.

Another group fought toward Little Dove and a group of women, but Sam and Little Bull plowed into them and the Volls were cut down. Tommy and another hunter fought off five Volls trying to get to another group of women. Tommy was wounded in the shoulder but kept fighting. He heard an arrow whiz past his head and bury itself into a Voll running at him. He glanced quickly to see Jinda nocking another arrow and firing at a Voll just ahead of him. She gave him a dazzling smile as she prepared for another shot.

There were five soldiers guarding the prisoners in the rear, but when the people saw what was happening they attacked the guards and beat them, even though their hands were tied.

It only took a few minutes until the soldiers who were not dead surrendered. A few scattered men still tried to fight but were killed quickly by the women.

Little Bull was yelling for the people to bring the prisoners to the square, but several of the people from the other villages had freed their hands and grabbed long knives lying on the ground and were killing the wounded soldiers around them. Little Bull shouted for his people to stop them and they were soon under control.

Someone yelled, "Fire!" and the people not watching the prisoners turned to see several houses and stores on fire. Flames were leaping from windows and doorways. Some of the fires had already broken through the roofs and were spreading to other structures.

Little Bull ordered everyone to gather buckets and go to the water barrels that were near every house in the village. There was always a fear of fire in the village, where homes and other buildings were built so close together, so they were prepared to fight a fire if it occurred.

The men and women rushed to the barrels and began dipping the water out and passing the buckets down a line of people that had already formed. The people who were new to the village were instructed by the others to get in the lines and help pass the buckets. Some women tied their hair up and the ones with cloth dresses tore them off to prevent them from catching fire.

They moved to the buildings not yet in flames and soaked the walls with water. Some women climbed on the roofs and as buckets were passed to them they soaked the roofs. It took over an hour, but soon the fires began to die. More than half the village had burned, but many homes were saved by the brave efforts of everyone.

Out of eighty Volls, only six were left alive and each was badly wounded.

A woman who had been a prisoner stepped forward and demanded, "Give them to us! They must die for what they did to our people and to our village. Those monsters have already burnt our villages to the ground!"

Little Bull walked over to the woman and spoke softly, "There has been enough killing. We will hold these men until our hunters return and then decide what to do with them."

Someone else shouted, "What about those whites over there with your hunter? They have no wounds and they must die!"

Now Little Bull said with anger in his voice, "Those men are guests in our village. They have fought to give you freedom and they have helped to fight the fires. If anyone harms them you will answer to me. They are friends and will be treated as such."

Someone else from the captives said, "He's right. I saw them kill the soldiers who were attacking the women."

Another one shouted, "I saw them going into a burning house, trying to save it."

Little Dove brought out her packs with matting inside, had the soldiers moved into the shade and began treating their wounds. Several other women were helping as well. Jason had a bad cut on his left arm and Sarah cleaned it and walked him over to Little Dove.

She asked, "Little Dove, can I have some of that for the man I love?"

Little Dove smiled at them both and handed some matting to Sarah.

Jinda walked over to Tommy, who had also suffered a deep cut to his shoulder, put down her bow and asked, "Can I help you take care of your wound? You were very brave. I saw you fighting two men at once."

Tommy said, "I would be honored if you would treat this small cut. What is your name?"

"I am Jinda and you helped save me at the mine."

Sam walked up to Little Dove and saw a sad look in her eyes.

He asked, "What is wrong, my warrior woman?"

Tears came to her eyes and she said, "Something has happened to one of our children. I don't know which one, but it is terrible."

Sam hurried over to Little Bull and spoke to him.

He then turned and said, "I am going to help our hunters across the prairie. Who will go with me?"

All the men had injuries and could not make the long run, so several young women moved toward Sam.

One said, "I will go! My husband is there and I will help him."

Sam finally had to choose four strong, young women and asked the rest to help watch the village.

He said, "Go pack supplies and we will leave in one hour. Meet me here in the square."

The four women turned and ran toward their houses, along with other women to help them pack. Nuuna and several neighbors ran to Sam's house to pack for him.

He sat next to Little Dove and said, "Honeybee, I will do what I can and bring our children home."

Little Dove smiled through her tears and said, "I don't know if I can trust you out on the prairie with four young women."

When all the women were back, Sawaan and Sirilak came running in, each with a pack and weapons they had gathered from the dead Volls.

Sam said, "We have enough people already. You stay here and help protect the village."

Malika Little Rose, Daniel's mother, stepped forward and said, "Sam, these two are very good with weapons and they are going to help my son, Daniel. I have told them to go."

Sam looked at the two beautiful young women and then at Little Dove and said, "I guess we will have to get used to women telling us what they will do."

He smiled and winked at Little Dove and led the group at an easy run toward the prairie. It would take at least three or four days of hard running to reach the hunters.

CHAPTER 30

Commander Harry King in the rear guard camp gathered a few trusted soldiers about him and said, "What I am about to tell you cannot leave this tent.

Something has happened back on Earth. The neutron bombs that were set off to kill so many millions of people hundreds of years ago have caused another large-scale discharge and millions more have died. The scientists believe it was caused by the light-speed drives on the ships returning to Earth. It was decided by the Planetary Governing Council to destroy all light-speed drive ships and rebuild later if a fix can be found. They remote detonated our ships and abandoned us wherever we are. From the reports I've read, they don't have a clue as to the real cause of the deaths, but they used this excuse to placate the people of Earth. It will take many years to build new ships, if they decide to at all."

One of the men asked, "How many years, sir?"

"We had five ships that took almost three hundred years to build. The first one took one hundred years from start to finish. Building the structural frame only took a few years, but the light-drives took over ninety years to assemble and synchronize."

Commander King looked at the soldiers and said, "I am going to break away and either join the Indians or go to find a place to live my life. If any of you wish to join me, you will be welcome. I had sent Sergeant Smith out earlier, but he was unable to make contact with the Indians. "

One of the men asked, "Sir! Isn't that treason? We will be hunted down and killed." King replied, "Treason from a world that has abandoned us? A world that believes in gathering slaves to do their bidding? A world that says people who are not white do not deserve to live a life they choose and make for themselves? We are given this chance to make our choices and I choose to try and live in peace."

CHAPTER 31

It was around three in the morning and all the hunters were set in their positions, waiting. About two hundred Volls moved quietly out of camp heading south. Their countenance was grim. They had all been told about their ships being destroyed, but only one or two knew the real truth. The others had been told the Indians had attacked and destroyed the ships. The few who knew the real truth wondered what the purpose of this war was.

Luke waited for about thirty minutes and then sent two men in to remove the small outpost guarding the rear of the camp. The rest of his men slowly made their way forward. When Luke saw the two hunters kill the outpost guards, he made a quick motion with his right hand, stood up and ran quietly toward the camp. May and two hunters stayed back with bows ready.

As the seven hunters entered the camp they found most of the soldiers asleep or resting. Two large tents nearby appeared to be empty. Luke gave a wild undulating yell and began slashing his long knife at anything that moved. The other hunters joined in the cry and brought death in their hands. Arrows flew in, not in waves but individually, striking targets as they rose. Soon the whole camp was up, some moving toward the attackers, but others stayed where they were to defend their area.

Luke yelled, "Move!"

His party started withdrawing back to the long grass, but the front of the tents opened and twenty Volls rushed to cut them off. Before the Volls reached Luke, Billy's party crashed into them from the side and cut many of them down. This allowed Luke's party time to withdraw. Luke was dragging a wounded hunter with him. Billy was fighting a big man that was very good. He could hear the *thunk* of Jamee's staff as it made contact with flesh and bone. She had not extended the blade for fear of injuring the hunters close at hand.

While Billy fought the big man, he could hear Daniel's great war-cry as his party moved into the Volls.

Using a move Silver had taught him, Billy sprang into the air over the head of the man he fought and brought his long knife down and across the back of his neck, nearly severing his head. He saw Jamee being overwhelmed and slashed his way toward her, but three hunters had already reached her and now she was in the open.

Billy yelled, "Move!" and his party quickly made their way into the long grass.

He ran northeast to circle back and engage the enemy again.

Jamee said loud enough for the others to hear, "Stay away from me when we go in! My blade will be out and I will need no help."

Billy could hear a loud roar from the large party coming in from the south as it tore into the soldiers. Luke had stopped, still to the north of the camp. He knew this next attack would be dangerous because they would come in from the same direction as they had before.

He heard May demanding all the arrows from the others and she said, "I will shoot alone. You two join the fight!"

The two hunters dropped their bows, handed the arrows to May and unsheathed their long knives. Every man had a fearsome proud smile as they watched May prepare.

Each hunter had a small pouch strapped to his belt. It contained matting mixed with a resin that was used to make the paint for their faces. If they were wounded, they would smear the resin and matting into the wound.

Jamee had come up with this before they had left their old camp.

The forward scouts had returned and reported to Major Vickers, "There's no one in the camp, sir. They have small fires, but they're gone."

Vickers swiveled his head and yelled, "Back to camp, now! Be prepared to fight!"

One soldier whispered to another soldier, "Does he think we weren't ready to fight when we got here?"

The unit maintained its order as they turned and ran back the four miles to camp. The Voll soldiers were not well trained in fighting with bows and knives, but they were in excellent shape and it would be a quick run back to the camp.

Jumping Horse's party fanned out as they entered the camp, fought for two minutes and withdrew. He lost four hunters but was able to bring the wounded and dead out with him. Once in the long grass they were not pursued.

He spoke to a hunter beside him. "Go tell Two Fists to bring up the others and attack from the southeast. Fight for two minutes, withdraw and wait for me to give the order to attack again."

Now he would send sixty-five hunters— all he had— against one hundred and seventy Volls. He did not know how many Volls were dead, but he knew he must hurry before the other two hundred Volls returned. He looked up as he heard Luke's party go in again.

As Luke stepped out of the long grass, he could hear the arrows passing one after the other over his head. Each one hit a target. Even in this situation he smiled with pride at May's work. The Volls were scattering as the arrows fell into their formation. Luke turned his men toward the west side of the camp to try and join Bert and Daniel as they attacked.

Bert and Billy came in from opposite sides, crashing into the confused soldiers. They had expected the attacks to come from the same place as before but they came in from the east and west. Daniel's great body broke into the flank of the line and with a knife in each hand he cut down every soldier within his reach. His yell struck fear into the hearts of many.

As they moved toward the north side of the camp they were joined by Luke's party. The Volls began to run, but there seemed to be hunters with wild painted faces everywhere. Many who saw the red and black face of Silver died. She had no fear and the anger in her heart and soul was released through her hands and feet. Everywhere she turned she saw Bert by her side but she ignored him.

Jamee led the party into the waiting Volls. Her staff's blade extended, she moved at a walk to let the soldiers see what she brought to them. Billy and the hunters swarmed to the sides. The soldiers recognized what she carried and all but a few tried to flee. The few that attacked her were cut to pieces and she continued her walk into them.

Billy yelled at her. "Jamee, enough! It is time to move."

She walked in a circle back toward Billy, her staff a blur with a ring of silver at its tip in the firelight.

The men in reserve and Jumping Horse's party attacked at the same time. They overwhelmed the soldiers as they fell back to the center of the camp.

After two minutes he yelled, "Move!" and both parties began to withdraw.

Of the one hundred and seventy soldiers, only twenty were still standing and crowded into the center of the camp.

Just as Jumping Horse reached the edge of the camp, the two hundred Volls sent out to his camp attacked and smashed into his party. Billy, Luke, Daniel and Two Fists saw what was happening and charged back into the camp. Luke and Billy's parties passed through the Volls left in the center, cutting many of them down. They continued on to join with Bert and Daniel to smash into the flank of the arriving Volls. It was a desperate time because the hunters were tiring. The Volls, not having witnessed the fight in the camp, were confident and looking for blood.

Many hunters lay dying or wounded, but there would be no surrender. They began to lose ground. Jamee was covered in blood, some of it her own. Even her staff could not move the tide as several spear points had come under her guard. Billy stayed as close as he dared, but he was wounded as well. Silver fought with the joy of released anger and had not been touched by arrow, knife or spear. Some of that was due to the courage of Bert, who was now lagging behind due to his numerous wounds.

As the battle became desperate and looked as if the hunters would finally be overwhelmed, a great undulating war-cry rose up from the west side of the battle. Red Eagle had arrived with one hundred hunters. Then from the east a loud cry of the prairie cat rose up as black men, one hundred-fifty strong, with faces painted for war crashed into the flank of the Volls. Daniel was almost brought down by a swarm of Volls, but suddenly the pressure in his battle eased.

A giant of a man stepped to his side and laughed. "Get up, son, and help me with these little ones."

It was Daniel's father, George, standing by his side and crushing any Voll who ventured too close to his great hammer.

What had seemed so desperate turned to quick victory. The Volls laid down their weapons and fell to the ground. The lust for death and blood overcame a few, but the leaders of the three parties soon had control. They moved the prisoners into the center of the camp and then gathered to decide their fate. As things settled down, one soldier jumped up and ran at a guard. It was Major Vickers.

The snick of his blade could be heard as he raised his Steer and cut down the guard directly in front of him. Vickers ran for the long grass, but one arrow and then another entered each leg, causing him to crash to the ground. May stood thirty feet away with another arrow ready, but she looked to Luke and nodded.

Luke walked up to Vickers and said, "My name is Luke Deer Catcher but you may call me Death. I will have that staff for my sister." Major Vickers swung the Steer at him, but Luke cut his right hand from his arm and then stabbed him in the throat. Death came quickly to Major Vickers as he watched Luke bend down and pick up the Steer. Jamee limped over to Luke and flicked the lever flat, retracting the blade, and then she kissed Luke on the lips.

Luke turned and walked to Silver, handed her the staff, kissed and held her.

He said, "This is yours, Silver. We will always remember Red and we want you to live. Your child will have many fathers and mothers and we will never leave you. I love you, my sister."

Silver looked up at Luke and the tears began to flow from her eyes as she said, "I will live as long as I can and I thank you for this gift. I love you, Luke, my brother. I love you all and welcome my brothers and sisters to help me raise our child."

Bert, still standing close to Silver, said, "Don't forget me. I made a promise and I will keep it."

Silver smiled, walked to Bert, kissed him softly on the lips and began to care for his many wounds.

Many hunters died and men were moving the bodies into camp to keep the animals from them. They would be buried at dawn in a marked grave so the tribe could come to pay respect when this war was over. A number of the People and black men had been wounded and were being treated with Bookus matting. The men who had come with Red Eagle moved through the group of hunters helping to treat the wounded and moving the bodies that were strewn about the prairie.

Red Eagle, Jumping Horse and Two Fists stood at the edge of the Voll camp and shook hands with the leader of the black men who had joined the fight.

Red Eagle said, "My name is William Red Eagle and I am an elder of the Eagle tribe. Our people owe you a debt of gratitude and you have my personal thanks for your help. How did you know of this battle?"

The black man that stood before them was as tall as George Quiet Badger but thin and sinewy. He wore leather clothing but in a much different style than the village hunters. He had a leather headband with the spiked feathers of a red Minerva, a small vest, loincloth, thin sandal-like shoes and a necklace of claws and teeth.

He spoke in a deep baritone voice and said, "I am the leader of Hopetown and my name is George Obama Tuce. One of our scouts saw a large patrol of these Volls passing near the edge of our territory. My men back-tracked them and found three large groups heading west. They reported back and we decided to come out in force to see what they were doing. This is something we rarely do because we want no trouble from you Indians. You do not disturb our territory, except for the occasional scout, so we respect your territory."

George continued, "Our scouts found evidence of several small battles between you and these whites and with the Koros, but they reported the whites were moving in force and there would soon be a large battle that you might not win. I decided it was time to help you Indians."

Red Eagle asked, "George, what are your people called? I wish to call you by a name that will not be disrespectful."

"We call ourselves Blackmen and Blackwomen. It is our color and we have become proud of this over the many years we have been here. We have kept to ourselves to darken our skin and keep our pride in what we are. After seeing how your people fought so bravely and with such skill, I think it is time for us to get to know the Indians of Prairie. You are a proud people."

Jumping Horse said, "You called this world Prairie. That is the name we also use. When we first came here it was known to us as Korostrata."

"Yes. We captured some maps and papers from the whites when they first came here. On the maps of the outer worlds they have named each one. Korostrata is called Prairie; QB-45 is called Ocean; QA-12 is Forest and QC-03 is Ice. We liked the name Prairie better than Korostrata so that is the name we use."

Red Eagle said, "I like that name as well. Now all the people of this land will know it as Prairie. I will ask the Council to send representatives to Hopetown, with your permission, to exchange ideas and perhaps set up a trading system. But first we have two more large groups of Volls to deal with and a few smaller groups."

George said, "I think it will be good to talk with your people, but I must warn you now we are intent on keeping our people pure. In the last few years our scientists have warned us about increasing our gene pool, so maybe there is room for mutual breeding."

Red Eagle looked sharply at George but kept his voice steady as he spoke. "The People do not breed. We live in a society of husbands and wives. When we first arrived on Prairie we were of many different tribes and a number with other blood in them. We decided not to try and separate the different tribes but to combine into the People. This is a name that many of the different tribes used to describe themselves. We live in peace but have always kept our fighting heritage alive. The People do not breed."

George looked at Red Eagle for a long moment and said, "You have given me something to think about. I believe we can exchange ideas and learn from one another. But now, what is your plan for these prisoners and the armies to the east and west of us?"

"We will hold these prisoners until a plan can be worked out, but it is not our way to kill unarmed men. As for the Volls left to fight, we will rest here for a few days until our wounded hunters are ready and then we will go out and meet these others who have invaded our land."

George looked over at the wounded men and saw many with grievous wounds and asked, "Red Eagle, do you think these men will be ready to fight in only a few days?"

"Yes. We have found something not long ago that heals wounds and injuries very quickly. You will see that your men will also be ready to fight as soon as tomorrow. For now I have sent out patrols to watch over the Volls."

"I see women and even a white man among your warriors. In our society it is forbidden for a woman to become a fighter and whites would not be allowed to live. Why are they here?"

Jumping Horse looked at Red Eagle, then at George and said, "Normally our women do not fight, but they train just like our men if they wish to. The three you see have recently joined our tribe and have fighting skills that must be seen to believe. The small woman is called Silver Dove and she came through this entire battle without being wounded. The white man is called Bert and his tactics helped sixty-five of us destroy over one hundred and fifty trained Voll soldiers. He is one of us but has not been challenged. One white man who was a member of our tribe was killed a few days ago fighting. He was a brave man and husband to Silver. His name was Jim Travis and we are proud to name him as one of us. If a person is accepted into our tribe, their color no longer matters."

George nodded but said nothing. He had much to think about.

His people had no contact with the whites for hundreds of years and the hatred for them had slowly lessened. They would never again be slaves to anyone, but he was unsure what to think about having whites live on the same world with the Black Nation. Now was time for thought and he would have to speak to his people. They would respect the wishes of the Indians for now and fight to destroy these aggressors.

Guards were set, scouts sent out and then food was passed out and the hunters lay down where they were to rest.

Silver had found a creek bed with a large pool of water and, aided by the hunters, carried water back to the camp. She helped clean and dress the wounds of those around her. She was crying the entire time, but it was a cleansing process that washed the hate from her soul. She would hurt for many years, but she would live and raise Red's child.

After the wounded were taken care of, Jamee brought Silver out to a rain berry clump and she lay her down with her family and they slept. Bert lay down at the edge of the rain berry bushes and kept watch.

Silver went into a deep sleep and dreamed of Red.

Red stood with her beside a vast ocean, holding her in his arms.

He said, "Do not worry, my love. We will be together again but not for a long time. You will live and have a good life and I will watch over you and our child. I want you to have more children. There will come a day when we are all together in a place of peace. I love you, Silver Dove. I love you enough to tell you to live your life and find another to help you in this life. Find a good man. Stay close to our family and that will make me content and happy. Watch over Billy. He will need his family's help in the coming years. He has many hard decisions to make and you must be a part of his strength. Silver Dove, I will love you forever and I will visit you in your dreams from time to time, but now you must let me go and turn back to living your life. You must do this for me."

Red turned her in his arms and kissed her and sent warmth surging through her and then he was gone and she fell back into a deep, life-giving sleep.

When she woke she smiled with a feeling of renewal. Jamee had snuggled close and Billy had an arm across them both. Luke and May were within reach as they slept holding each other. She could see Bert curled up at the edge of the bushes and she smiled. She eased her way out of Jamee and Billy's embrace and made her way out onto the prairie, enjoying the late afternoon sunlight. She saw a small group of people running toward the camp, but when the leader saw her he motioned the others to go ahead and he turned toward Silver.

He ran up to her and she exclaimed, "Father! What are you doing here? Is everything all right?"

Sam Walking Bear took his daughter in his arms and held her tight as he caught his breath.

He finally kissed her on the lips and said, "Daughter, it is good to see you are well. Tell me what has happened. Your mother told me something terrible had happened to one of our children but she didn't know which one."

The tears sprang back to her eyes as she told Sam everything that had taken place and of the death of Red. Sam sat on the prairie for a long time and cried for the loss of his son, but Silver comforted him and told him it was all right. When she told him that she was pregnant, Sam looked at her with warmth that thrilled Silver.

She could see the love grow in him even more and he said, "Daughter, you will make me a grandfather! I am so pleased. Why were you in this fight if you knew that you carried my grandchild?"

Silver stood next to Sam and laid her head on his chest and said, "I had to, Father. I came here to join Red, but my brothers and sisters made me see that I must live. There was so much rage and sadness in me I had to fight to release it. I am still sad and hurting, but I see what Red told me to do now. The night before he died I think he knew and he made me promise to live my life and love again. When he was wounded and dying I told him about our child and he was so happy and at peace. I know now I will live and care for our child and I will try to find some happiness."

Sam said, "We will miss Red and hurt for a long time. He has made me proud and will live on in my heart. Your mother and I will help you and you will live with us. Little Dove will fill your heart with love and I will give you and the child all the love he needs."

"I love you, Father."

They finally walked into camp and Sam found his other children waiting for him. They rushed to him, kissing, hugging and touching him. Silver noticed the commotion around the camp. Many people were laughing, smiling and talking excitedly.

She said, "What is going on? Everyone seems to be enjoying themselves."

Billy, Jamee, May and Luke all began laughing and finally Luke said, "It's all Father's fault. He brought the twins with him and as soon as they came into camp and found Daniel, they attacked him with kisses, knocked him to the ground and almost made love to him right on the ground with everyone watching. His father started laughing so hard he had the whole camp roaring. George said, 'Daniel! You must pick only one of them! No one has two wives.'

"The twins jumped up, ran to him and knocked George to the ground kissing him and calling him Papa and then Sirilak said to him, 'Papa, you better get used to it. We are going to marry Daniel and no one will stop us.' Then they started kissing George again. Finally George stood and held them away from him by their collars. He was blushing so much he looked like the second moon setting. Everyone was laughing, including Red Eagle and the black warriors. George looked at them for a moment, turned them and shoved them back toward Daniel saying, 'Son, this is your problem, but I wouldn't try to argue with them!' Daniel grabbed them up by the waists and ran out into the prairie and hasn't been back."

Billy and the others looked over to where George was talking to a group of hunters, looking like a very proud father and everyone began laughing.

Daniel ran with the two women under his arms out into the prairie. Once he had run for about one hundred yards, he put them down and took their hands and pulled them along. He found a creek bed and followed it until he reached a large pool of clear water. Neither Sawaan nor Sirilak had said a word. Daniel released them and fell into the water with his clothes on.

The twins smiled and started to undress, but Daniel roared, "Oh, no, you don't. Keep your clothes on!"

They stopped undressing but ran into the water and tried to move close to Daniel.

He pushed them away and said, "Stay! We have to talk and get a few things straight." The twins backed away from him but continued to smile.

Daniel looked at the two beautiful women and said, "This won't work. I can't marry both of you."

Sawaan asked, "Don't you want us, Daniel?" And Sirilak asked, "Don't you love us, Daniel?"

"Yes, I do. You are all I have thought about, but I can't have you both."

They both asked in their lovely singing voices, "Why not?"

Daniel looked into the water and said in a soft, quiet voice, "It's not done in our village. One man and one woman is the rule."

Sirilak said, "Malika said she thought it would be all right. She said there is no law of the People against it. It just hasn't been done before. She said that since we are twins and so close, she thinks it's a good idea."

Daniel exclaimed, "My mother said that?"

They answered together, "Yes."

Now Daniel was totally confused. He didn't know what to do. He did love them both and it had caused his heart to ache trying to decide which one he wanted more. He sat quietly for a long time. The sun was setting and the surrounding prairie was growing dark.

As the first moon rose and spread its silvery-gray light over the rolling hills of the prairie he finally asked, "Sirilak, why do you want to marry me?"

She moved closer to him and looked into his eyes and said, "Because I love you. I want you and need you. I want to make a good home for you and have your children."

He looked at Sawaan, but in the soft glow of the moon he could not see her face. The one difference he had found between the two women was Sirilak could express herself and was not afraid to say what she felt. He also knew that Sawaan felt many of the same things but couldn't or wouldn't put it into words.

He asked Sawaan, "Why do you want to marry me, Sawaan?"

She didn't move closer to him, but said, "I want you and need you, Daniel. I don't want to lose you. I never thought you would want to marry me. I thought I would be your woman and take care of you and make you happy."

"Why don't you want to lose me and why do you think I wouldn't want to marry you?"

He reached out and pulled her close enough to see her face. She looked down at the water, but he could see the tears in her eyes.

She said, "I was nothing on our old world. All I've ever had in my life has been Sirilak. We had no family or anyone to care for us. Men wanted to use us, but we learned very early how to fight and protect ourselves. When you rescued me, I knew I... I wanted to be with you. You are more than my protector, Daniel. I... I would have given myself to you and that would have been enough. I never thought you would... I never thought you would want to have children with me or marry me. It is enough just to make you happy and be close to my sister."

Daniel wanted her to say the words he knew were so difficult for her.

He said, "Sawaan, you have not answered my question. Why would you want to be my wife?"

Sawaan looked at him with tears running down her face and it almost made him take her in his arms and hold her, but he stayed where he was and looked at her. The tears streaming from her face fell into the water making ripples that moved out to him and Sirilak. She was linked to them, but fear nearly caused her to run. Sirilak was also crying but stayed back from Sawaan. She knew what Daniel was doing and she also knew how hard it was for Sawaan to say the words they both wanted her to say. Sawaan tasted the salty tears on her lips and knew it was time to say the words she feared.

She was so afraid of losing Daniel and she thought her words would drive him away, but she took a deep breath and spoke. "I... I love you. I love you! I want to be your wife and have your children and make you happy."

Daniel moved close to her and took her in his arms, kissed her lips and said, "I love you too. I guess I have known it since I saw you both at that tent, fighting to save what was yours to give. I want you to be my wife and have my children. I love you with all my heart."

Sirilak moved next to them and asked in a quiet tiny voice, "What about me, Daniel?"

Daniel released Sawaan and took her in his arms and kissed her hard on the lips and said, "Yes, I want you to be my wife and have my children as well. I love you with all my heart."

Then he pulled Sawaan to him and all three held on tight, kissing and touching each other.

"I don't know how this will work, but even if we have to leave the village, I won't let you go."

Sawaan's soul, finally free of the fear said, "It will be all right, Daniel. Mother said she would take care of everything."

Daniel laughed and said, "She was my biggest fear. I never thought she would accept me having two wives."

Sirilak said, "Oh, she was so excited for us and so happy to have two new daughters! She is so wonderful. It was even her idea for us to come here and tell you the good news."

They walked hand in hand back to the camp. Soaking wet, they walked up to Daniel's father.

Daniel spoke in a loud voice so those around could hear as well. "Father, I want you to meet the women I love and will make my wives."

George gave them a stern look, but then a smile broke across his face and he took the twins in his arms, kissed them and said, "I've always wanted a daughter and now I have two of the most beautiful daughters in the village!"

Everyone began to cheer and slap Daniel on the back and even made a few jokes about how often he would have to hunt to feed such a big family.

Someone shouted to the laughter of all, "You will have to change your name from Quiet Badger to Busy Badger!"

The next morning everyone was still in a good mood, but the coming battle was weighing on their minds. Hunters were sent out to gather more food and scouts were sent to relieve the ones already watching the other Voll camps. Around noon a scout came in leading a small group of Volls into the camp from the east.

Commander Harry King was at the head of the soldiers who entered the camp and was taken to speak with Red Eagle, Jumping Horse and George Tuce. Billy, Luke and a number of other hunters gathered around to hear what was said. King looked at the group and addressed Red Eagle.

The scout had told him who the leader was and he said, "I am Commander Harry King, second in command of this expedition. I have come to offer my services to you, along with these other soldiers. I will surrender if that is your wish but we come seeking a new life here on Prairie. We do not wish to fight you or control you; we only want to live in peace and be a part of this world."

"I am William Red Eagle, leader of the Eagle tribe, and this is George Obama Tuce, leader of the Blackmen warriors. You are no longer second in command. Your leader died in this battle so you may wish to change your words."

King looked directly at Red Eagle and said, "No. What I have said was as a man, not as a leader. I will, if you wish, do all I can to stop anymore fighting, but I must tell you that many of the soldiers will refuse to give up what they believe is their right."

George Tuce asked, in a commanding voice, "What do these other Volls believe is their right?"

King said, "They and many people from Earth believe it is their right to enslave you and control you."

Red Eagle asked, "Are these your beliefs, Harry King?"

King looked around him at all the faces waiting for his answer and said, "On Earth there are only white people and it has made it a world with no diversity or flavor. Even though I have been a soldier for many years, I have only fought white men before coming to the outer worlds. On Earth I grew to dislike the killing of people with different ideas and for my punishment I was sent to the Volunteer Outer League Legation, V.O.L.L., but only the color of the skin changed, not what I believe. I believe all men can live together, learn and enjoy their differences."

Red Eagle looked around at the hunters and warriors watching and then turned back to Harry King and said, "These are good words you speak if they are true. What will you do to help if we allow it?"

Commander Harry King reached up and tore the epilates from his shoulders and said, "I will speak to all the soldiers and let them make their choice and then you will do what you must to preserve this world and your way of life."

Red Eagle said, "Why would you go against your own people? You say you want to live here in peace, but there has to be more than that to make a man turn from his own people. Do you fear death?"

"I suppose all men fear death, but I am ready to die if I must. For many years I have known something was wrong with the way we white men have lived. On Earth there are only white people, but many of the books kept in secret told about a world filled with many kinds of people. I always wondered what it would be like to see different cultures and races, but until I was assigned to the Outer Defense Forces, Voll system, I could only read about it in books. Now I have been on all four of the outer planets, each one different from the others. I've studied the maps and reports and knew this world,

Prairie, was so remote from the others it would be the perfect place to live and avoid the cruelty of the Earth's government.

"Now that our ships have been destroyed, it will be many years before anyone will come to Prairie. It very well may be that no one will ever come. But to answer your question as simply as I can, I am turning against wrong, not against my people. The government I was a part of has nearly destroyed Earth and it wishes to destroy the outer planets and I will not be a part of that. There are good people, white people, on Earth and many were forced to the other outer worlds, but the majority have been influenced for hundreds of years to believe they are the only true race of people. That is wrong."

Red Eagle said, "We will talk on this. Until we decide, you are free to move around and you may keep your weapons." He looked at the other soldiers and said, "Talk to the People and to the Blackmen and see if we have a hate for your people. We will call you when we are ready."

Harry and his men walked away, led by one of the scouts.

Red Eagle spoke to the leaders of both groups and said, "We have no real choice but to trust this man, King, but even if we had many choices, I would believe him. I think we must use him and avoid more killing if possible."

George said "What you say is true, Red Eagle, but a choice will have to be made. The whites who will not agree to live in peace and as equals will be nothing but trouble for us. I say if they do not pledge to live by our standards, then they must die!"

Billy said, "George, doesn't that solution sound very much like what the whites decided many years ago when they tried to kill all people who weren't white? I have only known a few whites, but every one of them has been good people and they have learned our ways quickly. If these others give us no choice but to fight, then they will die, but I think there has been enough death."

George said, "We have many books in our towns that tell of what the white men did to both our peoples and we will not trust only words. We are many and you are few so we have no fear of what these whites will do. I can tell you that they will not be welcome in our towns, at least not to live there. In time we will see, but if you allow people bent on your enslavement to run free, then they will be a thorn in the Indian's side, maybe forever. We are here only to help you in your struggle and we will abide by your decisions. The East will not be a place for any people who try to control us."

They talked for several more hours, everyone speaking his piece, and then King was called to them.

Red Eagle said, "Harry King, we have decided to accept your offer to live in peace, but any trouble made by your people will be on their heads. We would also have you talk to the other Volls and try to avoid more killing. You may take whomever you wish when you talk to them, but we will also send people to listen. You will have no authority to make a pledge of peace, but we will listen to the offers made by the Volls and then decide."

Harry smiled and looked at each one of the leaders and said, "Thank you. I will do all I can for my new land and my new friends. I have spoken to several of the men you hold prisoner and would like to take them with me. They will tell of your bravery and lack of fear but also of how they have been treated since they were captured. I think I should first go to the forward battalion and then back to my old battalion. It will take several days, but I will require them to answer quickly. I must tell my new friends that if any refuse you must deal with them quickly and harshly. I say this with sadness but with truth."

To Bert's surprise, he was chosen to go with King, along with Luke, Jumping Horse, George White Bird and

Two Fists. At first Bert refused because he would not leave Silver's side, but Silver spoke to him alone and he agreed. A party of one hundred hunters and Blackmen escorted the group of twelve to talk to the soldiers.

CHAPTER 32

It was early morning when Flick woke Jamee from her sleep.

"Wake up, Jamee. You can't be tired. You haven't mated in a long time."

Jamee sat up and smiled. "Good morning, Flick. I guess things have been pretty dull for you lately."

"Yes and no. No mating is dull, but I have something that excites me more. I want you to wake Silver, Billy, May, Sam and those beautiful twins. We must leave quickly."

"Where are we going, Flick? There may be another battle soon and we can't just leave."

"You will be back in two days and this can't wait. If I tell you it is important, you must believe me."

"I believe you. All right. I'll get the others."

They were packed and ready to leave quickly, but it took some convincing for Daniel to let the twins go without him. Finally Billy talked to him and promised to protect them. The twins were excited to be included and promised Daniel they would be good and return soon. Everyone was armed and ready for whatever it was they were to do.

They headed southwest and it soon became obvious to Silver that they were going to pass near the place Red had died. She spoke to Jamee and Jamee spoke to Flick.

Jamee turned to Silver and said, "Flick won't tell me anything except that it is necessary."

Late in the day they stopped for a moment at the place where Red was buried, but Flick made them move on quickly.

They were headed for the Bookus grove where Red and Silver had been the night before he died. Flick had them stop in the middle of the grove and she spoke to Jamee.

"This is something that only happens every five hundred years. The Bookus will produce seeds tonight and they have selected Silver and you to bear them. You must both come with me. Tell Silver not to be afraid and that this is a great honor and responsibility. Look at the tree in the very center of the grove. Do you see the odd shape near the top?"

Jamee looked at the tree and saw a great bulge at the eighth level and she nodded.

Flick continued, "You and Silver will follow me there, but the others must wait here. Warn them not to climb in any of the trees until you return. It would be very dangerous for them to do that. They will be totally protected on the ground. They may light a fire and cook but gather nothing from the Bookus."

Jamee told everyone what Flick had said and the warning startled Billy.

"Will you and Silver be safe going into the tree?"

"Flick said yes. She says the Bookus are waiting for us and we will all be safe."

Billy did not want to let Jamee go, but he did trust Flick.

As Jamee and Silver climbed the tree Silver said, "Do you feel how the tree is moving and how warm it is?"

"Yes. It's almost like it is breathing."

They reached the eighth level and Flick had them stop before the entrance to the water cave. The opening was twice its normal size and the whole level was swollen. There was a strong but aromatic sweet smelling fragrance

Flick said, "Jamee, the Bookus, all the Bookus have asked for you and Silver. In the past the Ancients would come to receive this gift, but they have asked for you two."

Jamee asked, "Do you mean you can actually talk to them?"

"Yes. I am much more than you think and so are the Bookus. Now you and Silver must remove your clothes, enter the cave and do as you are told. Tell Silver that she will be able to hear and talk to the Bookus. Do not be afraid. You are very special."

Jamee told Silver what Flick had said and so they removed their clothes and walked into the cave holding each other's hands.

The water cave was hot and the walls and floor glowed in a golden light. They waited in the heat of the cave, still holding hands, and looked around. The floor and walls of the cave were smooth, hard and polished. The color of the wood was dark brown with golden growth marks weaving swirling patterns of what looked like a map of Prairie on the wall.

As Jamee studied the map, she could see the Great Prairie, mountains, forest and ice to the north. To the west was a great ocean. To the south was a great range of mountains, but beyond that it was dense forest. Lakes and a large river ran east to west. Beyond the river was a large structure completely enclosed by a great wall.

A voice startled them both and they moved closer together.

The voice said, "Welcome, Jamee and Silver. You have no need to fear. We have called you to give you a gift."

The voice was that of a woman and it seemed to come from everywhere. It was a gentle and soothing, melodious voice that put them at ease.

"We are pleased you were brought to Prairie, for the love and pureness of your hearts have brought us much pleasure. Jamee, you are the first one of the Ana, humans, we have allowed to mate within us. It pleased us to feel your love and see your pleasure. Silver, you are the second and your pleasure and love has helped us to allow this of all the Ana. We thank you both for sharing your love. You will tell the Ana of the red and white skin to come within us and share their love. The ones of black skin must learn to love and marry before they will be allowed our protection. Yes, Jamee, what is it you would ask?"

Jamee smiled and looked over at Flick and asked, "Do all the beings of this world enjoy watching people make love— mate?"

"Not all enjoy your presence here, but the Akasa, Flick's flock, have always told us how well the Ana mate and now we must agree. The visual of your love is stirring and gives us pleasure knowing that you were chosen.

"To answer your second question, Silver. Yes, the Ana were chosen, and Jamee and you along with some of the others of your family will play an important part. That is all we will say, for your free choice will be the measure judged. What we will say is it will take a very long time and you are not to hurry for you will know when it is time to act.

"As for your first question, it saddens us to feel your loss. You will take comfort in knowing your mate has gone to a place of joy, not pain, and even now a part of him grows within you. You will take another mate and he will give you pleasure, love and joy and you will have more children, if you wish. Do not worry that your love for the first does not fade, for there is room in your heart for another. Look to the twins and Daniel for assurance that love has the capacity to layer within the soul of the Ana. This example is a rare occurrence, but for love to grow more than once is not."

Silver felt the tears return to her eyes, but to know Red was in a good place gave her joy.

Jamee asked, "This gift you give us, what will we do with it?"

"Jamee and Silver, you will be given seeds to be sown. Plant one seed and an entire grove will grow from it. They can be planted anywhere on land, but remember we require room and we will make room, whatever may try to block us. You may keep the seeds for your lifetime and give them to your descendants or plant them all yourself. When it is time to plant you will know. Give one seed to each of the Ana we bring forward and to the ones we name. You need not worry about their care. They are indestructible and will only grow at your command. Fashion a necklace and wear one around your neck and it will give you safe passage in the land of the Ancients. However, they will not protect you from the Atowees, the ones you call Koros, and the other dangers of Prairie. Now, Jamee, go out and call your mate to this chamber."

Jamee walked out into the night. She went to the end of the limb and called down. "Billy, you are to come alone to me. I am on the eighth level."

As she waited for Billy, Jamee wondered what was to happen to them. The Bookus gave clear instructions but left much out. Jamee thought, *The Bookus said it was for our free choice, but how can we choose if we don't know the choices?* All she had wanted since meeting Billy was to live her life with him and be happy.

Billy appeared and she ran into his arms and held him.

He said, "Why are you so warm? Where are your clothes?"

Jamee smiled and said, "She wants to see you. You must remove your clothes before entering."

"Who is she?"

"You'll see, or at least you will hear. Come now, my love."

Billy followed, removed his clothes and walked with Jamee into the swollen and lighted water cave. When he saw Silver standing there nude he stopped, but then he noticed the cave and was amazed. Jamee pulled him to stand beside Silver and she stood on the other side of him.

"Welcome, Ana Billy," the beautiful woman's voice said to him. "You are to be the protector of these chosen. It will be your responsibility to help them in whatever they ask and to guard them in times of danger. Do you accept this labor?"

Billy had many questions, but this was something he would have done without being asked.

He answered, "I love my wife and sister and I will protect them with my life."

"Very well." The Bookus continued, "Now, stand apart and do not touch one another until this is finished."

They separated and a shower of thick warm liquid cascaded down on them from the ceiling. It adhered to them but was quickly absorbed by their skin. They felt a tingling and became very aware of the others' presence. Silver looked down at Billy's excitement and giggled. Billy looked down and started to turn away but remembered the words of the Bookus. He stood there and blushed at the giggles of both women.

The Bookus said with a touch of humor in her voice, "You have been tied to us and to one another. You will see in time that this will be important and will aid you on your quest."

After a moment the back of the water cave began to glow in a bright white light and a seam appeared. It began to swell and open. To Billy's surprise, the opening looked like a woman's flower and his embarrassment increased.

"Silver and Jamee, step forward and receive our gifts to you."

They stepped to the opening and a pouch appeared. Jamee reached out and took it. Then another appeared and Silver took that one. The pouches were made of a material Jamee had never seen before and the feel of it was soft and velvety. They moved back to Billy and waited.

The Bookus said, "Call the twins and May to come here, Billy."

Billy left and called the others, leaving only Sam on the ground. When they arrived they all giggled at Billy's condition. He told them that they too must remove their clothes and enter the cave. When Billy entered behind the three women his mind was full. He had seen May nude before, but the twins were things of wonder. Their bodies were identical and perfect. He was in a room with five of the most beautiful women he had ever seen and he was standing there with his excitement apparent. The twins took a good look at him and giggled nervously. Even May smiled and giggled.

As they settled down, the Bookus voice came to them all. "Silver, give each of the twins a seed and an extra one for their mate. When you return to your village give a seed to Little Dove and tell her she must come to a grove with her mate and spend two nights in a water cave and then she and Sam may wear the seeds on a necklace. The same is true for the twins, but they must both stay with their mate for the three nights."

Silver smiled as she reached into the pouch and removed three dark, walnut-colored seeds the size of a large acorn. As she moved to hand them to the twins, she brushed against Billy and they both jumped, causing the others to laugh.

"Jamee, give two seeds to May. One will be for her mate. They may wear them after a necklace has been fashioned. Give one to your father with the same instructions given to your mother."

After the seeds had been given, she said, "Silver, step forward and receive our last gift."

Silver walked to the opening and a dark red seed, larger than the others appeared. She took it and the opening sealed itself as if it had never been.

"Silver, go to the place where your mate lies and plant this seed. No commands are necessary. It will grow to be a single tree and will give tribute to the courage and sacrifice that he gave. It will also be our pledge to the Ana. If they continue to live their lives in service of the land and the Ana, then we will always be here for you to rest within us in safety. Now it is time for you all to rest. Go to the fourth level and sleep. Sam may join you."

Billy asked, "Can I get dressed now?"

With a laugh, she said, "If you must. And you may bathe after you wake."

As they were walking out the Bookus said, "Flick will be leaving you for a while, but she will return before the time you are needed."

When Sam arrived at the water cave and saw all the young women lying nude and fast asleep near Billy, he thought to himself, *Where's that bird? I know she has something to do with this. At least Billy is dressed.* He lay down and was asleep in a few seconds.

When Billy woke he felt as though he had slept for hours. He was completely refreshed. He moved to the back of the cave and cut into the floor to make an opening to bathe. He slipped out of his clothes and moved into the water. Jamee rose and moved into the water with him.

Billy took her in his arms and said, "I love you with all my heart, Jamee Soft Dove."

Jamee responded by kissing him and said, "I love you with all my heart, Billy Running Wolf."

The twins woke along with May and they all jumped in the water laughing.

May looked at Jamee and Billy and said, "Sorry. We didn't know."

Billy laughed and began to scrub himself clean. Silver woke looking like years of pressure had been removed from her.

Sam woke and sat up, seeing all the naked people, rose and started to leave.

Silver jumped up and took his hand. "No, Father; come bathe with us."

She looked at the others. The twins, May and Jamee rushed out of the water and began to take his clothes off. He tried to fight but finally gave up and was soon in the pool with everyone.

He looked at Billy and said, "I hope Little Dove doesn't hear about this. She'll never let me go off on my own again."

It was early morning when they left to join the others at the Voll camp. They stopped where Red had been buried and Silver planted the seed given her by the Bookus. They did not linger but hurried on. The women stayed close to Silver. Billy and Sam moved out front to scout ahead.

Billy had asked Jamee before they left, "Did you have dreams while you slept?"

"Yes. Many of my questions were answered about the Bookus and some things were explained that I didn't know how to ask. What about you?"

"It was the same for me. When we have time to be alone we will talk about what we've learned. I need you so much!"

Jamee leaned over and whispered, "I have a great need for your little buddy to visit me."

CHAPTER 33

Over the next week Harry King made several trips to each of the Voll camps trying to convince the soldiers to join this new world, live as equals and in peace with the people who already called Prairie home.

On the last trip to the western camp he approached the commander and asked, "Omar, have your men made a decision?"

Commander Omar Laden sneered at King and said, "You are a stupid fool, King! There is only one way to deal with these colored people. We will fight and kill you all."

King said, "Have you given the men a choice in this matter?"

"I am in command and I have decided."

With Luke, Daniel, Bert and George Quiet Bird ready to cut down any who interfered, Harry King said in a loud voice, "This is your last warning! If any of you want to live, come with us now. We will escort you to a place of safety until this battle is decided."

Several men stepped out of the ranks and were walking toward King when Commander Laden yelled, "Stop where you are! No one leaves this formation. I'll have you killed..."

He stopped yelling when three long knives touched his neck.

King said, "One more word and you won't have to worry about the outcome of this next battle. You men who wish to leave come ahead."

More men moved out of the ranks. In all, nine men were escorted away by giant George with his great hammer resting on his right shoulder.

Harry looked at Laden and said, "The next time we meet I will kill you. There will be no more talks."

He turned and walked away with the others of his party.

He made the same offer to the Volls in the eastern camp. Fifteen men came out with them. All the men who came from the opposing force were taken away from the battle area and put under guard in case any were spies. They were told they would be freed after the battles were over. The soldiers were well cared for and many of the hunters came to visit and talk to them, taking away much of their fear.

That night Harry was invited to the last meeting, where the final plans of the battle were made.

Red Eagle said, "Harry, you do not have to join in this battle if you wish not to."

Harry said as he waved another man into the group, "This is Jimmy Smith. He is the best man I have ever served with and we have both decided that if we want to live on this world we will fight alongside you."

Red Eagle smiled at Jimmy, thinking here is a man he would not like to face in battle.

Jimmy was forty-five years old. He had spent the last twenty-seven years as a soldier fighting anywhere he was sent. He had a face marked by many fights and a large body that could finish the battle. If Red Eagle could have looked inside him, he would have been surprised to see the kindness and intelligence within. As hard as his body was, he was a man who loved to read and think. His favorite books were on the subject of the American Indians and he was excited to be among these great people.

Red Eagle said, "You are both welcome to be with us. Is what Harry says true, Jimmy Smith?"

Jimmy gave him a hard stare and said, "Everything Commander... I mean Harry says is true, no matter what he is talking about. As for me, yes, sir, I am proud to stand with my red brothers. I have lived many years waiting for this day."

Harry spoke up, "Jimmy has read many more books than me on the subject of the American Indians and we have often talked about what it would be like to be an Indian."

Red Eagle smiled and said, "Tomorrow you will live as you have dreamed. Jimmy, you will fight with one of our best hunters. Billy Running Wolf is young, but he can be trusted in every decision he makes. Billy, meet one of your new hunters."

Billy stepped forward and took the hand of Jimmy Smith and said, "I welcome and thank you for joining with me in battle."

Jimmy didn't bat an eye at the youthful appearance of Billy as he said, "I am honored to fight by your side."

After the plans were discussed, Billy took Jimmy to meet his family and the others that he would be fighting with.

As they walked he asked Jimmy, "Do you have a problem fighting alongside women?"

"Well, I've never done that before, but after hearing how the women of your tribe defended your village, I don't have any problems."

"These women are much more than that. They are trained and could stand up to any man."

They were approaching a group of people sitting around a fire and Jimmy got his first look at the women he would be fighting with.

He stopped and stared at them saying, "Billy, they are all so beautiful!"

Billy laughed and said, "Yes, they are."

Everyone stood as Jimmy and Billy stepped into the firelight.

"This is Jimmy Smith, who has been in many battles. He is joining us to fight the Volls. Oh, he also says you are all beautiful."

Sam spoke up and said, "I hope he wasn't talking about me."

They all laughed and each woman stepped forward and introduced herself.

Jamee stepped forward and kissed Jimmy on the lips and said, "Thank you, Jimmy. I am Jamee and Billy is my husband."

May stepped up and kissed him hard on the lips and said, "I am May and Luke is my husband."

The twins stepped forward and took turns kissing Jimmy and said, "I am Sirilak and this is my sister Sawaan and we are going to marry Daniel!"

Jimmy blinked and said, "Both of you?"

They answered in their singing voices, "Yes!"

Finally Silver stepped forward with a sad smile and said, "I am Silver and I am Jamee, Billy, May and Luke's sister. Welcome, Jimmy."

She stood on her tiptoes, kissed and hugged him and then went back and sat down. Sam, Luke, Daniel, Bert and Apache Joe introduced themselves, without kisses, and they all sat down around the fire.

Billy said, "Jimmy, you might not believe this, but you have joined the most dangerous people on this prairie and you look as if you will fit right in."

Jimmy smiled and said, "After all those kisses, I'll believe anything you tell me." Silver walked back to Jimmy and handed him a bundle of clothes.

"Jimmy, I would like it if you would wear these clothes. You are a part of us now, as the man who wore these was also a part of us." She had given Jimmy a shirt, loincloth and leggings that had belonged to Red.

Jimmy stepped into the dark and changed. He walked proudly back to the group and smiled his thanks to Silver. They sat around the fire and the warmth of their companionship could be heard by many.

The next morning fifty Blackmen were sent to the eastern Voll camp to join the fifty hunters that were already there to hold them in place until the west camp was defeated.

One hundred hunters and one hundred Blackmen were assembled a mile from the western Voll camp and prepared to attack.

In the afternoon fifty archers who had moved to within thirty yards of the camp rose up from the grass and released their arrows. The Volls had expected quick flanking attacks similar to the tactics used on the main camp. The hail of arrows caught them unexpectedly, but they quickly sent out groups to kill the bowmen. Ten yards into the tall grass they were attacked by warriors and hunters that had waited patiently for them to come. The soldiers were slaughtered.

The main group of warriors and hunters attacked from three sides as one. The bowmen quickly moved to the north and shot anyone trying to escape. The great battle lasted twenty-eight minutes and all but seven soldiers were killed.

To Red Eagle it was a day of sadness, but he knew there was nothing else to be done to preserve their lives and freedom. After the battle was over, it was discovered that ten men were missing, including Commander Omar Laden. Hunters were sent out and followed the tracks, but the trail was lost in the mountains to the north.

Jimmy fought alongside the men and women of his group and showed his bravery many times as he put himself in front, trying to protect the others. He was wounded numerous times but was healthy within a few days thanks to the Bookus matting. Sawaan received a serious knife wound to her left arm but also recovered quickly. The small scar would be used in the future to tell one twin from the other. Silver did not join in the battle, wanting to protect the child that grew within her.

Two days later, with the soldiers at the eastern camp refusing to surrender, the battle was bloody and only three soldiers survived. No hunters or warriors were killed. It was decided that Red Eagle's tribe would take all prisoners with them and decide their fate.

The Blackmen warriors returned to the east with a promise of meetings and cooperation with the Indian Nation, as they now referred to the tribes. Harry King was also invited to visit Hopetown sometime in the near future.

Red Eagle decided to send Harry and Jimmy to visit the area of the Koro mine in case any of the Volls there survived. Billy, Jamee, Luke, May, Daniel and the twins volunteered to go with them. Sam, Bert, Silver and sixty hunters headed back to the village to start rebuilding while the remainder of the hunters slowly moved the prisoners across the prairie. They were to try and show the white men the kindness of the People in hopes they would decide to live in a world of freedom and peace.

CHAPTER 34

The small party arrived above the mine in daylight after seeing no sign of Koros or Volls anywhere. As they gazed down from the cliff ledge what they saw amazed everyone. The underground river had finally filled the mine and powerful cascades of water poured from the entrance of the mine to rush over the short piece of flat terrain in front of the entrance and fall a thousand feet to the valley below. The two small and one large air vents shot water two hundred feet into the air and streams made their way down in cascading waterfalls to the main flow. The view was spectacular. There was a beautiful rainbow reflected in the mist of the waterfall. Billy tried to describe what it had looked like before to Harry and Jimmy but soon gave up.

It had taken many more days than necessary to get to the mine. They had waited the three days required by the Bookus tree for Daniel and the twins to earn the right to wear the Bookus seed necklaces. Afterwards they had to travel slowly for two days in order for Daniel to recover his strength. The twins showed no a sign of fatigue and happily ran to everyone to show them the new necklaces they wore.

May had fashioned necklaces made of woven slivers from the May Tree in Green Hiding. The necklaces were incredibly strong and had a red glow to them. When the seeds were attached and placed over their heads, the seeds turned the color given to each person by Flick. Daniel's seed turned a honey-purple color. Sawaan's seed was a honey color and Sirilak's was purple.

In the last Bookus grove before they returned to the village Billy and Jamee sat on a platform at the top of the tree as the sun was settling in the west. The colors were so vivid that day Billy knew it was a special day. He sat holding Jamee in his arms.

He kissed her and then said, "Jamee, I love you with all my heart and it is singing because you are with me. I don't think life could be any better than this."

Jamee pressed her back into Billy's embrace, kissed his hands tenderly and said, "My love, I'm carrying your child inside me."

****

Tyler Hill's Decision

A young adult adventure that everyone will enjoy reading!

On his first camping trip to the Appalachian Mountains Tyler is attacked by bears and he becomes hopelessly lost deep in the mountains.

He meets an old Cherokee man who helps him find his way home and at the same time teaches Tyler about the mountains and the Cherokee people.

This is a story of a young man's search for answers about his heritage and the decisions he makes.

An unbiased look at Native Americans and the Cherokee people!

Read about author Dannie C Hill and all his upcoming novels at:
http://smallmountainpub.com

Dannie's blog with true stories about a writer living in Thailand can be found at:
http://danniehill.wordpress.com

In Search of a Soul

Have you looked out at the sea, felt its pull and wondered what it would be like to sail to exotic lands? At sea there are only three things that matter: the sea, the air and the boat.

Come along and join a man who sails alone upon the incessant waters just to survive his life. Douglas Durian is a former Navy SEAL that nearly lost his mind because of a tragic incident on his last mission. Now to save his life he seeks the solitude of the sea. His only companion is his boat and she holds him close and guides him until he is needed again.

Douglas is learning to live again and enjoy the magical ocean he rides upon and it's all because of a child he has rescued from the sea. Mei Yue escaped from servitude and sees her chance to be safe in Douglas, but he must remember his past. She is a willful and precocious child and guides Douglas and makes him live again because she knows danger lies in her future.

Together they explore the Pacific and all its beauty and danger. All the while there are people searching for the child.

Mei Yue is abducted and Douglas's world crashes down around him until a friend from his past and a love he thought lost forever come to him and aid in trying to recover Mei.

You will ride along on an adventure that will sooth your soul. Also witness desperate action as Douglas battles the sea, Mei's abductors and his past. He is willing to give up everything to get the child back—including his life.

What he finds may surprise you.

Note from the author:

I invite you to make a review of the books I have written at the site where you made your purchase. I would further invite you to let me know what you think of my books or any comments you wish to make at my website.

Readers are the life blood of writers! Tell your friends.

Thank you for reading.

Dannie C Hill